ICE CORPSE

Moak Stonetree gazed patiently at Ethan. "The tale says that in one part of the southern continent the ice has become a corpse."

"I don't know that term," Ethan said. "What's an 'ice corpse'?"

Stonetree picked up a half-empty goblet and ceremoniously turned it upside down. Water ran out on the stones, escaping into the cracks in the floor. "Do you now understand?"

"It's water," Ethan said. "When ice dies it becomes water. A corpse. Wait a minute. You're talking about open water; a hole in the ice sheet? That's impossible, even at the equator."

"Just so," said Stonetree. "It is perverse. It is...madness."

By Alan Dean Foster
Published by Ballantine Books:

THE BLACK HOLE

CACHALOT

DARK STAR

MIDWORLD

NOR CRYSTAL TEARS

SENTENCED TO PRISM

SPLINTER OF THE MIND'S EYE

VOYAGE TO THE CITY OF THE DEAD

... WHO NEEDS ENEMIES?

WITH FRIENDS LIKE THESE ...

The Icerigger Trilogy:
   ICERIGGER
   MISSION TO MOULOKIN
   THE DELUGE DRIVERS

Pip and Flinx:
   FOR LOVE OF MOTHER-NOT
   THE TAR-AIYM KRANG
   ORPHAN STAR
   THE END OF THE MATTER
   BLOODHYPE

THE DELUGE DRIVERS

DRIVERS

Book Three of
The Icerigger Trilogy

ALAN DEAN FOSTER

A Del Rey Book

BALLANTINE BOOKS • NEW YORK

A Del Rey Book
Published by Ballantine Books

Library of Congress Catalog Card Number: 86-91665

ISBN 0-345-33330-6

Manufactured in the United States of America

First Edition: June 1987

Cover Art by Michael Herring

In memoriam . . . Judy-Lynn Benjamin del Rey
Fate is an unkind editor, but at last the
genie is free of the bottle.
Soar.

I

The worst part of it wasn't that Ethan Fortune was freezing to death. The worst part of it was that he was doing so voluntarily.

Nudity was not favored by the heavily furred native Tran. For a human being to be standing naked on Tran-ky-ky verged on insanity. Despite this Ethan was not trying to commit suicide. He was supposed to be celebrating, though it was hard to pretend you were having a good time when you were turning blue and the goose bumps dotting arms, legs, and other sections of your anatomy were well on their way to settling in as permanent features of the epidermal topography.

That he had company in misery was no consolation. Skua September was just as cold, except for those portions of his face and neck that were covered by a heavy brown and gray beard. The old giant had both arms clapped tightly to his ribs.

There was also the matter of exposure to curious eyes as well as to the elements. Foolish to be embarrassed, Ethan told himself. He and Skua were the only the human beings in the royal hall of Arsudun. It was only natural their nude forms would draw attention, with their flat feet devoid of skatelike *chiv*, their *dan*-less arms, and their largely furless bodies.

Mousokka, who was second mate on the icerigger *Slan-derscree*, commented that he found the subtle change in color of their skin very becoming. The glares this observation drew quickly convinced him that the change was other than voluntary and he did not mention it again.

The hardest thing to do was simply to be quiet. Shivering was permissible: muttering and making other noise was not. Skua leaned over to whisper to his companion anyway.

"It's not so bad, young feller-me-lad. After a while the numbness kind of overwhelms the cold."

"Shut up. Just shut up, will you?" Ethan leaned forward around the nearest member of the honor guard and looked toward the cupola. "Surely they're almost through?"

Beneath an intricately carved dome of stavanzer ivory, a trio of elderly Arsudunian scholars were intoning the traditional marriage ritual. Overhead arched the stone walls and ceiling of the royal hall of Arsudun, the island-state whose corrupt Landgrave Ethan, Skua, and their Tran friends had recently overthrown. The new young Landgrave, Sev Gorin-Vloga, had given his blessings to the newlyweds-to-be and insisted they take their vows in Arsudun's ancient castle. Ancient, unheated castle, Ethan reflected as he tried to keep his teeth from chattering.

The two principles in this frigid romantic drama were Sir Hunnar Redbeard and Elfa Kurdagh-Vlata. Elfa was the daughter and heir of the Landgrave of Sofold, Hunnar the first Tran Ethan and Skua had dealt with after surviving their crash landing on this world eons ago. Ethan was delighted to share in their happiness. He would have given anything not to have agreed to share in the actual ceremony.

Not that he and Skua were alone in their nakedness. Guards and spectators alike had disrobed for the ceremony.

Only the bride and groom were dressed. But the feline-ursine Tran were clad in thick fur. They didn't notice the chill in the castle. Ethan and Skua had no such natural protection.

"Look, Ethan," Skua whispered, "when I accepted the invitation to this little soirée on our behalf I had no idea stripping down was part of the tradition. The way that guard captain explained it, by appearing without raiment in the presence of the beloveds we indicate that we're giving of our friendship and affection without any constraints. One holds nothing back. It's a sign of respect for the lucky couple. One hides nothing in their presence."

"That's for damn sure," Ethan growled.

Skua looked thoughtful. "Got its practical aspects besides. Hunnar there's going to be Landgrave someday, ruler of Wannome. When everybody's in a happy mood and celebrating would be a good time for a potential assassin to strike, but it's tough to sneak in a weapon when you've nothing to hide it behind."

"Damn shame, too. If I had one, I know who I'd use it on."

September spread his huge hands. "Now what could I have done, feller-me-lad? Turned down the invitation to our friends' wedding? A royal invitation at that, and what with us getting ready to leave this ball of ice once and for all. No reason for us to hang around. With Sofold and Arsudun in the north and Poyolavomaar and Moulokin in the south the Tran are pretty well on their way to breaking out of their feudal city-state cycle and establishing a planetary government. The rest of the independent states will have to join up because there's no way they can stand against that kind of strength."

One of the other spectators, an Arsudunian noble by the look of him, admonished them to be silent. It was disrespectful to converse during the sacred moments of the ceremony whether one be hero or commoner—or alien. Were they not conscious of the singular honor which had been bestowed upon them? Despite the presence of the human scientific outpost on the western shore of Arsudun this was the first time non-Tran had been allowed to witness the solemn, traditional rites which united male and female Tran in wedlock.

It was a delight Ethan could have forgone.

He kept quiet for Hunnar and Elfa's sake. The business of betrothing consisted of a lot of twitching and moaning and entirely too much talk. If not for the fact that the two principals were close friends he would have declaimed his discomfort to all and sundry and damn the consequences. He tried to tell himself he wasn't freezing, but his body wouldn't buy it. So he concentrated instead on the more enjoyable activities which had led up to this prolonged session of discomfort: the procession through the town, the entrance into the castle, the swearing of the nobles, even the formal divestiture of garments which had taken place outside the hall, the clothing heaped into two piles between which the wedding procession had passed.

Would he truly have blasphemed if he'd kept his underwear?

He should have been grateful. What if tradition had called for the ceremony to have taken place not within the castle but out on the bare plains of Arsudun? Inside the temperature hovered close to freezing. Out on the plains it sank far below the point where water moved in comfort. Only fires in a few stone basins held back the arctic climate. One blazed not far away. Sticking his naked backside, or for that matter any portion of his anatomy, close to the hot stone would have constituted an unforgivable breach of etiquette. But he was going to have to do something soon. Shivering and goose bumps were half funny. Frostbite was not.

"I can't take much more of this."

"Concentrate on the ceremony, on the movements. Ain't it beautiful?"

"What I can hear of it between my chattering teeth," Ethan replied.

"And ain't it great to see those two finally pledging their lives to each other?"

"Yes, yes, of course." Maybe marrying Elfa would at last put to rest Hunnar's groundless suspicions that she held some kind of perverse attraction for Ethan. "That warms my thoughts but not my tail."

"Think warmth, then."

"Easy for you to say."

Skua eyed him reproachfully. "No it ain't easy for me to say, feller-me-lad. I'm as cold as you are. You just ain't trying hard enough is all. Think about something else. Think about"— he grew suddenly wistful—"think about next week when the next supply ship will arrive and we'll be able to quit this world."

That *was* something to think about, Ethan told himself. Think about returning to civilization after spending almost two years living with well-meaning alien barbarians. Think about a modern, clean, warm stateroom on a new KK-drive ship. Think even about getting back to work. Time to put adventure behind him and get on with the business of everyday life. The ordinary was long overdue.

September gestured toward the chanting elders. "I think she's coming to a close, feller-me-lad."

"What makes you think so?"

He pointed across the open central aisle. "See those old Tran over there? The senior ladies of the court, I believe. They've been standing like trees for the last thirty minutes and now they're starting to gossip."

September's surmise was correct. As a final soliloquy crashed to a guttural close on a rising intonation, the assembled nobles gave out three loud shouts. Paws thrust ceilingward, they began to wave to and fro. This action caused their dan, the winglike membranes that grew from arm and sides, to move back and forth. The effect was to shower the happy couple with wind and words. Fortunately Ethan and Skua stood off to the side and so missed the brunt of the artificial gale.

The elders bowed out as the crowd surged forward to congratulate the newly joined. Hunnar raised both paws for silence.

"Newfound friends and allies: I thank you for your kindnesses and for your hospitality." He nodded toward the elders. "I thank you also for the splendid ceremony which you have made for us." Now he turned to face young Gorin-Volga. "Be assured that, pursuant to the new treaty made between our peoples, the citizens of Arsudun will be welcome in our home of Sofold as well as in the harbors of our fellow allies Poyolavomaar and Moulokin." He stepped back and Elfa moved forward.

"Great times are upon us, my friends," she began, her strong voice echoing through the hall. "Wonderful things are happening thanks to our friends the skypeople." She gestured in the direction of the two shivering humans, and a startled Ethan fought to look as dignified as possible under the circumstances.

"We have learned that there are worlds other than our own, worlds as numerous as the city-states of Tran-ky-ky. To share in their greatest glory and power we must give up some of our ancient ways. No longer can the Tran live apart from one another, fighting to settle the simplest of differences and disagreements. We must come together in peace, for strength, so that when we join our friends the skypeople among the stars, as they assure us we must someday do, we can do this thing with our heads held high and dans spread wide. As warriors and as a people proud of what we are and not as wards of a greater state. We join together seeking parity and equality. Charity is not for Tran!"

A rousing cheer rose from the assembly and reverberated around the royal hall. Elfa and Hunnar were all but overwhelmed by hugs and embraces. To Ethan it sounded unflatteringly like feeding time at the zoo. He followed Skua as the giant used his bulk to shove his way through the crowd.

"I, too, have something to say, Sir Hunnar," Ethan heard him ask.

"What is it, friend Skua?"

Ethan felt dwarfed by the mob of taller, wider Tran but not intimidated. He knew them too well for that. Besides, with all those furry bodies pressing close around him he began to warm up.

"It's about our clothes."

"Ah, in the emotion of the moment I did not think. You have lived with us for so long I sometimes forget you find our climate not to your liking. The ceremony must have been a strain for you and Ethan." He pointed to the small mountain of clothing stacked to the right of the entryway. "I think you will find your dress there. Attire of close friends and relatives is always stacked to starboard. Come, we'll help you." Taking Elfa's hand in his, he led them through the congratulatory crowd.

"I fear your strange clothing lies near the bottom," Elfa observed.

Ethan eyed the mound of alien attire. "Doesn't matter. I won't mind hunting for it. It has to be warmer under there than it is out here."

By the time he and Skua had recovered and donned their underwear and silvery survival suits, many of the chief nobles and knights of Arsudun had already presented their compliments to the newlyweds and made their exit. In another part of the castle the official feasting had begun. Shouts and snatches of half-sung, half-hissed song drifted into the royal hall.

He hung back while Skua joyfully participated in the raucous celebration. They couldn't return to the humanx settlement of Brass Monkey until Hunnar's crew, the sailors and soldiers of the icerigger *Slanderscree*, finished their reveling. This ended sooner than he'd expected. Not that it should have surprised him. The Sofoldians had been away from their home city of Wannome for more than a year. By now their many friends and relatives must be wondering if the great ice ship had come to grief and its crew of loved ones were no more than bones scattered on the ice. Ethan and Skua were not the only ones overdue at home.

Later that evening as the feasting was drawing to a close, Hunnar drew Ethan and Skua aside. They settled around a small table away from the noise of the main celebration.

"I wish that we could persuade you and your friend Williams to remain awhile longer among us. There is still so much we must learn."

"Milliken's sorry he was unable to attend," Ethan replied, simultaneously envying their schoolteacher friend his decision to skip the wedding and remain behind in Brass Monkey. "I'm sure he's as sorry as the two of us are that we have to leave, but we're just not designed to survive on a world like Tran-ky-ky."

"I would say you have survived well. You are as resourceful as any Tran."

September sipped at his tankard of brew, letting Ethan do most of the talking. "You're flattering us," Ethan told Hunnar, "but even if we could survive here, we want to return to our homes, even as your people want to return to Wannome. It's time. I'm not an explorer and adventurer by trade, you know. This whole business of Skua and Milliken and I coming to your world, landing among you—it was all an accident."

"Aye, that's a fact," said Skua. "He's a salesman, he is, and that's about as unadventurous a profession as a skyperson can pursue."

"You would give up all you have gained among us?" Hunnar stared at Ethan out of wide yellow eyes. "I could see you made a noble among my people. Vast tracts of land could be yours. The *Slanderscree* would be at your beck and call to carry you whence and whither you wished."

Ethan smiled gently. By Tran standards Hunnar's offer was magnanimous, but it was insufficient compensation for the lack of heated plumbing.

"Thanks, but right now all I want to see is a big city glowing with wasted light and full of naive customers with deep pockets."

"What of your intentions to do commerce among us, as you once said you had been sent here to do?"

"No offense, but I've kinda lost my taste for working this territory. I'll let some other representative of my company have that honor. I'm assuming that I still have a job, you see. Most companies frown on their employees' taking a couple of years off without explanation."

"But surely once you tell your"—Elfa struggled for the proper word—"master of what has happened he will be understanding and allow you to return."

"Not master, just employer," Ethan replied irritably, wishing he could scratch his chin but unwilling to pop the visor on his suit. "Although if I could talk to the big boss himself, I might be able to make him understand. I know my regional supervisor won't."

She turned her penetrating gaze on Ethan's companion. "And what of you, friend Skua? A warrior like yourself could command whole armies. There will be much fighting ahead. Not all will be persuaded to join the Union by sweet words. Your skills would be welcomed by our generals."

"You're a darlin', Elfa." Ethan tensed but Hunnar only grinned, showing sharp canines. September had indulged freely in the local liquor. "But you don't need me. With your combined forces you'll be able to overwhelm the most powerful recalcitrant city-state. Don't need me to make 'em see reason. I'd just be in the way, stealing the glory from some ambitious Tran warrior. Don't want to step on somebody else's career. Did that before, once, and it's never left me. Besides, I've got business of my own to attend to."

Ethan glanced sharply at him. "What business? You never said anything to me about having any business to get back to."

"What did you think I was about, young feller-me-lad? Retirement?" There was a twinkle in his eye. "There's this lady friend of long standing got herself a grant to do some studies on one of those out of the way recently discovered worlds Down-Arm. Fuspin—no, Alaspin the place is called. She's an archaeologist. Been after me for years to give her a hand with one of her projects. Ought to still be out there, poking into alien thises and thatses, getting dirt under her pretty fingernails. Told me this Alaspin's a jungle world. After our little stint hereabouts why, I'm ready for some sweat and humidity. That's where I'm bound soon as we can take passage off-planet." He smiled at Elfa.

"Second time, nothing personal. Your world's an invigorating place, but just a mite too much so for us human-folk. So you'll understand why we're taking our leave."

"We will strive to." She put a warm paw on September's forearm. "We can offer you many things, but not a substitute for home."

Home, Ethan thought. Did he have a home? Different nights, different cities on different worlds and then on again. If anyplace were home, it was the long emptiness between stars. Nothingness is my home, he thought, trying to be flip but finding that considering the matter seriously made him uncomfortable. Travel, sign a contract, travel on. It was hard even to remember his world of origin.

And what if he'd lost his job and couldn't get it back? What to do then? Proceed to the nearest civilized world and seek new employment?

No, he still had a job, was still a sales rep for the House of Malaika. He had to proceed on that assumption. It was all the security he had left. Maybe Elfa was right. Maybe his superiors would understand. One thing he could be sure of: they'd never heard an excuse for extended absenteeism like his.

He was wondering if his samples still sat in the customs warehouse as the *Slanderscree* docked again in the harbor of Brass Monkey. The icerigger would wait until its honored human passengers rode back toward the stars in one of their skyboats. There was also the matter of stocking the big ship for the long journey homeward.

One thing Ethan had already decided. If he were out of a job, he intended to claim his simple trade goods and give them to Hunnar and Elfa. Let the company sue him for the cost—if they could find him. A modern inert-element space heater would be worth a Landgrave's ransom to the Tran.

During their recent long journey to Moulokin, the outpost's engineers had received and installed a deep-space communications beam. For the first time since the establishment of the outpost, its citizens were able to communicate directly with the rest of the Commonwealth without having to wait for the monthly supply ship to carry out messages. The difficulty Ethan faced in trying to contact his superiors was that the beam was booked up for months in advance by long-suffering, long-silenced bureaucrats and researchers. Having been denied regular communication via null-space with the rest of civilization, they were making up for lost years by using the transmitter around the clock. Ostensibly it was all official business. In reality they just wanted to talk.

The solution to the problem of availability and cost was one and the same. Without it he couldn't so much as think of calling company headquarters.

Skua accompanied him to the gleaming underground communications center. Together they eyed the cluster of government functionaries and scientists gathered outside the broadcast console. The actual screen and its attendant instrumentation were enclosed in a bubble of smoked acrylic. As soon as one concluded his or her communication someone else entered the bubble. New hopefuls arrived in a steady stream. The number waiting to make use of the transmitter rose and fell without ever falling below a dozen.

September eyed the line of hopeful supplicants. "How are you going to break into that? And if you succeed, how are you going to pay for this? Use your retirement fund? This ain't like calling your old Aunt Tilly, you know."

Ethan smiled confidently. "You're right on both counts, but I'll manage. At least, I think I will."

He led September forward, pushing and excusing his way past irritated, curious members of the outpost population, until they were standing just outside the entrance to the broadcast bubble.

"Hey, you," snapped one of those in line, "there's a queue here."

"Sorry." Ethan flashed his most convincing smile. It was a salesman's smile, a professional smile; well practiced, endlessly rehearsed, subtly effective. "First-priority communication."

A smirk appeared on the face of the midlevel bureaucrat next in line. "First-priority? I don't recognize you. You're not government or research. You have any idea what a First-priority costs? Kitchen help couldn't pay for a First if the whole crew pooled a year's pay." He bestowed the dubious eye on both of them. Battered by the time spent out on the ice, Ethan had to admit that he and September probably didn't look like they could afford a short sentence between them.

He just smiled at the man. "We'll see. If you're correct, we'll be in and out of there in half a minute, won't we?"

The bureaucrat performed an exaggerated bow and gestured magnanimously with his right arm. "Leave us not waste unnecessary time then, shall we?" The woman standing behind him turned to her friend and giggled.

As soon as the functionary inside completed his business, Ethan and Skua stepped inside. Some of those farther back in the line might have disputed Ethan's right to try his luck even for a few seconds, but no one seemed inclined to strike up an argument with someone the size of September, which was why Ethan had brought him along in the first place.

The beam operator was tired, near the end of his shift, but not too tired to regard the newcomers uncertainly. He was blond and pale, and Ethan decided his ancestors would have been more at home on Tran-ky-ky than any other humans.

"What department are you two with? I don't see any insignia."

"No department." Ethan slid into the broadcast chair as though he owned it, trying to hide his nervousness. "I want to make a private call, First priority."

The middle-aged beam technician rubbed his golden crew cut. A single long, silver earring dangled from his perforated right earlobe. "A *private* call? First priority?

That means clearing the lines between here and wherever you want to call to."

"I'm aware of that."

"You know what that'll cost? The amount of time and energy involved? Even if it's Drax IV, and that's the nearest world with a receiving station, the number of relays involved are . . ."

"I don't want to talk to Drax IV. I want to talk closed-beam to the House of Malaika, which is located in the city of Drallar, on Moth. Can you set that up?"

The operator looked mildly offended. "I can set anything up—if you can pay for it. Right through Santos V and Dis and on to Terra. You're talking a lot of parsecs, friend."

"Devil take the parsecs. Set it up."

The operator shook his head. "I don't touch button one until I have some kind of financial clearance." A hand hovered over instrumentation that had nothing to do with chatting in null-space.

Ethan swallowed. "Enter code twenty-two double R, CDK."

Warily, the operator entered the information. "Mighty short code. This wouldn't be some kind of joke, would it? I wouldn't put it past Marianne and the guys."

A few moments fled before the words "Unlimited Credit" appeared on the small tridee screen near the operator's elbow. His eyebrows lifted. He gaped at the two words but nothing else materialized, no elaboration, no explanations. Just the two words.

"How'd you gain access to an account like this?"

September put just enough of a Tran-like growl into his voice to be intimidating. "You a cop or a beam operator?"

The man shrugged and turned to his instruments. "Hell of a distance," he grumbled. "Have to patch in fifty stations at least."

"You can set anything up, remember?" Ethan taunted him gently.

September leaned close and whispered, "How *did* you get hold of a code like that?"

"Colette du Kane," he reminded his tall companion. "Remember her? She said if I ever needed anything, to use that code."

"My kind of woman." September had not forgotten the plump industrialist's daughter who'd been marooned on Tran-ky-ky in their company. She'd proposed marriage to Ethan only to be turned down.

"Let's not make fun of her in her absence," Ethan chided his friend. "Especially since she's paying for this."

Despite his boasting it took the operator ten minutes to set up the call. Outside the communications bubble the functionaries who'd mocked Ethan cooled their heels while trying unsuccessfully to peer through the opaque plastic dome.

The static-filled screen in front of Ethan cleared slightly and the first sound filtered through. It was distorted and incomprehensible, not surprising considering the distance it had to travel. The operator cursed softly to himself as he adjusted his instrumentation.

Deep-space beams traveled in the mysterious region known as null-space, while KK-drive ships ploughed their way through space-plus. Sandwiched in between were stars, nebulae, and people in the region called normal space. Glory and a lifetime of ease awaited the physicist who could find a way for a ship to travel in null-space, a discovery that would reduce the travel time between the stars from weeks to minutes. Unfortunately, everything that ventured into that insane dimension came out scrambled, like eggs. Experimental animals sent through null-space arrived at their desintation as soup. This muted the enthusiasm of potential human followers. So far, pictures and chatter were all that the Commonwealth's men had figured out how to put back together again.

The picture cleared, revealing a figure as massive as September but not nearly as tall seated behind a hardwood desk. His complexion was ebony and his beard rolled out over his chest like waves across a beach. Though his frame occupied most of the image Ethan could make out a few details behind him. There was the desk of inlaid rare woods, a glass wall, and in the distance a city glowing with light. Drallar. Only a name on company documents until now. No reason for salespeople in the field to visit Moth. Actually, he'd heard it was something of a backward world, largely unpopulated, successful only because of its extreme laissez-faire attitude toward commerce. As a result it was headquarters for a number of major trading houses, among which was the House of Malaika.

Maxim Malaika regarded his caller across a distance of some seven hundred parsecs. The awesome gulf reduced his booming voice to a whisper.

"*Faida*, but this is a surprise. I don't take calls from lower-level field representatives, but then they usually don't call from such a distance." He paused while he glanced at a monitor whose screen was hidden from pickup view. "Tran-kee-kee, is it?"

"Tran-ky-ky." Ethan delicately corrected the pronounciation.

"And I *never* get calls from lower-level field representatives that they are paying for. I am intrigued, Mr. Fortune. What prompts this extraordinary communication on your part? You must have concluded quite a sizable transaction or two to justify such a transmission."

"Actually, sir, I haven't sold a thing in nearly two years." Malaika said nothing, nor did his expression change. He was accustomed to receiving explanations. Now he awaited one.

Ethan told him how he'd been outbound on the long run from Santos V to Dustdune when he'd stumbled into the kidnapping of the heiress Colette du Kane and her father, how they'd taken care of the kidnappers but crashed on the world called Tran-ky-ky, how they'd subsequently managed to strike up a friendly relationship with some of the natives, and how they'd spent the last year and more just surviving.

More than surviving, they'd set in motion the unification of fiercely independent city-states, thus putting the Tran well on the way to forming a planetary government capable of applying for associate status within the Commonwealth. The Tran proved to be intelligent, eager to learn, ready to adopt new ideas. As long as corrupt officials like the late Jobius Trell could be kept away from them, they should develop rapidly.

"I'm glad to hear that," said Malaika approvingly. "A developing race is a consuming race."

Ethan hesitated. "Then I still have my job?"

"Still have your job? Of course you still have your job. You did what you had to do. I'm sure you did not crash on this world on purpose. I don't fire competent people because they're caught up in circumstances beyond their control. I am impressed with your resourcefulness and skill in surviving. I am so impressed I'm not even going to dock you your base pay for the past couple of years. Of course, you gained no commissions during that time but there's nothing either of us can do about that."

Ethan was speechless. It was more than he had any right to expect.

Malaika leaned forward and his face filled the distant pickup. "And who is the large economy-size gentleman standing next to you, Mr. Fortune?"

"Just a friend. Skua . . ."

"Davis," September said. "Skua Davis."

"Nice to make your acquaintance, Mr. Davis." Malaika frowned. "That face. I've seen that face before. Have you always worn a beard, my friend?"

"Not always." September eased a couple of steps backward, taking himself slightly out of focus.

Ethan's expression twisted slightly. There had been several occasions when his friend had alluded to a checkered past. Ethan had pressed for details without ever obtaining any. Well, Skua's privacy was his own business and as his friend he was duty-bound to respect it.

"I can't thank you enough, sir."

"Yes, you're welcome." Malaika reluctantly shifted his attention back to his employee. "Great things are in the offing for the House of Malaika, young man, great things. This past year has been rich with the unusual. I have done some traveling of my own, entered new markets, overseen the expansion of the company. Also met this extraordinary child, a young adult really, wise in some ways beyond his years and in others the epitome of the naive." He shrugged. "But why burden you with the details of my life when yours has obviously been so much more interesting."

"Not by choice it hasn't been, sir."

"I understand."

"Thank you. I guess that's everything then, sir. The *Spindizzy* is due in orbit here next week and I'll be on it. I'll make contact with my district representative as soon as possible. I don't think it would do any good to try and resume my normal route where I left off, not almost two years late. For all I know my samples are a year out of date. Is Langan Ferris still my supervisor in this area?"

"Yes, Ferris is still out your way," Malaika said indifferently. "But why the rush? What's your hurry to be away?"

"What's my hurry?" For an instant Ethan forgot whom he was talking with. "Sir, I've been stuck on this ice ball for more than a year. I'd like to get back to civilization. I'd like to converse in Terranglo instead of Tran, enjoy some civilized company and companionship."

"Think of how you've positioned yourself, Fortune. Think of it! From what you've told me you're uniquely familiar with the natives and their ways. With their culture and their desires, their wants. You're best qualified to advise the new Resident Commissioner on how to deal with these Tran.

"If this local federation or union or whatever it is continues to mature and grow, these Tran will be ready to apply for associate status within the Commonwealth in a very short time. If they are accepted it means that their world will be upgraded from a restricted Class IVB to a IVA. They might even qualify for a special Class II. That means they would be allowed access to reasonably sophisticated goods and services. Goods and services which outside concerns would bid to provide." Ethan tried to inject an objection but Malaika raised a hand and rushed on.

"You have gained the trust of these people. I do not need to tell you how important trust is when you're trying to sell somebody something. You know the natives and what they would want. You could so advise the new Resident Commissioner."

"Please, sir." Ethan found he was starting to sweat. It was clear where Malaika was heading and Ethan searched desperately for a side road. "Any company rep could do what I've done. I'd be glad to brief anyone you decide to send out here. Myself, I'm looking forward to getting back to my old routine."

"Old routine. It defines itself." Malaika leaned back in his chair. "That's for your average, mildly competent, unimaginative salesman."

"But sir, that's what I *am*."

"Your modesty does you credit, Fortune. I couldn't

begin to ask a man like you, who's been through what you've been through, accomplished what you've accomplished, to go back to the dull, boring grind of visiting the same old places and talking to the same old customers. I wouldn't dream of asking it of you."

"Ask it of me, please."

Malaika went on as though he hadn't heard the last. Perhaps he hadn't, though Ethan doubted it. The head of the House hadn't missed anything else.

"I envy you, Fortune; yes, I do. To have enjoyed the experiences you have and emerged from them wiser and more knowledgeable is something the rest of us, chained to our computers, can only imagine. The life of a travelling sales rep is clearly not for you, no, clearly not."

"Begging to differ with you, sir, but I don't have an adventurous bone in my body. Everything that's happened has been an accident, and I'm tired of living an accident."

Malaika nodded. "I understand, truly I do, Fortune. You've tired of aimless wandering, you're tired of being bounced around the surface of a backward, primitive world. You want some stability, want to know where you're going to be from day to day. You want a regular routine again, want to know that tomorrow's work is assured and not radically different from what you've done today."

Ethan relaxed a little. For a while there he feared he wasn't going to be able to make his point. "Yes, that's exactly what I want, sir. If it's not too much to ask."

"Of course not. We are in agreement, then."

Ethan sat up straight in his chair. "We are?"

"Certainly. Taking into account all that you have told me, I have no choice but to appoint you as full factotum representing the House of Malaika on Tran-ky-ky. You will supervise the establishment and growth of a full-scale trading operation. With your unique knowledge and experience to draw upon, we will have a near monopoly on trade with the locals before any of the other great houses so much as get wind of the possibilities there. There are *possibilities*, I take it?"

"Yes sir, but as to the need for a permanent representative . . ."

"Every world no matter how recently opened to trade requires a permanent representative. A lucky man I am to have someone well qualified already on the spot!" Again Ethan hastened to argue and again Malaika overrode any incipient protests.

"Naturally such a promotion and increase in responsibility carries with it a hefty rise in salary. You can look forward to a better and earlier retirement, Fortune. You will have people under you to supervise. No more worrying about lost commissions and an irregular income."

"Even so, sir, I . . ."

"Don't thank me, don't thank me. You've earned this. It's an opportunity that comes rarely to one your age. Normally one serves twenty to thirty years before being appointed a factotum. And after our monopoly has been secured and you've trained a solid core of new people to handle the business, the House would consider transferring you to another world. Paris, say, or New Riviera."

Ethan hesitated. By themselves the promotion and increase in salary weren't sufficient to make him consider staying, but the possibility of obtaining both and then taking them with him to one of the paradise worlds, that was something worth thinking about. More than that, the offer was tempting. A factotum on a world like New Riviera could make an enormous amount of money while working in the most congenial surroundings the Commonwealth had to offer.

Even so, the memories of the bone-chilling arctic cold, the unceasing wind, and the more prosaic dangers of Tran-ky-ky were far fresher in his memory than tridees of warm beaches on unvisited worlds. Not that he didn't have a choice. He could accept promotion and promise or he could quit and take the next ship one way to Drax IV and start looking for a new profession. Drax IV was a nice civilized world but not a major one. Jobs there might not be so easy to come by.

"Don't thank me," Malaika said again. "I will make arrangements for an account to be opened in the company's name for you to draw upon. Within, oh, say a few weeks I'll expect to see a comprehensive report on our prospects there. I'll need to know what kind of approach you think we should begin with, what kind of assistance you'll need, what sort of office equipment, what trade goods will be admissable under the planet's current status, that sort of thing. I have complete confidence that you will do a thorough and businesslike job. Your raise in pay will be entered into the company's computers immediately. I think that's everything." He reached forward to break the connection, paused.

"One more thing. How did you manage to pay for this communication, anyway?"

"Through a gift from a friend," Ethan muttered dazedly.

"Ah. A very good friend indeed. Well, I have enjoyed our little conversation immensely, yes, immensely. Perhaps some day circumstances will allow you to visit Moth and we can meet in person. Lovely place, Moth. All the amenities with none of the concomitant restrictions and plenty of room for a man to stretch his legs as well as his mind."

"Sure." You wouldn't want to risk freezing your precious backside by coming out *here*, of course, Ethan thought. If he'd known Maxim Malaika better, he wouldn't have thought that. Or maybe he would have. He was mad: at Malaika, and at himself.

"Good-bye then, Fortune. *Kwa heri.* I'll be looking forward to reading that report."

The screen filled with static, then blanked. The operator fiddled with a few instruments, then swiveled in his chair to regard them both. "Transmission broken at the other end. Anything else?"

Unable to reply, Ethan simply shook his head as he stood. And he thought *he* was a pretty good salesman. The operator unsealed the bubble, letting them out. The line of waiting bureaucrats gaped at them as they strode silently out into the corridor.

"There now, young feller-me-lad, everything's going to turn out all right." September put a comforting arm around Ethan's shoulders.

"Sure it is. For Malaika."

"What about the money?"

"Money can't buy happiness, Skua."

"Well now, lad, it appears our philosophies differ on that point. You have to admire your boss. Made the whole thing seem as much your idea as his. He never actually gave you the choice to make."

They turned a bend in the corridor. "The raise and the promotion are gratifying, sure. I just wish they applied on a slightly more benign world." He nodded toward one of the insulated windows at the perpetual snow and ice outside.

"What's this? Losing your affection for good ol' Tranky-ky? I thought you'd feel right at home here by now, feller-me-lad. It ain't as though you're going to be skidding across the ice in the *Slanderscree* for the next few years. You're going to have underlings to do the fieldwork for you while you sit back here in the commercial building in your nice warm office, staring at entertainment tridees and reading good books. With the deep-space beam in place you don't have to feel cut off from what's happening in the rest of the Commonwealth. There'll be news, and new visitors—maybe you can hire a few competent young ladies to help you out—and in a few years, if all goes well here, you'll get yourself boosted over to Paris or some place soft."

"You make it all sound so reasonable and inviting. You sure you don't work for Malaika on the sly?"

"Not likely, lad. And if the Tran qualify for associate status, you'll be able to use a skimmer when you do have to make checks on your people out in the field. Your promotion will be good for you and good for our friends."

"If it's all so wonderful, why don't you call Malaika back and offer to take the job?"

September's eyes widened. "What, d'you think I'm crazy? I'm getting out of here on the next ship!"

II

Every building at the outpost where humans could expect to meet with Tran was equipped with a transition room, a chamber where the temperature was lowered to just above freezing. It enabled humans to talk unburdened by survival suits, while the Tran found it bearably tropic; a climate where different races from different temperatures could get together. Hunnar Redbeard was to meet them here. They waited in the corridor for the Tran to arrive.

Maybe Skua was right. The decision had been made. Nothing to gain from moping and moaning about his fate. There were plenty of people who would gladly have traded places and opportunities with him. And if he changed his mind, he could quit anytime. Sure he could. Just throw away his job, his career, his seniority within the House, and, as Malaika had so irresistibly put it, the chance of a lifetime for someone his age.

"At least I'll have one old friend to keep me company."

"Oh, you'll make plenty of friends here," September readily agreed. "Not all of them are likely to be as stiff-necked and tight-assed as that bunch back in communications. You'll strike up all sorts of friendships as you get to meet the personnel."

"I wasn't talking about new friendships."

"What's that?" The giant eyed him askance. "Whoa now, feller-me-lad, you know better. When the *Spindizzy* settles herself in orbit, I'm up and away for Alaspin, I am. For Alaspin and a warm climate and the understanding solicitudes of a lady friend."

"What was all that then about Tran-ky-ky's wonderful opportunities and its delightful people?"

"All true, all true, young feller-me-lad, and just think of the good you'll sip from that glass. I'd gladly stay and keep you company save for my prior obligations."

"What obligations? A two-year-old half promise to join some archaeologist on a distant world? She's probably forgotten all about you by now."

"Ah, now, feller-me-lad, there you're mistaken. Those who meet old Skua don't forget him so fast, and a promise is a promise even if I am to be a bit late fulfilling it."

Ethan nodded disgustedly. "That's it then? You're just going to run out on me?"

"Now, lad." September looked hurt. "I'm not running out on you. You've chosen to stay here. You can still leave with me if you want to."

"Sure I can."

"Sure's the word. Would you really deny me the choice you deny yourself? After all, I don't have so much as a job here."

"I can give you one. I'm going to be in charge, remember. You could be my executive assistant. I'm sure I could arrange a good salary for you."

"Not good enough, feller-me-lad. Old Skua, he ain't much for regular employment. I like to kind of keep moving around, if you know what I mean."

Ethan turned away from him. "All right, then, go on, leave, forget it. Forget me, too. See if I care."

"I had hoped," September told him softly, "that our final parting when it came would be under more pleasant circumstances. We've been through too much this past year and more to say farewells without smiles, feller-me-lad." Ethan didn't reply. "Let's put it another way. Would you ask anyone else to stay here if they didn't have to?"

The younger man considered, slumped against the wall. "No. No, you're right, damn you. It's wrong of me to expect you to stay just to make it easier on me. You're carrying around enough emotional baggage without me dumping extra guilt on you." He managed a smile. "Maybe it'll help if I can think of one of us enjoying himself someplace else relaxing and taking it easy in the sun."

"I think you've a false conception of what archaeology's all about, feller-me-lad. From what I've heard this Alaspin's as primitive as they come. Don't think they've got a deep-space beam dug in there yet. But if warmth can be transmitted by telepathy, I'll do my best to share some with you. Maybe one of these days we'll both meet under more comforting circumstances." He looked past Ethan, through the transparent walls that lined both sides of the transition room.

"Let's put made decisions aside. Here come our friends."

Ethan turned. Hunnar and his two squires, Suaxus-dal-Jagger and Budjir, were approaching from outside. They halted at the entrance to the chamber, then stepped inside, waving at their human friends. They couldn't come any farther since the temperature in the outpost would lay them out with heatstroke inside fifteen minutes.

As Ethan and Skua passed into the meeting room, a blast of cold air struck their exposed skin. Leaving the comforting confines of the outpost was always a shock, and this wasn't even outside. Out on the ice beyond, the midday reading hovered between twenty and thirty below zero—on a clear day. Near the poles it was so cold that if not for the steady circulation of the atmosphere, the air itself would have frozen and fallen to the ground like dust.

Hunnar looked a little heavier than usual, Ethan mused. Marriage was already showing its effects. Greetings were exchanged.

"Well, friend Ethan, were you able to talk across the night to your Landgrave?" At the look on Ethan's face the Tran adopted a tone of concern. "It went badly?"

"No, not badly. It's just that—well, it was decided that I'm to stay here and continue with my work."

"Here?" Suaxus's pointed ears twitched forward. "With us? But that be wonderful news, Sir Ethan!"

"It is good," Hunnar agreed. "I understand if you will not be able to return to Sofold with us, but because we now have the *Slanderscree* we will be able to come and visit you."

"Yes, and one day I'll be able to travel in a skimmer." Despite what Malaika had said about letting employees do the fieldwork Ethan knew he could hardly turn a bunch of innocents lose on the surface of Tran-ky-ky without personal supervision. They wouldn't last a month. The Tran would eat them alive, perhaps literally.

"I know that our climate and some of our people are not to your liking," Hunnar said perceptively, "and that mayhap you wish still to return to your home, but when and wherever possible we shall strive to make a home for you here, among us."

"It won't be bad," Ethan assured him, talking as much to himself as to his friends. "For a salesman, home is where you plug in your order screen." And he had friends here already, he reflected. Unlike humans, when you made friends with a Tran you had a friend for life. He clapped a hand on Hunnar's arm, feeling the thick bristly fur through the sensitive glove of his survival suit. "Let's go see how the *Slanderscree*'s repairs are coming along. Now that I hold an official position here, I'm going to be able to help you a lot more. Anything Captain Ta-hoding requires in the way of joints or glue or bolts, I'll be able to requisition from outpost stocks and charge to the company. I can put it all down to priming the customers." He flipped up his hood but kept the ice visor unsealed. Maybe he couldn't help himself but he could damnwell help his friends.

"That's the spirit, feller-me-lad." September hung back. "While you're out looking over the old *Slanderscree* I'm going to be getting what personal possessions I have together. The *Spindizzy*'s shuttle should be arriving pretty quick now and I won't want to be late."

Ethan turned at the exit to grin back at his friend. "You know these commercial shuttles. Some of them are pretty small." September was six foot ten and built like a tank. "What if they don't have a seat wide enough to fit you?"

"Why in that case, lad, I'll have the factotum for the House of Malaika order me up a special crate and I'll ship myself out as cargo." He winked. "Happens as how I know the factotum himself and he owes me a favor or two."

In fact, September was not quite ready for departure when Ethan thumbed the privacy buzzer set in the door of the small apartment the giant had been allotted. Several days had passed and the *Spindizzy*'s shuttle rested in the outpost hangar, still taking on cargo and comments.

The door slid into the wall to reveal an awesome sight few human eyes had encountered, or would want to—Skua September clad only in his underwear.

"Come in, young feller-me-lad, come in. In a little while I'll be off and there'll be time only to recall the things you wanted to say and didn't." He put a hand over the close control. Ethan stayed outside.

"You won't be off like that, I hope."

"Not on this world. It's cold enough in the hanger.

Come in, why don't you, before we shock some passing technocrat?"

"I'm afraid I can't, Skua. You're going to have to come out."

The giant's huge bushy eyebrows drew together. "Don't talk riddles with me, feller-me-lad. Not now. I've no business remaining here that requires my presence."

"There's someone who disagrees with you."

"And who might that be?"

"The new Resident Commissioner."

September glared at the floor. "How so? If they need some kind of deposition or statement from me, they can get ahold of me on Alaspin—if they can track down Isili's site."

"It's not that simple, Skua. She's flagged your boarding pass."

"Splendid," he muttered. "If some bureaucratic mama thinks she's going to keep me off that shuttle, she's got another thing coming."

"She sure does. You and me." He checked his chronometer. "In twenty minutes, to be exact. In her office."

"What's the point?" September made no effort to conceal his exasperation. "We've already entered everything that happened outside Moulokin in the official records."

"Don't get excited," Ethan advised him. An excited September was something even his friends didn't want to be around. "I'm sure it's just a last-minute formality of some kind. In five minutes it'll be done with and you'll be out of there and on your way. We don't even know what she wants to see us for. Maybe just to say hello and, in your case, good-bye."

"She wants to see you, too, huh?"

Ethan nodded. "Before you get yourself all exercised and overwrought let's just go up there and see what she wants. Besides, aren't you curious to see who the Commonwealth has sent out as a replacement for that schmuck Trell? It's crucial to the future of the Tran."

"Aye, but not to the future of the September." He sighed resignedly. "If she's flagged my boarding pass I don't have any choice. Wait while I find something to put on. Perhaps if she's young and inexperienced she'll need to have a private chat with old Skua to learn what this world's really about."

"What about your shuttle?"

"For the important things in life, one can always make time, feller-me-lad."

The office of the Resident Commissioner occupied the apex of the triangular structure which housed much of the local Commonwealth administrative complex. From its top it commanded sweeping views of the outpost of Brass Monkey, the modest Tran community which had grown up around it, and the fjordlike ice harbor beyond. Tran ice ships sat tied up to low stone docks, seeking protection from the stronger winds that blasted the open ice ocean.

Ethan's apprehension and Skua's anticipation both turned out to be misplaced. The new Resident Commissioner for Tran-ky-ky was a pleasant, handsome woman in her mid-seventies. She wore a severe dress suit of light blue with Commonwealth insignia to match. Touches of the exact same shade of blue formed two parallel streaks in her otherwise silvery hair. She did not look like anyone's grandma. Her movements were slow and her speech patient. Her name was Millicent Stanhope.

"Be seated, gentlemen."

"Look, ma'am," September said, starting in without waiting to be asked, "I can't stay long. I'm booked on the *Spindizzy*, as you know, and I don't want to miss her. I've been stuck on this world for too long already."

"Gently, September. I read your formal reports. I know

that you're anxious to be on your way. I won't detain you long." Her eyes flicked over to Ethan. "And you, Mr. Fortune, I understand will be staying with us for a while longer. That's good. I'll want to draw upon your unique body of experience."

"I'll be glad to help whenever I can," Ethan assured her, simultaneously realizing the truth of Maxim Malaika's assertions.

September was in no mood to be coddled. "If you've read our reports, then why the need for this meeting?"

"Please try to relax, Mr. September, however much an effort it may be for you. I promise you won't miss your flight."

September leaned back in the big chair but continued to glance pointedly at the wall chronometer even though ample time remained before the shuttle was scheduled to depart.

"There is this business of the death of my predecessor, Mr. Jobius Trell." Ethan shifted uncomfortably in his chair. "According to your report he was killed while making use of advanced weaponry in an attempt to enforce an illegal and extortionate trade monopoly on the native populace."

"That's right," Ethan told her.

"Your description of the manner of his death is fuzzy as to details. I was wondering if you could be more specific." Ethan glanced at September who regarded the ceiling with single-minded intensity. The awkward silence lengthened.

"You see, gentlemen, I have a reason for asking," Stanhope finally told them. "I have spent forty-three years in the diplomatic service. I am retiring in six months and I want nothing, and I mean absolutely nothing, to mar my record. I am searching for neither scapegoats nor assassins. I just don't want any surprises. That's all. I promise you that anything you tell me will remain confidential and will go no further than we three, but if I am to treat knowledgeably with the locals, I must know everything that happened."

Ignoring September's silent protest, Ethan related the incidents which had led to the death of the former Resident Commissioner, telling Stanhope about his treacherous alliance with the former Landgrave of Arsudun and how he had manipulated the mad former Landgrave of Poyolavomaar. When he'd concluded the story, Stanhope leaned back in her chair and nodded gratefully.

"Thank you, Mr. Fortune. I appreciate your candor. That is a word rarely employed in the diplomatic corps."

"Six months, you said." Ethan strove to change the subject. "If you don't mind my saying so, I'm surprised they'd send someone like yourself to a place like this with retirement so near at hand."

She laughed lightly. "Oh, but I requested this post."

That brought September out of his pout. "You *asked* to come here?"

"That I did. This is an outpost world, not even a formal colony, about as low a classification as you can find that rates someone with my seniority. Nothing happens here. Once a month the KK-drive ship that travels between Santos V and Drax IV pauses here. That's it. For a diplomat, Tran-ky-ky is a dull, boring, and unprestigious place to be stationed, and that's precisely why I wanted to come here." Her tone darkened slightly, steel beneath the smiles.

"Six months, gentlemen. Six months I have left. I want them to be as quiet and undisturbed as though they never were. I came here to be forgotten for half a year. Then I can retire to my modular on Praxiteles and work on my laserpoint."

"What are you going to do about the Tran?" Ethan asked her.

"Actually, I think they're cute, your Tran."

September guffawed. "About as cute as cannibals on ice skates."

"That may be. But as they appear to be progressing nicely on their own, thanks to your own philanthropic efforts, I propose to do absolutely nothing. I will stay out of their way. Out of everyone's way, hopefully. If there are any matters that require my attention, I expect my aides and involved civilians such as yourself, Mr. Fortune, will bring them to my attention. In return for this advice I will do my best to stay out of *your* way.

"I know that you intend to establish a formal branch of the trading house of Malaika here. I will do what I can to expedite your work by burdening you with as little red tape as possible. In return I expect you and the others like you to serve as my eyes and ears among the natives. As for myself, I will count my tour of duty here a success if I never have to step outside this office save to eat and sleep. I hope I have made myself perfectly clear."

Ethan nodded. "Perfectly, Ms. Stanhope."

She glanced at September. "And I expect you to say nothing about your difficulties here, particularly as they concern the late Mr. Trell, for at least six months."

September adopted a dignified mien. "Ma'am, I assure you that unburdening myself to government officials is right near the bottom of my list of permanent priorities. I'm on my way to a world that makes this one look advanced so I can lose myself in an alien jungle for a year or two."

"Then we are all in agreement as to the direction of our futures. Good." She rose. It was a dismissal. "Mr. Fortune, I imagine you have a great deal of work to do. Mr. September, you must have some last-minute preparations to conclude prior to your departure."

September approached the desk and took her hand in his. It vanished inside his massive palm. "Good to know the future of Tran-ky-ky's in such understanding hands, for half a year, anyway."

"Mr. September, you are gallant." She retrieved her fingers, sat back down. "Now if you will both excuse me, I have a great deal of nothing to do and I am anxious to be about it."

September wore a thoughtful expression as they took the elevator back to ground level. "Interesting old gal. Wish I'd known her twenty years back."

"A bit stiff for my taste," said Ethan.

"Don't be too quick to judge, feller-me-lad. You never can tell about these steely-eyed types. Why, underneath that hard-shelled exterior there probably beats a heart of pure concrete."

The lift doors parted. As they exited they nearly stumbled over a preoccupied Milliken Williams.

Like Ethan and Skua, the diminutive schoolteacher had also been in the wrong place at the wrong time when the kidnapping of the wealthy du Kanes had taken place, and like them, he'd been carried unwillingly to the surface of Tran-ky-ky. He was full of self-deprecation and apologies except when he was doing something like introducing the Trun to gunpowder and crossbows. Ethan thought he looked worried. That was William's usual state of mind. He was always worrying about what was going to go wrong next, and if nothing went wrong, he worried why it hadn't.

"I was just coming to get you." His eyes darted from one face to the other. "Could I have a moment of your time, do you think?"

September rolled his eyes. "Everyone wants a minute of old Skua's time. I'm running out of minutes, Milliken."

"Please. This is terribly important."

"What isn't? All right." He looked around, gestured resignedly toward the administration cafeteria. "I could use a bite to eat before getting on the shuttle."

It was between meal times and the room was almost empty. Tran furs and handicrafts decorated the walls and gave the otherwise bland hall a little character. Automatic food machines lined one wall. Ice particles formed abstract patterns on the exterior of a curved, triple-paned window as the wind smashed them against the glass. They ordered food and drink and settled into a booth near the window.

"Skua," Williams asked earnestly, "how set are you on leaving Tran-ky-ky?"

September said nothing, simply sat and stared. "Is there some sort of conspiracy at work here that old Skua knows nothing about? First you, feller-me-lad, and now our over-educated little friend here."

"There is no such thing as overeducation," Williams replied primly. "I asked you a perfectly straightforward question. And if we're going to make comments about size, let me say I'd ten times rather be my height than a grotesque variant of a macrocephalian like certain people I know."

"You mean macrocerebral," said September. "Forget it. It's just that you're not first in line."

"What's going on, Milliken?" Ethan asked him.

"There seems to be a bit of a problem. More than a bit, actually. A very considerable problem."

"What kind of problem?" Ethan was patient with the teacher. He had a way of talking around a subject rather than going straight to the point. You had to prod him or the conversation would languish among irrelevancies.

"It involves Tran-ky-ky."

"I figured that much. I don't want to sound impatient, Milliken, but Skua has a shuttle to catch."

"Plenty of time before liftoff. I know. I checked the schedule. I was just wondering if you'd mind listening to a full discussion of this problem."

"Anything to get this over with." September swallowed the rest of his snack in a single gulp.

"You said it involves Tran-ky-ky," Ethan reminded the teacher. "In what way?"

"We're not sure. The entire planet may be at risk."

Ethan sipped at his drink. "The sun's not going nova or anything like that?"

"No, no, nothing so immediate or dramatic. It's just that, well, there's a climatological anomaly that nobody has a decent explanation for and it's driving the meteorology staff crazy. By now the members of the local scientific community know about the three of us and our experiences. They know that our knowledge of Tran-ky-ky isn't theoretical, that we've had 'hands on' dealings with the world beyond Brass Monkey."

"Hands on for sure," said September. "I don't know that participating in the bashing of hostile locals qualifies us as scientific experts on much of anything."

Williams didn't so much as crack a smile. "This is a serious business, Skua."

"Deity save us from serious business. What you're saying is that some folks just want to ask us a few questions, right?"

Williams nodded.

"Milliken, you're the only one of us who's had anything that could be called scientific training. You've been everywhere Skua and I have. Why don't they just talk to you?"

"First because no one is yet positive this matter is of a wholly scientific nature and second because some of the staff doubt their own conclusions. They're desperately searching for as many possibilities of confirmation as possible. They're afraid of being ridiculed. Since the three of us have been out there and know what Tran-ky-ky is like, they're fairly certain we won't ridicule them. Argue and dispute, yes, but not ridicule."

September pushed away from the table. "Don't let 'em be so sure. Let's get on with it."

"Do we have to go outside?" Ethan stared through the cafeteria window at the blowing snow.

"The main research center is reachable via the underground walkways, but it would be faster to cut across open ground."

"We'll walk the extra meters," Ethan told him.

III

During their brief stays in Brass Monkey neither Ethan nor Skua had had any reason to visit the research complex. It was the oldest group of buildings in Brass Monkey and the rationale for the outpost's establishment in the first place. Scouts first, scientists after, lastly bureaucrats. Like the rest of the outpost complex it was largely buried beneath the ice and permafrost.

The large meeting room Williams led them into lay several levels beneath the surface of Arsudun. Half a dozen curious faces turned to inspect them when they arrived. Out of this pack of intelligent speculation emerged a woman even shorter than the schoolteacher.

She wore a bright blue jumpsuit with green and white insignia and patches. Ethan had expected a white lab smock. Her hair was straight, jet black, and cut off in a straight line just above shoulder level. She might have been thirty or sixty. Her handshake was firm.

"I am Cheela Hwang. There are my fellow crisis mongers." She introduced each of her companions in turn. "In case Milliken hasn't told you, I am in charge of the meteorology department at Brass Monkey. As you might imagine, knowing Tran-ky-ky, we constitute a fairly large contingent here."

39

"Weather'd be about the only thing worth studying on this world," September commented, "excepting the locals, of course."

She tilted back her head to try and meet his gaze. "Milliken forewarned me about your attitude as well as your sense of humor, Mr. September."

The giant grinned slightly. "I'll try to comport myself in a civilized manner and not eat any of your subordinates."

"What's this problem all of you are so exercised about?" Ethan asked her.

"Over here, please." She led them toward the far wall, fingering a small remote control she took from one of the jumpsuit's pockets. The wall came to light. It was an integrated tridee screen, which explained why it was the only partition in the room devoid of pictures, photographs, or other hangings.

"Perhaps you recognize this, Mr. Fortune."

"Just Ethan will do fine." He stared at the wallful of whorls and swirls. The colors were bright, the outlines regular. "Infrared photographs, but of what?"

"The ground we're standing in, young feller-me-lad." September gestured at the wall. "That blob up there, that's Arsudun. Those smaller spots represent the Landgrave's town, Brass Monkey, and the like."

"You have a fine eye for information." Hwang sounded approving.

September shrugged. "I've had some experience identifying topographic features from above. Why the infrared? Why not just a straight satellite photo?"

One of Hwang's colleagues spoke up, a touch of bitterness in his voice. "This is a minor outpost. We don't rate a fully equipped survey satellite. No high-resolution cameras. Just straightforward instrumentation."

Ethan wanted to ask his friend where he'd gained experience "identifying topographic features from above," but

Hwang was pressing on, using her remote's built-in pointer to trace features on the wall as the image changed.

"Do you recognize this?" The center of the picture was an intense orange.

"Looks like Sofold," Ethan ventured. "The home island of our Tran friends. The central volcano is unmistakable."

"That is correct. And this?" The two men stared hard at the image and looked blank. "That's not surprising," Hwang told them. "There's no way you could recognize it because you haven't been there. No human has. It lies far to the southeast of Arsudun." She ran the wall through a rapid sequence of similar images.

"This is an infrared mosaic of the large southern continent." Her pointer moved over the images like a two-dimensional insect. "Notice these features here. These big clouds and"—she dipped the pointer—"this heat shadow on the ice ocean."

"What about them?" Ethan asked.

"They shouldn't be there." This from Gerald Fraser, an assistant "They're all wrong. We've been studying Tranky-ky's climate for quite a while now. We've done mapping for years and the climate's been under intensive examination ever since the establishment of the outpost here. There haven't been any big surprises. Everything involving the weather has been pretty predictable and very consistent. Then this." He waved a hand at the wall. "It's like finding a lump of coal in your ice cream."

"Gerry's right." Hwang's pointer moved. "These clouds and this shadow on the ice are all wrong. Right for Kansastan maybe, but not Tran-ky-ky."

"So it's wrong." Ethan was getting interested. "What's its significance? What's it indicative of?"

"A change in the climate."

Ethan and Skua exchanged a glance. "I don't understand," Ethan told her. "Less freezing or more freezing, what's the difference?"

"It's not freezing here."

Ethan's gaze narrowed. "I beg your pardon?" He stared at the infrared image anew, trying to see things that weren't there. Meanwhile Hwang's pointer continued to flutter over the wall.

"This small area exhibits a radical difference in temperature from its immediate surroundings. In addition to the inexplicable rise in temperature spectroscopic analysis also reveals a radical change in the composition of the atmosphere directly above this portion of the continental plateau."

"Volcanism," September said immediately. "Tran-ky-ky's full of it. I don't see what the problem is."

Hwang smiled. "You're full of surprises, Mr. September. Yes, there are many volcanoes on this world, and sufficient volcanism in this area could possibly be responsible for what we're seeing, but we don't think volcanism is the cause. Low-resolution or not, our satellite is capable of resolving fairly small details on the surface; there's no evidence of cratering anywhere in the vicinity of the anomaly."

"What about venting?" September asked her. Ethan looked at him in surprise and September smiled back. "Done some geology in my time, feller-me-lad."

"We thought of that also. We've even considered purely speculative and fanciful rationales. None of them fits the magnitude of what we're observing. If we had a really decent satellite, with high resolution cameras on board . . ." Her voice trailed off momentarily. "But we don't. Our orbiter was designed to aid in measurements of the atmosphere and in making weather predictions. We have better equipment on order but you might imagine how difficult it is to obtain expensive instruments for use in studying these backward worlds."

"Don't let Hunnar Redbeard hear you call Tran-ky-ky backward," Ethan told her. "The Tran may not be sophisticated or technologically mature but they're not dumb either, and they're proud as hell."

"Don't be so defensive," said one of the other researchers. "We're here to try and help these people, not insult them."

"We suspect volcanism," Hwang continued, "because we don't have anything else to go on. We know the planet's internal heat helps drive its weather in the absense of open bodies of water. We could write the whole thing off until new equipment arrives. But we're worried."

A tall geophysicist with the unlikely name of Orvil Blanchard waved at the wall with a lanky hand. "Keep in mind we can't find any natural features that might explain what's going on in this region. Despite that, the changes in the atmosphere are increasing steadily. Volcanic venting varies dramatically. It doesn't increase at a steady, measurable rate the way this anomaly does. At least, not any volcanic vent I've ever encountered. It's as if something's thrown a switch inside the planet."

Hwang shut off the concealed tridee projector. "We could put it down to volcanism anyway, but we want to be certain. Since our modest survey satellite is unable to resolve the problem to anyone's satisfaction, all that's left to us is an on-site inspection. Which presents us with a problem. Because of restrictions governing the deployment of advanced technology on a Class IVB world like Tran-ky-ky, we have no access here to aircraft or skimmers. It was assumed we could get all the information we required to continue with our research via the satellite. Normally that would suffice.

"Administration had a skimmer for emergency use, but

that apparently was destroyed when the previous Commissioner ran afoul of some unfriendly natives. Or so your report—which everyone here has read by the way—indicated."

"I've seen ice cycles around the outpost. What about using those?" Ethan asked her.

"Strictly short range," said Blanchard. "We could pack extra fuel cells, maybe even enough to make the journey there and back, but we couldn't carry sufficient additional supplies. And from what we know of the weather out on the ice ocean, something as small as a cycle might get blown two kilometers back for every one it advanced."

"Besides that," Hwang went on impatiently, "none of us has ventured any farther from Brass Monkey than the shore of this island. It was circumnavigated and mapped by geologists as the base here was being established. That's about the extent of our long-range exploration. Everyone's still new to a new world. That's why we've devoured your official report. It's been invaluable to every department. But we've no personal experience or knowledge of what it's like out on the oceans. None of us here at the outpost, for example, has ever seen one of these extraordinary creatures the natives call stavanzers.

"We'd be traveling blind and ignorant and with no aircraft or skimmer to back us up. I think you'll agree that it would be exceedingly risky, foolhardy even, for people like us without your kind of experience to undertake a journey to the southern continent."

"Can't argue with you there," said September, blithely ignoring the hidden plea.

Subtlety having failed, Hwang put the request directly. "Then surely you can see that we need your help."

Realization dawned more slowly on Ethan. "Oh, no. I mean, we'll be glad to help you with preparations and suggestions and advice, won't we, Skua?"

September pointedly checked his chronometer. "That we will, young feller-me-lad, so long as they don't take more than a few hours. A nova *might* have kept me off that shuttle. Nothing else will."

Hwang turned to gaze earnestly at Ethan. "What about you, Mr. Fortune? Milliken tells us you're going to be staying here anyway."

Ethan shot an angry look in the schoolteacher's direction. Williams didn't turn away from the glare. Why be upset with Milliken anyway? Ethan asked himself. Truth was truth.

"Yeah, I'll be based here for a while. But my responsibility is to the House of Malaika. I have to set up a formal trading station. Right now that consists of myself and a few cases of samples that are probably frozen solid in the warehouse. I have to arrange for construction or leasing of offices and / storage space, hire an assistant from administration, and begin the search for suitable employees off-world. There are forms to be processed and filled out and filed, and I don't know where to begin."

"We can help you with that," said another of the meteorologists. "We've been dealing with the local administration for years."

"From a scientific standpoint, not a commercial one," Ethan argued. "I also have to arrange quarters for myself."

"We could find you a permanent apartment here." Blanchard grinned. "Not entirely on the up and up, but we did lose a couple of geologists a few months back. You could have two apartments, one for yourself and another for a temporary office. Better than what administration would assign you."

Ethan felt like a man climbing a ladder to escape a pack of carnivores. He was rapidly running out of rungs. "Look, I appreciate your offers and I sympathize with your situation, but I don't have a minute to spare for myself, I've got a ton of work to do, and I just can't disappear for weeks on end again. I just got *back* to civilization. If it's an ice ship you want, I can make contacts for you in Arsudun Towne. You can hire transportation to Poyolavomaar. Once you're there, I'm sure you'll be able to hire a ship and crew to take you farther south."

"Where we have to go is uncharted territory. It's a long way from this Poyolavomaar you describe in your report. We don't know the natives or their ways."

"Why not just wait for your new satellite instrumentation? Then you can get all the answers you need from the safety and comfort of your offices."

"It's not our safety and comfort that concerns us at the moment," Hwang told him. "It's the safety of the natives, the Tran. You see, while we don't share your unique experiences we do interact with the natives here in Brass Monkey. We know many of them by name and we've come, as you have, to like and admire them. We don't want to see anything happen to them."

"Now hold on a minute." September looked confused. "We've been talking about an unexplained localized meteorological phenomenon affecting a part of the southern continent. Nobody's said anything about a possible planet-wide disaster."

"It's difficult to speak in such terms without hard evidence," said another of the scientists. "That's why we're so anxious to go and see what's happening for ourselves. We hope no disaster is in the offing—planetary or even continental—but we need to go there and find out. And we need to do it as soon as possible. We can't wait for answers on advanced imaging equipment that might or might not ever arrive. We're probably overreacting, but we need to know what's going on out there, Mr. September."

"It doesn't matter." Ethan fought to keep a grip on his emotions. "Unless you hire an ice ship to take you to

Poyolavomaar and then try to proceed south from there you won't find out. Because there's no other way to reach the region you're talking about. You just ran through all the options yourself. It's too far for ice cycles and there's no skimmer or aircraft available."

"What of the remarkable ice ship you built?" Hwang asked him.

"We didn't build anything," Ethan told her, more sharply than he intended. "The Tran built every meter of it themselves."

"Excuse me. The ice ship you designed. It's far sturdier and faster than anything we've observed locally. And it's a proven long-distance traveler. If we could . . ."

"Out of the question." It struck him then that the main purpose of the meeting had been to obtain the use of the *Slanderscree*. He and Skua were incidentals. "The *Slanderscree*'s going one way—and that's west. Not east, southeast, or anywhere in that vicinity. It's going to take a long time for it to get home because it's going to have to tack into the wind.

"Its crew has been away from home for over a year. They may have membranes between their wrist and waist, they may have vertical pupils instead of round ones, but they're people. They've been away from their families, their friends, and their lives for much too long, just because of us. They want to get back home as badly as Skua does."

"We're aware of their concerns." Hwang made placating gestures as she spoke. "We sympathize with them just as we do with you and Mr. September. We've read everything you wrote about Sir Hunnar Redbeard and his people. But this matter concerns them more than it does us. This is their world that may be in danger. You must convince them to help us."

Ethan shook his head. "It wouldn't matter if we went to

them stark naked and did tricks and somersaults until we froze in midair. Hunnar is now heir to the throne of Wannome. He has political as well as personal reasons for returning home. They're our friends but we're still aliens and they're still Tran. They don't owe us a thing. Quite the contrary—Skua and Milliken and I owe them for keeping us alive. No amount of talk on our part is going to convince them to put off their journey homeward for another six months or whatever in order to help you resolve a dispute about some variance in the weather hundreds of kilometers southeast of Arsudun."

Hwang's eyes dropped to the floor. "I understand. You must also understand that we had to ask. Milliken said it would be difficult."

This is crazy, Ethan thought. Why do I stand here listening to this? What difference does it make what is causing the rise in temperature far to the south? They've already admitted it was probably due to volcanism.

But if it wasn't due to volcanism, what was responsible?

It was none of his business. He was a trader, a man of commerce, not a scientist. It wasn't his business to intercede with the Tran on behalf of Cheela Hwang and her associates. He had enough problems of his own to worry about.

She wasn't finished. "We have neither the right nor the power to compel you. We know that you and Mr. September have endured a great deal these past months. We won't impose on you any further. But we had to ask." She spread her hands in a gesture of helplessness. "We had to ask because we had no other choice."

What a terrific way to begin his relationship with the rest of the outpost's permanent staff, Ethan thought. Not that he was likely to ever need their help. If only they wouldn't be so damn gracious in defeat! Why didn't they yell a little and curse him? What the hell did they expect?

Even if he did confess to temporary insanity and agree to go off with them, didn't they understand there was just no way he could convince Hunnar and Captain Ta-hoding and the rest of the *Slanderscree*'s crew to do likewise?

Because Hunnar and his friends had to return home. Even if Hunnar was in no hurry to assume the mantle of Landgrave's heir and even if he and his people were interested in exploring still another unvisited region of their world, he was technically on his honeymoon. Did Tran *have* honeymoons? Maybe newlyweds were expected to go out and butcher a Droom or something equally adventurous.

It made no difference. They had to return to Sofold if only to inform their friends and relations of their continued existence. For all Elfa Kurdagh-Vlata's father knew his daughter was dead and the crew of the icerigger with her, the great ship destroyed, the bones of her crew gnawed by scavengers. Regardless of how they might respond personally to Cheela Hwang's request they were obligated to return home if only to convey news of their survival. The citizens of Sofold were unaware they were now members of a great and growing union of city-states. Hunnar and Balavere Longax were obligated to inform them of their future. There were relationships to be renewed, songs to be sung, deeds to be told. No choice in the matter.

He said as much to Cheela Hwang and her colleagues, hoping it would satisfy them and put the matter to rest in a manner which would preclude any need for future defensive recriminations on his part. He forgot he was dealing with people who were used to extracting answers from meager data. Blanchard found one before Ethan could excuse himself.

"What you're saying, then, is that if you could convince them to take us, they'd be prohibited from doing so because of their need to report back home."

Ethan nodded vigorously. "Circumstances beyond my control, or Skua's, or anyone else's."

Blanchard looked gratified. "Not necessarily. What's the minimum crew for a ship like your icerigger?"

"I don't know," said Ethan, taken aback. "I never really thought about it. I was just a passenger. If you're talking about sailing, you don't need near as many as the *Slanderscree* normally carries. If you're talking about exploring a new part of the planet and defending yourself while you're doing it, that's something else again."

"This would be a journey purely for research," Blanchard argued. "We don't anticipate any fighting."

"You never do," Ethan told him, "but Tran-ky-ky isn't exactly a benign world. There's plenty of hostile fauna around besides uncontacted Tran."

"We would go properly equipped," said another of the scientists. "No advanced weapons because that's strictly forbidden, but we could take other equipment which would be of help. And if you're trying to frighten us you're wasting your time. We've discussed this among ourselves and we know what we'd be letting ourselves in for. We've traveled on and around Arsudun. We're not entirely innocent of the dangers of this world."

Ethan didn't bother trying to explain that a jaunt of a few days around a relatively stable, civilized island like Arsudun bore no relation to a journey of many weeks into unexplored regions of a hostile world. Why waste the time? They weren't going anywhere anyway. But Blanchard wasn't through.

"What we could do is hire a merchant vessel to take the elderly, the injured, and the chronically homesick back to this Sofold. We have some discretionary income in our budget and we know how starved the Tran are for metal. I'm sure we could find a captain willing to undertake the trip. Those of your friends who insisted on returning wouldn't have to work or fight on the trip back. They could relax. They've earned it. And we'd still have plenty of funds left to hire your icerigger."

"This Balavere Longax, the senior soldier you speak of in your report, could be put in charge of the returnees," Hwang added. "As a respected member of the court of Wannome his report would be believed and honored. In fact, you could argue that it's his place to deliver such a report and not the younger knight you call Redbeard. The remaining crew could sail us to the southern continent."

"Let this Longax person," Blanchard went on, "assure the people back home that all is well. He can tell them about this union you've instigated, about the exploits of his comrades and friends, and of the royal marriage you attended recently. He can also explain the delay in the *Slanderscree*'s return and the importance of this journey we have to undertake. As to payment, we want to be sure we don't offend the dignity of this Redbeard person."

"There ain't a Tran alive adverse to taking money," September said, "but you won't hire the *Slanderscree* and its sailors for a few chunks of iron."

Hwang smiled. "The outpost has its own compact smelter, Mr. September. There's ore deep in Arsudun which the natives cannot make use of but which we can. The smelter is here so that we can build and repair outpost facilities. That doesn't mean we can't use it to turn out ingots, bars, tubes, nails and bolts, swords and arrow points, and whatever else would please your Tran. We can fill the hold of their ship for their return journey. They can give us a detailed shopping list and we'll fill it."

Hwang had just made the closest thing to an irresistible offer one could propose to a Tran. Trade in sophisticated goods like electronics was still forbidden on Tran-ky-ky save for a few simple devices which would eventually break down. Nails and swords would last on a world where steel was more valued than gold. Even one as homesick as Hunnar would find it hard to turn down the offer.

"You can also tell them," Blanchard continued, "that they would be expanding their knowledge of their own world and extending the hand of friendship and union to new peoples."

That was as much an appeal to him as to the Tran, Ethan knew. By going along he would be doing business, making new trading contracts, perhaps finding new goods to buy. In a civilization like that of the Commonwealth, where electronics and goods and services were available cheaply and readily, exotic handicrafts and artwork were among the most highly prized of new goods.

Why the hell not? He was stuck here anyhow.

"I'm still not sure if this is a good idea or not or if it wouldn't be better taken care of by some kind of remote survey craft, but I'll put your proposition to Hunnar and his people. They have the right to turn you down themselves."

"That's all we're asking." She glanced up at September. "What about you, sir?"

"Me wishes all of you the best of luck, but my ship departs orbit at oh-eight hundred tomorrow morning. I'll wave on my way outsystem. I've been cold long enough."

Hwang was persistent, stubborn, or both. "The region where we're going is warmer. That's the problem."

"Your problem, not mine. I'm off to where it's warm all the time. Maybe I'll regret not taking you up on your offer —in a year or two."

She turned to Ethan. As far as she was concerned now, September had already departed. "I'm sure you'll put our offer to your Tran friends as openly and honestly as we have put it to you. I only wish I could convey the importance of ascertaining the cause of this meteorological disturbance as rapidly as possible. There are crucial contradictions that require immediate resolution. Try to convey that to your friends along with our offer of cargo and transportation home for those who won't come with us."

"I'll make sure they understand all the details. Why don't you come with me since you feel so strongly about it? Tell them yourself."

She shook her head. "I'm not good with people and I don't know the language. None of us do. In that way our translators are electronic crutches. Speaking in person is infinitely more effective than talking through a device. Besides, these are your friends. It'll sound much better coming from you. If they agree to help, then maybe I'll be able to think of them as my friends as well." An approving murmur rose from the scientists.

"We'll see," Ethan said, "but I can't make any promises. As to convincing them of the urgency, that's going to be tough."

"I'll take care of that," said Williams quietly but confidently. "You soften them up, Ethan, and I'll finish the argument off."

Ethan looked dubious. "Hunnar Redbeard and Captain Ta-hoding are going to take more than just softening up when I try to convince them it's not time for them to return home."

"We've been a long time gone."

As Hunnar finished his little speech his sentiments were echoed by the other Tran in the room. They included Balavere Longax, senior warrior among the crew of the *Slanderscree*; Ta-hoding, her captain; Elfa Kurdagh-Vlata, daughter of the Landgrave of Sofold; and Hunnar's two squires. Ethan and Milliken Williams spoke for the staff of the research station while a dour Skua September glowered in the background. Ethan had asked him to join them and since his shuttle's departure had been postponed to an early morning liftoff, he couldn't very well decline. But he wasn't happy about it.

The humans required survival suits for this extended parley, but to the Tran the temperature in the transition room was positively tropic, barely a few degrees below freezing.

As Hunnar sat down Ta-hoding leaned over the plastic table. "They wish us to take them where, friend Ethan?"

Williams unrolled the map Cheela Hwang and her colleagues had prepared. Transfers had been made from the survey satellite's infrared photos. He wondered how the Tran would react to it, never having seen their world from above. They navigated by wind and stars, landmarks and tradition. If any could make the mental leap necessary, it would be those in this room. The concept of maps was not unknown to them, but aerial photography was something else again.

Tran measured distance in units called *satch*, and he'd had the outpost cartographer put all measurements on the crude map in those familiar numbers. It helped.

Elfa eyed the map uneasily. "No one has ventured so far south and east. That region is unknown to us."

Ethan thought she looked wonderful in her furs and leathers. Exotic, very feminine in a feline sort of way, and wholly alien. You're anthropomorphizing again, he warned himself.

"Until you made the journey in the *Slanderscree* no one from Sofold had ever been this far east before, either." He used a finger to trace a route on the map. "We'll head south to Poyolavomaar. That much is familiar territory and we can resupply the ship there if necessary. From there we turn southeast until we cross the equatorial ice pressure ridge— the 'bent ocean' as you call it—somewhere in this vicinity. Then it's straight on to the edge of the southern continent. The continental plateau runs almost due east-west at that point and we'll be able to keep the west wind hard behind us. I doubt we'll run into anything we haven't already met up with."

"That is a promise oft disproved before," Budjir quipped softly.

Ethan rerolled the map. The research department's publications section would have copies prepared and laminated prior to the icerigger's departure.

"It's not like Hwang and her people are asking you to sail them to the south pole. They're going to make the trip worthwhile. Each member of the icerigger's crew will share in the profits to be realized upon your return home to Sofold."

"What of those left behind who wait anxiously for word of that long-delayed return?" Balavere Longax inquired. His fur was tipped with silver and his beard gray instead of ruddy.

"The humans here intend to hire the best ship available to take a portion of the *Slanderscree*'s crew back to Wannome. They can report for all."

"No other merchant vessel has ever made such a journey. Until we came to this place the people of Sofold had no knowledge of Arsudun, nor they of us," Ta-hoding pointed out.

"Exactly. Now that the route is known and the journey once completed, other Tran should be more willing to attempt it. The owners of the ship we hire will be well paid."

"We had the wind always behind us."

"The return trip will involve more time and less danger, since the obstacles are now known. Those of your crew who make this journey will do so in comfort. Others will raise the sails and cook the food. When you stride together into the great hall at Wannome to speak of our adventures you will be honored. There will be more honor to come when the *Slanderscree* finally returns weighted down with its cargo of metal.

"I've talked to the metallurgist in charge of the smelter here. She'll be glad to fulfill your requests for spear points, nails, small tools, and pipes. Whatever you wish. The humans who want to engage your services will pay for everything. With this one cargo Wannome will leap beyond its neighboring city-states in wealth and prestige. It will make it easier to strengthen the new union. When the people of Ayhas and Meckleven see the benefits to be gained from membership, they'll rush to join."

"You tempt us, friend Ethan," said Balavere. "You tempt us greatly. Were it not for the need to inform our loved ones and our Landgrave that we still *chivan* o'er the oceans of our world, I would be inclined to stay with you myself. Such a cargo as you describe has never been imagined. I would like to be the one to unveil it."

"As friend Ethan says, it is not as though we are being asked to sail 'round the globe." Suaxus-dal-Jagger clearly had no doubts as to which course they should take. "What his friends propose is a journey no longer than the one that took us from here to Moulokin. Those lands also were unknown to us until we visited them. By making the journey we gained knowledge and allies. Why should not this one prove similarly beneficial?" The squire grinned, showing razor-sharp canines.

"And if there is to be a fight or two along the way, why, it would keep us from boredom. That is the only place I fear to visit."

"I should think you'd had enough adventure to keep you from boredom for the remainder of your life." Elfa's gaze shifted from the exuberantly enthusiastic squire back to Ethan. "Still and all, your scholar friends offer a city's ransom in payment for a little transportation. Long as it has been since my father has seen me, I know what he would advise."

Hunnar had been studying his right paw, extending and retracting his claws. Now he looked up to where Skua September leaned against the door that led back into the outpost complex.

"What think you, friend Skua? Should we accept this proposition?"

"Yes, what *do* you think?" Balavere asked.

September let his gaze touch on human and Tran alike. "I think you're every one of you fools. Some of you are furry fools and some of you smooth-skinned, but you have warm blood and idiocy in common. I think Ethan's a fool for risking the dangers of your world on still another journey into unknown regions. I think the rest of you are fools for not returning home right now."

"We know what to expect, Skua," said Williams, adjusting his glasses. "It would be discouraging if we didn't encounter one or two new things on such an expedition."

"Something new ain't what would worry me. Surprises wouldn't worry me. What would worry me, Milliken, is that sooner or later a man's odds will catch up with him. You don't go give those odds any help against us. Fate's already on their side. Me, I've been tiptoeing on the far edge of disaster most of my life. Just because I haven't fallen off yet doesn't mean I'm going to start dancing. I don't think you should go."

Williams turned to the watchful Tran. "Certainly there may be dangers to be faced. This is your world. I believe Cheela Hwang and her colleagues when they say that it may be in danger. The kind of danger that can reach across oceans and continents. We seek an explanation because events that cannot be explained have a way of coming back to haunt you. We *must* find out what is happening to the weather along the edge of the southern continental plateau."

"What threat could it pose to us in far distant Sofold?" Budjir wanted to know.

Williams struggled to persuade. "I realize you're still trying to grasp the concept of a world as one place, a single home. It took my people even longer to do so, to their detriment. A world is like a living organism. What happens on the other side of the globe can affect us here in Arsudun. Think of it as a creature without arms or legs. If one area is infected and not treated in time, the infection can spread and kill the whole body. We need to find out if this is an infection of that kind."

"The scholar speaks truth. I agree with him," said Balavere.

Hunnar and Elfa exchanged a look. She nodded once, slowly. But the final word did not rest with them. Not here, on this matter. This was not an affair of state. He turned to the captain of the *Slanderscree*.

"What of the ship? What repairs would have to be made before she could undertake such a journey?"

"None, Sir Hunnar. The ship is sound. While I would rather return home myself, the thought of another long journey does not frighten me. Our vessel is solid. She could use a thorough cleaning, but then what ship could not?

"The thought of sailing so far south with less than a full crew does not cheer me, but it can be done. No reason be there why thirty could not handle her well enough, particularly if we take our time and put out anchors early."

"We'd like to reach this place as quickly as possible," Williams commented, "but our actual speed would be up to you. Whatever's affecting the climate isn't going to alter radically one way or the other in a day or two."

Ta-hoding looked content. "As long as we are not hard

pressed, then, I see no reason why we cannot send half our complement and more home to cheer those we have left behind. We know her well by now, our icerigger, and those who agree to crew her on this voyage will be volunteers. If those who do so are promised a greater share in the promised cargo, I foresee no difficulty in securing willing sailors."

"Naturally the captain's share would be proportionately larger," said September from his corner.

Ta-hoding coughed, looked slightly embarrassed. "It would not be unnatural. It is the traditional manner of such payments."

"Clearly there would be plenty for all." Hunnar shook a massive paw at Williams. "This will be the last place the *Slanderscree* docks before the familiar portal of Wannome harbor. Absolutely the last! The lamentations of my family echo loud in my ears."

Williams nodded assent. "I promise. After this you can all go home, richer as well as wiser."

"It is settled then," said Elfa. She glanced up at Ethan. "But this I say to both of you: This is a thing we do not for the fortune your metal wizard has promised to us, nor out of friendship which has its limits. This thing we do because Milliken Williams asks it of us. Because we owe him a debt that has not yet been repaid."

"Truth!" declaimed Balavere Longax loudly.

Ethan knew what they were referring to. If not for the schoolteacher's application of some ancient practical knowledge, both the battles for Wannome and Moulokin would have been lost. Elfa, Hunnar, and the rest of the Tran owed Williams not only their independence but their lives.

"Yes, well." The teacher dropped his eyes and voice and tried to vanish from view. "Anyone else in my position would have done the same. I just happened to be in the necessary place at the required time."

"Anyone else I do not know," said Hunnar. "Milliken Williams I do know. You overdo your modesty. This then is our repayment. We Tran do not like to leave debts lying loosely about where consciences can stumble over them in the night."

"We're all set then." Ethan pushed back his chair. "Milliken, why don't you deliver the good news to Hwang and Blanchard and the others? I'm sure they've chewed their nails down to the quick wondering what our friends' answer will be."

"With the greatest pleasure. They'll be delighted for a minute or so. Then they'll get to work making preparations for departure."

"Yes, preparations," said Ta-hoding. He didn't rub his paws together but came close. "And while provisioning is going on I can meet with your metal wizard to discuss what we will want in the way of cargo for our trip back to Sofold. In that way it can be ready and waiting for us as soon as we return."

Elfa was smiling. "It will be good to return home with something more than stories to give the people."

Laser-bright, the sun of Tran-ky-ky cast the rocky features of Arsudun island into silhouette as it rose in the east. Ice particles bombarded the glass sealing in the second-floor observation deck that overlooked the shuttle runway.

Ethan watched as the shuttle rose from its underground hangar like a skeleton from the grave. It rested on wide blue ice skids, the stern of the sleek delta-wing shape pocked with rocket and jet exhaust ports. It would accelerate rapidly down the smooth runway, using standard jets to carry it into the upper atmosphere where ramjets would take over and increase its velocity further. Beyond the en-

velope of frigid air that cocooned Tran-ky-ky, rockets
would take over and propel it into orbit where it would be
overtaken by its mother ship. After passengers and cargo
had been distributed, the KK-drive would be activated,
tugging the interstellar craft out of Tran-ky-ky's system and
into that strange region known as space-plus, where faster-
than-light travel was possible.

As he stared, the shuttle's stern glowed with life. The
thunderous roar of the jets was muffled by the thick glass.
The ship began to move forward. Slowly at first, gradually
gathering speed, its great weight forcing the skids through
the ice onto the solid stelacrete beneath. Behind him other
members of the outpost's complement turned away. The
once-a-month departure of the shuttle was not enough of a
novelty to hold their attention longer.

They chatted easily, relaxed, their thoughts back on the
business of the day. Ethan's rode aboard the shuttle, alongside the large, extraordinary gentleman who'd been his
close companion and friend for the year and more they'd
spent surviving on this frozen world together.

Carried aloft on a column of superheated air, the shuttle
lifted from the far end of the runway. Ethan followed it
with his eyes until it vanished like a lost leaf in the perfectly clear blue sky. He continued to stare into the distance
until the echo of the little vessel's thunder faded in his ears.
Then he turned away from the window.

There was plenty to do. Establishing a formal trading
station would require the completion of an enormous quantity of paperwork, no matter how accommodating the new
Resident Commissioner. If he started on it immediately he
might be able to scratch the surface before the *Slanderscree*
departed for the southern continent. Then there were spe-
cialized computer programs to be ordered, files to be set
up, requests for personnel to enter. If he were lucky and
everything he needed reasonably available, he might be

able to relax in three or four months. If he could at least get some programs operating, it would look to Malaika's subalterns like he was doing his job.

It was going to be a lonely one. Administration and supervision demanded he read, not shake hands or other appendages. The most entertaining computer program was a poor substitute for close companionship.

So preoccupied with planning was he that he almost ran into the large figure that had stationed itself at the far end of the corridor. The individual was leaning against the jamb, arms crossed and an angry expression on his face. Ethan's jaw dropped.

He jerked around to stare back toward the observation window. No, the shuttle had not returned when he wasn't looking, nor had he imagined its departure. Any more than he was imagining the massive, familiar figure that blocked the doorway.

It was just as well September spoke first because Ethan was utterly at a loss for words.

"This is all your fault, young feller-me-lad."

The accusation called for a response. "My fault? What are you talking about, my fault? What's my fault?" He gestured helplessly back at the window. Beyond, ground crew in small individual vehicles were out on the runway, already commencing preparations for the arrival of next month's shuttle.

"Why aren't you on the shuttle?"

"I'm not on the shuttle because I'm here. Can't be in two places at the same time, now can I?"

"I don't know what you're talking about, Skua."

"Really? I thought I made it quite clear. We're talking about my being here being your fault. That's not overly obtuse, now is it?" He unfolded his oversize frame, stood straight. "It's because of your damn archaic sense of responsibility. Your innocence and your filthy ingratiating personality. Hell, if I pulled a gun right now and blew your grinning head off, your last words would be an apology for the cost of the power surge. Where do you come off making me feel guilty, you and that midget mine of arcane trivia and those tiger-toothed furballs with pretensions of civilization?"

"Nobody can make another person feel guilty like that, Skua. You've managed it all by yourself."

"Oh, now that's a pithy homily, it is. Here I was, all set and ready to be on my way, and that runt Williams had to go and drag us to that damn meeting. Dangerous meteorological anomaly, my butt! And here I am still stuck on this lousy chunk of slush because somebody sees an anomaly in a fogbank a few thousand kilometers away."

Ethan knew it was an inappropriate time to smile, but he couldn't help himself. It was clear Skua was raging not against his friend but against himself.

"Skua, it's not the worst thing in the world to admit to somebody else that you're a decent human being."

"But that's just it, young feller-me-lad. I *ain't* a decent human being. I've never been a decent human being. I could give you proof."

Ethan tried to calm the giant. "You're confused; that's all."

"Confused, hell. I'm mad and I'm frustrated because I don't know what I'm doing here." He jabbed a thumb ceilingward. "When I should be up there, relaxed, warm and outbound."

"Whatever you're doing here you're going to be doing it for at least another month, until the next shuttle arrives. What about your archaeologist friend?"

"Who? Oh, Isili. Isili Hasboga." He shrugged. "I'm two years overdue. I don't expect she'll fly into a rage if I don't show up next week. In fact, I have the feeling she won't

even think about it. Me now, that's something else." He
turned, ate up distance with enormous strides.

"One thing I'll warn you about now, Ethan, and you can
pass it along. When we're out on the ice none of those
sniveling scientists better thank me for coming along or
he'll find himself skating all the way back to Arsudun on
his backside."

"So you're coming with us, then?"

"No," September snapped. "I purposely missed the
shuttle so I could squat here and glower at the robots. Of
course I'm coming along."

Ethan struggled to repress a broad grin. "That'll be nice.
Knowing in what regard Hunnar, Elfa, and the rest of the
Tran hold you, I'm sure their spirits will be boosted just by
your presence."

"Further proof of how primitive they are and how far
they still have to go," September muttered. "Showing respect for a fool like me. I am a fool, you know. I've just
gone and proved it again."

"Quit bawling, already. And you still haven't convinced
me I'm in any way shape or form responsible for your
continued presence here."

"Ain't it obvious, feller-me-lad? How could I leave with
a clean conscience knowing you were all set to run off and
get yourself killed. You would, too, without me around to
watch after you. If not for old Skua, you'd be dead a dozen
times over this past year."

That was true enough, Ethan knew. It was also true that
he'd returned the favor by saving September at least as
many times as September had saved him, but he forbore
pointing that out. He was too pleased to have his friend
back for the forthcoming journey to belabor him with
logic.

"What makes you think I'm going to put myself in a
position to be killed? You heard Hwang and the others. A

straightforward little scouting expedition to check out some weather, that's all. No barbarian hordes to battle. No exotic cities of unknown persuasion to win over to the union cause. Why should we have any trouble?"

"Because there's still this world to deal with. Tran-ky-ky. Damned little we know about it after more'n a year sailing its ice. No, you'd get yourself killed for sure without me to yank you back from the brink of disaster, young feller-me-lad. You're too nice, too empathetic, and far too understanding for this business. Me now, I'm none of those. So I'm still alive when I should've been deaded ten times each of the past forty years.

"And if you persist in committing suicide in spite of anything I can do, at least I'll be around to see to it that you get a decent burial, or cremation, or whatever form of final send-off tickles your soul."

"Your concern for my welfare is touching, Skua."

"Yeah, well." The giant looked over his head, up the corridor. "Just don't mention it to anyone else, okay? Give me a bad name in certain circles. Let's get out of here, get something to eat." He headed up the corridor that led to the central part of the outpost complex. Ethan had to hurry to keep pace with him.

"What do you want me to say if someone asks me why you chose to stay behind?"

"Tell 'em I overslept," said September irritably.

Only later did it occur to Ethan wonder if his friend might have had some other reason for missing the *Spindizzy*'s departure. As September had admitted on more than one occasion, he was a man with a varied and not altogether benign past. Something might have convinced him that it would be in his own best interests to remain on an isolated, unvisited world for another month or so. Maybe there was someone on the KK-drive ship he didn't want to encounter. Maybe he didn't want to go where it was going just yet. Maybe, maybe . . .

Too many maybes for a mind already swamped with plans for the new trading station and the forthcoming expedition. If September was frustrated by his own inability to leave Tran-ky-ky, Ethan knew that frozen world would provide the giant with numerous opportunities to work off his unease.

IV

Provisioning and preparation of the *Slanderscree* proceeded apace, thanks to the scientific establishment's open-ended credit account. In a couple of days the ice-rigger was bulging with supplies. Only Hunnar's embarrassment finally put an end to Ta-hoding's unending requests for still more food, still additional extra rigging and sail. If they didn't depart soon, the clever and acquisitive captain would have overstocked the ship to the point that no room would be left for her crew. As it was, by the time they were ready to leave, the icerigger was almost bursting.

Those Tran who had volunteered to crew the *Slanderscree* bade farewell to their colleagues and cousins who would be riding a hired merchant ship back to Sofold. Ethan and Skua had made many friends among the crew and there were handshakes and backslaps to be given in addition to the traditional Tran gestures of parting.

Cheela Hwang, Blanchard, and the four other scientists who'd been nominated to go on the expedition were busy checking over their gear. Besides Hwang and the geophysicist there was another meteorologist, a glaciologist, a geologist, and a xenologist. Moware, the last of the half dozen, had been included not for the help he might provide in determining the cause of the climatological anomaly but because the chance of a long trip away from already over-studied Arsudun was too valuable to pass up. He'd already expressed his intention to do photos and in-person studies of everyone they met during the course of the journey.

"Just don't study them too close up," September advised him. "You never can tell about the Tran. Why, they can be chatting with you friendly as can be one minute and slip a knife across your throat the next. There's them that would spill your guts just for the metal in your belt kit."

Ethan overheard and sidled over to stand next to his tall friend. "Come on, Skua, you know that isn't true."

"Do I now? Are we already experts on the Tran? Just because we've spent some months among them doesn't mean we really know them. We know their language, the habits and culture of a few, the attitudes of several more, but we don't *know* them. For all their cheery hellos and how-do-you-dos they're still an alien people. They're not human. They're not even anthropoid." He turned and stalked away.

Moware was the oldest member of the scientific team. He had the visor of his survival suit flipped back, as did all the humans, and he regarded September's retreating back with interest. "I don't know your big friend very well, but I think he carries a considerable mental burden with him wherever he goes. He jokes with his words but not his eyes." He looked over at Ethan. "You're good friends, though."

"Very good—I think." Ethan searched for September, but the giant had already disappeared. "He's right, though. We don't really know the Tran."

And I don't really know you, do I, Skua September?

He strolled over to where Hunnar and Elfa were bidding a final farewell to those members of the crew who were staying behind.

"In Wannome we will meet soon and drink and sup by the great fire in the Hall of the Landgraves." Hunnar clasped the old warrior by both shoulders and Balavere Longax returned the gesture. Then Longax was embraced by Elfa.

"May the good spirits stay with you, princess, and carry you safely back to us. Your father will be disappointed to find you not among us."

"My father will grumble and return to his business," she replied with a smile. "You'll still have stories to tell him when we finally enter Wannome harbor, for we'll be back before your voice and imagination run dry."

Then it was Ethan's turn. When the ceremonials had concluded, Longax searched the busy crowd behind them. "Will not the great September come to bid us farewell?"

"He's sulking," Ethan explained. "Making a big show of how upset he is at coming with us."

Longax made a gesture of understanding. "The September is much like a small meat-eater called the *toupek*. It is solitary, hunts by itself, joins with others of its kind only to mate, and roars like thunder, but it is only this big." He held his paws a foot apart.

"I don't know. Skua talks about us not knowing you. Sometimes I think I know you and Hunnar and Elfa better than I know him."

"A strange one, your large friend," Longax agreed solemnly, "even for a human being. I think he prefers to sail against the wind."

"Why should that bother him?" It took Ethan a moment to realize he'd just made a joke that only another Tran could understand. Translated, it would have meant nothing to someone like Cheela Hwang. He'd been here a long time for sure.

Longax's party left the icerigger and lined up on the stone dock. A blast of subzero cold slapped Ethan in the face and he snapped shut the visor of his survival suit. Through the polarized glass he watched while Longax and his companions bowed somberly toward the ship.

Ta-hoding took up a stance behind the ship's wheel and bellowed commands. The wind which had stung Ethan bothered the captain not at all. Tran mounted the rigging and adjustable spars. Sails woven from pika-pina fabric began to unfurl.

Quite a crowd had gathered to watch the icerigger's departure. There were a number of humans from the research station, running their recorders while murmuring notes into the aural pickups. A three-masted, arrowhead-shaped ice ship mounted on five huge skates fashioned of metal salvaged from the ruined shuttle craft which had originally brought Ethan and Skua and Milliken Williams to this world, the *Slanderscree* was a wonderment to all who set eyes on her, Tran and human alike. There was nothing to compare to her anywhere on the planet. Her ancestors had once carried tea and porcelain and passengers across the two great oceans of Earth. Milliken Williams had adapted those designs to the necessities of Tran-ky-ky and its frozen oceans.

Using the wind as skillfully as a flutist, Ta-hoding backed the huge vessel away from the dock. The watching humans were too busy with their recording and note taking to cheer, while the Tran observing the departure had no reason to do so. Formal farewells had been concluded. As far as Balavere Longax and his companions were concerned, their friends and shipmates were already out of sight.

Under Ta-hoding's direction the icerigger pivoted neatly around its fifth skate, the stern rudder which was used to steer the ship. Wind filled the sails as the spars were adjusted. Picking up speed, the *Slanderscree* headed up the narrow ice-filled fjord that formed Brass Monkey's harbor.

On our way again, Ethan mused as he watched the frozen terrain slide by. Outward bound and still not for home.

He expected that Hwang and her people would keep to their cabins; the deck of the *Slanderscree* under full sail was not a relaxing place to be. But he was wrong. Having been confined to a single island for their tours on Tran-ky-ky, the researchers were delighted to finally find themselves out on the great ice sheet itself. They embarked on a nonstop round of activity and experimentation, to the point where nighttime measurement taking began to interfere with normal shipboard routine.

"I was sleeping soundly, Captain," Second Mate Mousokka explained to Ta-hoding while Ethan and Hunnar looked on, "having seen to the setting of the anchors for the night, when suddenly I hear the sound of many feet on the deck above. Too many for the night watch and in the wrong place. So I arise from a warm hammock and steal onto the deck to espy what's happening. I am thinking perhaps we have been attacked and the night watch has already had their throats cut.

"But all I see are the furless beings—no offense, Sir Ethan—prowling about the deck setting up strange metal tubes. They stare through these and I look in the same direction, but all there is to see is the ice."

"They were studying the phosphorescent algae that grows on the ice," Ethan explained uncomfortably, having familiarized himself with that particular experiment. The second mate and the captain looked puzzled while Hunnar was merely amused. "*Eorvin*," he told them, finding the proper Tran name.

Mousokka squinted at him. "They were looking at eorvin? In the middle of the night? In the cold dark?" Ethan nodded, a gesture that meant the same among the Tran as it did among humans.

The second mate thought this over before replying. "I

will tell the others that they must watch your friends carefully, lest in their single-minded staring they fall beneath the ship or out of the rigging."

"Not a bad idea, but they're not as crazy as you think."

"They are scholars." Hunnar punctuated the comment with a grunt. "It is much the same thing." There was no literal translation in Tran for scientist, Ethan knew, and the natives had decided to use the nearest formal equivalent.

"I would not know," said Mousokka. "I am but a simple sailor."

"Just make sure they keep out of your way," Hunnar instructed him. "We don't want them interfering with normal routine *or* hurting themselves." He glanced at Ethan to insure this met with his approval.

"Don't be obvious about it and it'll be okay. I doubt they'll notice anyone keeping an eye on them anyway. They're too busy with their work. Preoccupied. You have to understand that because of Commonwealth regulations, they've been cooped up in Brass Monkey ever since the place was established. Now that they've been allowed out to see more of your world, they don't want to miss a single thing. They want to see everything."

"Eorvin." Mousokka left muttering to himself.

The activities of the human scholars remained a mystery to the Tran, but at least the sailors and soldiers were sufficiently sophisticated not to ascribe everything Hwang and her people did to witchcraft or sorcery. It was much simpler just to explain that the scholars were all slightly daft.

Such as the morning when a ravenous flock of carnivorous *snigaraka* was driven by hunger to move against the ship. A lookout spotted them and gave the alarm as they wheeled above the ship's path and prepared to attack. When they finally dived at the deck, unarmed personnel had already taken refuge below and the soldiers were ready to meet them. Arrows and crossbow bolts picked one fanged flyer after another out of the sky.

One fell close by Ethan's feet. It was two meters long from nose to tail, with a gaping mouth lined with spikes. The latter were not teeth but the sharp, jagged edge of two horny plates which formed the jaws. Like every successful Tran-ky-ky lifeform it was covered with a coat of fine fur. Unlike the Tran, the bristles of the snigaraka were hollow to conserve weight while maximizing heat retention. Their wings were short and broad, more like those of a hawk than an eagle. The tails were the most distinctive feature in that they were held vertically instead of horizontally, and there were two of them.

With sharp projectiles and grasping talons flashing around him, Moware sat high up in the rigging preserving the battle on his recorder, calmly adding explanatory notes where necessary. Tran yelled at him to come down. He ignored them, and it was possible he never heard them. Two snigaraka could easily have plucked him from his webbing and carried him off, or he could have been knocked from his perch to the deck or the ice. Of those potential disasters he appeared blissfully unaware, a delighted smile creasing his face as he imaged the attack for posterity, not to mention future study.

Later that day, after the aerial assault had been beaten off, the xenologist played back his recording for the benefit of his fellow scientists. They sat clustered around the recorder as it played back the battle, offering comments and asking questions and completely ignoring the obvious danger Moware had placed himself in. It was wholly incidental to the information obtained. When an attacking snigaraka swooped down on Moware and the lethal jaws momentarily filled the recorder's lens, the only comments to be heard involved the structure of the jaws: were they true jaws or a flexible beak?

All the grumbling about the strange and disturbing actions of the scholars finally came to a head when one of them asked Third Mate Kilpit if they might seek out another flock of the airborne assassins in order to complete their documentation of the snigaraka's method of attack.

"It is one thing to convoy these alien creatures to an unknown land," Kilpit told Ta-hoding, "another to deliberately place ourselves in danger to satisfy their strange and inexplicable desires."

"Did anyone get in your way during the attack?" Elfa asked the mate.

"Well, no, my lady." Kilpit dug into his pelt for a persistent nibbler and looked uncomfortable.

"Was anyone injured because of something the humans did?"

"No, of course not."

"Then you have no complaint."

Hunnar was more understanding. "Some of the crew are confused. That which is new and different is always confusing. I will talk with the scholars."

What he did was convey the disquiet to Ethan, who agreed to have a chat with Hwang's group.

"You have to understand," she said when he'd finished relaying the Tran's concerns, "that it's difficult for us to restrain our enthusiasm. After years stuck in offices, we've suddenly been given a whole world to examine." Her manner was formal without being standoffish.

"I understand," Ethan replied, "and Hunnar understands, and Elfa and probably Ta-hoding understand, but the common sailors and soldiers in the crew, they don't understand. And they're nervous about what they don't understand. They watch while you run your experiments and engage in inexplicable activities and they conjure up all sorts of superstitious nonsense."

"We keep too much to ourselves. You and Milliken and

September move freely among them, have for a long time now, so they accept you and your individual idiosyncrasies." Blanchard supported his chin with his left hand. He wore his mustache, Ethan mused, like an afterthought. "We may not be athletes, but after two years and more on this world we're in pretty good shape. You have to be to qualify for posting to a world like Tran-ky-ky." He glanced up at Ethan.

"Because of our arrangement which involved sending a large portion of the ship's complement home, it is presently minimally crewed."

Ethan nodded. "That's so."

Blanchard regarded his colleagues. "We've all done heavy work in survival suits. Perhaps we could help."

"No, no," Ethan told him. "Ta-hoding looks like a jolly, easy-going type, but he's not where his ship's concerned."

"We wouldn't try anything we couldn't handle." Almera Jacalan, the resident geologist, flexed an arm. "We're intelligent enough to know what we can and can't do."

"Put it to the captain," Hwang decided. "It might be fun." Murmurs of agreement came from her colleagues.

"Sure." Jacalan laughed at the prospect. "I can pull a pika-pina cable with the best of them, and we know we won't have to swab the decks. You can't wash outside on this world because any liquid freezes instantly. Besides," she added, "the crew ought to know that in a tight spot they can call on us for assistance."

"I'll suggest it." Ethan sounded doubtful.

He was honestly surprised when Ta-hoding agreed. "A couple of extra hands, be they furred or not, would be welcomed. By all means let the scholars learn the ways of the *Slanderscree*. One need not be an experienced sailor to help pull in an anchor."

It was as Blanchard had hoped. With the humans working alongside, the crew came to know them as individuals.

They gradually put aside their fear and suspicion and before many more days had passed were enthusiastically demonstrating how to do everything from adjusting the spars to scraping the sails. Everyone was able to relax because all knew the arrangement was only temporary. They would take on additional, experienced hands at Poyolavomaar.

Everyone was relieved at the cessation of tension and surprised at the feeling of camaraderie that quickly developed. While learning how the icerigger was handled, some of the scientists began to give the Tran short courses in geology and climatology. The lessons generated grudging admiration among the sailors, while the scientists ceased to view their furry, big-eyed companions as primitive aborigines.

Meanwhile the *Slanderscree* followed its zigzagging course southward to Poyolavomaar as Ta-hoding made skillful use of the ceaseless wind.

Not long ago they'd traveled that same section of ice. It should have looked familiar to Ethan, but he wasn't a Tran. Ice was ice. Ta-hoding or any of his crew, on the other hand, could have pointed out specific cracks in the ice sheet, could have identified individual folds and subtle discolorations. Streaks and striations were as clear to a Tran as lines on a road map. For beacons they relied upon the stars, for direction the wind.

He wondered how much Commonwealth participation would change his friends. Civilization dulls the senses.

Having learned their lesson, the snigaraka stayed clear of the icerigger. So did the rest of Tran-ky-ky's lethal lifeforms, though they did encounter a rarity called a *dyella*.

To Ethan it resembled a gigantic snake, though he knew that was impossible; a cold-blooded creature couldn't survive long enough on Tran-ky-ky to reproduce. The dyella was twenty meters long, legless, and covered with fine maroon and pink fur. Flanks and top were rounded and it slid along on its flattened underside, special glands secreting a hot lubricating slime which enabled it to slip quickly across the ice. Twin rills or sails ran nearly the length of its back. By twisting and turning these to catch the wind it sailed along as efficiently as the *Slanderscree*.

Several of the sailors yelled to Ta-hoding to swing sharply to port so that the icerigger's metal skates would cut the carnivore in half, but the human contingent would have none of it. Moware was frantically trying to reload his recorder while Jacalan and the rest of the nonbiology specialists fought to make records of their own. In coloring and size the dyella was far and away the most impressive lifeform they'd yet encountered.

The creature let out a rumble incongruously like a threatening mew and moved slightly sideways, parallelling the icerigger at a distance of some thirty or forty meters. It neither attacked nor retreated.

"One small bite . . ." said Ta-hoding as he stood by the rail watching their unwelcome escort. He brushed the points of his claws against the palm of his other paw. "Dead meat. Poisonous."

Ethan looked forward. Moware and his colleagues were all but falling overboard in their haste to snap close-ups. "Don't tell the scholars. They'll want to obtain a sample of the toxin." He turned his gaze back to the dyella, fascinated by its supple, seemingly effortless method of propulsion. It had no trouble keeping up with the *Slanderscree*.

"What do they eat out here? That's a big animal, and you don't need poison to take down pika-pina."

Ta-hoding leaned forward so he could peer toward the bow, grunting as his belly was indented by the railing. After a few moments he pointed sharply to the southeast. "There, *achivars*!"

The herd to which the captain was referring soon came

into view and Ethan realized the dyella hadn't been following the icerigger. It had been pursuing the herd of herbivores. Each achivar was about the size of a pig. In addition to their fur, the achivar were covered with meter-long spines. At the tip of each spine was a small winglike membrane. By raising and lowering their spines and adjusting how they lined up, the achivar could catch the wind and sail efficiently across the ice, like the dyella and the *Slanderscree*, and dozens of other ice dwellers.

The icerigger plowed into the herd without running over a single member of the group. Even the youngsters spun and turned with incredible agility, their massed spines flashing as they caught the sun. They had large, brilliantly intense red eyes, tiny heads that hugged neckless bodies, and broad flat feet that had evolved into flat, slick pads. The dyella raised its long rills to catch the maximum amount of available wind and tried to cut the herd off, to steal the wind from their spines much as ancient seagoing men-of-war tried to capture the wind from an enemy sailing ship in order to deny it speed and maneuverability. The tactics of consumption instead of the strategy of war, Ethan reflected.

The dyella was having a hard time. The achivar were as fast and much more agile. September joined Ethan in viewing the spectacle.

"Ice-skating porcupines," he grunted, glancing at Tahoding as the captain yelled a casual command to his helmsman. "Are those spines as sharp as they look?"

"Every bit of that," Ta-hoding replied. "Their small wind-catchers notwithstanding. The trick in hunting achivar is to surprise them when they are resting or feeding and their spines are relaxed."

"Moware asked me to come up here." September gestured toward the bow. "They'd like to capture a specimen to take back to Brass Monkey. I tried to tell him and the others you wouldn't go for it."

"These achivar are neither asleep nor feeding, and if we were to come to a stop the dyella might decide spineless Tran are more agreeable prey than speedy, spiny achivar. Therefore we will not stop. You must convey my apologies to your scholars."

"Not me. I agree with you completely."

Ethan stepped away from the railing. "I'll tell 'em. They're the ones who are in a hurry to get to the southern continent. I'll remind them that you're only doing as they requested." Ta-hoding nodded his approval.

As the icerigger left the achivar herd and its tormenting dyella behind, Moware fumed but had to be content with the images and sounds his recorder had captured. Much later the frustrated xenologist drew Ethan and Skua aside. "Who's paying for this trip?"

September merely grinned and turned away to continue his surveillance of a line of distant granite teeth poking through the ice. "Ask that of Hunnar or Ta-hoding or any of the other noble Tran and you'll have the chance to study how tight a U-turn this ship can execute."

"Surely it would not destroy their scheduling for us to stop occasionally to gather specimens."

"You're the ones who wanted speed, remember? The Tran agreed to take you to the southern continent as fast as possible. That's what they're doing. You don't alter plans in midjourney. It's not their way. These *people* have put off seeing their friends and loved ones for another few months to help you out. Be satisfied that you're on this ship at all. Don't push your luck with the Tran. They have short tempers and long memories. Irritate them now and you'll have the devil's own time getting them to help you in the future."

Moware mulled over September's advice. "If you say so—but I'm not happy about this."

"Nobody said you had to be happy."

The xenologist bridled slightly but his position was weak and September knew it. His colleagues might sympathize but they wouldn't risk the good will of the Tran to advance his argument. The meteorologists needed to get to the southern continent, and the geo people like Jacalan and Blanchard had nothing at all to study out on the ice. They weren't about to insist on detours and unscheduled field trips.

The next day they entered the first extensive pika-pina field and no more was heard from Moware as he embarked on a detailed study of the vast reservoir of flora. He was too busy recording the new wonder to argue about stopping. All he had to do to collect a week's worth of specimens was drag a collecting net alongside the speeding icerigger for ten minutes.

Ta-hoding guided the ship through the endless field of greenery, avoiding the larger, thicker stands of pika-pedan. The icerigger's metal skates sliced cleanly through the water-filled greenery, leaving pulp, other organic detritus, and new shoots already climbing in its wake.

"Noticed something different here lately, young feller-me-lad?" September joined Ethan in staring over the bowsprit.

"That's an open question." Ethan idly checked the thermometer built into the wrist of his survival suit. It was a brisk ten below that morning. Not bad considering that just before sunrise the reading had fallen to minus sixty.

"It's our good friend Williams."

"What about him?" Ethan stared up at September curiously from behind his survival suit's visor.

The giant nodded toward the four scientists clustered together amidships. Ethan recognized Williams immediately by the teacher's battered survival suit, so different in appearance from the shiny unmarred attire of his companions.

"That's our friend Hwang he's hanging around with."

"So? They're observing together. I'm not surprised. After over a year of having to try to make conversation with a couple of simpletons like you and me, I'd expect him to spend as much time as possible with people of a similar mental bent."

"Been doing nothing but observing together. Ever since we left Arsudun."

"You wouldn't be insinuating that there might be something more than a professional relationship developing between them, now would you?"

"Oh, no, not me, not me, lad."

"Why don't I believe you?" Ethan watched as Williams put his faceplate close to Hwang's. Natural enough, given the limited range of the suits' speaking membranes. "I'm not sure our friend Hwang is capable of anything more than that."

"Don't let her attitude fool you, feller-me-lad. Even steel can smolder, given the right conditions."

"Sorry. I just can't think of our Milliken as a right condition."

"Can't you now? Adjust your perspective, feller-me-lad. Among that lot Milliken's stature is considerable, and I ain't referring to his size. He's seen stuff these stay-at-homes can only dream about—and lives to tell about it. And he's a bona fide hero to the Tran. Don't think our calculating friends miss things like that. Someone like himself comes marching into Brass Monkey on a ship of his own design, crewed by Tran he's helped to make allies of, and the status of a fancy degree goes right down the chute. Can't you see how someone like Hwang could be taken with a figure like that?" There was definite merriment in September's voice.

"Maybe so, but all that time we spent out on the ice, I kind of got the feeling that maybe Milliken was . . . you know."

"I thought similarly, feller-me-lad, which makes recent developments all the more intriguing. You think about it, though, and everything matches up pretty well. Our friend Cheela's a bit on the domineering side, for all that she's a petite little package, and . . ."

"Don't you have something of more consequence to speculate on?" Ethan said disgustedly.

"I sure don't," September replied cheerfully. He waved at the ice sheet speeding past, the broad monotonous plain of pika-pina. "Not out here I don't. I was just wondering what the Tran would make of such goings-on. Species or no, this is a bunch of sailors we're keeping company with. Sailors are sailors no matter what shape their pupils or feet."

"Just keep it to yourself, Skua. What you find amusing they might consider blasphemous or bad luck or something. We don't know their attitude toward shipboard romances."

"Tran wouldn't be like that, but you're right about one thing, young feller-me-lad. I should keep my big mouth shut." He nodded toward the quartet of scholars. "It ain't going to be easy to keep it a secret the way those two are carrying on. Why, do you realize that yesterday they. . .?"

The wind roared over the bow, drowning out the rest of his words as he strolled away.

Now that the idea had been planted Ethan found his gaze drawn back to Williams and Hwang like filings to a magnet. Damn September anyway for distracting him with inconsequentials. It was none of his business or anyone else's what the two were about. If it were true, though, he was happy for Milliken.

He discovered he was grinning to himself.

The following afternoon they encountered not a herd of the achivar but a veritable spiny army, sweeping toward them from the south. Brown and blue spines stretched from horizon to horizon. Females and offspring swerved neatly around the *Slanderscree*'s skates while an occasional larger male would try to jab the metal supports with his forespines. The icerigger sailed on through an ocean of flag-waving spikes.

"Must be a hundred thousand of them!" yelled the ecstatic Moware as he tried helplessly to decide which way to aim his recorder.

Hunnar and Ethan watched the astonishing spectacle side by side. "Never have I seen or heard of a migration so large. It is not the proper time of year."

"Maybe their habits are different in this part of the world," Ethan suggested.

Hunnar executed a gesture of concession. "Perhaps. You would think they would stop in such a rich region to graze, yet they push steadily northward. One would almost think they were running away from something."

V

"Poyolavomaar on the horizon!"

All eyes turned to the lookout's bin atop the mainmast. Then there was a concerted rush forward as crew and passengers alike strained for their first sight of the powerful city-state which had allied itself with Sofold following the battle outside Moulokin. The scientists were anxious to set eyes on the seven islands they had been told about, while Ethan, September, Williams, and the Tran wondered what kind of government had been established in their absence. Would they still be welcomed as friends, let alone as allies?

An hour later they were in among the outer islets, steep-sided volcanic buttes whose tops projected up through the frozen ocean. Neatly terraced hillsides were dotted with farmhouses of dressed stone. Smoke rose from tall chimneys. The first of the seven large islands that were home to the majority of Poyolavomaar's population lay dead ahead.

Ethan scanned the slopes for signs of war or discord and allowed himself a silent sigh of relief at finding none. Their deposition of the homicidal former Landgrave had not sparked a civil war in their absence. "Looks peaceful enough."

September nodded. "Someone's taken control here, and without a heavy hand. I see new decorative wood carving on some of the buildings and the docks. Oppressed people don't decorate. Wonder who the new Landgrave is. Maybe that young officer T'hosjer T'hos who finished off Rakossa."

"Could be, but I think the nobles would choose someone with a closer connection to the throne if they could find a distant relative who wasn't as crazy as Rakossa. We'll find out soon enough."

Small ice craft were turning from their courses to parallel and escort the *Slanderscree*. There was no mistaking the icerigger for any other ship on Tran-ky-ky. Those Poyolavomaarians who had been present when it had passed through on its way to fabled Moulokin recognized it immediately. Citizens of the city-state filled the rigging and lined the rails of their much smaller vessels to offer whistles and shouts of greeting.

One sleek, high-sailed ice boat pulled alongside long enough for a member of its crew to perform a feat of acrobatic derring-do which had even the hardened sailors of Sofold cheering. Using his strong claws to maintain his grip on the wood, he crawled out on the starboard rigger of his ship until he was squatting directly above the single skate at the end. Then he lifted one paw long enough to wave to his helmsman. As that individual delicately manipulated sails and wind, the ice boat's starboard rigger rose slowly off the ice until it was careening along at sixty kilometers an hour on its fore and aft skates only. A hair more to port, and the boat would roll, smashing itself and its crew against the ice. Back to starboard too suddenly, and the impact would certainly jar the precariously balanced rider loose, to be battered against the ice or thrown beneath the massive skates of the *Slanderscree*.

Neither happened. With his boat heeled as far to port as possible the daredevil young Tran gathered himself and leaped, his claws and fingers slamming into the scaling

ladder built into the icerigger's side. Immediately his own
boat dropped back level with the ice. Several of the *Slanderscree*'s sailors roared their approval. Others extended
willing paws to help the boarder onto the deck.

He was a tall, sleek male, not long out of adolescence.
His fur glistened with youth and his eyes shone with excitement as they tried to take in everything at once. They
stopped moving only when they caught sight of Ethan and
September.

"It is you who helped us to regain our freedom from the
tyrant Rakossa. You have come back to us."

"Just passing through," said September. "As for regain-
ing your freedom, you did that yourselves."

"Who reigns in Poyolavomaar now?" Ethan asked.

"T'hosjer T'hos, he who deposed the tyrant."

"Picked the right individual instead of the right blood-
line," September murmured. "Sensible folk, our Tran."

"We are looking forward to meeting with your new
Landgrave," Ethan told their visitor.

"And he glad will be to greet you. I hight Neravar Blad-
Kagenn, soldier in the Island Guard. I would be honored to
accompany you to the castle."

"Glad to have you aboard." September looked past the
young warrior. His small ship had sped away, probably to
convey news of the *Slanderscree*'s arrival.

Blad-Kagenn's gaze traveled from one part of the huge
icerigger to the next. "I am almost enjoying myself."

"Any reason why you shouldn't?" Ethan inquired curiously.

Blad-Kagenn turned yellow eyes on him. "Because the
world is going mad, of course. Have you not heard in the
northern lands?"

"I guess not.

"What is such talk?" Hunnar had joined them in time to
overhear the warrior's last comment. Redbeard's attitude

was more formal than that of the two humans, though not unfriendly. For his part Blad-Kagenn lowered his voice out of respect for the senior knight. . .

"The world is going mad, or so it is said. Perhaps it is nothing more than a rumor."

Hunnar glanced at Ethan. "Something we should be looking into?"

Ethan shrugged. "Too soon to say. We've business of our own to take care of. One crisis at a time." He returned his attention to Blad-Kagenn. "Tell us of your new Landgrave. We met him only briefly when last we passed through your territory, and at that time he was only a soldier, not a ruler."

Blad-Kagenn told them of how Rakossa's line had been formally deposed and how the nobles, to make peace quickly, had settled on the young soldier to lead them. None were sorry to learn of Tonx Ghin Rakossa's death. His madness and not-so-private depravities had been both an embarrassment and threat to the population for many years. Rakossa's spies had been everywhere, but when T'hosjer removed the head of the monster, the body dissipated quickly.

The *Slanderscree* was in among the seven main islands now. Ta-hoding slowed the ship lest they run over one of the smaller vessels plying the iceways. At the main island more cheers awaited them, though Ethan thought the shouts and roars oddly subdued.

Blad-Kagenn proudly escorted them around the harbor and up the steep slope that led to Poyolavomaar's castle. T'hosjer T'hos was still the tall and, by Tran standards, slim soldier Ethan barely remembered from their previous visit. He greeted Ethan and Skua as friends and embraced Elfa and Hunnar, his recently acquired allies in the Union of Ice. Court retainers looked on approvingly. It was a good thing, this alliance. There was none of the nervous whispering or sidelong suspicious glances that normally attended such a meeting. The sycophants and fawning bodyguards who had surrounded Rakossa were gone.

Chairs were brought forward. They were wide enough to accommodate folding winglike dan—or a loose-fitting survival suit. Drinks arrived in the company of a court recorder who would write down whatever was said between Landgrave and visitor.

"I did not expect to see any of you so soon again," the young Landgrave told them.

"Nor we you," replied Elfa.

T'hos adjusted his dan and leaned forward. "I think I preferred soldiering to administration, but I could not refuse the honor to my family. Tell me now: What changes in the north? What have you seen, where have you been, and how does the Union progress?"

"The Union is solid as the rocks and grows larger and stronger every day," Elfa told him. "As for what changes there have been"—she nodded demurely toward Hunnar—"I have taken a mate."

T'hos smiled broadly at the Sofoldian knight. "This means that I will not be able to strengthen the Union by a marriage between our two states."

Hunnar nodded and kept a straight face. "There are many young females of marriageable age and noble birth in Sofold." His tone turned serious. "Much have we seen and learned since last we made landfall in Poyolavomaar. Enough to last a curious soldier several lifetimes." He nodded toward Ethan and Skua. "Our new friends have ships that fly through the sky and devices that enable them to talk across more satch than separate Sofold and Poyolavomaar. As soon as the Union becomes strong enough and we are able to join in this greater union they call their Commonwealth, we too may be permitted to make use of such wonders."

T'hos's whiskers rose. "This is a time I must live to see! I have sent emissaries to Warreck and Vem-Hobar asking them to join in our Union. They have reacted with suspicion and evasion, which is to say, normally. I have hopes of winning them over together with several smaller outlying city-states. We could compel them to participate by force of arms but"—he glanced sideways at Ethan—"you say this is not how your government prefers a union to be formed."

"Not really." It wasn't much of a prevarication, he reflected. Actually the Commonwealth didn't care how primitives created their planetary governments. Conquest was as acceptable as argument. But the Tran were warlike enough. By giving soldiers like T'hos no option Ethan hoped to preserve lives and property. A union that came into being with as little bloodshed as possible would be the stronger for it.

"Continue your discussions."

"Such is what we are doing," T'hos assured him. "In the end I am confident reason will prevail. It is merely a matter of time. It is only that I am personally impatient to qualify for these benefits you spoke of when last you paused among us." A puzzled expression crossed his face. "Was I then wrong in believing that you would not return here?"

Elfa dipped her head slightly and cut her eyes sharply toward her human companions. The double gesture was rich with suggestion, not all of which Ethan comprehended despite the months he'd spent living among the Tran.

"It seems that Sir Ethan and Sir Skua found our company so pleasing they decided to remain awhile longer among us."

"Not on your whiskers," September growled, not caring if he insulted half the organized government of Tran-ky-ky.

"I came along to keep him out of trouble and that's the only reason I came along." He nodded toward Ethan.

"We know well what a rugged and unfeeling person you are," Hunnar said sardonically.

T'hos was staring past them, toward a high window which overlooked the harbor below. "Do you wish to know what I have thought of every day and night since you left? To ride one of your sky boats and see my world from above, as the long-winged *urlus* do. I have climbed all the major peaks of Poyolavomaar but it seems to me not the same." He extended both arms to display his veinous *dan*. "These flaps of skin make chivaning a delight, but they will not allow us even to glide."

"I promise," Ethan told him, in defiance of any relevant regulations, "that as soon as the Union is accepted by my government, as representative of the Tran I'll get you up in a skimmer or a shuttle somehow. I'll have to have an aircar to carry out my new work here and I'll bring it to Poyolavomaar just so you can have a ride."

"Wonderful, wonderful!" The young Landgrave clapped his paws like a cub. "If only the world does not end before this happens. Some say it is going mad."

"We heard the rumor," September commented. "Maybe you could tell us a little more about exactly what—"

"Your pardon for interrupting." Ta-hoding had been waiting patiently off to the side until he could stand it no longer. "We have a problem that is based on fact and not rumor, good Landgrave. As many of our crew were desirous of returning to their homes, we have sailed here with a minimal crew. My people are exhausted and in need of relief. The humans who are our passengers have been as helpful as they can be, but experienced ice sailors they are not." He indicated Williams, Cheela Hwang, and the rest of the research group who were studying the wall hangings and stone carvings that decorated the Landgrave's hall.

"They are willing, but sometimes they cause more trouble than their well-meaning efforts are worth."

September nodded ready agreement. "I saw Jacalan trying to raise a sail in a seventy kph gale. We're lucky we didn't lose her."

"Tell me what you require," said T'hos unhesitatingly.

"We know that Poyolavomaar is home to many fine sailors of the ice. We would take some temporarily into our company to aid us in our journey. It would make much smoother our expedition to the southern continent."

"The southern continent? Why would you wish to go there? Are you returning so soon to our friends in Moulokin?"

"No. We go another direction entirely; not south by southwest but by southeast."

T'hos frowned. "You sail upon empty ice. Though that is far from the routes our traders ply it is said there is nothing in that direction for thousands of *kijat*. No cities, no towns, not even barren unclaimed islands. A few dealers in furs and metal have penetrated that far to tell us only that there is no reason to go farther."

"Nevertheless, that's where we're going," Ethan told him.

"You should not." The Landgrave looked troubled. "That is the part of the world they say has gone mad."

"Should've guessed," September murmured. He jerked a thumb back toward the rubbernecking researchers. "Our thoughtful associates apparently aren't the only ones who think something out of the ordinary's going on down there."

"The travelers who described this madness heard it from others who heard it from another who heard it from one they say was probably half-mad himself," T'hos muttered uneasily. "One must be cautious in such matters. The credulous are all too ready to believe whatever they are told.

As Landgrave I must be more careful. But it is one thing to deal with one who is mad, as Rakossa was, and another to think of what someone means when they talk of the whole world going mad." He rose half out of his chair and gestured to his right.

The Tran who shuffled forward was older even than Balavere Longax. His chiv had seen so much use they had been worn down nearly flush with the thick pads of his feet. No more for this elder long hours of carefree chivaning across the ice. Like the poor humans his wizened eyes touched upon he was reduced to walking.

He listed slightly to the left, like tree that has been permanently bent by the wind. The long staff he leaned on was pointed like a skier's pole. His mane and facial fur had gone snow white. His eyelids opened halfway only, afflicting him with a perpetually sleepy air. His infirmities notwithstanding, he managed two-thirds of a respectful bow.

"I greet our friends from Sofold and from the sky. I remember you from your previous visit, though we were not then formally introduced." He smiled, a patriarch who had outlived his tormentor. "I was not in favor in the court of Tonx Ghin Rakossa. I am afflicted with a disarming habit of saying what I think."

"Get you run through every time," September said knowingly.

T'hos had resumed his seat. "This is Moak Stonetree, my most respected adviser. He it was who first learned of the rumor you would seek in person."

"What's all this nonsense about the world going mad?" September had never been much on protocol or subtleties.

Stonetree made certain the point of his staff was driven into a crack between two smooth flooring stones. His gaze narrowed as he fixed on the tall human. "A rumor proven is a lie confounded. Truth balances itself precariously betwixt the two. I have passed along only what I have learned from others."

"Trappers and outreachers will say anything to draw attention to themselves." Elfa snorted derisively. "The more their tall tales are believed the readier they are to embellish them. They enjoy frightening with imaginative stories of the world beyond the wind those who remain safe and secure in their cities."

Stonetree nodded respectfully. "All that you say is true. Yet so wild and bizarre is this particular tale that one can only wonder at the inventiveness of whoever initially declaimed it. It has the singular virtue of remaining unchanged through several retellings."

"Means little," observed Ta-hoding. "Such travelers take care with what they swap far out on the ice, be it money, skins, or stories. Keeping such an odd and elaborate fantasy coherent would only add to its effectiveness, and to the amusement of telling and retelling it."

"I hope that you are all right," Stonetree said solemnly. "I hope that this is but a fanciful invention with which to afright children. However, it is sometime since my childhood and I find that *I* am frightened."

"Is that all the stories say," Ethan asked him, "that the world is going mad? Or are there details or descriptions? How does a world begin to go mad?"

The old adviser turned his patient gaze on the smaller human. "The tale says that in one part of the southern continent the ice has become a corpse."

Ethan had to ask the oldster to repeat himself. September wasn't sure he'd understood clearly either. The giant looked for explanation to their fellow Tran, but Ethan spoke up before Ta-hoding or Hunnar could do so.

"I don't know that term. What's an 'ice corpse'?"

By way of reply Stonetree picked up a half-empty goblet and ceremoniously turned it upside down. Water ran out on the stones, escaping into the cracks in the floor.

"Do you now understand?"

September shook his head in frustration. "I never was one for oblique explanations."

"It's water," Ethan told him. "When ice dies it becomes water. A corpse."

"Okay, I buy the relationship. That still doesn't tell us why someone would think the world's going mad down there."

"It is wrong," Stonetree told him firmly. "We make ice corpses so we can drink. That is natural. To find it where we have made it not is unnatural. It is perverse. It is— madness."

"Wait a minute," said Ethan suddenly. "You're talking about open water? A hole in the ice sheet?"

"Just so," said Stonetree, relieved that the skypeople had finally grasped the notion.

"That's impossible. Even at the equator it's impossible."

The old adviser sounded tired. "Just so."

Ethan swallowed hard. At its thinnest point, the ice sheet that covered Tran-ky-ky from pole to pole was thirty meters thick. Because of the planet's perturbed orbit the equatorial regions would not warm sufficiently for standing water to form on its surface for at least another several thousand years.

"It's got to be volcanic activity, like Milliken and Jacalan and the rest suggested." September was staring hard at the stone floor as though seeking inspiration in the cracks. "Nothing else could cause this damn ice to melt like that. Nothing!"

"How large do the travelers claim this ice corpse to be?" Ethan asked T'hos's sage.

"There the tale becomes slippery. Some say it is no more than a small pond as might be made by hunters who have built themselves a fire upon the ice. Others declare it to be *kijatin* in extent. There is no proof because no one wants to go there. Demons make corpses of Tran as well as ice."

Ethan tried to imagine how a group of unsophisticated Tran would react if they stumbled across a large area of open water. What would Earth's ancient Polynesians have thought if the tropical seas surrounding their island homes had suddenly begun to freeze solid?

"Nobody makes a corpse of me, not while I'm alive," said September with a disarming grin. "We'll find out what's going on there because that's where we're going."

"If there is too much truth to this, I fear you will not return." Stonetree shifted his stance, resting his aged legs. "A pity, for you have done much good for Poyolavomaar and for all Tran." He gestured with a withered finger. "One piece of advice I will give you: If you encounter demons, leave them alone. Let them have what ice they wish. Perhaps they will claim only a small area and leave the rest of the world sane."

Ethan indicated the scientists, who had concluded their tour of the royal hall and were casting impatient glances in the conference's direction. "Our scholar companions have instruments which will take the measure of any demon. Whoever comes with us need not fear."

T'hosjer considered. "I will find sailors for you who are not afraid of traveler's tales. I will also give you a guide to help lead you to this place of seeming indecision."

"We don't need—" Ethan started to say, intending to explain that Hwang and company's instruments and satellite reconnaissance measurements would take them straight to the region in question without the need for a guide, when September cut him off.

"We'd be very grateful for a guide and for all your help, T'hosjer. Anyone brave enough to lead an expedition of aliens to a land of demons is someone I'd like to have riding point for me. So long as your sailors aren't tempted to bail out if the going gets rough."

T'hosjer drew himself up to his full height. "The sailors of Poyolavomaar will do as their Landgrave bids them, no matter their own feelings. You need not fear desertion. Stonetree will make the arrangements." As the Landgrave turned to bark orders at his adviser September leaned over to whisper to Ethan.

"Have to watch your thoughts, young feller-me-lad. T'hosjer here's already offered to fill out our crew. To refuse his guide, who'll probably also serve as his personal spy on the trip, would be a bit of an insult."

Ethan looked abashed. "I let my enthusiasm get the better of me. Sometimes I forget the Tran aren't regular folks."

"You're right about that. They're a damnsight finer than regular folks. For a salesman you ain't much of a diplomat."

"Sorry. They're not always the same thing." He sat back in his chair as T'hosjer turned his attention back to them.

"Stonetree will speak to Orun Malc-Vierg, who is marshal of our fleet. He will find volunteers from among his bravest and most experienced sailors. There is honor to be gained in traveling with you, and much to be learned. I do not think there will be trouble filling your requirements. Fleet sailors are not superstitious trappers. As for your guide, it will be someone from my own court, knowledgeable, brave, and close to me." He turned and beckoned toward the crowd of silent courtiers.

An extremely attractive and unexpectedly young Tran female slid over on an ice path to join them, moving with leonine grace and power. By Tran standards she was even prettier than Elfa Kurdagh-Vlata, but there was nothing soft-looking about her. Her attitude as her eyes flicked over them bordered on the imperious. She was silently challenging each and every one of them to object to T'hosjer's selection of her as guide.

"This is Grurwelk Seesfar," said T'hosjer by way of introduction. "As a child she explored that very same distant land you seek in the company of her father, a well-known and respected explorer." He nodded to her. "You have the honor of guiding our allies back to that region."

"I have been listening to your conversation. Too much talk. But I am pleased that I have been chosen to assist our friends from the sky."

"You mated?" September asked casually. "And if so will your mate be coming along also?"

She looked sharply at the giant. She had yet to blink, Ethan noted. Among the Tran the absence of a gesture could have considerable significance. Not blinking for long periods could be construed as silent defiance.

"Mated I was. Widowed I am. My mate and my father vanished during a visit to that same area you aim toward during a hunting expedition more than a year ago. Since that time I have tried and failed to find others willing to accompany me on a search for them. All the fault of these childish stories. I was preparing to go by myself, and now providence has brought you and your curiosity to Poyolavomaar. I will be glad of your company and gladder still of your aid."

"Whoa," said September. "You're coming along to help *us*, remember?"

She ignored him as she turned her icy stare on Ethan. "I know you have strange weapons and devices, instruments capable of dealing even with demons. I know this because of what you did to destroy Rakossa the tyrant and because of what I have just overheard. If demons have imprisoned my mate and my father, you will destroy them for me!"

"We don't know that any demons are involved," Ethan said quietly.

"There are!" Light flashed from her nictitating membranes. "They stole away my father and my mate. I will find them and bring them back." So saying, she spun on her chiv and skated back into the crowd without waiting politely for a formal dismissal from Landgrave. T'hos simply smiled tolerantly.

September looked at the ruler of Poyolavomaar. "Not a good idea. She talks tough and looks tough, and I'm sure she knows the area as you say, but she's in on this because she's after revenge on something or somebody that probably doesn't exist."

"She will do as she has promised to do," T'hosjer assured him.

"She can pledge her loyalty a thousand times over. That's not the kind of reassurance we're after."

"I am curious that you think no demons dwell where you are going. If not demons, what then is causing the ice there to die?"

"We don't know that's what's happening there," Ethan reminded him. "There's a system of internal heating that—" The expression beginning to appear on the Landgrave's face made him stop, turn, and beckon Milliken Williams.

The teacher did his best to give T'hosjer a crash course in volcanism, geophysics, and plate tectonics. It was impossible to tell how much of it made sense to the young ruler. Finally September stepped in.

"We're searching for the cause. Whether volcanoes or demons or hot springs or whatever, we don't know. That's why we're going there. Whatever it is, we'll find it and find it fast." He leaned back in his chair. "I have a ship to catch." He nodded toward the crowd of courtiers which had swallowed their guide-to-be. "And I'd still prefer someone to lead the way who doesn't have a personal, highly emotional stake in the outcome of our travels."

"Seesfar *is* high-strung," T'hosjer admitted, "but she is the only one to have traveled in the region you intend to visit."

"That's settled then," Ethan said quickly before September could think of another objection. "I'm sure she'll be a great help."

T'hosjer T'hos rose. "I will see to it that you are provisioned with whatever you require." Ta-hoding started to speak and Hunnar was quick to silence the greedy captain. "The additional crew you asked for will arrive at your dock no later than this evening so that you may have time to instruct them prior to your departure. Come, Stonetree. I would talk more on this matter."

The aged retainer bowed again, holding on to his pointed staff for support. They left together.

Ethan caught September by the wrist. "You ignored your own advice. What was that you told me about accepting the offer of a guide or else we'd insult our host?"

The giant looked uneasy. "I expected someone interested in topography, not revenge. She could steer us wrong, looking for her relatives."

"Use your head, Skua. All we have to do is listen politely to her suggestions, nod approvingly, then go where our charts and measurements tell us."

September nodded slowly. "I hope you're right, young feller-me-lad. What's done is done. But I've seen that expression and heard that tone from humans and nonhumans alike, and I'm telling you now that if that smoky little Tran sees something she wants, she'll use the *Slanderscree* and the rest of us to get it for her."

"Ability and determination don't necessarily go hand in hand, Skua. We'll be able to handle her."

"Could be." His eyes still searched the crowd without

finding the shaggy-maned head he was looking for. "Could be also that if she's convinced demons have shanghaied her father and husband, she'll find a way to steer us straight to hell."

"You've seen the survey satellite readouts," Ethan reminded him quietly. "What makes you think we're not headed there already?"

VI

As they prepared to depart the following morning it seemed as though half the city-state's population had gathered to watch. Poyolavomaarians sat on the docks, stood along the harbor wall, and chivaned on the ice, the adolescents showing off to see who could execute the most intricate and dangerous maneuvers. A few of the icerigger's sailors were doing a brisk trade in goods they'd brought with them from Arsudun, still little more than a name to most of the islands' inhabitants. Ta-hoding complained that he was fast becomeing captain of a crew of merchants instead of sailors and that the *Slanderscree* was so loaded down with trade goods it wouldn't steer properly.

Nevertheless, despite his complaints Ta-hoding was justly renowned for his tolerance. The trading was allowed to continue until the ship's cook attempted to bring aboard a disassembled, intricately carved Poyolavomaarian house, for which he'd traded several barrels of dried vegetables from the ship's stores. Ta-hoding let loose with a barrage which had his people scrambling to sequester their purchases belowdecks before he could throw them overboard. The next sailor or soldier who attempted to swap so much as a button would find himself tied to the stern of the icerigger to be dragged like baggage all the way to the southern continent, Ta-hoding roared.

The crew griped about lost opportunities for profit but returned to their stations and jobs. Ta-hoding might be overweight and slightly comical-looking, but there was nothing amusing about his authority or his willingness to bring it to bear on those under him. For their part the Poyolavomaarians applauded each of the captain's inventive imprecations and urged him to still more elaborate flights of verbal-anatomical fancy. Or as September put it: "Nothing like a little cultural exchange to cement friendships among new allies, feller-me-lad."

While exchanges, verbal and commercial, were taking place, Grurwelk Seesfar clung to the foremast rigging and sneered at her jostling fellow sailors.

It was Suaxus-dal-Jagger, Hunnar's senior squire, who apologized for intruding on September's observation with a comment of his own. "Perhaps you could lend your wisdom to a small problem, sirs."

"What kind of problem?" Ethan sighed. For some unknown reason the Tran believed he possessed great powers of reconciliation and understanding.

"Two of them, actually. They're right behind you."

Both men turned. Members of the ship's crew were going about their business, storing last supplies, cleaning the deck, pouring water to form fresh icepaths, and defrosting frozen pika-pina rope with a lamp. A few were instructing recruits from Poyolavomaar's navy in the fine points of the icerigger's operation.

He was just turning back to dal-Jagger when a blur near one of the main loading ramps caught his attention. His first thought was that two of the new crew were midgets. As they slowed and he saw their pudgy faces, he knew they were preadolescent cubs.

That in itself was not a surprise. Wherever they docked

cubs loved to play around the great ship, chivaning around its tall metal skates and climbing on the cables that secured the ice anchors. What was surprising was that they were on board. Their antics drew angry comments rather than smiles from the busy crewmembers.

"They're in the way," Ethan commented. Dal-Jagger nodded approvingly. "Why not shoo them off, then?"

"That is the problem, Sir Ethan. They are the offspring of this Seesfar person who has been forc—assigned to us by the Landgrave of Poyolavomaar. It is beyond normal protocol." The squire was obviously upset. "I understand as do most of us that we must accept her because to refuse would be to insult our new allies, but it is beyond common sense to expect us to accept her entire family as well. The *Slanderscree* is not a nursery."

"Why not just let it slide?" September suggested. "What harm can a couple of cubs do? The trip's bound to further their education."

"The *Slanderscree* is also not a school. Nor is it a passenger transport. The crew are already complaining."

"Absurd. Next you'll be telling me it's bad luck to have a female on board."

Dal-Jagger eyed him oddly. "Why would I say a thing like that, Sir Skua? All who sail know it is the contrary, that it is good fortune to have a mixed crew. Not to mention more enjoyable for all involved. But you are not Tran."

"Nope. Every race to its own prejudices, I guess."

"This has nothing to do with prejudice. It is a question of what is practical and sensible," dal-Jagger said firmly. He gestured toward the loading ramp. "Several times they have almost caused others to fall."

"No need for a cabin boy or two, is what you're saying. Our traditions ain't the same either. Ah." His tone changed to one of satisfaction. "The captain has been informed.

"Come on, feller-me-lad. This ought to prove interesting."

Grurwelk was hidden behind Ta-hoding's mass, though they could hear her stating her case as they approached.

"They come with me because I am all they have left. They are my family."

"While you are on my ship your crewmates are your family," Ta-hoding shot back. "T'hos rules in Poyolavomaar. Out on the ice, I am lord. They must remain here."

"I'm taking them with me," she growled, "so that they may see their father again soonest, *if* he still lives."

Something bumped into Ethan from behind, nearly knocking him off his feet. When he turned he found himself staring down into a wide furry face. Its owner took a step backward and stumbled into his brother. Both of them fell to the deck. Awed eyes flicked from Ethan to September and back again. The cub let out a peculiar whoosh of chilled air, the small cloud like a visual exclamation mark. Ethan knew it as the Tran equivalent of gosh-gee-whiz.

"Look," breathed the cub, "it's the great lords from the sky!"

"Not great lords," Ethan corrected him.

The pair scrambled to their feet. "It is as we were told. You are as modest as a great lord, sir."

On the edge of puberty, Ethan decided as he studied them. Cute as could be. As he looked on they both bent double and rested their paws on the deck.

"We are honored," they said in unison.

"Charming little buggers," September commented. He glanced at Ta-hoding. "You sure they'd be in the way, Captain?"

That worthy looked uncomfortable but he stuck to his

guns. "If you were a scout or a pilot, Sir Skua, you would know how out of place cubs are on a warship."

"Warship?" Seesfar seized on the claim immediately. "I see no preparations for war. Only for travel and exploration."

"We go not to fight but we must be prepared to. We have had to do so in the past."

"You speak of my offspring as being in the way. What do you call these foolish humans who dash back and forth and run into each other much as my children?"

"Scholars. Scholars are often absent-minded because they are constantly thinking on scholarly things. This is something that is the same among the skypeople as it is among us."

"What better place for a pair of cubs, then, but among a host of scholars? Think of what they could learn."

Ta-hoding flashed his dan at her. "I will not sail this ship out of this harbor with those infants aboard!"

Eyes locked. Sailors pretended to continue their work. When the end came it was a surprise to everyone.

Seesfar nodded, just once. "This is your ship. While I am on it, I will abide by your decisions."

Ta-hoding relaxed uncertainly. "Well, I—that is right of you. Very right. It is decided, then."

"Yes. Decided." She put her dan protectively around both cubs. "Come, sons of Seesfar. My body will go but my heart will stay still upon the ice." As everyone stared she led them down the ramp and off the ship.

"See?" Ethan said smugly. "She's perfectly responsive."

September was following the departing guide with his eyes. "Or perfectly subtle."

"I don't follow you."

"Any Tran who's ever sailed a ship knows that cubs aren't wanted aboard." He nodded toward the dock. "She knew that when she brought them aboard. She was also aware of our worries about her. What if she brought them on just so we could see how docile she could be when push came to shove? What if the whole confrontation was a sham, staged so she'd have a chance to demonstrate how 'cooperative' she could be? To allay our lingering concerns?"

"I hadn't thought of that. I've been out of sales for too long." Ethan considered, finally said, "Maybe we should try to keep her off even at the risk of insulting T'hos?"

September shook his head. "Too late for that. Besides, anybody that clever—if she is that clever and I'm not reading motives into her actions that weren't there—could be a definite asset on a trip like this. I just can't escape the feeling she was smiling inside all the while she was arguing with Ta-hoding."

Exasperation colored Ethan's response. "Skua, make up your mind! Do you want her off the ship or not?"

"I really don't know, young feller-me-lad, and that's the truth. Hard enough to know what to make of an enigma when it's human."

Ethan walked off, shaking his head in frustration. September continued to stare into the crowd until what really troubled him finally struck home.

Feloursine or not, he was startled to realize, Grurwelk Seesfar was a lot like him.

As the *Slanderscree* departed Poyolavomaar and turned south toward the equator, Ethan saw little of Grurwelk Seesfar. When not counseling Ta-hoding about ice conditions and weather, she remained below in her hammock, quiet and unobtrusive. It would be easy, he mused, to forget she was aboard, so little did she show herself on deck. Perhaps that was what she wanted.

The great ice sheet slipped beneath the *Slanderscree*'s runners. Uninhabited islands poked their heads through the white pavement off to starboard while great fields of pika-pedan, pike-pina's giant relative, dominated the western horizon. Though stories of iceships becoming trapped in such fields were a staple of sailor lore, such tragedies were rare in reality. That didn't keep Ta-hoding from giving the forest of towering succulents a wide berth wherever possible.

Four-legged furry crunilites scurried the length of the growths, nibbling at the soft sides, while a pair of Oroes drifted from the crown of one stalk to another, the sacs on their backs fully inflated.

It was instructive to view the fauna of the pika-pedan forest—from a distance. He hadn't forgotten, never would forget, the day when he'd nearly been dragged beneath the ice and consumed by a kossief during their journey to distant Moulokin. The ice sheet was home to all manner of creatures in addition to the far-ranging root system of the pika-pina and pika-pedan.

Each night Ta-hoding would park the icerigger with its stern facing into the west wind, the ice anchors would be set out, and all but the night watch would settle into a deep, unbroken sleep. Cheela Hwang and her companions slept as soundly as the *Slanderscree*'s crew. The cold itself was exhausting.

Ethan didn't know what woke him. His breath was a distinct, pale cloud in the moonlit air of the cabin. Here near Tran-ky-ky's equator the nighttime temperature fell no farther than a mere forty or fifty below. He looked around in the dark and tried to remember what had disturbed his sleep. His survival suit lay nearby. Some of the scientists chose to sleep in their suits, but he and September had long since abandoned the practice. They slept instead beneath small mountains of thick furs. Besides being more comfortable, it gave the suits a chance to air out.

As a precaution he reached out and touched a contact on the suit's sleeve to prewarm the interior. At the same time the sensation was repeated: movement. There shouldn't be any movement. Multiple ice anchors locked the icerigger in place and if anything it was unusually calm outside. Sudden gales were not unknown at night, but this was different. He had experience of wind-induced motion and this wasn't it.

A third time and he was sure. Not movement to port or starboard, bow or stern. More like a settling sensation.

"Skua? Skua, wake up."

Across from his bed a massive form stirred beneath an avalanche of blankets. "Hy—what?"

"We're moving, Skua. The ship has moved. Several times."

"So what? Everything on this world moves. The wind sees to that."

"No, this is different. It's more like—" The *Slander-scree* shuddered again. A moment of uncertainty until the motion ceased, then September rolled over to peer across at his companion. White hair gleamed in the moonlight.

"Now that did not feel proper, feller-me-lad. Damn if I don't think you're right, but something else ain't."

"I don't understand. If something's wrong, the night watch should have sounded a warning by now."

"If it still can." September reached out to flip the prewarm on his own survival suit. Meanwhile Ethan took a deep breath and slid out from beneath the mass of furs. The cold stung his naked body and then he was secure inside his suit. He snapped down the visor and sealed it to the collar. The suit's thermostat immediately began to raise the temperature inside the garment to a comfortable level.

The two men quickly discovered that Ethan was neither the first nor the only one who'd been awakened by the peculiar motion. The corridor outside their cabin was packed with crewmembers, recruits from Poyolavomaar, and others. He watched Elfa Kurdagh-Vlata moving toward the gangway while struggling to don a hessavar-hide vest. Even here near the equator the nighttime temperatures were still a bit brisk for an acclimated Tran.

As Ethan tried to catch up to her the ship shook again, violently this time. Sailors spread their arms to brace themselves against the corridor's walls. Ethan stumbled, was caught by September on his way to the floor.

"Bad and getting worse." The giant's expression was grim as he stared toward the gangway. "Something's happening outside and we'd damn well better find out what in a hurry."

Natural phenomenon or otherwise, the daughter of the Landgrave of Sofold was prepared. She drew her sword as she mounted the gangway. Sailors parted to make way for the skypeople following her while those Tran not previously awakened began to stumble sleepily out of their beds and hammocks.

Elfa and Ethan emerged on deck simultaneously, side by side. With both of Tran-ky-ky's moons up, there was ample light to see by. Ice glistened, stark and barren beneath the unwinking moons. The wind blew steadily if unspectacularly from the east. Ethan estimated its velocity at no more than twenty or thirty kph, not near enough to shake a well-anchored vessel.

Hunnar crowded close behind them. "Check the anchors first thing." Ta-hoding had yet to put in an appearance and his evaluation of the situation was the one Ethan most wanted to hear.

They moved away from the hatch. Soldiers and sailors emerged from the opening in a steady stream, spreading out in several directions.

"All clear off the bow!" came a shout.

"All clear to starboard!"

"All clear to—" The cry was cut off abruptly as something like a flexible pine tree reached over the *Slander-scree*'s railing to pluck the unfortunate sailor off the deck as easily as Ethan would have removed an olive from a martini. It was followed by a second gargantuan limb, then a third.

"Shan-kossief!" screamed one of the sailors as he joined his companions in a mad dash for the open hatchway. Hunnar managed to slow the panic by pointing out that no matter how far they stretched, the huge tentacles or whatever they were could reach no more than a meter or so beyond the railing. If you stayed clear of the ship's flanks, you were safe. Warily, the sailors began to spread out again, keeping to the center of the deck. The tentacles would vanish, then reappear farther along the portside in hopes of grabbing another victim, but Hunnar was right: their range and reach were limited.

Ethan knew what a kossief was from personal experience: an ice worm, a carnivore with a tubular body that lived within the ice sheet itself. It traveled by melting the ice in front of it, digging a continuous tunnel until it sensed prey somewhere on the surface. Then it would stealthily melt its way up beneath its intended victim, strike and grab with long tentacles, and drag its struggling meal down into its lair. Expelling water from its own body, it would re-form the ice sheet and settle down to consume its food in an icy cocoon. That was a kossief. What was a shan-kossief?

In Tran "shan" meant variously "big," "huge," and "too-vast-to-be-imagined." As he tried to decide which interpretation would best apply, the ship shuddered anew. There was that settling sensation again.

It didn't take an expert on local fauna to hypothesize what was happening. If the shan-kossief's method of acquiring prey was similar to that of its smaller namesake—

Ethan shivered, and not from the cold. What would a monster like that think of the icerigger? It must be very confused. Here was prey the size of a small stavanzer. Edible prey, if the unlucky night guard had gone to the fate Ethan imagined. Yet most of it was inorganic and inedible. Probably the carnivore could sense the other warm, edible lifeforms aboard. It couldn't get at them, and the ship was probably too strong for it to tear apart. What else would it do but attempt to employ its instinctive method of obtaining food?

Not enough to guess. Before they could implement defensive reactions, they had to be certain. He started slowly toward the portside rail.

Elfa put a restraining paw on his shoulder. "You cannot. It will take you as well."

"Not if I keep down and don't expose myself," he told her without much conviction.

"Ethan is right." Hunnar moved up to join them. "We must know what is happening. I will go."

"No. I'm a lot smaller and maybe my suit will shield my body heat from its receptors." Hunnar thought this over, then nodded reluctantly and retreated to rejoin the rest of the onlookers.

Ethan went down on his hands and knees and resumed his approach to the railing. The anxious murmurings of both Tran and humans filled his ears. Hwang and her companions had joined the Tran on deck and were bombarding September and Hunnar with questions neither could answer.

He bumped his head against the wood. Nothing reached over the rail to grab him. Carefully he sat back on his haunches and began to straighten. His gloved hands reached over the top of the barrier. A moment later he found himself staring over the side.

Initially it seemed nothing was amiss. Then he leaned

out over the edge and saw that the portside bow runner was half gone. Water lapped at the brace that secured it to the underside of the ship. The long pool was spreading slowly beneath the *Slanderscree*. If the shan-kossief was big enough, it could conceivably drag the entire vessel beneath the surface where it would proceed to pick them off as efficiently as an anteater would glean a termite nest.

Something beneath the ice caught his attention. He found himself staring in fascination at a set of immense phosphorescent eyes. Beneath them lay the faint outline of a hollow space wide enough to swallow a skimmer. The ice sheet was a window through which he could peer into the frozen depths. The eyes were hypnotic and complex, not the light-sensing organs of a primitive invertebrate.

A rubbery cable shot out of the ice to snake itself around his right arm.

He'd leaned out a little too far, made himself a little too obvious. He tried to brace himself against the railing and the wood creaked. His arm felt like it was being torn from its socket. The pressure was irresistible. He felt himself being dragged up and over the side. Then he fell back onto the deck and Skua was standing over him, clutching the monster axe an admiring Tran smith had fashioned for him.

"Better than a beamer for this kind of work." With his free hand he reached down, grabbed Ethan by the collar of his survival suit, and began dragging him back amidships. He didn't let go until they were back with the others.

"Can you stand?"

"That's not the problem." Ethan straightened, winced, and leaned to his right as he felt gingerly the place where bones and muscles came together to form a limb. "I think I might've dislocated my shoulder."

"Lucky you didn't dislocate your skull, leaning over the side like that." Ethan was surrounded by a circle of concerned faces, most of them alien.

"It's trying to melt the ice out from beneath us. That's why we keep shaking. Every time another few centimeters of ice is dissolved we settle deeper. The portside bow runner's already half under."

Hunnar growled. "It will exhaust itself, I think. It would take days to melt enough ice to swallow the whole ship."

"Evidently," September said dryly, "it thinks we're worth the effort. Probably thinks the *Slanderscree*'s a giant cookie box."

"We have some time, then, but we'd better do something fast," Ethan commented. "All this shifting and settling might break one of the runners off and we're a long ways from repair facilities."

"What can we do?" Hunnar asked. "If we approach the rail, far less go over the side to attack it on the ice, it will take us one at a time. Nor are crossbows and spears likely to hurt it, even if we could force it up from beneath the ice, which we cannot."

"What about bringing in the anchors and letting the wind take us where it will?" the third mate wondered.

Hunnar shook his head doubtfully. "Too late now, if what Ethan says is true. With even one runner sunk beneath the surface the wind would not move us from this place. If we were to set our sails and catch the wind it surely would snap that runner's brace."

"What we have to do," September said, "is convince it that we're more trouble than we're worth." He glanced at Blanchard. "Don't suppose you or any of your friends smuggled along an illegal beamer or needler?"

"You know the restrictions on importing advanced weaponry to a primitive world." Blanchard sounded disappointed. "I wish in this case one of us had disregarded them." He was eyeing the rail where one of the shankossief's tentacles was probing the deck in search of something else worth grabbing. The short length September had amputated lay motionless off to one side.

Ethan brushed ice particles from his suit. "Should've brought along some kind of gun anyhow and damn the regulations."

September patted him on the shoulder. "Probably don't matter anyways, young feller-me-lad. I'm getting the feeling that to budge our submerged brother you'd need a cannon at least. Besides which you'd have to melt through the ice to get at it and melting's what we're trying to stop." The icerigger gave another lurch as it settled lower.

"Why not threaten it with your moral superiority?"

Ethan glanced sharply at Grurwelk Seesfar, thought of a response, but turned back instead to confer with September.

"Wishing for guns isn't going to get us out of this. We'll have to make use of what we have." He plucked at his wrist. "We have our survival suits. What else?" He looked over at Hwang. "You brought instruments along. What kind?"

The scientists looked at each other and ran through the inventory of devices regulations had permitted them to bring on the expedition. Ethan wasn't encouraged. Sensors for determining the rate of glacial advance or sampling humidity weren't likely to be of much use against a carnivore the size of the *Slanderscree*. The research team had devices for measuring the varying intensity of Tran-ky-ky's magnetic field, for recording tremors, for analyzing its intense and worldwide aurora, for on the spot chemical analysis, and for collecting and cataloging samples both organic and inorganic. All were useless.

He looked to Milliken Williams, but this was one crisis where the teacher's basic knowledge could not help them. "I've made gunpowder twice, but there's nothing here to work with: no nitrates, no sulfur, nothing. Only ice."

"Maybe there's some way to use the ice against it."

"Sure there is, feller-me-lad," said September sourly. "We could mix it up a gigantic cocktail and get it dead drunk."

"Hey, that's a thought."

The giant's eyes widened. "For a moron, maybe. We'd need a ship full of alcohol just to daze something that size."

"I didn't mean that," Ethan said, thinking hard. "I meant that there might be something we could feed it that would upset its metabolism. We're stocked to bursting with supplies. Maybe there's something in stores that could poison it."

A hurried inventory was taken but the results were discouraging. Most of the food the shan-kossief would gratefully consume and hope for more. Some strong spices might have done something but they were stocked in small quantities. What they needed was a couple of barrels of pepper, or the local equivalent.

"We didn't just bring instruments," Cheela Hwang reminded her companions after the feeding idea had been discarded. "Besides our survival suits we have knives and other tools."

"What about the stove?" Jacalan looked excited. "How could we use that?"

September let out a snort of derision. "Easy. We'll plop it in the pot and set the old dear up to boil."

"No, Almera's got an idea." Hwang displayed about as much enthusiasm as she was capable of. "The stove runs off a thermocouple fuel cell that can put out a lot of juice. It's designed to cook enough for a dozen people at one time. What if we locked it on its maximum setting and someone got the creature to ingest it?"

Ethan hunted for the flaw in her reasoning. "It still

might not put out enough heat to injure this thing, much less kill it."

"We don't have to do either," she argued. "All we want is for it to leave us alone. To become discouraged, as you said earlier." The ship lurched to port and people fought to keep their balance.

Ethan looked to Hunnar. "What do you think?"

"It would depend how much heat this machine emits. Remember that the shan-kossief generates much heat itself. It might not notice the difference."

"It should notice this." Hwang was adamant. "This is a tough piece of equipment, designed to function under difficult conditions. It should survive long enough to draw attention to itself even in something's belly."

"I have no better idea. We might try your idea, friend Hwang." The knight glanced toward the gangway. "Bring it forth, then, and let us see what it may do."

Moware and Jacalan hurried below. Meanwhile Ta-hoding instructed the ship's cook to bring up the biggest carcass in the icerigger's stock.

The stove wasn't much larger than a computer storage block with a square heat plate sealed on top. After some discussion, Jacalan set the controls and the doubts of the Tran were dispelled by the intense heat the device generated. On maximum setting you couldn't bring your hands within half a dozen centimeters of the cooking surface without burning them.

The stove was inserted in the carcass and the opening sewn shut. Ethan, September, and Hunnar dragged it to the rail.

"Carefully go here, feller-me-lad," September whispered as something moved in the moonlight below. "Now!"

They heaved it over the side. It struck the looming tentacle and bounced away. For a moment they were afraid the carcass would roll across the ice and be ignored.

But the shan-kossief was more sensitive than that. Noting the presence of something edible, it began to melt the ice beneath the carcass, which vanished into a puddle even as Ethan and his companions looked on. They retreated from the edge lest they follow the butchered corpse into oblivion.

No one spoke. A few looks of despair crossed faces when time passed and the ship shuddered anew.

"It didn't work," Ethan mumbled. "We're going to have to think of something else."

"I don't understand." Blanchard was shaking his head in puzzlement. "On a world like this a few hundred degrees should feel like thousands."

"Not in haste." Ta-hoding wasn't looking at them. He was listening, listening and perhaps employing senses only someone who'd spent a lifetime sailing the ice sheet possessed. Again the *Slanderscree* quivered.

"Ethan is right," said Hunnar. "It is not working."

"Something is. Be calm, relax, and feel the ship."

Hunnar frowned, then slumped slightly. Once more the icerigger shook. Ethan stared at one, then the other, until he couldn't stand the silence any longer.

"Would one of you please tell me what's going on?"

"The last few times the ship moved it was not from settling," Ta-hoding told him without shifting his gaze from the ice beyond. "I am sure of it. I know this ship's balance as well as I do my own, maybe more so." As he finished, the *Slanderscree* was wrenched violently—but to the side, not downward.

Ethan and the others made a cautious concerted rush to the rail. No tentacles rose to the attack. A glance showed that in the subarctic night air the water which had been sucking at the port bow runner was already refreezing, the ice sheet re-forming around the duralloy. Hal Semkin, Hwang's assistant, produced a small flashlight and played the powerful beam over the surface below. It was likewise refreezing. There were no visible weak spots for tentacles to burst through.

"Sonuvabitch," Ethan muttered in surprise, "we did it."

"Don't be so quick." Seesfar pressed close behind him, staring at the ice below. "The shan-kossief is crafty. It may simply have gone deeper and waits there for us to grow careless."

"Not if he's trying to get rid of that stove," Hwang argued. "I don't care how big the thing is. That's all that'll be on its lumbering mind for a while."

"You do not know the shan-kossief," Seesfar snapped.

"Maybe not, but I do know some biochemistry. The creatures of your world are no more different in makeup than you and I. They're flesh and blood, even if their blood is pumped full of natural antifreeze."

"We cannot in good conscience send workers over the side to cut us free until we are sure the shan-kossief has departed," said Hunnar.

"*You* can't." Ethan extended a gloved hand toward Semkin. "Let me have that light." The meteorologist obediently handed it over. "Somebody get a rope. If I run into trouble down there you can yank me clear."

September divined his friend's intentions. "May not be time enough to yank, feller-me-lad."

"I don't think it'll matter. I think Cheela's right. Our subsurface nemesis has gone off in search of a nice quiet place to try to throw up." He nodded over the side. "Everything's already refrozen. Surely if the shan-kossief was still around it wouldn't let that happen. It would have to start all over again. We'll fix the rope around my arms and shoulders so that if I'm grabbed I won't slip out of my suit."

"If it's still down there and it does get a grip on you, it

won't matter," September warned him. "All the Tran on this ship won't be strong enough to pull you free."

"Somebody's got to make sure it's gone. I'm lighter than you are and our thoughtful friends don't have my experience out here. Besides, I know what a kossief is like, if not its big brother. And I don't want to spend the night wondering about it. If it is gone and we sit around here and debate its intentions, we might give it time to come back."

September shook his head. "I think your common sense is frozen, like everything else on this iceball." When Ethan started to comment September stopped him. "Spare me any more of your logic. It's your neck. And everything above and below it."

"That's right," Ethan agreed. "It's my neck."

The rope was secured and double-tightened. Thankfully no one wished him good luck. Not verbally, anyway. He slipped over the rail and started down the boarding ladder cut into the icerigger's side. When he reached bottom he took a deep breath and let himself drop the rest of the way to the ice.

The silence on the ice was total. He couldn't hear the soft whispering of his companions up on deck. As he scanned the surface he saw that the ice sheet was broken and cracked where it had been thawed by the shan-kossief and then had refrozen in the creature's absence. Assuming it *was* absent, he reminded himself.

Trying to float above the ice, Ethan made his way toward the bow. Nothing moved under the ice sheet. The few puddles he encountered were freezing underfoot. His light penetrated the ice more than a meter in places and revealed nothing.

The starboard bow runner was intact. As near as he could tell so was its portside counterpart, though it was buried two-thirds of the way into the refrozen ice. Shouldn't take a crew of energetic, muscular Tran equipped with spears and ice picks long to chip it free, he mused. Then they would have to hack a sloping channel so it could slip free without damage when Ta-hoding gave the order to put on sail.

He leaned back, saw anxious faces and visors staring down at him. "It's all right. We can get out of here without any trouble. The runners and braces are intact. Just going to take a little hard digging. I'm coming up." He turned and started briskly back toward the boarding ladder. He was halfway there when the ice gave way beneath him.

The rope harness brought him up short. Somehow he hung on to the light. Now it danced crazily off smooth ice walls as he spun like a top at the end of the cable.

Nothing had reached up to grab him and pull him down, he saw as he fought to still the pounding in his chest. He'd fallen through a thin layer of ice into a sizable cavern. It dawned on him that he was dangling in the middle of the cavity the shan-kossief had occupied. He felt like bait on a line.

Bringing the light under control as his spinning slowed, he was immensely relieved to see that the cavity was empty. Peculiar undulations marred the otherwise smooth walls, reminding him of watery ripples on a smooth sandy beach. His beam revealed a huge tunnel stretching off into the distance. Residual heat trapped beneath the surface continued to melt water in a few spots. The steady, metallic drip was the only sound in the cavern besides his own breathing.

He was still slowly spinning when he picked out a large mound of white powder off to one side. At first he thought it was pulverized ice. It was a different shade of white, however, and the riblike projections which emerged from the pile were not ice crystals. He wondered if any of the crushed skeletons were Tran, but not hard enough to insist

on a closer look. The cavern was too much like a cata-
comb.

His light lingered on the mountain of dissolved calcium
as he was pulled up through the hole.

"I'm okay!" he shouted as he reemerged. A swing on
the rope brought him into contact with the ship's side and
he was able to secure the grip on the boarding ladder he'd
been walking toward. Still shaking, he forced himself to
climb the rest of the way to the deck.

September's anxious face was the first one he saw. "You
disappeared on us, feller-me-lad. I thought you were a
goner."

"I fell through a thin spot into a big cavity. The shan-
kossief's lair, I think." He sucked fresh air. "We'd better
make sure we angle to starboard when the time comes to
move. That's a *big* hole down there. If you could tame one
of those things, it'd be a heckuva help in building underground communities on this world."

September glanced over the side, saw the dark pit into
which Ethan had stumbled. "You might be able to train it,
but I don't think you could find anybody who'd volunteer
to feed it."

Ready hands helped Ethan slip free of the harness.
"There's a big tunnel stretching from the lair northward.
That's where it took off. You can bet if the stove doesn't
kill it, we'll see it again."

"We will not," Ta-hoding assured him, "because we will
no longer be here." His breath formed a small cloud in
front of him as he turned and began shouting orders. There
was a noticeable reluctance on the part of the crew to
comply with the captain's directives. No one rushed to
scramble over the side and test the accuracy of the human's
assessment.

Eventually, two soldiers braver than their comrades cautiously made their way down. Using picks they started

hacking at the ice which imprisoned the *Slanderscree*'s port bow runner. When nothing materialized to grab them, they were joined by two dozen of their fellows. Picks rose and fell with increasing confidence.

Meanwhile Suaxus-dal-Jagger and a trio of Hunnar's bravest soldiers lowered themselves into the shan-kossief's lair to stand guard before the tunnel. At least those working on the exposed surface would have time to flee if the monster returned.

The pit was not reoccupied. "Busy trying to salve the worst case of heartburn it's ever had" was how Blanchard described the shan-kossief's situation. If it could survive the heat, the creature would pass the stove much as it had passed the bones of its prey. Then hunger would drive it again.

That was the hypothesis put forth by Moware. No one planned on staying in the area to check its validity. As soon as the runners had been freed and paths for them sliced through the ice, they brought the excavators aboard and the ice anchors in.

Wind filled the icerigger's sails. Wood groaned. The great ship began to move forward. Shuddering and scraping the ice, the *Slanderscree* emerged from its temporary imprisonment. Moments later it was standing even with the surface of the frozen ocean.

Soldiers and sailors cheered, then returned to their tasks. Despite the fact that many of them had been chipping ice all night, no one rested until they had traveled a reassuring distance from the shan-kossief's cavern. A safe number of satch away, someone remembered the unfortunate night watch and the ship paused long enough to hold a brief, somber double ceremony. The wind would have to be satisfied with words alone since there were no bodies to return to the ice.

There had been some tension between the more experienced sailors from Sofold and the newcomers who'd joined the expedition at Poyolavomaar. The confrontation with the shan-kossief had taken care of that. Of the two night-watchers who'd been lost, one had been a citizen of Wannome, the other of Poyo. Tragedy was a powerful unifier.

A few guttorbyn, aerial carnivores resembling furry flying dragons, swooped down on the ship in hopes of picking off an isolated meal. Each time, they were met by alerted, armed Tran who would drive them off, shrieking their disappointment. After the shan-kossief, the guttorbyn seemed almost comical, with their long, narrow mouths and outraged cries. By the time they reached the equatorial ice pressure ridge which the Tran called the Bent Ocean, the crew had become blasé about danger.

The ridge was a much more serious if less life-threatening obstacle to their progress than any carnivore, however. Forty thousand years ago that line was where the previous warm cycle had ended. Pack ice from the north had run into pack ice advancing from the south. The two ice sheets had crunched together and pushed up and out, forming a solid wall of blocks and slabs that girdled Tran-ky-ky at its equator.

Ta-hoding barked at his helmsman and the icerigger slowly swung eastward. They sailed parallel to the ridge with the wind behind them, searching for a break the crew could enlarge to create a passage.

During their previous journey to Moulokin, far to the west, they had found such a pass. After enlarging it with picks and axes, they'd used the power of a rifs storm to force the ship the rest of the way through. It was not a technique anyone wished to employ again since it could just as easily result in the destruction of the icerigger as in its safe passage to the southern ice sheet.

Days passed without sighting anything more encouraging than slight variations in the height of the ridge. Ethan and his companions grew discouraged.

"Surely," Cheela Hwang said to him, "there has to be a place where the ice has collapsed under its own weight, or been cracked by continuing pressure, or has melted enough for us to make a passage?"

"Not necessarily. Any change we've observed has been organically induced, as by that shan-kossief thing." Zima Snyek, their resident glaciologist, was the butt of jokes among the Tran since he spent as much time working with the ice as a kossief. "We know the ridge circles the whole planet. It's conceivable it might do so without interruption."

"We haven't the time or the resources for a circumnavigation." Hwang was studying a small electronic map. "We've already sailed too far to the east. We shouldn't continue much farther this way." She glanced up at Ethan. "You told me you broke through the ridge once before."

He nodded, gestured sternward. "On our journey to Moulokin. It was a do-or-die situation. Break through or get torn to shreds by a rifs."

"Why don't we just retrace that route and utilize the existing passage?"

Milliken Williams had been listening, as was his preference, but now spoke up. "First because it's a *long* ways to the west. Second because we could easily miss it and sail on by, and lastly because we barely slipped through the first time. Between the weather and subsurface movements, the gap may already have been at least partially filled in. If that's the case, we'll never find it. We'd be a lot better off if we could find a suitable way through right here. You're talking about spending weeks searching for a break that might be undetectable." He shrugged. "You're right about one thing, though: If we don't find something soon, we won't have any choice but to go back."

It was Ta-hoding who brought the search to a halt. Like most of them he'd spent endless hours scanning the unbroken barrier parralleling them off to starboard, the wind ruffling his mane and the fur on shoulders and neck. He was very patient, Ta-hoding was, but he, too, had his limits. The day came when he requested a conference.

"It is time to decide how we intend to make our way southward from this region. We cannot sail around the world only to meet ourselves in the same places we have already visited."

"There is no other way." Hunnar was as frustrated as any of them. "We have already determined that."

First Mate Monslawic nodded. "Still we must find one. Let us think hard on this matter as we continue as we have for another day or two. If by then we have not found a place to make a passage, we must turn about and retrace our course. Better to sail all the way back toward Moulokin to search for a way through we know exists than to continue endlessly on an unprofitable heading." Clearly the *Slanderscree*'s first mate had given their situation much thought.

"We cannot go back," Ta-hoding informed him. "We must cross the Bent Ocean within the next couple of days."

"Why the hurry?" September wanted to know.

By way of reply Ta-hoding pointed toward the bow. Ethan joined the others in staring forward. A few scattered clouds marred the otherwise pristine horizon. Not rain clouds, of course. It never rained on Tran-ky-ky. Most of the planet's moisture lay permanently frozen on its surface. Even snow was rare, though more common in the planet's warmer regions. Clouds were seldom seen, even here near the equator.

Ethan wondered what Ta-hoding was pointing at. As it developed it was something visible only to an experienced sailor.

"For the past several days the winds have been erratic," he told them. Ethan knew the winds of Tran-ky-ky blew with extraordinary consistency from west to east. "That is a strange formation but not an unknown one." Then he *was* talking about the clouds, Ethan mused. "Also it is the season."

"Season for what?" Williams asked.

"Comes soon a rifs. Not today, not tomorrow, but soon. Out of the east. Usually they come from north or south. This comes out of the east. It will be very bad."

That went without saying, Ethan knew as he stared at the innocuous-looking puffs of cumulus. It meant a complete reversal of normal wind paterns. The atmospheric disturbance required to accomplish that would have to verge on the demonic. Yet Ta-hoding sounded so sure.

"What's a 'rifs'?" Jacalan asked.

Hwang let her colleague Semkin explain. "A local superthunderstorm. Several thunderstorm cells cluster in the same area. They start feeding off each other, the way a firestorm feeds on its own heat. On Tran-ky-ky very little actual moisture's involved. That only seems to make the storm worse." He was gazing thoughtfully at the clouds.

"I've never actually experienced one, of course. None of us have. They're nearly nonexistent away from the equatorial regions. But Cheela and I have studied them via satellite reconnaissance. The thunderhead crowns will boil up tens of thousands of meters until they scrape the limits of the upper atmosphere. There's lightning, lots of lightning, and surface winds approaching hundreds of kilometers an hour. Not good kite-flying weather. Any animal with any sense immediately goes to ground to try and wait it out."

There was silence as his colleagues absorbed the implications, which were obvious even to non-Tran and non-sailors. You couldn't tack into a three-hundred kph wind, nor could you safely anchor yourself anywhere on the barren ice sheet. The only reasonable chance of safety lay in a protected harbor. There were no harbors of any kind out on the naked ice.

A ship caught in the open and overtaken by the rolling storm front of a rifs had one chance and one only to survive. That lay in adjusting the amount of sail and turning about to run directly before the wind, praying that sails, masts, and crew held together long enough for the storm to pass over.

Once before the *Slanderscree* had done that and survived, battered and bruised. Attempting it a second time would involve tempting whatever fate had thus far watched over her. Even if they tried it and managed to ride out the storm, it would shove them, probably damaged and unstable, far off their chosen course. The planet itself seemed to be conspiring to keep them from reaching their destination.

Ideally they would make it through the pressure ridge, put on all sail, and fly southward beyond the storm's reach. Ideally. Ideally, Ethan thought, they would have ignored regulations and smuggled along a few explosive devices with which to blast their way through the barrier. No time left now for what-ifs and maybes.

They had no explosives, no beamers, no appropriate modern technology. All they did have, they realized as they took stock of their resources, was a lot of muscle and determination. That would suffice to chop a path through the ice ridge. In weeks. They needed to break through within forty-eight hours.

What sophisticated scientific instrumentation they did have consisted largely of devices for measuring and calibrating and weighing, not for concentrating brute force on a specific area. A pair of drills designed to take core samples from the ice would help. A hundred such drills would be needed to accomplish their ends. The drills could melt some ice but not nearly enough fast enough.

The alternate solution did not occur to the Tran because as Tran they would never have conceived of something like it. For once the obvious was voiced by Skua September and not Williams.

"It's pretty damn clear to me that since we can't go through this stuff we have to go over it."

Ethan added his own expression to the sea of astonishment that greeted this blithe observation.

VII

"Are you proposing," Williams said finally, "to turn the *Slanderscree* into an aircraft?"

September didn't bat an eye. "Something like that."

Since September was considering it semiseriously, the teacher did likewise. "Even if we could pack on sufficient sail the wind isn't strong enough."

"Funny, that is." September looked thoughtful. "Though with a rifs behind us and enough sail I wouldn't be surprised if we *could* get the ol' scow airborne. Controlling her would be something else again." He glanced past Williams until he found Snyek. "Going to need those coring drills you mentioned. Have to melt some ice and then let it refreeze."

"What in heaven's name for?" Hwang demanded to know.

September grinned at her. "Your corers aren't big enough or powerful enough to melt half a path through that ridge, but we can use them to take the sharp edges off, if you know what I mean. Some of those ancient ice blocks that form the ridge are pretty big and pretty solid. If we could just sort of melt them together and even them out, doing the fine work with ice picks and axes, why, we might end up with something."

129

"Like what?"

His eyes twinkled and he turned his grin back on Williams. "Like a ramp." He let them mull that thought over, then continued. "See, we form and shape this big ramp out of ice using the coring drills and hand tools, run it right to the crest of the pressure ridge. Then we back the *Slanderscree* off a fair ways"—he illustrated the necessary maneuvers with great sweeps and twists of his long arms— "as far to the west as required, put on all sail, and bring her in to the ridge at an angle with the wind strong behind us.

"We go *up* that ramp," he said as he slid one palm sharply against the other, "and over the top. That's it, we're through. We don't have to cut through the damn ridge, all we have to do is go over it." He coughed into a closed palm. "And make a respectable landing on the other side, of course. One thing about ice: It may be sharp-edged and cold and uncomfortable, but as long as you've got some tools, good cold weather, and a heat source or two you can sculpture it as easy as you would a bar of soap."

His companions' response was underwhelming. "I would prefer to transit the ridge another way," Williams said finally.

"So would I." This from a doubtful Ta-hoding. "I find your thoughts intriguing but impractical, friend Skua. As you have said, the critical problem is one of velocity."

"Are you kidding? The *Slanderscree*'s only put on all her sail once or twice. You know how fast she could go."

"On the level ice, yes," the captain admitted, "but uphill? Such a thing has never been done in a large ship. It is a maneuver left for sport, on chiv or in a very small light craft."

September looked at Hwang. "Run some calculations. Mass and velocity, wind speed—let's find out if it's theoretically possible, at least. We can make the ramp as graduated, as long as necessary."

"Not too long." Ta-hoding the sailor had an excellent grasp of elementary geometry, not to mention the physical capabilities of his crew. "We have only so much time."

"We'll manage," said September impatiently. "We'll do whatever we have to do. I'm sure we can gain the necessary speed and hold the ramp."

"That is not what troubles me." All eyes turned to Hunnar Redbeard. "Let me see if I understand this novel sky-people notion." He employed his arms and paws in rough imitation of September's aerodynamic gestures. "We retreat a certain distance, put on all sail, and catch the wind full behind us."

"That's it, that's right," said September excitedly.

"We sail up this ramp you propose to construct"—he raised one paw skyward—"and launch ourselves over the top of the bent ocean with enough force to carry us across the far side of the barrier and onto the navigable ice on the southern side."

September looked pleased. "You've got it, Hunnar."

"I have no doubt we can attain the required speed, and I believe it may be possible to maintain enough control at that speed to sail up this ramp. Yet I worry still."

"About what?"

"The *Slanderscree* is a large, heavy ship. It was designed to chiv"—and he made a shoving gesture with his right paw—"across solid ice. It is a strong vessel and many times have we learned the strength of the wondrous metal we cut from your small ship to fashion the great runners and their braces. Still, for all it has accomplished and all it has survived, it was not designed to be dropped from a considerable height." He stared at September.

"If all goes as you plan and we overfly the Bent Ocean, what will happen to us when we strike the unyielding ice on the far side? The ocean will not break. That is something that cannot be said of the *Slanderscree*. What would it profit us to cross the barrier if we destroy our ship in the process?"

"That's one thing I don't have any way of predicting," September replied somberly, "and despite all their instruments and learning, I don't think Williams and his friends do either."

"The ship's whole weight will come down on the bow runners, then the stern and the rudder," Ethan murmured. "If we try this, and I don't have any better idea, we need to pull everything out of storage that can be used for padding. Spare clothing, extra pika-pina rigging, everything we've got. If we cram it all between the runners and their braces, it'll help absorb the shock."

"That's the spirit, feller-me-lad!"

"Those braces can only cope with a certain amount of shock," Ta-hoding reminded them.

"They're duralloy from the skin and guts of a lifeboat," September said. "So are the bolts and sheet bracing. The woodwork's the product of Wannome's finest carpenters and shipwrights. Even if we do bust a brace or two we can still rig something temporary to hold the runners in place until we can get the ship back to a repair yard."

"If only it were that simple." Ta-hoding gestured toward the bow. "If we break off more than one runner, we will have to anchor the ship so that we can make these temporary repairs you speak of so casually. Remember that the rifs can catch us as easily on the southern ocean as on this side, should we become trapped in this place. With damaged runners we could not even run before the wind. The ship could be torn to pieces."

For a moment or so only the wind talked. Then Ethan spoke up quietly. "Doesn't look like we have much choice. We're much too far from Poyolavomaar or any other known shelter to try to make it to safety before the storm hits. If we sit around and wait for it, we'll be in real trouble. If we try and outrun it and it overtakes us, it'll blow us so far off course we might as well go back to Poyo and start over again."

"Might we not find shelter in the lee of an island?" Elfa wondered.

Ta-hoding shook his head. "We've seen none that would be suitable."

"Then Ethan and Skua are right. We must try this."

Hunnar looked sharply at his new mate. "I always knew you to be conservative. Have we spent too much time among the skypeople?"

She put two fingers to his lips, letting him feel the claws. "Not that. In your company I would dare anything, lifemate."

Hunnar let out an appreciative hiss. "Whatever the daughter of the Landgrave dares, can I dare less?"

She withdrew her hand, turned to face Ta-hoding. "Royalty does not command the ice. This is your dominion, your ship. The final decision rests with you. You know what the icerigger is capable of better than anyone else. What are our chances of surviving such a mad enterprise?"

Ta-hoding sighed deeply, executed an intricate gesture with the fingers of his right hand. Fifty-fifty. Ethan had hoped for better odds.

"One is ready to risk all, the other tells me nothing," Hunnar grumbled. Cat's eyes turned on Ethan. "What think you, my friend?"

"Why ask me? I'm just a passenger on this boat. I have no authority here. Why don't you ask Milliken?"

"Because you are no adventurer, by your admission. Because you and not friend Milliken are a counterweight to tall Skua's opinion. You are cautious where he is rash. You consider where he dares."

"Well, in the absence of a better alternative I'd have to

say that you don't get anywhere in life without taking a chance now and then. I admit we've taken our share, this past year, but that doesn't alter the situation we're facing now. That's all easy for me to say. It's not my ship."

"No, but it is your life," Elfa pointed out.

"Let us do this." Ta-hoding spoke without looking at them, already making preparations in his mind. "Everyone who is not a member of the sailing crew will disembark and cross the Bent Ocean on foot, to wait for us on the other side. That way if catastrophe strikes not all will be at risk."

"Then you have decided," Hunnar murmured.

"Boldness is not in me. I play only the dice that are given to me. Here we must roll as best we are able and hope for a twelve to show itself. If I cannot have confidence in my ship and my crew, what is left to me?"

"So it is to be tried." Hunnar could not bring himself to show false confidence. "I wish there was another way. Were there, we would not be proceeding with this insanity." He turned to Hwang. "My soldiers will work side by side with you to shape the ice. You will choose the angle of the ramp and instruct us accordingly." He stood. "Now that we have determined our course of action let us move quickly. The sooner we begin, the sooner we will be finished."

"And the harder we work," Elfa added, "the less time we will have to think about what we are really going to attempt."

Blue sky had given way to roiling blackness on the eastern horizon by the time the ramp was ready. Like questing scouts, the first gusts of wind from the advancing storm front slammed into the steady west wind, sending confused air swirling in all directions. Ice devils, miniature whirlwinds composed of ice particles, danced crazily across the flat surface of the frozen ocean. Occasionally one would stumble into the workers, forcing them to drop their tools and hug the ground. One caught Ethan with his visor up and brought tears to his eyes. It was like being battered by cold sand.

Jacalan and Blanchard shut down the two overworked drills and joined the rest of the refugees in slipping and sliding down the south flank of the pressure ridge. Ethan and September hung back, settling themselves in the shelter of a huge upturned ice block. Someone had to watch, Ethan told himself.

Like the approach to a giant's castle a long, relatively smooth ramp had been hacked and melted out of the ridge's north slope. The scientists and Hunnar's soldiers had done their work well. How well there was no way of telling until the icerigger actually attempted its run.

Everyone knew that if the ramp collapsed while the *Slanderscree* was making its climb, the great ship would be imprisoned on the ridge. Then they would be well and truly trapped in this isolated region, far from human or Tran civilization. They'd built us solidly as possible, given the limited amount of time and equipment at their disposal. Semkin had supervised the work with the drills, making sure that all the gaps between the massive ice blocks had been filled and sealed.

At last there was nothing left to do but to do it.

A glance to his right showed figures standing and waiting on the southern ice sheet: the icerigger's fighters and the members of the research team. Only Hunnar and Elfa had joined Ethan and September atop the ridge. With the wind whipping his fur Hunnar stood tall and straight as one of the icy spires surrounding them. He shaded his eyes with his right hand.

"I can barely see the ship." Ethan squinted and looked northward but saw no sign of the *Slanderscree*. That would change shortly, he knew. "They are putting on sail. Ta-hoding has the spars turned into the wind. Ah, now they are being adjusted. The sails fill. She comes."

They waited. A few minutes later both men could make out the sleek arrowhead shape of the icerigger racing toward the ridge at high speed. Ethan was startled to realize that this was the first time he'd actually seen the ship under full sail and from a distance. For a hybrid cobbled together from a schoolteacher's memory it was quite beautiful. There was none of the ungainliness one might have expected, though the absence of a curving hull was disconcerting. The underside of the icerigger was perfectly flat, since there was no water for it to cut through.

"Wish Ta-hoding had given better than an even chance," he muttered.

September had his visor up so it wouldn't interfere with his view. "Hell, young feller-me-lad, that's better odds than life gives most of us."

Ethan turned his attention eastward. Lightning split clouds black as coal dust. "When will the rifs get here?"

Hunnar Redbeard looked down at him, then turned to face the oncoming storm. "Soon, but not so soon as it might. A bad storm, very bad, but I think it may be moving slightly to the northwest instead of due west. We have been gifted with a few precious additional hours of manageable weather. If it continues to turn, it is possible it might miss us entirely. A *haylak* full of irony there would be in that!"

"It might also not miss us," Elfa put in. "And if we do not do this thing we will be no better than where we were before the storm was sighted. We must still cross the Bent Ocean. Now is not the time for hesitation."

"I was not hesitating, my love. Ethan asked my thoughts."

"Here she comes!" September roared, bending slightly

and pointing. "I swear Ta-hoding's got his clothes on the line trying to coax another tenth of a kph out of the west wind."

Ethan found he had to lift his own visor in order to see properly. Cold stung his exposed skin, pins on his cheeks. The icerigger seemed to be accelerating with every extra meter of ice it crossed. Five rooster tails of ice particles flew from the base of each duralloy runner as it cut across the flat surface. When it was half a kilometer from the pressure ridge, Ethan guessed its velocity at between a hundred and fifty and a hundred seventy kilometers an hour. Sails billowed taut from the masts and rigging. The whole vessel appeared to be leaning forward, straining, struggling to gain every last possible ounce of speed. It was near enough now for Ethan to pick out Ta-hoding and his helmsman. They were leaning on the large wooden wheel, fighting to keep the flying *Slanderscree* on course.

The captain must have shouted a command because as they looked on the adjustable spars suddenly pivoted. Heeling over on both port runners like a skater fighting to maintain his balance, the great ship swung sharply southward. The maneuver might have cost her a little speed.

Old instincts made Ethan crouch in anticipation. If the icerigger hit the ramp at the wrong angle, it could fly off in any direction, including straight toward them. Hunnar and Elfa likewise sought shelter. Only September held his ground, looking like some misplaced sculpture in his silvery survival suit.

On board the *Slanderscree* those sailors who weren't trimming the spars reached for something solid and gritted their teeth. Ta-hoding and his helmsman clung to the wheel. Driven by the full force of the west wind the icerigger reached the base of the ice ramp and came rocketing upward, looking for all the world like some alien version of the Flying Dutchman about to sail off into the sky against the wind.

As it ascended it slowed perceptibly. Ethan found himself urging it onward, trying to lift it the extra thirty, twenty, finally ten meters toward the top. His help was not required.

Still traveling at upward of a hundred kph, the *Slanderscree* shot off the top of the ramp and over the crest of the pressure ridge. For an instant it seemed to hang in the air, frozen as if by some cosmic artist. Then it began to descend in a slow, graceful curve.

Hunnar and Elfa rose, while down on the southern ice sheet soldiers and human scientists watched breathlessly as the icerigger came soaring toward them. For a brief moment it was a ship not of the ice but the air, a visitor from a long-forgotten legend. The beauty of those few seconds impressed itself strongly on all who witnessed it. None would forget it.

The beauty was replaced by a shattering reality as the huge ship smashed down onto the ice sheet.

Ethan winced as it struck. Most everyone did. The hull held as the icerigger bounced once, struck again, and slewed sideways. Sharp *ping*ing sounds rose above the wind as several spars as thick as a man's leg were snapped off and went flying over the bow, carrying their sails with them. The loss actually helped to slow the ship.

Hunnar and Elfa were already chivaning down the far side of the ridge like a pair of champion skiers. The chivless humans followed more slowly, slipping and sliding in their boots.

The soldiers who'd been waiting on the ice were scrambling up the *Slanderscree*'s boarding ladders to assist the dazed sailors, many of whom had been knocked unconscious by the force of the ship's touchdown. When Ethan stepped onto the deck, Hunnar's troops were already work-ing to bring order out of chaos.

Snapped rigging and torn sails littered the deck. The broken spars dangling forlornly from the bowsprit were a bigger problem, but the icerigger could sail without them. Thanks to the extra bracing and rigging Ta-hoding had laid on, the three mainmasts had held, though one swayed dan-gerously in its braces.

The captain greeted them with shining eyes. He held a thick cloth to his nostrils. It was stained red, but Ta-hoding didn't seem to notice it. Nor did he mention a newly ac-quired limp.

"Is that what it is like to ride one of your sky ships, friend Ethan? A glorious experience, if painful. The ship" —and he looked around proudly as he spoke—"survived better than her crew."

September looked on approvingly. "She seems to have taken the concussion very well." Blood stained cabin walls and decking. A couple of sailors were going to need rest and repair, but most had suffered nothing more serious than bruises and contusions.

Third Mate Kilpit came running to join them. His left arm hung loosely at his side but he saluted briskly with the other. "Starboard bow runner is almost broken through at the bracing. Portside bow appears to be all right, as do the stern runners and the rudder. As you predicted, Captain, the front third of the ship took most of the impact."

"How bad is the brace?"

"To fix it properly requires the services of a shipyard, but"—he hesitated—"if we use enough cable I think we can secure it temporarily. I would not advise trying any sharp maneuvers to starboard."

"We won't," Ta-hoding assured him. "Gather a repair team and set to work." He glanced back over the ridge and eastward, toward the oncoming storm. "We need to be moving again as soon as possible. The brace will hold. We are not preparing for a fight. There is nothing to battle here save our own injuries and the weather. When we are safely away southward we will talk and remember this moment, but not now." The mate saluted again and jumped down to the main deck, gathering his work crew around him as he headed toward the bow.

"I thought when last I looked that the rifs was turning somewhat to the north," Hunnar said.

"I noticed that also. It could as quickly turn south." Ta-hoding's gaze and his thoughts were roving the damaged foremast.

Everyone pitched in to help with the repairs, including Hwang's group. They knew nothing about sailing craft but any extra hand was eagerly accepted for fetching and carrying, even if that hand was devoid of fur. The ship was under way again far sooner than anyone dared hope.

They didn't escape the rifs entirely. Its southern edge caught them long after the pressure ridge had fallen out of sight astern. Somehow the damaged starboard bow runner held, wrapped in enough tough pika-pina rope to rig another whole ship. Bandaged and limping, they used the rifs kiss to increase their speed as they fled southward.

The rifs gale was exceeded only by the windiness of those sailors who had actually guided the *Slanderscree* up and over the Bent Ocean. The altitude it had reached and the distance it had traveled through the air increased with each retelling of the experience. For a few wondrous seconds they had flown just like the skypeople, and in a craft of their own manufacture. Ethan listened to the enthusiastic recitations and smiled. If their union continued to expand and solidify, someday soon these Tran would be permitted to fly skimmers of their own, then aircraft. Eventually they would find themselves traveling from their world to others aboard massive KK-drive starships. He wondered if it would mean an end to their enthusiasm. To be technologically advanced is to become jaded, he told himself.

Eventually they outran the rifs, though not the crew's enthusiasm for reliving that glorious flight. The soldiers who had crossed the pressure ridge on foot began to grumble and a few fights broke out. No one took any notice of this. The Tran were a naturally combative lot. Betting on the outcome of various fights helped to pass the time.

Days became weeks. The change in the climate was almost imperceptible at first, but before long everyone was commenting on it. As they sailed steadily south from the equator it grew warmer instead of cooler. The hundred-meter high cliffs of the continental plateau were still out of range when the Tran began to divest themselves of their clothing.

Outer furs went first, followed by hessavar-hide armor, then rough pika-pina fabric vests and undergarments. Soon the *Slanderscree* sailed on manned by a crew of naked Tran, bare save for their short brown or gray fur. As the temperature continued to climb Ethan found himself wondering how long it would be before he and his companions joined them. Of course, while the climate had turned outrageously hot for the Tran the thermometers still sat below the freezing mark. Not yet shorts and bare chest weather. Yet as they continued due south the temperature gauges continued their inexorable climb toward zero.

By now the Tran were not merely uncomfortable, they were suffering visibly. There was talk of trimming fur as short as possible, an unheard of aberration made necessary by the soaring temperature. A hasty vote indicated that no one was bad off enough yet to suffer the indignity of being shaved.

The humans commiserated as best they could, but silently they were delighted. It was possible to move about inside the ship clad only in long undergarments, and to stand on deck with hoods retracted.

Once before, Ethan, Milliken, and September had encountered similar temperatures. In the land of the Golden Saia lived an isolated group of pre–ice age Tran whose bodies had never been forced to readapt to the onset of frigid weather. They clung to territory warmed by permanent hot springs. Perhaps they were sailing toward a similar region, he thought, since extensive volcanism was still the most credible explanation for the inexplicable climatological shift Hwang and her colleagues associated with this region.

Five days later they encountered something which had not been seen on Tran-ky-ky in forty millennia.

The lookout who detected the phenomenon raced down the rigging, gestured voicelessly and wide-eyed toward the bow, and vanished below deck before anyone could ask her what she'd seen. Third Mate Kilpit tried to run the woman down to reprimand her for making such an inadequate report, but couldn't find her. By then the phenomenon was visible to those on deck, many of whom were tempted to follow the lookout, Kilpit among them. As a ship's mate he was not allowed to succumb to personal fears. Shaking, he made his report to the captain.

Not all reacted to the discovery by panicking. A few were defiant, others simply curious. With Milliken Williams to provide reassurance, Ta-hoding managed to calm his people with an explanation. They drifted back to their stations, muttering nervously under their breath as they regarded a childhood nightmare come to life.

Open ocean.

Well, not quite that, though that was what it looked like to the uneasy Tran. A layer of water, liquid water, the kind of water that was only encountered in its free form on Tran-ky-ky in homes and galleys where fire was present, covered the surface of the ice sheet. Though less than a centimeter deep, it was more than enough to rattle the collective Tran psyche. Ethan checked one of his suit gauges. The temperature here read just slightly above freezing.

The icerigger's bow runners were now throwing up watery roostertails instead of ice particles as the ship cut through the liquid layer. Suddenly the *Slanderscree* resembled a seagoing hydrofoil.

The sailors began to relax when it was apparent they weren't going to plunge into the inside of the world. The depth of the watery layer remained constant. Williams and Hwang's people were at pains to reassure their Tran companions that the hundred-meter thick ice sheet wasn't about to vanish beneath them.

It better not, Ethan knew. The *Slanderscree* was no boat. Its seams were caulked to keep out the wind, but they weren't waterproof. If it fell into deep water, the caulking wouldn't hold for more than a few minutes. Then the graceful craft, so solid and steady on the ice, would sink like a rock. Ethan wasn't sure there was a word for *float* in the Tran language.

As they sailed on southward, all eyes were alert for signs of volcanism. There were heavy clouds clinging to the south horizon, but no plumes of smoke or towering cones. Blanchard's readings indicated that the sea floor lay an average of five hundred meters beneath the icerigger's runners, so the possibility of subsurface heating was ruled out. In any case, oceanic volcanoes would melt the ice from below, not from the top.

And still the temperature rose, albeit reluctantly, as they continued south by southeast. In places the ship sliced through water six centimeters deep, though that was the maximum depth they encountered.

"The effect feeds off itself," Snyek explained. "Only the circulation of subsurface currents driven by the planet's internal heat and external gravitational forces keeps the sea from freezing solid all the way to the abyssal plain, but if the ice sheet should ever melt all the way through, then the melting would greatly accelerate because the air temperature here has risen, or been driven, above freezing. Warm air would interact with the warmer water below the ice to expand any opening in the sheet."

"Ice corpse," muttered one of the Tran who'd been listening to this translated explanation.

"It's just a localized phenomenon," Ethan explained. "There's no need to panic."

"Who is panicking?" Seesfar turned to the taller sailors. "Will you get back to your jobs or do I have to do them for you?"

Grumbling, the group of Tran moved off, still talking to themselves.

"Thanks," Ethan told her.

She glanced sharply back at him. "Thank me not. Just find my mate." She stalked off in the wake of the others. Stalked or stomped or marched, Ethan mused, there was tenseness even in her stride. A bomb ready to go off at any moment. He hoped he wasn't in the vicinity when that happened.

Hunnar whispered in Ethan's ear. "'Tis becoming more and more difficult to keep even the most loyal sailors in line." He nodded over the side. "This is a thing never before seen. They listen to the explanations of friend Williams and his companions, but in their hearts they believe this water to be the work of devils and demons."

"They know the *Slanderscree* and our tools aren't the work of supernatural forces. They know about science."

"The ship is real to them. It is something in the world. This melting of the ice is something that affects the whole world. It is not easy for them to nod understanding. How would you feel if the solid land beneath your feet were to suddenly reach up and grab you by the ankles? That is what water does if you try to chivan through it."

"I hadn't thought of it that way." The *Slanderscree*'s runners could cut through six centimeters of water with ease, but an individual Tran trying to travel across such a surface would have trouble. It would be the equivalent of a human trying to run through mud. He tried to imagine what it would be like to be walking down a concrete path only to suddenly see his feet sink into the ground.

"There are only natural forces at work here. There's no danger."

"Tell that to the crew." Hunnar nodded toward the busy deck. "These are but simple sailors and fighters, gatherers of pika-pina, workers in wood and stone. They are the bravest Wannome and Poyolavomaar can produce. Think what the reaction would be among the general population should this aberration spread to the homelands. There would be as much panic as though the sun had not risen."

"They'll be all right." Ethan tried to sound confident.

"They will have to be," the knight agreed.

VIII

The cliffs of the southern continent were still out of sight over the horizon when the mainmast lookout let out a cry of "Guttorbyn!"

Soldiers scrambled tiredly to arm their crossbows while others picked up spears and bows. They had dealt with attacks by flying carnivores often enough to become bored with the routine. The spearmen would hold off any of the large meat-eaters which came close while the crossbowmen reloaded and picked the attackers out of the sky one at a time.

Considering how many of the large flying carnivores they'd slain while defending the ship this past year and more it was a pity they weren't better to eat, Ethan reflected as he picked up the sword which had been a gift to him from the whole crew. Skua September joined him, his oversize war axe held loosely in one fist.

When the lookout reported he could see only one of the flying creatures coming toward the ship, half the defenders put their weapons aside and returned to their work. Those still armed argued over who would be permitted to shoot first. It was not a decision to be made lightly. There could be no indiscriminate firing. Crossbow bolts were tipped with metal, and metal was too precious to waste.

"It's a big one!" the lookout cried. "Biggest I ever saw!"

"Maybe it's not a guttorbyn." Ethan strained to pick out the airborne dot arrowing toward them. "I'm sure there are hundreds of lifeforms Hunnar and his people from Sofold have never encountered."

"Strange sort of flyer." September was leaning over the rail, trying to make out details. "There's none of the swooping, arching flight you see in a guttorbyn. Coming in much too low, too." If you were winged on Tran-ky-ky, you stayed a respectable distance above the ice sheet when airborne, out of the reach of shan-kossiefs and other sub-surface ambuscaders.

"That's no guttorbyn," the giant murmured tightly, "but recognize it I do."

Hunnar joined them. "Is that not one of your flying boats?"

"It's a skimmer for sure. What the hell is a skimmer doing down here?"

"Maybe Trell left behind some partners we never found out about," Ethan said, referring to the late, unlamented Resident Commissioner.

"Unlikely." September was trying to pick out faces on the oncoming craft. "They would've turned themselves in by now. The body isn't much use when the head's been cut off." He turned and bellowed toward the nearest hatch. A sailor obediently turned and raced below to inform the scientists.

Cheela Hwang was first on deck. Williams said the meteorologist slept less than four hours a night. Ethan forbore from asking the teacher how he'd happened to come by that bit of information.

By now the skimmer was flying parallel to the icerigger, close enough for those on board to make out individual shapes.

"Not one of ours," Hwang said, "because there aren't

any of ours. Skimmers aren't permitted at Brass Monkey. Too advanced for use among the natives."

"Like beamers, which I wish we had." September gestured. "They're sliding closer. Doing the same thing we're doing, I expect. Checking us over."

"What about the government people?" Ethan asked her. "Could some department have one they've been using on the sly?"

Hwang shook her head impatiently. "Brass Monkey's too small a community to hide something like that. If a skimmer were available, everybody would want to use it. You couldn't keep it a secret. There are no aircraft, nothing bigger than the ice cycles you saw."

"Could the Commonwealth have another outpost on Tran-ky-ky whose existence they're deliberately keeping secret from everyone at Brass Monkey?"

"Governments can do anything, feller-me-lad," September assured him, "but in this case I expect they're innocent. This world's too hostile a place to be playing such games."

The skimmer wasn't the only surprise. As it drew quite close to the icerigger, those on board were startled to see that there were no humans on the little craft. It was crewed and operated solely by Tran. This provoked a good bit of comment among the *Slanderscree*'s sailors. The reaction among members of the icerigger's human contingent was a good deal stronger.

"Allowing locals the use of this type of technology is an imprisonable offense." Moware was beside himself. "Just letting them *see* a skimmer is criminal. Letting them operate one. . . ." He shook his head numbly, unable to countenance such egregious disregard for regulations.

"Someone trusts these Tran a lot!" was all September had to say.

Ethan noticed Grurwelk close by. "Those aren't demons. They're your own kind."

She hardly glanced back at him. "Demons come in many shapes, skyman."

By this time the skimmer had slid close enough for those on board the icerigger to make out individual details. The skimmer's operators wore vests of leather strips and similar loose-lying kilts. All wore caps or helmets of dark leather decorated with bits of wood and metal straps. The latter were informative: They didn't look like the crude iron work of the Tran. They threw back too much sunlight, a hint that they'd been machined. Of course, anyone renegade enough to provide the Tran with a skimmer wouldn't hesitate to supply them with scraps of metal for decorative purposes.

Two of the flyers moved to the edge of the skimmer facing the *Slanderscree* and shouted. Ethan considered himself fluent but the words were unintelligible to him. Even Hunnar appeared to be having some trouble with the accent. Through gestures and repetition the skimmer's occupants eventually got their point across.

"They want us to change course and follow them," Hunnar announced. "No, wait, that is not entirely true. They are *ordering* us to follow them. By the Seven Devils!" He turned to yell toward the helm. "Hold to your heading, Captain!"

·The admonition proved unnecessary, since Ta-hoding had already independently determined to do just that. The Tran on the skimmer appeared to consult someone out of view. There was much waving of arms and violent gesticulations. Then one of the talkers vanished below, to reappear a moment later with something small and shiny in one hand. A tool.

A hand beamer.

It was an old, outdated model, but still plenty effective

enough to burn a hole in the *Slanderscree*'s hull or anyone unfortunate enough to get in its way. Its operator proceeded to demonstrate the weapon's effectiveness while everyone on that part of the icerigger ran for cover.

"Beamers." September peered over the top of a storage locker. "Where the hell did they get beamers? And a skimmer."

"Outrageous." Hwang was lying prone on the deck. "Whoever is behind this is a candidate for mindwipe!"

Upon concluding his demonstration the Tran with the beamer waved it carelessly in the direction of the sailing vessel and repeated the demand that it turn and follow. The Tran at the controls handled the skimmer smoothly, keeping it equidistant from the icerigger and the frozen surface below. Clearly he'd been taught how to drive the advanced vehicle.

"What are they saying now?" Ethan asked Hunnar.

"Strange accents. They say that if we do not turn immediately to accompany them, they are going to disable us." The knight turned cat's eyes on his human companion. "Can they do that with weapons so small?"

Hunnar's query was prompted by the fact that the hole the strange Tran had burned in the side of the icerigger was barely a centimeter in diameter. What the knight didn't comprehend was the beamer's range. Its operator could stand off at a safe distance and pick off the crew one at a time, or force them to abandon the *Slanderscree*'s helm, or slice up the rigging like so much spaghetti. Yet they hovered within crossbow range.

Crossbows were not a native development. The Tran of Sofold had been instructed in their construction and use by Milliken Williams. There was a chance the icerigger's marksmen could pick off the Tran with the hand beamer. A hasty conference was called while the participants lay flat on the deck.

Three soldiers were chosen. Hunnar replied to the ulti-
matum with a long-winded reply, stalling the skimmer's
occupants until the crossbowmen were ready. Then he
ducked down as they rose and fired.

All three bolts struck their mark. The reaction of those
on board the skimmer was almost as extreme as the reaction of those on the ice ship to the skimmer's appearance.
The belligerent Tran wielding the beamer clutched at his
chest where the heavy bolt had penetrated his leather
armor. He tottered sideways and fell over the side, vanish-
ing astern like a leaf on the water. His body bounced several times as it receded behind both craft.

Another Tran had been trying to bring a second beamer
to bear on the icerigger when one of the bolts slammed into
his shoulder and the third grazed his ribs, ripping a hole in
his right dan. He dropped the weapon and tumbled back
into the craft.

The skimmer bobbed and ducked wildly as its driver
momentarily lost control of his ship. It lost altitude,
glanced off the ice and threw up a spray of ice particles,
nearly crashed into the side of the *Slanderscree*, and finally
regained operational altitude as it zoomed toward the
southwest before the crossbow operators could reload and
fire a second time. Growls of defiance from the rigging and
deck of the icerigger spurred its flight.

Premature, Ethan thought. A pity they hadn't been able
to hit the driver. In that event the skimmer would have
gone to automatic and they might have been able to board
it and take control. As it was, they remained ignorant of
who their assailants had been, where they'd come from,
and how they'd come into possession of advanced Commonwealth technology.

Humans and Tran conferenced and argued on the quarterdeck.

"Maybe there's another independent research team out

here studying the change in the weather," Jacalan suggested.

"That's crazy," Hwang insisted. "Even if there was, no halfway reputable observer would give advanced weapons to the sentients of a Class IVB world. And why give commands like that? Friendly people who want to talk don't take potshots at you."

"I think we should turn about and head for Brass Monkey," Ethan said firmly. "Yes, I know we've come a long way and I'm sorry to see all of you return empty-handed, but this is something we didn't count on. They showed two beamers. Maybe they have more. Right now I'd say survival's more important than time. In fact, it's always more important than time.

"The obvious conclusion to draw from our recent visit is that there are humans or other advanced people operating in this area, doubtless without authorization. They're engaged in something probably illegal. They've provided local allies with weapons and transportation. I'm sure they weren't expecting us to show up or we wouldn't have been able to surprise them with crossbows the way we did."

Second Mate Mousokka joined them. "Your pardon, honored ones, Captain, but the bindings securing our port bow runner have weakened. It is slipping free of its brace. I have been over the side to check it myself. If it is not fixed soon we will loose the runner completely."

Ta-hoding muttered an old sailor's curse, looked at the expectant cluster of humans. "We cannot make the necessary repairs while moving. We shall have to stop."

There was nothing to discuss. Sails were reefed and spars turned into the wind. The *Slanderscree* slowed, came to a complete halt. Ice anchors were set out to hold her steady while workers poured over the side and began work on the crippled runner. Worn lengths of pika-pina cable were cut away and replaced with fresh. Undamaged rope was unwound and retightened.

They were three-quarters finished when the skimmer returned with company. Two of the small, open airships flanked the immobilized icerigger this time. Once more exposed crew scrambled for cover while the crossbowmen loaded their weapons and prepared to defend the ship. Once more a beam was fired from one of the skimmers. It took the form of a thick, intense beam of bright orange light and it ripped right through a mainmast spar. The heavy length of wood fell to the deck like a severed limb, scattered sailors.

"Laser cannon." September spat to his right. "That takes care of that. We can't impress 'em with crossbows this time." He squinted in the direction of the skimmer. "You sure there ain't any humans on board?"

"There are no skypeople on either sky boat," Hunnar assured him. "I see only the Tran of strange dress and speech." As he spoke, the smaller of the two craft edged close to the icerigger while its larger companion hovered well out of range. For the second time that day they were ordered to follow.

"Do we want to go with these people?" Cheela Hwang wondered aloud.

"Do we have any choice?" September said.

Ta-hoding was thinking fast. "Tell them, Sir Hunnar, that we cannot follow because they have disabled us. Tell them of our troubles with our port bow runner. Explain that we are but inoffensive merchants exploring new territory and that we wish only to be allowed to continue on our way."

A dubious Hunnar conveyed this assertion of innocence to those on board the skimmer. The craft immediately moved around to the stern of the *Slanderscree,* where a Tran with a hand beamer used the small weapon to cut through the thick pika-pina control cables that linked the rudder runner to the wheel on the quarterdeck. The big wooden wheel immediately spun loosely. Until the cables were replaced or repaired Ta-hoding would be unable to steer the ship.

"Laser cannon," Moware was muttering disconsolately. "Skimmers. Vile people have been at work here."

The meaning was clear enough to everyone. Whoever had committed these violations of Commonwealth development policy for unsophisticated worlds would be unlikely to have any compunctions about disposing of a few traveling scientists and their companions. They needn't necessarily be human, either.

While motives and origins were debated, the first skimmer moved from the *Slanderscree*'s stern to her bow. A heavy braided fabric cable was attached just below the bowsprit. By shouts and gestures those on the skimmer indicated that repairs to the bow port runner were to be completed as fast as possible.

"Don't have much choice," September told Ta-hoding, Elfa, and the rest. "Not with that sticking down our throats." He nodded toward the second skimmer and its heavy artillery.

"I have regretfully reached the same conclusion," Ta-hoding said.

By late afternoon the work was finished and the icerigger was taken in tow. Advanced or not, the load strained the skimmer's engine. Their progress southwestward was slow. While the first skimmer pulled, the second paralleled the ice ship, the narrow muzzle of its heavy weapon focused amidships.

"What about putting some of our best people over the stern," First Mate Monslawic suggested, "to repair the steering cables?"

"A thought," said Ta-hoding. He looked neither fat nor

lazy as he glared at the bigger skimmer. "Perhaps we could outrun these sky boats."

Ethan shook his head. "You'd need twice the wind we have now. They're more maneuverable than the *Slander-scree* as well as faster. And it would only take one shot from that cannon to disable us permanently. This way if we do get the chance to make a run for it all we have to do is fix the cables." He frowned. "I wonder why they haven't taken the precaution of disabling us further."

"Perhaps they wish the ship for a prize," Hunnar suggested.

"My beautiful *Slanderscree*," Ta-hoding moaned. "Everyone wants my ship. Truly it is the greatest prize on all Tran-ky-ky."

The captain's pride-filled exaggeration was pardonable, Ethan mused. There was nothing to be gained by pointing out that Tran who had access to laser cannon and hand beamers and skimmers didn't need ice boats, no matter how great or graceful.

The long, slow tow offered those on the icerigger ample opportunity to study their captors. Despite access to advanced technology the Tran manning the skimmers didn't look particularly prosperous. Some wore armor and attire that looked battered and worn while their distinctive headgear was more outré than impressive. The dichotomy was as puzzling as it was obvious. It was as if they had encountered a knight of old mounted on the most magnificent charger, only to discover on closer inspection that he was clad in rusty, broken armor and torn underwear.

They were much closer to the southern continent than they thought. They would long since have seen the expected hundred-meter high cliffs of the continental plateau but for one thing: there weren't any. Not here, where the usual vertical walls of rock had given way to collapsed, eroded slopes. A few isolated granitic spires loomed like lonely sentinels surveying the results of millennia of erosion.

There was also much more vegetation than usual, due to their proximity to the equator. Disintegrated rock had collected in cracks and crevices to form soil. Even so, the land plants which clung to a subfreezing existence were a sorry lot, nowhere near as impressive as the pika-pina and pika-pedan which thrived out on the ice sheet itself.

They sailed parallel to the rubble-strewn slopes all that evening and through the night before morning saw them towed into a deep harbor much like that at Moulokin. Unlike Moulokin's haven, no sheer walls towered above the ice here. Gentle slopes rose gradually from the edge of the ice.

Ethan knew from their previous journey that such harbors were actually subterranean river canyons which were submerged when the ice sheets melted during Tran-ky-ky's warm cycle. In twenty thousand years, this inlet would be completely under water.

If not sooner. The new thought was as disturbing as the presence of the laser cannon.

Before long they found themselves in among other, much smaller ice ships. Poorly put together, scarred and battered by heavy use and poor weather, they clustered around the *Slanderscree* like jackals around a lion. Some of those on board conversed animatedly with the crews of the skimmers. No surprises there.

As they neared the harbor's end the first cliffs hove into view. Thick clouds hid the edge of the continental shelf. Hunnar and the rest of the *Slanderscree*'s crew were panting nonstop now. The water beneath the icerigger's runners was nearly ten centimeters deep, and to those accustomed to normal temperate zone readings, the climate within the harbor was sweltering. According to Semkin, by high noon the thermometer might reach an astonishing two degrees *above* zero centigrade.

A city had taken root on the southwest rim of the harbor. Ethan hadn't expected a real town, but the presence of so many small ice ships was sufficient to suggest a thriving community. It was a dull-looking place, the stone structures sprawling haphazardly along the shoreline and back up into the hills. Across the harbor from this egalitarian community, a fairly steep slope climbed several hundred meters from the edge of the ice sheet, leveled off, and vanished into the clouds. This prompted him to query Jacalan, their resident geologist.

"Sorry. I know there's a lot of cloud cover here, Ethan, but I've been watching my instruments closely and there's no evidence of plutonic activity anywhere in the vicinity." He nodded toward the mountain that rose from the north side of the harbor. "If that's a volcano, it's dead or dormant."

"Then what about all this cloud cover? It's not a rifs storm. *Something* has to be generating all that moisture."

Jacalan shrugged. "Ask Hwang or Semkin. Weather's their department."

He did, but neither meteorologist had a ready explanation for the dense layer of clouds that hung over this area of the continent. It was part and parcel of what they'd come to investigate, and thus far their studies hadn't produced anything particularly informative. Hal Semkin clung to the hot springs theory despite Jacalan's counterarguments, while Hwang was trying to put together a theory allowing for warm subcrustal emissions of heat and moisture which would not conflict with the geologist's findings.

Ethan moved to the quarterdeck. Ta-hoding still stood by his useless helm. "Know anything about this place?" Ethan asked him, fairly sure of the captain's response.

"Nothing." Next to the captain the great wooden wheel spun aimlessly.

"What about the sailors from Poyolavomaar?"

"The questions have been asked." Ta-hoding sounded irritated but Ethan knew it was only frustration that made his replies short and sharp. "This land is as foreign to them as to those of us of Sofold. At this end of the world only Moulokin was spoken of, and as you know it, too, was unknown until we went there and made allies of its people." He stared at the low-lying city they were approaching. "Would that the soldiers of that fine metropolis were here to aid us now." He pointed toward the port.

"What a poor place this is. See, with all this broken stone lying loosely about, their homes and storehouses are still ineptly fashioned. There is no profit to be made trading with such a community. The wonder of it to me is that it exists in this place at all. Who do they trade with? We encountered nothing between here and Poyolavomaar."

Indeed, the closer they drew and the better view they had, the more Ethan found himself wondering what this city was doing in this isolated region in the first place. There was little use of mortar or cement. Gaps between undressed stones were chinked with smaller rocks and pebbles or stuffed with raw pika-pina. Roofs were fashioned of large flat stone slabs instead of the dressed and cut slate common to developed communities like Wannome or Arsudun. Except for a single multistory structure which overlooked the town from off to the left and resembled an oversize hut with battlements, the entire city conveyed the impression of being nothing more than a hasty afterthought.

"No walls, either," observed Ta-hoding professionally. "No gates. It is evident they do not expect to be attacked. There are no other city-states nearby to threaten them."

"Who would want to?" Hunnar commented contemptuously. "What is there to plunder? New buildings that are already falling down? Citizens clad in rags and tatters? All the loot this place could offer would not be worth the life of a single warrior."

None of which, Ethan reflected, squared with the presence of skimmers and energy weapons.

The skimmer with the cannon was moving inboard. Hunnar and September barely had enough time to debate the possibility of jumping her crew when it was already too late. Their captors were prepared to repel boarders not with swords and shields but with hand beamers. It hovered alongside the *Slanderscree* only long enough to let off a couple of its crew. Then it drew away to a safe distance again, the cannon muzzle still trained on the icerigger.

No one bothered the boarders. If they hadn't been completely confident of their safety, they wouldn't have exposed themselves to those on the icerigger in the first place. The pair wandered the deck, ignoring the surly stares of the sailors, inspecting rigging and woodwork. Despite their ownership of beamers and skimmers they were obviously impressed.

The one in charge was a large, powerful individual who to Ethan's surprise was on the elderly side. Not as old as Balavere Longax, but older than anyone still on board the *Slanderscree*. His squire or bodyguard clutched his sword convulsively in his right paw and tried to hide his nervousness. Neither of them carried a beamer. Naturally not, Ethan mused. They weren't going to put themselves in a position where someone could take any of those precious weapons away from them. Whoever had engineered the capture of the *Slanderscree* knew what they were doing.

Both the presence of the weapons and the tactics their captors had employed were alien to Ethan's experiences on Tran-ky-ky. He said as much to Hunnar, who readily agreed.

"Indeed, it would appear that in addition to tools from your people these hostiles have received advice as well."

For an instant Ethan wondered if these Tran could have ambushed some illegal expedition and stolen their equipment. It was a theory quickly discarded. The Tran were clever, but you didn't figure out how to operate something as complex and advanced as a skimmer without some kind of instruction. Whether that instruction had been given voluntarily or under duress was, like practically everything else that had happened during the day, still a matter for speculation.

The older boarder had a thick brown beard as opposed to Hunnar's red one. Ethan left Ta-hoding guarding his useless helm as he joined Hunnar, Elfa, Skua, and several others in confronting their visitor.

The peculiar, thick accent was easier to understand up close than when shouted over a distance between two moving craft. "I am Corfu. Formerly Corfu of Kerkoinhar."

"Never heard of it." Hunnar's admission was echoed by his companions.

"Few have." The older Tran did not seem troubled by the slight. "It was a good place to live and prosper. Only, Corfu did not prosper with it. There was a disagreement involving ethics. It was said that I cheated a relative of the Landgrave. It was said that I did not. In such a confrontation I was bound to lose. I was exiled.

"I am just a merchant, not a hunter. Exile is hard on a merchant whose property has been confiscated. Yet despite the fate my enemies intended for me I survived—and found a place here." He gestured toward the city as they turned toward a dock and the towing skimmer maneuvered them in close.

"Yingyapin. Not much to look upon now, but that will change. Is changing."

"A lot of construction going on, but none of it what

you'd call impressive," September commented thoughtfully.

Corfu glanced at the giant in surprise, studying his face
carefully. "You speak our language without a translating
device."

Their visitor wasn't the only one who was surprised. In
addition to skimmers and beamers this Tran also knew
what a translator was and spoke of it as though he was
familiar with it. Was there any advanced technology they
hadn't been given access to?

"Humans are not supposed to speak Tran except through
such machines."

"Is that what your human friends have told you?" Ethan
asked him.

Corfu's attention switched to him. "And another who
speaks." He studied the humans who had gathered around
him. "How many of you speak Tran?"

Ethan cursed himself for speaking. He'd been doing it
for more than a year and it was a natural reaction, but on
reflection he realized he should have let September do all
the talking. It would have been better to keep their linguis-
tic talents a secret. Too late now. This Corfu looked sharp
enough to figure out that those humans not wearing translators were the ones likely to be fluent in his language.

Still, Milliken Williams kept his hands at his sides and
their captor seemed content to let the matter pass as he
extolled the virtues of his new home.

"It is not impressive, true, but one day all will bow
before its Landgrave. You are looking at the most important city in the world."

"There are no important cities anymore," Hunnar informed him. "There is only the Union."

"The Union? What foolish talk is this? There are no
unions among Tran."

"There are now. The city-states of Wannome, Moulokin, Poyolavomaar, Arsudun, and many others are joining together to form a great Union so that we may join with our human friends and others in the greater union of the night sky."

"Ah, you are talking of membership in the Commonwealth." Corfu smiled.

Ethan thought he was beyond shock. He was wrong. "How do you come to know of the Commonwealth?"

Corfu looked smug. "We, too, have our friends. I am not displeased to hear of this Union between your city-states. I welcome it. It will make our administration of Tran-ky-ky that much easier."

"If you think you're going to conquer the world with a couple of skimmers, a few beamers, and one cannon you're badly mistaken," Ethan told him.

Hunnar nodded in the direction of the merchant's uneasy bodyguard. "Especially not with the likes of that for your army."

Corfu nodded at the speaker. "By your bearing you are a noble, I see. I have had my fill of nobles, Redbeard. When we of Yingyapin take power, we will do away with them. A new order will arise in place of the old, one founded on ability instead of false aristocracy."

Hunnar growled and displayed his long canines. "I earned my knighthood, as did every knight of Wannome."

The merchant wasn't impressed. "Influence begets training; birthright, education. Heredity counts. And you may kill me if you wish." He didn't turn to face Grurwelk Seesfar, who held a knife concealed in one paw and had been slipping up behind him. She hesitated.

"If I do not return unharmed to my companions, they will destroy this wonderful vessel and everyone aboard. Your human friends will tell you what our weapons can do."

"We already know." Hunnar glared at Seesfar, who

backed off but kept the knife in her fist. Then he indicated the city beyond the dock. "I see nothing to fear here, no irresistible army, no relentless ranks of warriors."

Corfu smiled at some secret thought. "We will conquer without the need of an army. We do not need to fight. Indeed, we will conquer without recourse to these light weapons."

"How do you stand the heat here?" Ethan asked him. "I wouldn't think any Tran would find this land a comforting place to live."

"You think this is too warm? I find it pleasing myself."

"So you are diseased in body as well as in mind," Elfa commented.

Corfu's smile faded slightly. "Think you so? Soon you will see."

Milliken Williams stepped forward. "Listen, on behalf of my colleagues I demand to know. . ."

The much bigger Tran caught him across the face with a powerful backhand, sending the schoolteacher staggering backward. Blood trickled from the corner of his mouth. Cheela Hwang was at his side instantly. Several of the *Slanderscree*'s sailors tensed but Hunnar gestured for them to stay where they were. Corfu ignored the threatening body language and glared down at Williams. There was no doubt the merchant was enjoying himself.

"You demand nothing here, little human. You are not my superior. We use your technology, but we are not afraid of you. You are not gods; only people like us who have lived longer. So you have a little more knowledge and much more metal. We make use of your knowledge, we make use of your metal and your machines, but that does not mean we need always make use of *you*." He turned and stalked off toward the quarterdeck, indifferent to the hostile stares that followed him, unconcerned as to whether anyone might chose to put a spear through his spine.

Ethan leaned over the rail and stared at the crowd that had gathered to inspect the icerigger. They were no more impressive up close than they'd been from a distance; a poverty-stricken, tired group of migrants. They didn't look like conquerors. They looked beaten.

Hunnar joined him. "I know this is a strange place, but something here speaks to me besides the unavoidable decrepitude. Everything here is different." He nodded toward the crowd. "So many different costumes. If you listen to them speak you hear not one odd accent but many."

Having concluded his inspection of the quarterdeck, Corfu rejoined them. "You observe accurately, noble. What you must realize is that until recently Yingyapin was far poorer than this.

"It could have been otherwise had we founded a city elsewhere. There are better harbors waiting to be developed, richer land to cultivate. Here there is little of that. But this city is founded on something else: hope. The kind of hope that sustained me in my time of troubles. It was hope that brought me to this place and hope that has kept me here." He made a sweeping gesture.

"All you see before you fled troubles in their homelands. Some are outcasts, some criminals, others simply poor. That is why you hear so many dialects, why you see so many different modes of dress. Yingyapin is a refuge for the dispossessed and displaced, for those who have left poverty and disappointment behind."

"Looks to me like they've just exchanged their old disappointments and poverty for new."

"Do not forget hope, human."

"What hope?" Hunnar gestured toward the ramshackle buildings. "I see naught but destitution and aimlessness."

Corfu waxed unexpectedly eloquent. "Sometimes hope is not like a fine hide or a good sword. It is not always what you can hold in the palm of your hand or feel beneath your feet. For all that, in our case it is intangible yet still has weight. Our hope is as real and solid—" and he chuckled at some private joke—"as the ice of Tran-ky-ky. When it is held up before you to marvel at, you will understand. Then you will not be so quick to disparage the judgment of the poor wretches you now see before you. A wise Tran measures his decisions on all the facts."

"The fact is that we have been kidnapped by pirates," Hunnar snapped.

"If you choose to join us all of your goods and property will be returned to you," Corfu replied unexpectedly. "Even unto this grand vessel. Nor will you be harmed in any way. We seek allies, not enemies." He raised a paw to forestall Hunnar's instinctive protest.

"I know what you are about to say. It has been said before by those equally as proud and foolish. Wait and see what is offered before you refuse your cooperation." His tone darkened as he turned to face Ethan.

"As for you and your kind, you cannot join us because we have already joined you."

Ethan wasn't given a chance to delve into the meaning of this enigmatic comment. A loading ramp slid from the dock onto the deck of the icerigger. The ramp crew had been forced to improvise, never having had to deal with a ship the size of the *Slanderscree*. Ethan noted that the cannon-armed skimmer continued to float off to one side. Its crew hadn't relaxed their vigilance one iota.

Escaping from this place wasn't going to be easy. And what was all this talk of joining? What was there here to join that could possibly appeal to the likes of Hunnar Redbeard and Elfa Kurdagh-Vlata? Corfu told them they'd find out.

The merchant chivaned down the iced ramp, returned soon with a ragtag, poorly disciplined guard to escort a dozen representatives from the ship into the city.

Yingyapin did not benefit from close inspection. If anything, Hunnar's and the other Trans' opinion of it fell a notch. It remained a puzzling, unimpressive collection of falling-down structures cobbled hastily together out of broken, undressed rock. The least building in Wannome would have seemed a masterpiece of the mason's art compared to any edifice in Yingyapin. Only the squat, ugly pile at the southern end of town looked like it could survive a strong wind. Corfu called it the palace.

Only half a dozen Tran guarded the visitors, but each was armed with a hand beamer. They were slightly better clad than their urban compatriots and they handled the advanced weapons as though they knew exactly how to use them. September was certain they hadn't merely acquired a few minutes casual instruction in their use. They'd been drilled. Any attempt to overpower them and take their weapons would have been suicidal. Far too soon to give thought to such extremes.

Even the renegade former Resident Commissioner, Jobius Trell, whose plans had depended so much on his Arsudinian allies, hadn't trusted his native friends with advanced weapons. Clearly someone hereabouts felt differently.

A pair of tall Tran hefting traditional weapons flanked the nondescript entrance to the palace. The lack of a heavy guard was itself instructive. They were marched through the dingy, badly lit structure until they emerged into a larger chamber only slightly better illuminated than the hallway they'd employed to reach it. The decor was unimpressive and reflective of the general poverty of the community—with one notable exception.

Suspended from the ceiling two thirds of the way down the room was a meter-wide, self-powered lighting fixture. It might have been transposed straight from a modest auditorium on a far-distant Earth. Its presence in that crumbling bastion of barbarian penury was as unexpected as a conservationist's triody in a hunter's igloo.

Seated on a throne hammered together out of scrap sheet metal was a twisted little Tran whom Ethan first took for a juvenile but who on closer inspection was revealed to be only an extremely short adult.

"All bow," Corfu grandly declared, "in the presence of Massul fel-Stuovic, first emperor of all Tran-ky-ky!"

IX

Ethan didn't know whether their guards would have shot Hunnar, Elfa, or any of the other Tran in the visiting party for laughing, but all of them somehow managed to restrain their instinctive reaction to this astonishing pronouncement. Even the acerbic and combative Seesfar restricted herself to a single sharp bark of amusement.

By the look of him Massul fel-Stuovic wasn't emperor of anything. Any one of them, including the ladies of the group, could have beaten him up without strain.

Corfu frowned and lifted the muzzle of his own beamer. "All will *bow*."

September shrugged indifferently. "What the hell. It's only a gesture. Not much point in getting shot over a gesture." He bent from the waist. Ethan and Milliken mimicked the movement.

Their Tran companions were not as ready to comply. Corfu aimed his beamer between Hunnar's legs and scorched the floor with a single shot. Hunnar's expression tightened, but he held his ground. The merchant was about to fire again when the diminutive ruler tiredly waved a paw.

"It doesn't matter, Corfu. Leave it be. What good to kill a potential convert?"

Corfu's gaze narrowed as he stared at Hunnar Redbeard. "Not this one, I think. Too stubborn to save himself."

"Stubbornness can give way to fanaticism, and if channeled, that can be useful." Massul waved a second time.

The merchant hesitated, his eyes locked with Hunnar's. Then he shrugged as if it were of no consequence and reholstered his weapon. "As you command, my lord."

"There are no emperors on Tran-ky-ky." Elfa didn't request permission to speak. "There never have been and never will there be."

"Never is a long time, female."

"Besides, we've already unified four major city-states and are preparing to accommodate more in a union of our own making. We have no need of would-be emperors."

"A union, you say? Good news, if true. It makes our own work that much easier." The emperor appeared no more distressed by this news of a competing planet-wide government than had Corfu. On the contrary, it was a development he seemed to welcome.

"Just what is your 'work'?" Ethan asked him.

Massul studied him out of small, sharp eyes. "Curious, you humans. Always asking questions. When you're not giving orders."

Suaxus-dal-Jagger was craning his neck to examine the hall with exaggerated interest. "Where are the banners, the insignia of family? What kind of court is this?"

"A new kind," the emperor informed him. "One based on achievement instead of nobility. I do not count myself the product of an ancient line. I merely have been fortunate enough to be in the right place at the right time. As have many of us." He gestured casually in Corfu's direction. The merchant acknowledged the gesture with a nod. Even here, in the castle's inner sanctum, the wind penetrated sufficiently to ruffle the fur and dan of the visiting Tran.

"Words do not make a ruler," Hunnar snapped.

"Truly. Only deeds make rulers. One cannot achieve great things without proper preparation. We are in the process of preparing. The results will become apparent to all Tran soon enough." He looked past him. "What I do not understand," he said, addressing himself to Hunnar and Elfa, "is what a grand vessel crewed by warriors like yourselves is doing convoying a group of humans to this part of the world."

"We are friends," Elfa replied simply.

Cheela Hwang stepped forward and spoke through her translator. "We have come to observe an anomalous meteorological phenomenon. The air here is much warmer than it should be. Surely you have noticed."

"You do not find our climate to your liking?" Massul was clearly amused. "I thought you humans preferred warmer weather."

That was as much as an outright confession that the emperor and his people were being aided directly by a group of people operating illegally on Tran-ky-ky, Ethan thought.

"Yes, we do. We prefer much hotter temperatures than you. That's not what we're concerned about," Hwang explained. "The weather here shouldn't be this warm. The upper part of the ice sheet hereabouts is melting."

"Not only the upper," Massul informed her, not in the least perturbed by the thought, "but from below as well."

"Then you must know what's going on here," Williams blurted, "and yet it doesn't seem to bother you."

"Why should it bother us? Everything changes sooner or later."

"Yes, but in the case of your world it should be later. Ten to twenty thousand years later, according to our calculations. Something is very wrong here."

"No!" Massul leaned forward. "Nothing is wrong here —except you. You should not be here. Something will have to be done about that. Everything else here is very right."

Dal-Jagger leaned over to whisper in Hunnar's ear. "My lord, I am not afraid of these light weapons. No matter how efficient the spear it must still be wielded with courage and daring. We can take this lot without much trouble."

Hunnar turned his squire down. "There may be others watching us armed with similar devices, or machines we know nothing about. We do not yet know enough to risk all. Hold."

Dal-Jagger stood back, disappointed but obedient. September had overheard and now bent over the squire. "Answers first, then fighting. If I'm going to get shot, I don't want to go down full of unanswered questions. Time enough later for grand gestures. Let's make sure we know the reason for them before we go making 'em." The squire nodded reluctantly.

"Something else that interests me." September addressed himself to Ethan while Hunnar and Elfa talked to Massul. "I'm still not sure who's master here; emperor or merchant. Corfu lets his emperor do all the talking, but when he has something to say he says it and doesn't ask permission. Doesn't look to me much like your usual Landgrave–noble relationship, even if he did back off on shooting Hunnar. Maybe he's got reasons for keeping himself in the background. Sometimes the people with the real power aren't the ones you see on the tridee. They're the ones to whom real power's more important than ego-boosting. They hang in the background and shun the publicity. In that respect, based on what we've seen this past year or so, the Tran ain't that much different from the rest of us."

Massul was picking at one paw. "What are we to do with you humans?"

"I would think that our friends would have some suggestions," Corfu said.

"Yes, yes, of course. Well, see to it. I have had a long day and I am wearied. Take them up to Shiva and let him decide."

September and Ethan didn't react to the name, but Williams and most of the scientists certainly did. As they were marched out of the court chamber the teacher fell back with his friends.

"That's not a Tran name," he informed them.

"Didn't think it was," said September. "Didn't sound right."

"It's human, from one of the ancient babel-tongues. Pre-Terranglo. It's from a dialect that was known as Sanskrit. In the Hindu religion Shiva was the god of death and destruction."

"What's in a name?" September muttered. "I was born in July."

"Are you saying," Ethan said, "that on top of the beamers and skimmers and lights we're supposed to believe that there are ancient human gods wandering around here?"

"As Skua says, it's just a name. I just thought you should know."

Their escort marched them out of the castle, but instead of turning back toward the harbor they headed west and out of town. Corfu chatted with his own people, unsuccessfully tried to engage Hunnar in casual conversation. He had better luck with Grurwelk Seesfar, much to everyone's surprise.

They turned up a well-worn path that led between a pair of ruined buildings and found themselves climbing a trail that switchbacked up the steep slope on the far side of Yingyapin harbor. Ethan tilted his head and regarded the ascent ahead uncertainly. The slope was climbable for about three-quarters of its height. Above that the broken talus and boulders gave way to sheer cliff. None of their guards carried ropes, grappling hooks, or any other kind of mountaineering apparatus. Surely they weren't going to be expected to climb *that*. For one thing, humans were much better climbers than Tran.

At the base of the cliff Corfu turned to the left. A much narrower trail wound its way northward along the base of the sheer rock wall. Whether poorly cleared or intentionally camouflaged Ethan couldn't decide. It was an excruciatingly difficult hike for the Tran. They were used to having the wind propel them effortlessly across the ice. Here, on rough ground, their huge clawlike chiv tended to be more of a hindrance than a help. Obviously used to the climb, Corfu bore the strain uncomplainingly. Hunnar, Elfa, and the rest of the Tran in the visitors' party grimaced and tried to ignore the pain in their feet. It must have been, Ethan reflected, like walking in too-tight boots balanced on six centimeter–high spikes. You had to move slowly and carefully or you'd twist an ankle or worse.

As a result even Milliken Williams, who was not the most athletic of men, managed to keep up easily with their escort.

Ethan was only mildly surprised when Corfu finally halted outside what looked like a bare rock wall, touched a hidden switch, and caused a large slab of gray schist to swing aside to reveal a well-lit tunnel beyond. They'd endured so many surprises in the past twenty-four hours he was sure he was beyond being surprised anymore.

He was wrong.

The tunnel they entered had not been chipped from the solid rock with picks and hand shovels. The walls were smooth and straight, the ceiling gently curved. Before they'd walked very far the rock gave way to metal, the metal to plastic as the passageway opened into an endless, hangar-sized cavern full of machinery. The air was alive with humming and whistling, electronic Muzak. It stank of lubricants, steam, and electricity.

Sight and smell alike were foreign to Tran-ky-ky. Pipes and conduits snaked off into the distance. Suddenly the presence among the Tran of Yingyapin of a few beamers and skimmers seemed but a trifling breach of regulations. If whoever had provided them to Massul's minions was a candidate for mindwipe, here was interference on a scale sufficient to qualify the perpetrators for physical dissolution.

Whatever the installation's purpose, it was clear it hadn't been put in place overnight. Design and scale suggested years of preparation and actual construction. It still wouldn't be difficult to keep the whole business a secret, as September pointed out.

"We're a helluva long ways from Brass Monkey and what with the weather on this world being like it is, why, you could build a whole city a few kilometers from the outpost."

A city this was not, though it employed a small army of human technicians. They looked up curiously from their work as the parade passed them by. None tried to engage the visitors in conversation. Ethan found that odd. The presence of strangers within the complex ought to have provoked more than curiosity. Surely even the most ingenuous among them knew they were participating in an illegal operation. That might have something to do with their reticence.

"I don't recognize any of this." Cheela Hwang was studying the complex machinery intently. "I wish some of the people from our engineering department were here."

"Be glad they're not," Ethan told her.

"Some kind of mining operation?"

"Possible." September was as puzzled as any of them as

to the complex's purpose. "Maybe they found a big ore body here and they're digging it out on the sly. You'd have to do it that way, since you wouldn't be able to get permission from the authorities. On a Class IVB world any minerals would be left untouched, kept in trust as it were for the locals. Maybe whoever's responsible—and they've sunk a lot of credit into this operation—is paying off Massul and Corfu and the others with beamers and skimmers and such."

The deeper they marched into the complex, the easier it became to sense the vastness of the installation. The temperature here had risen to just below human optimum. Corfu and his troops seemed halfway acclimated, but Elfa and the other Tran from the icerigger were suffering, their long tongues hanging out as they panted incessantly, their bodies fighting to rid their systems of excess heat. Ethan and his companions had switched off their survival suits.

Corfu directed them into a large service elevator. It barely held all of them and would have been a good place to try overpowering their captors. Once again September vetoed dal-Jagger's suggestion. At close quarters even a badly aimed beamer could do horrible damage to mere flesh and bone.

The lift ascended slowly, eventually depositing them in a deserted hallway. Corfu led them to a pair of doors which parted to reveal a spacious circular room. Free-form windows spotting the far wall looked out over sandstone monoliths completely enshrouded in fog. When the mist parted Ethan could see gentle slopes lining a smoking valley. Taller plumes of fog or smoke streaked the otherwise cloudless sky.

Here then was the proof of the volcanism which Hwang and her associates had been so sure existed. Yet there was something about the massive plumes that didn't look right. They did not vary in thickness or intensity and showed no signs of fluctuating in strength. Ethan had visited a few hot springs in his life and their output was never this consistent.

"Perhaps the installation we walked through utilizes the subsurface volcanic heat for power." He nodded toward the windows. "This vented steam could be a by-product of energy generation."

"Probably is," September agreed, "but I don't think volcanism has anything to do with it."

Any chance of pursuing September's thoughts further was eliminated as they were pushed into the room, which on closer inspection most resembled a conference chamber combined with an office. Their beamer-wielding guards split up to flank the entrance. Corfu strode toward the windows and bent over a high-backed chair, whispering.

A small, dark-skinned man (though not as dark as Williams) rose from the chair. His back was to them and he was staring out at the smoking valley. Ethan wondered what this room would look like from the outside. Unless you stumbled into it, he was sure it would blend perfectly into its rocky surroundings. Even the free-form windows would be difficult to identify from a distance. He didn't have to debate whether this was the result of camouflage or aesthetics.

As the man turned to face them he continued listening to Corfu. Ethan saw no evidence of a translator in the man's ear. It followed that he was as fluent in Tran as any of them. His manner was preoccupied, nervous, and intense. He was smaller than Williams and his structure was delicate without in any way being effeminate. When he spoke he sounded preoccupied and almost apologetic.

"Please, all of you, sit down. I am sorry for the manner in which you were brought here, but as you will learn it was necessary. Until I have determined how your purpose and intent in being here will affect our functions, I must be cautious."

"We're more interested in your purposes and intent," said Williams.

The man turned to him, tight-lipped. "Already I don't like you. Please keep your mouth closed until you are spoken to."

Not very apologetic, Ethan mused. Not all the fires here burned beneath the smoking vale beyond the windows.

Williams bristled but kept quiet. Their interests would not be served by provoking a confrontation before they'd learned anything. September stepped forward and performed introductions for human and Tran alike. The man listened politely while Corfu smirked in the background. When Hunnar and Elfa were introduced and what they represented described, the man began shaking his head slowly while gazing at the floor, giving the appearance of one who's just lost a paper clip and whose sole desire was to find it immediately.

"I've never heard of your union," he said when he finally looked up at them. "Unfortunately, cut off as we are here in the southern part of your world it is impossible for us to keep up with native affairs elsewhere. I am going to believe you because I'd like to. Your union suits our purpose here."

Ethan pointed to Corfu. "That's what he said."

"Yes." The man smiled thinly at the merchant. "Corfu has been a great help to me." Ethan noted that there was no mention made of Massul fel-Stuovic, emperor of all Tranky-ky.

"You must forgive my forgetfulness. I have been very busy and it has been some time since I was required to practice anything resembling the social amenities. I am Dr. Shiva Bamaputra. I am in charge of the installation here at Yingyapin."

"Quite a setup," September commented.

"It is fairly impressive, isn't it?"

"Enough to impress even a Commonwealth inspector-ate. Why don't you apply for a permit for whatever it is you're doing here? It would make things a lot easier for you."

"You choose to affect the air of an uneducated bumpkin, Mr. September, but I think I know better. I think you know as well as I why I cannot do that. Why do you think we built underground here if not to escape detection from those who would disagree with our intentions? We would have had to do this in any event in order to preserve heat. Heat is very important to what we are doing, you see, and even fusion stations are not unlimited in what they can achieve."

Then volcanism wasn't involved, Ethan reflected. "Just what is it you *are* doing here?"

Bamaputra looked past him, past all of them. "Some-thing the Commonwealth would not approve of, I think. The reaction of the Councilors of the United Church would be stronger still. They're all so stiff and formal, so tradi-tion-bound and conservative that even if they saw the chance to help those in need, they wouldn't do so if it didn't fit their precious regulations. They would shut us down in an instant despite the benefits that are accruing to the people of this world." He turned back to face the win-dows that overlooked the valley.

"We are Tranforming."

"That's a contradiction in terms," Hwang said. "This world is already 'Tranformed.'"

He glanced back at her. "How familiar are you with the physiology and history of the Tran?"

"We've made a few interesting discoveries," Ethan told him.

Bamaputra eyed him a moment, then nodded. "Yes, I've

noticed that several of you seem very comfortable with these people as well as with their language. I will presume you are cognizant of the basics, then. If I go too fast for you or mention something you are not familiar with, please interrupt and I will elucidate.

"There is nothing complex about what we are doing here. Three fusion plants have been installed deep within this part of the continental plateau. We are using the production of these plants not only to power our installation but to melt the ice sheet from the underside up. You will be interested to know that where it clings to the continental shelf in this area the oceanic ice sheet is in places less than twenty meters thick. That is one reason why we chose this peninsula as our base of operations. The warming of the atmosphere in this vicinity and the concurrent melting of surface ice is the by-product and not the principal intent of our operation."

"Why?" asked Blanchard.

"Because this atmosphere needs more of two things: water vapor and carbon dioxide. In addition to melting the ice sheet we are pumping water vapor back into the air. To produce the carbon dioxide that accompanies it we extract oxygen from the air and add carbon from large coal deposits directly beneath this station. There are substantial archaic seams of anthracite in the area. It seems strange to burn a fossil fuel for no other reason than to intentionally pump it into the atmosphere."

No scientist, Ethan was struggling to follow the conversation, which was why Bamaputra was making everything as simple as possible.

"The greenhouse effect on Tran-ky-ky is weak. We intend to artificially increase it to the point where enough of its sun's heat is retained to raise the surface temperature as much as eighteen degrees."

"What is all this talk?" Hunnar finally asked his friend.

Ethan replied without taking his eyes off Bamaputra. "He is talking about raising the temperature of your planet considerably, to well above the point where ice becomes a corpse."

"You're talking a long time," September was telling their host. "You won't live long enough to see it to fruition."

"Ah, but that is where you are wrong, my large friend. Because the climatological balance on Tran-ky-ky is so delicate, it is in fact possible to effect substantial shifts in temperature over a surprisingly short period of time."

"What I don't understand," Ethan told him, "is why you're bothering. All that's going to happen naturally."

"Yes, but the change will take ten to twenty thousand years. The planet will enjoy its briefer warm cycle before swinging back out in its perturbed orbit and freezing again. Then the down cycle of life will resume. The oceans will refreeze, the temperature will drop permanently back below freezing, and the Tran will once more be forced to cower in their caves and feudal castles, reduced to devoting their racial energies just to surviving. No, you are wrong about the time we require to change this. You forget your elementary physics." Several of the scientists grimaced. If this reaction pleased Bamaputra, he gave no sign of it.

"Once the ice sheet has melted through, the defrosting effect will accelerate even in the absence of above-freezing temperatures since the exposed dark water will absorb and distribute the sunlight which the ice has previously reflected. The result will be accelerated shrinkage of the ice sheet and the expansion of open ocean into the northern and southern temperate zones. The level of the seas will rise fifty meters and more. Those Tran inhabiting low-lying areas will be forced, as would be the case in fifteen thousand years or so, to abandon them and move to higher ground. There will be a mass migration from the low islands to the higher land of the continents. As the air warms, these will become inhabitable, as they historically have been before when the climate moderates. In point of fact, they will come here.

"Our initial research suggested that this, the southern continent, was the area of highest population density in warmer times. There will be a corresponding migration and physiological change in the animal population as well. There will be some deaths among the Tran because their necessary physical change from a cold state to a warm one will also be accelerated." He shrugged. "This is unavoidable."

"How many deaths?" September's voice was very low.

"Impossible to predict with accuracy. They are certainly to be regretted, but you might reflect that in earlier times such deaths occurred naturally as a consequence of the long, arduous journeys from the islands to the continents. These deaths will be prevented."

"How?" Blanchard asked him.

"When the Commonwealth learns what is happening here by means of relay from the outpost, regulations will have to be put aside in favor of rescuing as much of the native population as possible. Their arcane restrictions do not apply in the face of a 'natural' catastrophe affecting large numbers of sentients. The Tran of Yingyapin, quietly aided and abetted by us, will do likewise. It is not in our interest to have anyone die unnecessarily."

"Nonetheless, you're willing to accept those deaths as an inevitable consequence of what you're doing as opposed to modifying your goals," Jacalan said.

"You must consider what the final result of our work here will be," Bamaputra said emphatically. "As the temperature rises the Tran will begin to change physically. They will lose their dan and chiv and long fur and adopt the golden-furred Saia state millennia earlier than other-

wise. A much more natural state of affairs. They will become land dwellers instead of ice dwellers.

"Don't you see what this will mean for them? They will
be given a boost no other generation of Tran has ever had.
In a congenial climate they will be able to develop properly, to achieve the advanced civilization they are capable
of but which was always aborted by the onset of this bru-
tally cold climate. For the first time in their history they
will be able to reach a level of civilization high enough to
enable them to retain it through any future onsets of frigid
weather. As a result they will be ready to enter into not
associate but full membership in the Commonwealth thousands of years earlier than would otherwise be possible.

"Furthermore, the inevitable consequence of emergency
Commonwealth aid will permit them to retain their newly
achieved civilization regardless of what happens to the climate if our artificially enhanced greenhouse effect cannot
be maintained. It will be the dawn of a golden age for
Tran-ky-ky."

Like the rest of them September had listened quietly to
Bamaputra's exculpation. Now he frowned and scratched
at the back of his neck.

"You know, monkeying around with something like a
world's climate is strictly forbidden by just about every
primary Commonwealth directive I can think of. Folks are
only allowed to play god on uninhabited worlds. Trying to
make permanent changes on one populated by intelligent
locals, well, if word of what you're doing here got back to
the right parties I wouldn't give half a credit for your prospects."

"Ah, but we have the advantage of operating on such an
isolated world. By the time the 'right parties' "—he formed
the words with barely concealed contempt—"get wind of
what we are doing it will be too late to reverse the process.
The seas will already have begun to melt, the Tran will

have begun to change physically, and shutting us down here would be more harmful than permitting the process to continue."

"What I can't figure," Ethan said, "is what's in it for them." He nodded toward Corfu, who looked a little startled at abruptly being included in the skypeople's conversation. "I mean, you've obviously managed to secure his cooperation and that of this self-proclaimed emperor and the rest of the local population. I don't see that they're necessary to it. You could just as easily lock yourselves inside this mountain and ignore them."

"You are correct, Mr. Fortune. They are not necessary —but they do make life here easier. Eventually we will need the aid of some Tran. Corfu and his fellow citizens will provide that for us."

"It has all been very carefully explained to me by the scholar." Corfu indicated the diminutive Bamaputra. "It is very simple. Even a fool could see it." No one in his audience, human or Tran, accepted the bait. He was forced to continue, slightly disappointed.

"I—through the good offices of the emperor, of course" —and he smiled sufficiently to show who stood where in the local Tran hierarchy—"saw to it that information and labor were supplied to the skypeople to help with their project. In addition we have served as scouts, recruiting new citizens for our growing city, co-opting the curious and educating them about the nature of the Divine Plan, driving off those who appeared unsuitable for participation."

When he said the last Ethan glanced at Grurwelk Seesfar. She was staring intently at Corfu but said nothing.

"We did not expect to capture so fine a prize as a great ship crewed by both humans and Tran, but as you saw we were equipped to deal with any eventuality."

Are you? Ethan thought. Do you really realize what's

going to happen to you and to your world if this little maniac is allowed to continue his work here? Does Bamaputra really have it worked out so precisely? Playing around with a world's weather isn't quite like building a new castle or fighting a rival clan.

"Mayhap you can fool the skypeople," Elfa said sharply, "but you cannot darken our eyelids so easily. There is more to it than that."

"Oh, there will be changes," Corfu murmured with a smile. "Many changes."

"Indeed." This explanation didn't seem to interest Bamaputra as much as his previous one. "As the sea level rises and the Tran abandon their city-states to migrate here they will initially be dependent on those Tran already securely established on the continents. That is where Massul's people come in. My successors and I won't have the time to deal with local matters. Someone else will have to take care of allotting land, setting up and administering refugee stations, and generally running the new unified government. Emperor Massul will by then be well prepared for coping with the increased migratory influx to the southern continent."

"And my family," said Corfu, "my despised and degraded family will be in charge of all commerce, supplies and clothing, tools and housing, homes, and local transportation. All at a price. This I may not live to enjoy, but my children will. The name of Corfu ren-Arhaveg will be resurrected, and all Tran will do it homage!"

"My financial backers have already agreed to a long-term commercial arrangement with Massul and Corfu. It will assist in accelerating the integration of the Tran. They will be compelled to unite in the face of a common problem. Those who insist on trying to retain their feudal independence will drown or starve. Those who survive and work together will bring about a new age on Tran-ky-ky."

He spread his hands and a trickle of real emotion seeped through the carefully controlled visage.

"Don't you see? We're not engaged in anything unnatural here. All we're doing is speeding up something that's going to take place anyway. We're giving the Tran a ten thousand–year head start. Everything we're trying to accomplish: the melting of the oceans, the warming of the climate, the physical transformations—those are all going to come about sooner or later. Why not sooner?"

"Now we know what's in it for him." September jerked a thumb in Corfu's direction. "We still don't know what's in it for you and your 'financial backers.'"

"Me?" Bamaputra drew himself up to his full height. "I am 'in it' because I am a scientist. Because I want to help these people achieve their potential. Because I wish to see certain theories of mine come to pass." He relaxed slightly. "Of course my triumph will be a private one. There will be no public acclaim, no honors or honorary degrees. Since this is highly illegal, my name and that of everyone else involved in the actual work will have to be kept secret." He looked thoughtful.

"Perhaps after I am dead, as Corfu says of his offspring, some relatives of mine may seek proper enshrinement for my name. In my lifetime, I know I must be satisfied with internal contentment alone."

"I am confused." Ta-hoding looked at his human friends. "This all sounds very much akin to what you have been doing for us."

"This isn't the way to go about it, Ta-hoding," Ethan responded. "You don't unify people by threatening them with drowning and starvation. You don't bring them closer together by forcing them from their homes, destroying their existing culture, and interfering with the natural order of things."

Bamaputra's lower lip pushed forward. "When the

oceans melt of natural causes many die. Perhaps more than would die without us here to aid them."

"The Commonwealth will be around to help the Tran in ten thousand years or it won't be worth joining," Ethan shot back.

"Why should these people have to wait that long?" Bamaputra looked shrewdly at Hunnar and Elfa.

Hunnar didn't reply immediately. He eyed this peculiar little human warily, fond neither of his accent nor his attitude. In the almost two years he'd lived and traveled across the world in the company of Ethan, Skua, and Milliken Williams, he'd learned much about the ways of skypeople. Some his friends had explained to him. Other things he had learned from quiet observation. Something about this Shiva person disturbed him.

Not his treatment of Tran. This Corfu creature he treated well. There was a distance in him, a deliberate if silent barrier erected between himself and those he spoke with. Not contempt. It was almost as if he believed himself to be the only person in the room. Instead of humans and Tran he might as well have been speaking to machines. Was that because he thought of others as nothing more than machines or because he was so machinelike himself? Hunnar wasn't intimately familiar with sophisticated machinery, but he had observed enough of it in action at the human outpost of Brass Monkey to gain some idea of its characteristics.

"What are you talking about?"

"In coming to this place you have demonstrated courage and resources beyond the Tran norm." Bamaputra's expression of false jollity didn't fool Hunnar in the least. "Now you know what is going to happen to your world. While our facilities for receiving large numbers of migrants are not yet in place, you could still return home and inform your people of what is forthcoming. But for those already living in Yingyapin you could be the first. You could partake of relevant advantages by moving here and helping us in our work before the real changes begin."

"A moment." Corfu was more than slightly taken aback by this unexpected offer from his human ally. "We could not possibly cope with . . ."

Bamaputra cut him off. "There are ways. We could manage. I will talk with my backers. When all is explained to them I am sure they will be able to find a way to come up with the requisite additional funds to commence settlement by outsiders, particularly as energetic and advanced a group as this. Development on the continental plateau could begin ahead of schedule." He turned his attention back to Hunnar.

"You see, my friend, you and your people could dominate. In time you could rule Tran-ky-ky."

"What about the line of your emperor?" Elfa asked sarcastically.

"Massul fel-Stuovic's family is small. Over a period of time, who is to say which group would emerge as the most powerful? That is up to you. Internecine conflicts among your kind do not interest me. I am willing to work with whoever is on top at the time. So are my backers." He looked over at an obviously upset Corfu.

"Relax, my friend. You would still be in charge of the distribution and sale of all supplies and equipment, including any new devices we choose to provide."

"Where do the people live?" Ethan asked.

"Which people?"

"The engineers, the technicians who run this place."

"We have constructed an extensive underground facility for their comfort." Bamaputra was obviously annoyed at the interruption, feeling he'd been making progress with Hunnar and Elfa. "Given the climate, underground living is much more practical. That is one of the things we will change, of course. Why do you ask?"

"I was just wondering," Ethan told him evenly, "if they're all aware of what the end result of their work here is going to be."

"It wouldn't be practical to try concealing our aims from those who work for us. Each has his own reason for being here. You see, my idealistic friend, there still exists a sufficiently large segment of humanity which is not concerned with the fate of alien races as much as they are with improving their own circumstances—the thranx excepted, naturally. We pay very well and our method of payment ensures that the taxing authorities have trouble tracing such disbursements.

"Even so, not all know everything. Safer to keep as many as possible in the dark. They prefer this as much as we do. Should they be discovered and arraigned they will be able to plead honest ignorance before the truth machine. It's not hard to find competent people to perform under such circumstances, provided you phrase your job offer appropriately. The number of zeroes at the end of financial statements is likewise efficacious."

September was looking around the conference room/office. "You're right about one thing. Somebody's put a lot of money into this. I imagine they expect they're going to get it all back by selling vital supplies and equipment for the development of a new civilization to the grateful survivors?"

"I would not know. I am not much interested in commerce myself, though in order to deal effectively with my backers I have been forced to learn something of the financial world, yes. Your supposition is correct insofar as it goes, but it does not go far enough. It is not only the Tran who will be dependent on my backers for favors.

"When the sea level begins to rise, low-lying harbors

such as Brass Monkey will be flooded. Much of the island Arsudun will likewise become untenable. The Commonwealth will need a new location for its outpost, not to mention its refugee centers. Not enough of Arsudun will remain above water to suffice.

"Here, the government will find not only facilities suitable for human habitation already in place, but also the new center of Tran civilization. Uncertainty over how this all came about will be overwhelmed by the need to establish a new base quickly."

"To help the migrants," Ethan muttered.

"Precisely. In any fight between necessity and morality the latter never wins."

"It's still not the right way to do things," Ethan argued.

"What is the right way anymore?" Everyone turned in surprise to Mousokka, second mate of the *Slanderscree*. "So much has changed since these people have come to our world."

"For the better," Elfa reminded him, "because we know that Ethan, Skua, and Milliken are our friends. This have they proven not with words but with deeds."

"They are changing us. The skypeople are changing us. Why is one group better than another? None of them are Tran!"

"Why don't you talk over my offer?" Bamaputra suggested with a smile. "Return to the familiar surroundings of your beautiful ice ship. Discuss it among yourselves. I would much prefer to have your cooperation than not, though it will not make any difference in the end either way."

"And if we don't cooperate?"

"You people have this charming way of dispensing with diplomacy." Bamaputra retained his good humor. "That can be discussed if and when it occurs. Do not trouble yourself with such thoughts. We are not barbarians here."

"No," echoed Corfu proudly, "we aren't barbarians here."

"I don't like giving ultimatums. But keep in mind that nothing is going to stop this project. There is too much invested. You can be part of it or not, as you will. Go and talk in private. If you have any more questions, Corfu will see to it that they are relayed to me.

"Meanwhile I need to talk about *your* unexpected appearance here." He was staring straight at Ethan as he spoke. "Devin Antal is plant foreman. It is his responsibility, too."

"Any preliminary thoughts on the matter?" September asked easily.

Their slightly built captor tilted his head back to regard the giant casually. "When any occur to me, Mr. September, I assure you that you and your companions will be made aware of them immediately."

X

Hunnar was too nervous to sit. He paced the *Slanderscree*'s dining room, ruffing his dan and clicking his canines.

Escape was out of the question. The icerigger's anchors had been wrapped around heavy pilings, and Corfu had mounted a guard on the deck. Upon returning from the installation their situation had been explained to the crew. Now the sailors and soldiers were conferencing out on deck while Hwang and her companions anxiously discussed their own options in the cabin that had been reserved to them.

Elfa was present, of course, as were Ethan and Skua. Ta-hoding, Suaxus-dal-Jagger, and the *Slanderscree*'s mates sat off to one side.

"What I do not understand is what's so bad about the offer we have been made." The second mate, Mousokka, leaned against a wall and crossed his arms.

"You can't let someone turn your world upside down like this," Ethan tried to explain.

"Why not?" The mate eyed him sharply, then let his gaze rove around the room. "I don't know about the rest of you, but I like the idea of being warm all the time. Simply because our weather is always cold does not mean it is to be enjoyed. The north winter wind never delights me. If our bodies will adapt themselves to warmer temperatures, why should we not welcome their arrival?"

"And we could also," the third mate put in, "gain an advantage over all other Tran, as this human says. With the *Slanderscree* to lead the way, all of Wannome could move to this place."

"It would mean starting over with nothing," Elfa argued. "Would you then abandon the homes of your forefathers for a promise?"

"If what this human says comes to pass, we will be forced to do that one day anyhow. We will become like the Golden Saia." Kilpit looked at Ethan. "Is this so?"

Ethan nodded. "But we're talking ten thousand years or more before the change occurs naturally."

"Why not start now? This human says his people will help us. We will be given light weapons and sky boats for our own use."

"At a price," Hunnar snapped. "And a price we know nothing of."

Kilpit looked to Mousokka for support, then shrugged. "Everything comes at a price. We can pay these humans now or pay the world later."

"What about your union?" September asked him. "What happened to the idea of all Tran cooperating and working together for a common goal?"

"We will all be united as the world warms and the seas die. Only some of us have a chance to be united before everyone else."

"Such thoughts go against the whole idea of union. Either we work together as equals or we cannot work together at all," Hunnar insisted.

"Too much to decide on in one day," murmured Ta-hoding. "Too much. Of course we cannot accept this divisive proposal. It is unthinkable."

"Unthinkable to you, perhaps," growled Kilpit. "What

will you do when the seas melt and you have no ice ship to captain?"

"I will learn to steer one of these sky boats. Or I will learn another trade. What I will *not* do is compromise my ideals or the world of my birth because some skinny furless creature from elsewhere says it is best for me." He glared hard at his third mate. "That is what you and Mousokka seem to be forgetting. Always have we Tran made our own decisions. Not always for the best of reasons or motivations, but at least they have been ours. I dislike the idea of my future and that of my cubs being determined by someone else, no matter that he may be well intentioned."

"I don't think he's as well intentioned as he's trying to be." September dug at a tooth. "Never can tell about some of these pure-research types. They live in their own little worlds. So long as they can prove an occasional theory or so, they're happy. As far as they're concerned, the rest of the universe can go hang. He argues well but not plausibly."

"Then this is settled," said Hunnar firmly. "We will refuse his offer."

"But not right away," Ethan cautioned him. "We have to make it look like you're hesitating, have to buy some time until we can figure out a way to break out of here so we can warn the authorities. If this is such a benign enterprise whose primary beneficiaries are supposed to be the Tran, let's let the Commonwealth Xenological Society debate its merits, not us."

"It does not matter." Kilpit suddenly rose and headed for the door. "You have made your decision. We have made ours."

"We?" Hunnar's fur bristled.

Ta-hoding rose and his eyes narrowed. "Kilpit, you have been a good and faithful mate, but now you go too far. You forget yourself."

"On the contrary, Captain mine," the third mate said with a hint of the old deference still detectable in his voice, "it is myself I must not forget." Mousokka moved to join him in flanking the exit. "Myself, my relatives I have not seen in more than a year, and my friends." His eyes darted around the room.

"Listen to yourselves! You have been among skypeople so long that you have forgotten what it is to be Tran. I have not forgotten. It is about surviving the best one can. It is striving to obtain an advantage for yourself and your family."

"We had no argument with the concept of a greater union," Mousokka said, "since within it, Sofold would always be first among equals. You are prepared to cast aside a still greater opportunity. We are not." He opened the door.

Armed sailors filed into the room. Though they held tightly to their weapons few of them could raise their eyes to meet Hunnar's or Ta-hoding's. That they were carrying arms at all was enough to explain what was going on, since Corfu's troops had disarmed the crew earlier. Ethan strained to see past them, out into the hallway, trying to count the number of mutineers.

"You have cast night soil on your heritage," Hunnar said tightly. "You have foresworn your duty to city and Landgrave and have gone over to a foreign king."

"We have done no such thing," said Mousokka uncomfortably. "It is you who have gone over. Over to these skypeople." He jerked his head in Ethan's direction.

"And who have you gone over to," Elfa asked contemptuously, "if not to skypeople?"

"Massul is Tran. So is Corfu. The human thinks he uses them; they think they use him. It does not matter. These skypeople have light weapons and sky boats. They cannot be stopped. Martyrs are fools. I am not a martyr."

"They can be stopped," Ethan told him, "once we break out of here and get back to Arsudun."

"You are not breaking out of anything." Corfu shouldered his way into the room. "Thoughts of flight are futile. At least these right-thinking Tran"—and he indicated Mousokka and Kilpit—"have sensed which way the wind is blowing."

"The wind," declared Ta-hoding with dignity, "blows always to the east."

"Not always." Corfu grinned. "These skypeople have machines that can bend the very wind and sun to their needs. These things they can do on behalf of those willing to work with them." He allowed himself a slight chuckle, which among the Tran consisted as much of whistling as anything else. "Did you truly believe we would let you hold council and make a decision which might not be in our interests without taking care to secure allies among your own people as rapidly as possible?" He looked past Ethan and September to Hunnar and the other Tran in the room.

"Come, use your heads, my friends. Join us. Your city-state or union or whatever you want to call it can become first among all Tran-ky-ky. Do the sensible thing for your children and grandchildren if not for your yourselves. For it is certain a new age is upon us."

"It became necessary to destroy the world in order to save it," September murmured, but in Terranglo so only his fellow humans would understand him.

Corfu glowered in his direction, executed an expressive gesture with the short sword he carried. "No talking in skypeople words. In my presence you will speak properly." Ethan noticed that not all the armed Tran who had filed into the room were members of the *Slanderscree*'s crew. Corfu was making sure Hunnar's eloquence could not sway the hesitant mutineers at the last minute. Not a good idea to change your mind with a beamer stuck in your back. The merchant's people would not be affected by Hunnar's outrage, Elfa's contempt, or anything he or September could say.

Ta-hoding was talking to the deck. "My fault. All my fault. A captain who cannot maintain the allegiance of his crew is not worthy of the title."

"Do not blame yourself," said Kilpit compassionately. "This is nothing to do with you or your abilities, Ta-hoding. It is to do with what we think is best for ourselves and our future."

"We linger too long." Mousokka stepped aside, gestured at the open door with his sword. "We have spent too much time already listening to the words of these skypeople and doing as they ask without question."

"Who do you think pulls this puppet's strings?" Hunnar nodded toward Corfu.

"No one pulls my strings but me!" The merchant waved his sword a centimeter from Hunnar's muzzle.

The knight replied with a thin smile. "Yes, it is evident what a brave warrior you are on your own."

The two glared at each other for a long moment. Ethan held his breath. Then Corfu took a deep breath and stepped back. "I am bound by agreement—agreement, you hear, not an order—not to harm any of you for now. I agree to this to please my *friend*, the skyperson Bamaputra." He looked around the room.

"Those who have joined with us will be watched, but eventually all will be given an important place in the new ruling caste. The rest of you will be given time to think and hopefully to learn whence your true destiny lies." He gestured with his sword. "Come now."

"Wait a minute," said Ethan. "I thought we were going to be allowed to stay on the *Slanderscree*."

"You were allowed to return to have your discussion in

familiar surroundings. Nothing was said about letting you remain longer." Corfu smiled wolfishly. "If you were to be allowed to remain here, you might waste your time on thoughts of escape instead of considering where your destiny lies. Thoughtful as he is, Bamaputra would spare you such wasteful distraction.

"For myself, I do not think you could escape all the guards and slip away with this ship, but I have learned that skypeople do not like to take chances. You are to be returned to the skypeople's house to meditate upon the error of your ways."

This was bad, Ethan knew. As long as they were on the ship there was always the chance of cutting the anchor cables, slipping their bonds, and overpowering or eluding Corfu's minions. If they could maneuver the *Slanderscree* back out onto the open ice where the wind blew hard, they might even be able to outrun a skimmer.

Within the installation their every breath was likely to be monitored by advanced surveillance devices. They wouldn't be able to go to the bathroom undetected, much less break through a real door. Bamaputra wasn't taking any chances.

"What about our friends?" He indicated Elfa, Hunnar, and the others. "They can't stand the heat inside the installation."

"Their health is not my concern," said Corfu brusquely as they were herded out of the mess under the watchful eyes of beamer-wielding guards. Those members of the icerigger's crew who'd gone over to the other side made way for the column. Some of them looked as though they might already be having second thoughts, but no one had the guts to express that kind of opinion in the presence of the handguns. Ethan thought most of them could be made to see the error of their ways, but doubted he or anyone else would be given the opportunity to win back their loyalty.

"Understand," Kilpit was saying earnestly as they were marched onto the deck, "we do this thing for our families and for the traditions you have forgotten. Wannome first, last, and always. So it has always been among the Tran of Sofold and so it will be again."

"It doesn't have to be," Hunnar was muttering. "It doesn't have to be. Sometimes times themselves must *change*." No one paid any attention to him.

Once more they found themselves forced to make the steep climb from Yingyapin to the underground installation. With night beginning to fall the humans were grateful to reach the Earth-normal temperatures inside the mountain.

A quick head count revealed that less than half the ice-rigger's crew had joined Bamaputra's domesticated Tran (that was how Ethan had come to think of them). The mutineers did not join in the ascent but were left in possession of the ship.

The sheer number of captives presented a problem. Despite their insistence that they be allowed to remain together, Tran and their human friends were separated. No doubt Bamaputra hoped to convince the reluctant to join him. Hunnar, Elfa, and the others were herded into a large, empty food storage room where the internal temperature could be kept at a level more to their liking.

As the humans were thoroughly searched by Bamaputra's security team, Ethan noticed that Skua was eyeing one of their captors with particular intensity. He remarked on it.

"Funny, young feller-me-lad. Time passes in a twinkling but it's hard to forget certain faces."

Ethan gaped at him, then at the big man who appeared to be in charge of security. "You know that one?"

"That's the Antal Bamaputra mentioned. Devin Antal.

He and I were in a bit of a war together, on opposite sides. If he's the same man he was, then he won't make things easy on us. A real do-as-you're-told type, but if push comes to crunch, the type who'll make sure to look out for himself. There might be an opening there for us, if we pay attention."

Sure enough, the man Skua called Antal introduced himself as Bamaputra's foreman. He showed them their new home, an unused workers' dormitory that could be sealed from the outside. After a short speech warning them to stay put and not make trouble he departed for parts unknown.

In a war together. On rare occasions September had alluded to a conflict in which he'd played some important role. That was hardly pertinent to their present predicament, Ethan mused dourly as he sat down on the flexibunk. It was more comfortable than any bed he'd slept in since leaving Brass Monkey, but he still didn't think he was going to rest easy.

"Our guests are situated." Antal flopped down on a couch in Bamaputra's above-ground observation room-cum-office. "Didn't have any trouble with the people from the outpost. Their Tran were a little more rambunctious. Corfu's boys had to crack a couple of skulls."

Bamaputra turned away from the window. "I don't want anyone killed. Each of them is potentially useful to us."

"Hey!" Antal raised both hands. "I told Corfu I'd hold him personally responsible. He didn't like it, but he got things quieted down. I should have taken some of our own people off the line instead of letting Massul's stooges handle it. You know how these natives are."

Bamaputra pursed his lips. "Fractious. Undisciplined, combative, unable to live in peace among their own kind.

At times they remind me of humanity prior to the Amalgamation. The Dark Ages."

Antal casually struck a narcostick alight. "What are you going to do with them?"

The installation director frowned at the cloying smoke that filled the room, but he didn't demand that his foreman extinguish it. The relationship between the two men was of almost equals, like a pair of boxers who never fought because they were ganging up on a third opponent but who fully expected to face each other in the ring one day.

Not that they wouldn't have enjoyed a good fight, though it wouldn't have been much of a contest. Antal was a big, broad-shouldered individual in his late thirties, a menial laborer with a degree. He outweighed Bamaputra by forty kilos. But he didn't think of taking a swing. They needed each other everyday. Antal ran the day-to-day operation of the complex installation that was gradually transforming Tran-ky-ky's atmosphere and melting the ice sheet. If anything went wrong mechanically, he knew how to get it fixed. If anything else went wrong, well, that was Bamaputra's business. He knew why things broke. He also saw to it that the credit kept flowing.

It was an awkward relationship, but it worked. The installation had suffered a minimal number of breakdowns under their dual supervision. None of the clandestine shuttle drops had been detected by the government people at Brass Monkey. No reason why they should be: Tran-ky-ky was a big world, difficult to survey. Their supplies always arrived timed so they would not conflict with the arrival of the regular Commonwealth liners.

So what was a Tran ice ship doing probing the continental shelf with a half dozen human scientists aboard?

"I thought they'd get curious about the warming trend hereabouts, but I didn't expect they'd be able to make an on-site inspection."

"It would not have been possible," Bamaputra muttered, "without this extraordinary ice ship and the cooperation of its Tran crew. That, and the three men who have apparently lived for some time among them. A strange story, that. If not for their intervention, albeit involuntary, these Tran would still be huddled inside their own city-states doing traditional battle with their neighbors and the plundering nomadic hordes which migrate around the planet, not setting off on missions of unification which can only inconvenience us."

Antal puffed on his narcostick and relaxed. "Damned inconsiderate of 'em."

Bamaputra glanced sharply at his foreman. "Are you mocking me?"

"Would I do that, Mister Bamaputra, sir?"

The administrator let it pass. Now was not the time for him and his foreman to get into one of their little fights. "It's fortunate we spotted them and were able to bring them in. If they'd been able to turn and run before the skimmer with the cannon had been able to arrive all might be lost."

"Yeah, but they didn't and we've got 'em."

"I'd hoped this was a problem we would not have to deal with until both you and I were dead of old age."

"Well, we're not. What do you want me to do with them?"

"The Tran we will sit on and try to bring over to our camp. As for these other meddlers, I would much prefer to dump them into a hole in the ice and then allow it to freeze over. While that is an appealing scenario, I fear it is impractical. If they do not return, they will be missed. Not that those bureaucrats at Brass Monkey can do anything without skimmers, but in the event of a mass disappearance they might be able to secure a waiver of regulations. That would mean more of the same types snooping around here.

We can do without that kind of attention. Therefore we cannot kill them—yet. Nor can we let them leave.

"Those Tran who remain obstinate can of course be disposed of."

"What about this trio of outsiders, this guy Fortune, the schoolteacher, and September, the big guy? I don't imagine they'd be missed."

Bamaputra shook his head. "Killing them would only make the rest that much more obstinate."

"Are you thinking of persuading some of them to work for us?"

"The thought had occurred to me. I don't know any of them yet. Money is available for such purposes. That might swing one or two of them over to us, but not all, I'm afraid. I fear several are idealists." He sniffed. "There is no place in science for idealism."

"What if we kept the women here as hostages?"

"Too risky. It would only take one to give us away. The ones we allowed to return to the outpost might harbor hidden dislikes for those we held here. We absolutely cannot allow any of them out of the installation."

"So what do we do?" Antal put his feet up on the couch. Bamaputra eyed him distastefully, but said nothing.

"If we cannot persuade them to join us and we cannot dispose of them, we will simply have to keep them alive and quiet. There is no hurry. They will not be expected to return for some while and so we will have time to think. In time we will come up with an appropriate solution. Or they may. For now let us do this: We can have them make a recording. Let's say our studious guests have encountered an unexpectedly advanced Tran community boasting a unique social order which they wish to study while they pursue their investigations of local meteorological anomalies. The Tran in question have agreed to put them up until they have completed their studies. All of this can be put on a recording chip and sent back with some of our own Tran in a small ice ship. These people did bring recording equipment with them, I trust?"

"Yeah. We've been through all their stuff. Gauges and samplers and so forth. What you'd expect. No weapons." He grinned. "Can't break regulations, you know. They had a good field recorder."

Bamaputra nodded approvingly. "Everyone on the recording will be all smiles and contentment. Its arrival should allay any worries on the part of both the outpost scientific and government administration. And I understand the new Resident Commissioner has arrived. She will be too busy settling in to concern herself with a group of explorers who by their own admission are in no danger. What do you think? Will they cooperate and make the necessary recording?"

"I don't think there'll be any problem with that. I'll stick a beamer in somebody's ear and threaten to pull the trigger. That ought to eliminate any hesitation. This doesn't strike me as an unusually brave or foolhardy bunch."

"Fine. Meanwhile we will continue operations normally. When the next supply vessel arrives we will relay news of this awkward development back to headquarters. Let them chew on the problem and come up with a final determination. That way it will be out of our hands. I don't want the responsibility. Our task is to see that our work here continues uninterrupted."

"Sounds good to me."

"What kind of watch do you have on them?"

"Watch?" Antal sucked in smoke, exhaled a small cloud. "They're well secured. Standard camera surveillance. You want me to put guards on their rooms? They're not going anywhere, and I'd rather not spare the personnel."

"If you're sure . . ."

"The Tran are sealed in an empty perishables storeroom and the others in a safe dorm. Now and then I have somebody check on them and they'll be fed three times a day. The Tran don't know enough to start looking for a way out and that dormitory has magnetic seals on the door. No locks to pick. The cameras make thirty-second room sweeps. They're unbreakable, regular security equipment. Why take somebody away from his job so he can go to sleep in front of a door with a beamer in his hand? These are machinists, programmers, and fusion engineers, not peaceforcers.

"If anyone in either room tries to fiddle with the door, the cameras will show it to security central. We'd just tell the fiddlers to knock it off or else. They're as aware of their predicament as we are. I doubt they'll try anything."

Bamaputra hesitated, then nodded. "This isn't my area of expertise. You know best."

"It's not my specialty either, but I wouldn't worry. They can't go to the bathroom without being seen. There's no camera in the Tran dorm but they wouldn't know how to break a magnetic seal even if they were told what it was." He pulled a fresh narcostick from his vest pocket and extended it toward the administrator. "Sure you won't try one of these: Helps you forget where you are."

"I prefer to know where I am." He sniffed disdainfully. "What is the point in distorting your perceptions when there is so much of interest to observe while they are functioning properly?"

Antal sat up. "Maybe mine aren't functioning right, then, because it beats the hell out of me how anyone could find anything of interest to observe on this spherical ice cube. All I'm interested in observing are my quarterly credit transfers. I've gotta check Number Three. Been having some overheating problems. Minor stuff, but I want to look into it. You know how temperamental those magnetic containment fields can be." He rose, started toward the exit.

"You going to stay here and stare at the steam?" he asked curiously.

Bamaputra had turned to face the windows. "For a while."

"Suit yourself." Antal left the administrator to his contemplation. What a weirdo. He'd long since given up trying to understand the smaller man. For a while, Antal thought he might even have been an extremely well-built, cleverly programmed robot. The theory was quickly disproven. He'd encountered a few pure humanoid machines and without exception every one of them was friendlier and warmer than Bamaputra. He was too distant, too cold to be a robot.

September lay on two bunks placed end to end and put his hands behind his head. "Well, young feller-me-lad, how do we get out of this?"

"I don't know," Ethan told him as he stared at the single door, "but they daren't kill us."

"Daren't say daren't. Anyone willing to sacrifice a few tens of thousands of intelligent locals to further a commercial end is more than capable of bumping off a few members of his own species."

"I don't doubt they'd do it in a minute if they thought they could get away with it, but they must know we'd be missed back at Brass Monkey."

"I'm sure they do or we'd probably be sucking ice by now. The longer we sit here and don't report back, the more curious Hwang's colleagues back at the outpost will become. So whatever this Bamaputra fellow decides, he's going to have to do it pretty quick. You're right about one thing, though. I don't think our imminent demise is one of their primary options. There's plenty to dislike about our captors, but they don't strike me as rash. I wouldn't be surprised to see them try to co-opt Hwang and her people."

"Surely not." Ethan was shocked by the suggestion.

"If you work on somebody long enough, it's been proven you can alter their attitudes no matter how dedicated they are. This Bamaputra's sharp. And he's a scientist himself. He can talk to folks like Blanchard and Semkin in their own language. He might eventually be able to convince some of our friends that what he's doing really is in the best interests of the Tran, his backers' ulterior motives notwithstanding."

"You know, that whole business still bothers me."

September turned to look at him. "How do you mean, feller-me-lad?"

"Well, I'm in the same sort of business. Trade, commerce, you know. There are other, less expensive ways to secure a trade monopoly than by changing around a whole world's climate."

A broad grin spread across the giant's face. "I was wondering when that would occur to you."

Ethan was startled. "You've been thinking along the same lines?"

"Have to be blind not to see it, lad. For instance, your company could simply apply for such a monopoly. Even though getting it's an outside shot, if you paid off the right people and demonstrated your good intentions to the rest, you just might get permission. At least you try."

While they mulled over the obvious, Hwang and her colleagues were engaged in animated discussion across the room. When it concluded, Williams and Cheela Hwang came over to join them. They brought confirmation of Ethan's suspicions, but not in the manner he'd hoped.

It was much worse than anything he'd thought of.

"We've been doing calculations."

"Isn't that what you always do?" September quipped.

She didn't even glance in his direction. Her expression was ashen. "We've been plodding through what we know and combining it with what we can extrapolate in the absence of actual raw data about the actual rate of melting of the ice sheet and the warming of the atmosphere in this region. We've had to guess as to how long this installation has been in operation. We do know, of course, that it can't be longer than the existence of Tran-ky-ky has been known. The chances of it having been discovered by these people prior to the first official Commonwealth survey are slim." She looked at the scientific calculator on her wrist, shoving back the sleeve of her survival suit to expose the small rectangular readout. It was filled with dancing figures.

"We're pretty sure of our results. I wish we weren't."

Milliken Williams looked stricken. "They show that this Bamaputra is being much too modest when he says they're going to change things on Tran-ky-ky over a period of time. The surface will indeed warm rapidly once the ice sheet begins to retreat. The trouble is that Tran physiology can't adjust nearly as fast. The climatological shift will occur much too quickly for our friends to adapt to it.

"Those who live close to the equator have a chance of surviving, with help and care. Those in the northern zones, from the temperate to the subarctic, will die of heatstroke long before they can reach the southern continent, despite anything short of massive intervention on the part of Commonwealth authorities. Even if such intervention is forthcoming, we don't see how a relief effort of that size can be mounted in time." He made a disgusted sound. "Politics."

"We're not talking thousands of deaths here," Hwang whispered. "We're talking millions. Genocide. Not mass extinction, but close. Those Tran who survive will do so as government wards, not as the progenitors of a new 'golden age.'"

All Ethan could do was gape at the two of them and say, "Why?"

"I'll tell you why," said Hwang evenly. "You recall what Bamaputra said about this Massul and Corfu being in charge of refugee relief efforts? This is going to simplify their work. Massul will be emperor of nothing."

September was nodding his head understandingly. "All adds up, don't it?" He looked at Ethan. "What happens, feller-me-lad, to a world that gets warmed right up real quick, too quick for the Tran to handle the change? What's the result down the line when the ice melts and the temperature starts staying above freezing day and night?"

"I don't follow you, Skua."

September tapped the side of his white-haired head with an index finger. "You gotta learn to think in global terms, lad. See, if it gets too hot for the Tran, it becomes real comfortable for humans. You end up with a nice, temperate, attractive, watery world where what's left of the native population is confined to a single land mass much larger than they need to support them. A native population so reduced and weak that it would be dependent for its very survival on the largess of the Commonwealth."

"Precisely," said Hwang. "This installation has been carefully concealed so that the change in the climate can be made to appear the result of natural causes. Giving the prevailing ignorance about this world that is still possible to do. The Commonwealth will be forced to step in to insure the survival of the Tran as a race. In the confusion many relief organizations will be establishing footholds here. Bamaputra's people will be the first of many and the best positioned to take advantage of the catastrophe."

"Maybe Bamaputra's fooling everyone under him.

Maybe they're not aware of what he's really doing here." Ethan knew it sounded naive but felt it had to be said.

Hwang shook her head. "The calculations are too simple, too obvious. People like this Antal aren't stupid. They must know what the end result of their operation here is going to be. It is possible that the lower echelon workers are being kept ignorant."

"Don't you see, young feller-me-lad? Bamaputra's backers aren't interested in commerce. They aren't interested in trade monopolies. They're interested in real estate. A world's worth. Colonies are allowed on uninhabited worlds and Class I worlds with the consent of the dominant race, but not on anything in between. Tran-ky-ky's real in between. Not that anyone would want to settle on Tran-ky-ky the way it is. But raise the temperature fifty degrees or so and melt the ice and this could be another New Riviera."

"For the Tran it would become a literal hell," said Williams. "For those who managed to survive, anyway. The racial remnants would eventually change into the Golden Saia state, but their numbers would be too reduced to object to an influx of settlers."

It was quiet for a long moment, each of them lost in their own private contemplation of a horror greater than any had previously encountered or ever expected to.

"Are you sure about the rate of warming and melting?" Ethan finally murmured.

"Even if we are off by a factor of ten or twenty percent," Hwang told him softly, "it still spells doom for the Tran as a developing race. They will never have the chance to build the advanced civilization Bamaputra talks about because they will not have the numbers to do it on their own. They will become wholly dependent on Commonwealth refugee agencies—or on this project's backers."

Williams smiled humorlessly. "I can see Bamaputra's

people displaying great concern for the survivors. It will be excellent public relations for them."

September nodded knowingly. "They've figured it down to the last weld. Right from the start—except for us. We shouldn't be here. At least we've managed to start 'em looking over their shoulders. Not surprised they're handling us so careful. They know any of us gets back to Brass Monkey and starts talking, the Commonwealth itself won't be big enough for them to hide in."

"Then they'd better start running," said Cheela Hwang softly, "because we're leaving."

"I'm willing. There's just one problem or two." Ethan nodded toward the exit. "We're stuck behind a metal door with magnetic locks on it, under constant video surveillance and imprisoned deep inside solid rock." As he finished, his objections were punctuated by the gentle whir of the spy-eye motor drive swiveling the camera across the floor.

Cheela Hwang reacted as though she hadn't heard a word he'd said. "Getting out of here is the easy part."

Ethan looked at September, who shrugged. "Say we manage a miracle and do make it back outside. Our troubles would only be beginning. How do we get from here back to Brass Monkey? You've seen the size of the guard Corfu's mounted on the *Slanderscree*—not so much because he's worried about us taking it back as to keep his fellow citizens from stealing it for themselves. Then there's the matter of the thirty or so mutineers still living on board."

"We'll manage."

"You got to hand it to her, young feller-me-lad," September said. "She's nothing if not confident."

"We'll do it because we have to." She indicated her companions, who were sitting nearby making loud, casual conversation to overload the aural pickup that was almost certainly observing the room along with the camera. "We thought of trying to steal one of the installation skimmers, but those are surely more heavily guarded than our ship. Once we get out, we must find a way to take back the *Slanderscree*."

September flexed his huge hands. "Once we're out we might be able to manage all sorts o' things. The problem is vacating this particular suite. You don't seem too worried about that."

"If there is one thing we still have it is a surfeit of brainpower." She smiled at him. "I have talked it over with Orvil and the others. The security system watching over us is very simple. This room must have been set aside to hold those employees who become abusive or drunk or break rules and regulations. It was not built to restrain hardened criminals or"—and her smile widened slightly—"dedicated, knowledgeable people who are compelled to find a way out. This is something which Bamaputra or his foreman may soon realize. If they plan to hold us here for any length of time, I'm sure they will begin arrangements to make this area more secure. All the more reason for us to leave as soon as possible."

"We've decided that it would be an advantage to move at night," Williams put in, "even though technically there's neither night nor day inside this place. From what we were able to observe on the way in we determined that this installation functions according to a typical twenty-four-hour day/night routine. Much of the equipment we passed is automatic. Probably everyone except designated nighttime supervisory personnel sleeps during the Tran night." He checked the chronometer built into the sleeve of his survival suit. "Everyone should try to rest some. We'll see about breaking out of here around midnight."

"Security won't sleep," Ethan pointed out.

"It won't matter because we'll be gone," Hwang told him.

"No, you don't understand." He nodded inconspicuously in the direction of the methodical, roving spy eye in the ceiling. "Whoever's watching that camera's monitor will raise the alarm immediately."

"Not if there's nothing to watch."

Ethan smiled. "You can't throw a blanket or something over the lens. That'll provoke just as quick a reaction as if we start hammering on the door. For the same reason you can't bust it. If the monitor at their security station goes blank they'll be down here in seconds to fix it."

"We're not going to do either of those things," Williams assured him. He looked at Hwang and the two of them shared some secret joke. "Whoever's watching the security monitors isn't going to see anything unusual all night. Meanwhile we'll be on our way out of here."

Ethan shook his head. "Then I confess I don't have the faintest idea what you have in mind."

"Good." Scientist and schoolteacher stood together. "That means they won't either."

"So what's our first step? What do we do now?"

Williams stretched elaborately. Next to him, Hwang yawned. "We go to sleep."

XI

One of the most difficult things to do is maintain the illusion of sleep when in fact you are so keyed up you can hardly lie still. That was what Ethan and everyone else in the room had to do for the rest of that day and on into the night. At the appointed time it was all he could do to remain silent with his eyes tightly closed.

Faint noises came from the cluster of bunks the scientists had grouped together. That would be Blanchard moving about. He and his companions had rehearsed all that afternoon, but even if it worked it was going to be close. The spy eye swept the room every thirty seconds. There would be no second chance. It had to work the first time.

A hand gently touched his shoulder and he slipped silently out from beneath the thin bedcovers. He could sense other shapes moving in the darkness. As time passed without armed guards appearing to check on the sudden rush of nocturnal activity their confidence grew.

They had been allowed to keep their survival suits and the harmless equipment the suits contained. Using their bodies to shield their efforts from the tireless spy eye, Blanchard and his freinds had cannibalized portions of that equipment. The result was a tiny, ultrashort range transmitting device.

They couldn't disable the spy eye because that would bring an immediate response from installation security. But Blanchard had devised a way to achieve the same result. Instead of recording what it saw every half minute, the transmitter he and his colleagues had constructed and trained on the spy eye jammed the recording circuitry. Instead of displaying a new recording every thirty seconds, the camera now continued to play back only what it had observed in the half-minute interval between twelve fifteen and twelve fifteen and a half A.M. All the spy eye had seen in that particular thirty seconds was a room full of sleeping people. It would run back that sequence over and over until either the deception was finally noticed or the recording began to deteriorate from repeated replaying.

By which time they hoped to be elsewhere.

Eventually it should occur to whoever was assigned to watch the monitors that no one in the dormitory prison had yawned, turned over, or so much as twitched in his sleep. They were gambling on the boredom inherent in such a job. It was much more likely that the monitor-watcher glanced only occasionally at his screens, and therefore unlikely he'd notice anything out of the ordinary for some time. With luck, their disappearance wouldn't be noticed until it was time for the morning meal to be delivered.

Compared to fooling the spy-eye system defeating the door lock was an easy matter. A single window was set in the door. By peering through it was possible to ascertain not only that there was no one immediately outside but also that the plant did indeed shut down during the nighttime hours. Only a few dim lights glowed in the corridor.

After everyone had quietly slipped outside, Blanchard removed the lock defeat he'd improvised and listened as it sealed itself shut once more. Anyone happening by who tried the door would find it locked tight. Should they also happen to glance through the window they would be able to see lumpy, motionless shapes lying on the dimly lit cots. Williams had supervised the artistic rearrangement of blankets and pillows to simulate sleeping human forms.

From Blanchard they shifted their reliance to Skua September, who as it turned out had the best memory of all for places and passageways. As they crept down corridors and stairs they remained fully alert, but no one appeared to confront them. Machinery hummed and fussed around them, masking the noise of their footsteps on the metal catwalks. Clearly the installation was attended by a minimal night crew.

"Down this way, I think," Williams whispered.

September shook his head in disagreement. In the poor light, his white hair served as a bobbing beacon for all to focus on. "Over here. After we left the Tran they took us up one more level." He started toward a stairwell, silent as a ghost.

In a few minutes they found themselves standing across from the oversize door that sealed the refrigerated storage room where their Tran compatriots were being held. Williams had to admit that he'd been wrong. September accepted the apology as his due.

This would be the trickiest part of their escape attempt, for naturally there was no thought of trying to flee without freeing Hunnar, Elfa, and the rest of their Tran friends.

"Can you see anything?" Ethan and the others looked on anxiously as Blanchard put his face to the window in the door and stared into the room beyond.

"Two dimples in the ceiling. They might be spy eyes, or they might be something else. Can't make out details."

"Sprinkler heads," Semkin suggested hopefully. "Why would anyone put spy-eye cameras in a freezer?"

"I don't know." Blanchard stepped back, rubbed at his eyes. "We'll just have to slip inside and hope that if they are cameras I'll have a chance to jam them before anyone wakes up." The abrupt stirring of the fifty or so Tran in the room would be bound to draw the immediate attention of even the sleepiest of security personnel watching the monitors.

They waited while the geophysicist used his homemade device to interrupt the magnetic flow which kept the door sealed. In the darkness the faint clicks sounded preternaturally loud. September wrapped one huge fist around the oversize handle, nodded at Blanchard, then slowly eased the door aside.

Several Tran stirred. One sat up and stared in the darkness but said nothing. Blanchard hurriedly moved to aim the jamming unit at one of the dark spots in the ceiling, relaxed with a sigh. Sprinkler heads. No reason, just as Semkin had said, to put security cameras in what was essentially an enlarged refrigerator. Ethan didn't doubt such devices would eventually be installed to keep an eye on the Tran as well as the humans. For now it wasn't an immediate concern of Bamaputra's or Antal's. Besides, a primitive native couldn't defeat a magnetic lock. The cold room was perfectly secure.

As secure as the dormitory.

They spread out and began waking the Tran, admonishing them to silence. Dark furry shapes began to rise and gather. Faint light shone eerily through raised dan, giving their native companions the appearance of enormous bats. Within minutes the entire group had been awakened. Hugs and greetings were postponed until they could be exchanged under more amenable circumstances. They still had to get out of the installation.

The corridor was empty as a newly dug grave and they began filing out of the room. The mere movement of so many bodies produced a certain amount of sound, enough to rise above the soft muttering of machinery. Still, by itself the noise wouldn't be enough to raise an alarm. Some-

one had to hear it first. Blanchard resealed the chamber
door while Ethan and the others discussed their plans with
the newly liberated Tran.

"We've got to try and retake the ship."

Hunnar nodded, that odd little down and sideways
movement of the head that Ethan knew as well as any
human gesture. "It will be good to fight."

"Even if we should fail," whispered Monslawic, Ta-
hoding's first mate, "better to die fighting than rotting
away in a cage."

September clapped the Tran on a furry shoulder. "We
ain't going to fail. Not after having made it this far."

They followed the giant as he struggled to retrace the
path they'd taken when they'd been marched inside the
installation. There was no way to muffle the clatter of
clawlike chiv on metal, which sounded like an army of
dog-sized insects. A single night tech left his dials and
gauges to find out what was making the strange noise. He
found out. His eyes widened as half a dozen of the
Slanderscree's sailors jumped him. They would have cut
his throat save for the intervention of the humans. Ethan
pointed out that the unlucky man wasn't responsible for the
installation or its raison d'être. It required all their powers
of persuasion to dissuade the Tran, who were eager and
anxious for someone to kill. In the end they settled for
gifting the technician with a mild concussion.

Cheela Hwang and her companions descended on the
man's equipment belt and pockets like so many scientific
scavengers, appropriating everything that might prove useful later.

No one guarded the entrance to the installation. It would
have been a waste of manpower. The human inhabitants
rarely went outside and unauthorized Tran were never admitted. Nevertheless, Blanchard and Moware wasted what
Ethan and September thought were precious minutes

double-checking possible alarm relays. The Tran milled aimlessly behind the humans, fancying they could already smell the frigid freedom that lay on the other side of the heavy barrier.

The geophysicist, Hwang, and Semkin worked with the door mechanism for several minutes. Then they all stepped back. Blanchard made a connection, a motor sprang to life, and the door swung up and back quietly. Everyone held their breath, but no sirens screamed behind them, no horns shattered the night silence. On the barren slope outside the ceaseless wind moaned invitingly.

There was no holding back the Tran. Sailors and soldiers poured through the opening and gathered on the cleared, flat area that had been sliced from the granite. They sucked in the fresh cold air, spread their dan, and danced pirouettes on the frozen places out of sheer exhilaration.

Off to their left lay the path that led down toward sleeping Yingyapin. Tran-ky-ky's multiple moons illuminated the switchbacks, a dark ribbon drizzled among lighter rock. A few lights burned late in the would-be capital of all Tran-ky-ky.

Ethan started down as Blanchard closed the door behind them. A clawed hand held him back and he turned to see Hunnar Redbeard's cat's eyes glowing down at him. The knight smiled with satisfaction.

"There is a quicker way, my friend." He turned, exposing his broad back. "Climb on. Put your legs around my waist, just below where the dan is attached."

"I don't . . ."

"Do not argue. In that place we rely on your wisdom. Out in the real world you must listen to us. See." He pointed and Ethan could see Hwang and the other scientists crawling onto the backs of strong sailors.

As the door closed, Blanchard came rolling out beneath

it, just clearing the descending lip of the barrier. He rose panting, the visor of his suit temporarily fogged. His tone was exultant.

"I haven't done anything like this since I was at university. Rather like a complex game." He turned to face the doorway, a part of the hillside once more. "The thirty-second repeat is still fooling them."

"Let's hope it continues doing so." Ethan climbed onto Hunnar's back and wrapped his fingers around the straps that held the two pieces of the hessavar-hide vest together. He locked his legs around the knight's waist. "What now?"

"This now."

Hunnar trudged to the edge of what to Ethan looked like a sheer drop. Closer inspection revealed that the slope wasn't *quite* vertical. He'd never been very fond of heights. Water had been dumped here to create a smooth ribbon of ice down the embankment. In the moonlight it gleamed like a frozen waterfall.

He started to say, "You can't . . . !" as Hunnar pushed off into emptiness.

They were falling. Wind roared around his visor. The knight spread his powerful arms, opening his membranous dan to their maximum extent—not to catch the wind this time but to brake their descent. To Ethan it didn't feel like they were slowing down at all. His fingers dug into the hessavar straps while his heart commenced a rapid migration up into the vicinity of his throat.

This was how the local Tran, Corfu, and his ilk, returned from the installation back to Yingyapin. Not for them hours wasted trudging down the switchbacks. It was like descending a ski jump except there was no upcurving jump ramp waiting at the bottom. Only solid rock and what looked like far too small an area in which to stop.

Daring to open his eyes, he saw the rest of the Tran screaming down the ice flow. Some carried his fellow humans. One husky sailor balanced Skua September on his back. As Ethan stared, Skua saw him and waved wildly in his direction. His large friend was apparently enjoying the near-suicidal descent immensely.

Miraculously they arrived at the bottom of the drop intact. Trembling, Ethan slid down off Hunnar's back and struggled to regulate his breathing and heart rate. As he did so he tilted his head back and stared up at the ledge which marked the entrance they'd just fled. It showed as a thin line against the lighter stone impossibly far above. September strode over to him, his eyes shining, and clapped him on the back.

"Was that a ride or weren't it, young feller-me-lad?"

"I could have lived without the experience." Ethan was still gulping air via his visor membrane. Much as he wanted to, there was no thought of pushing back his hood or visor, not during the coldest time of night.

If their captors had thought ahead, they would have appropriated the research team's suits, exchanging them for normal coveralls or similar attire. That would have precluded any possibility of escape more effectively than the strongest locks or thickest doors. Antal hadn't bothered. Why worry? The prisoners were secured in a locked room under constant video surveillance. They couldn't possibly flee.

The breathtaking descent had deposited the escapees on a rocky ledge just outside the city. While the humans recovered from the precipitous drop, the Tran were conferencing. Hunnar, Elfa, Grurwelk, and Ta-hoding rejoined them moments later.

"We think it safer to avoid the city. Though none should be about this time of night, you can never tell when you might encounter a watch. The harbor is ringed with easy icepaths. The farther we stay from inhabited areas the better. It will take a little more time." Hunnar traced a course over rock and ice in the moonlight. Across the harbor, her sails reefed and still tied to the dock where they'd arrived, the *Slanderscree* waited like a sleeping princess in a dream.

"We will go around there, and there, and then cross the harbor."

September studied the proposed route thoughtfully. "We'll be mighty exposed out there on the ice. No cover."

"Corfu's guards will be huddled around a fire or one of your magical heaters on the city side. They have no reason to believe us anything but tightly imprisoned inside the mountain. As for the traitors on the *Slanderscree*, if their consciences trouble them as they should, they will not rest as easy, but neither would they bother to mount guard over a vessel already under guard. By approaching the ship from the harbor side we will avoid the gaze of any who may be awake."

"I don't see that we have any other choice," Ethan ventured. "Besides, the faster we move the better our chances. Speed's stood us in good stead so far."

Hunnar grinned at him. "Ready then, friend Ethan, for another ride?"

"So long as it's not vertical."

They moved out, Tran in the lead, humans in the middle, more Tran under First Mate Monslawic's command bringing up the rear. The Tran traveled on the icepath that paralleled the coastline while the humans had to make their way across the bare rock nearby. From time to time they had to slow and detour around an isolated shack or stone hut, but no lights burned in these habitations. If any held occupants, they slept on unaware of the desperate column that marched so carefully around them.

Any fighting to be done would be left to the Tran. While the human's survival suit material was tough and durable it was not designed to serve as armor. It was intended to keep heat or air conditioning in, not sword points out. A stab or slice at the right angle and with enough force could penetrate the inner lining and render a suit useless. If they were to escape, they would need the suits functional.

Elfa insisted they were worrying needlessly. There was no reason to mount a guard on the harborside of the ice-rigger. They would approach undetected.

Then it was time for Ethan to mount Hunnar's back again and a moment later the entire party was moving out onto the ice. Hunnar lifted his arms, letting his outstretched dan catch the wind. Ethan could feel them picking up speed, accelerating steadily, until they were chivaning silently across the harbor. The layer of melt water which covered the surface slowed them somewhat and Ethan readied himself for a fall or two, but the Tran adapted to the presence of the water well and had no difficulty in maintaining their balance.

Hunnar's guess proved correct. As they neared the great icerigger even the most myopic among them could see that the railings and masthead lookout bins were unoccupied. Ship slept as soundly as city.

Jacalan and his companions kept throwing nervous glances in the direction of the buried installation they'd just fled, only to be reassured by the continued absence of flashing lights or blaring alarms. Their departure had yet to be detected, and it would be hours before anyone needed to check the dormitory in person. If all went well aboard the icerigger, by breakfast time they would have left the harbor behind and would be flying across open ice. The more kilometers they could put between themselves and Yingya-pin before their escape was discovered, the better their chances of outdistancing one of the short-range skimmers.

Hunnar turned and let Ethan slide down. It was hard to walk on the ice in survival suit boots but not impossible. The layer of water didn't make things any easier. They had to move more cautiously than usual. The sound of so many feet sloshing about seemed deafeningly loud to Ethan.

Half the loyal Tran began to climb the boarding ladders cut into the ship's side while the rest chivaned beneath the hull. They would board from the starboard side. A third group led by Skua September headed for the dock. They would silence any guards ashore and then give a signal, whereupon the final attack on the icerigger would begin.

Unfortunately, Corfu's minions were neither as lazy nor sleepy as everyone hoped. Instead of continued silence, the night air was broken by a hoarse scream. Ethan tensed at the faint, unmistakably whispery hiss of a beamer being fired. Hunnar muttered something incomprehensible in Tran and started up the boarding ladder nearby. No point in holding back now. Staring into the darkness Ethan could see the soldiers and sailors of the Slanderscree climbing frantically and knew that on the starboard side of the ship others would be doing likewise. They outnumbered the mutineers, but that was no guarantee of success. They had no way of knowing how many guards Corfu had put aboard the ship itself or what type of armament they carried.

He found himself scrambling up the roughhewn steps, up over the railing and out onto the moonlit deck. Muffled sounds filtered up from below where what fighting there was was taking place. He immediately rushed to the far rail and stared toward the city. Shouts and yells came from the small building at the far end of the dock where the guards had barricaded themselves. The occasional flash of a beamer was shockingly bright against the night. Lights were already appearing in other buildings as those awakened by the noise fumbled for their lamps. Anxiously he glanced up and back toward the mountain that dominated the far side of the harbor, but there was still nothing to indicate that the alarm had been carried to their captors.

Dissension and fighting were as natural to the Tran as

eating and sleeping. With luck anyone observing the goings-on in the city would put it down to normal internecine argument. It couldn't have anything to do with the recently acquired prisoners. After all, didn't the security monitor continue to show the captured visitors from Brass Monkey sleeping soundly in their beds?

No, there was no reason to believe the nocturnal ruckus was due to anything out of the ordinary. Even if word eventually reached Massul fel-Stuovic or Corfu it would take time to raise the alarm up at the underground installation. Unless Bamaputra's allies had the use of a communicator. Even if they did, it would take a while to wake someone like Antal who had the power to make decisions.

His attention was drawn to an alien shape emerging from belowdecks nearby. Moonlight glanced off a sword wet with blood. Seeing the look on his face, Elfa hastened over to reassure him.

"Little enough killing there has been. We surprised them in their hammocks. The traitors Kilpit and Mousokka were in Ta-hoding's cabin. Among those who remained true there was some sentiment for butchering them all, but Hunnar, sweet-tongued devil that he is, insisted that those who rebelled had been swayed as much by the difficulties of the long journey as by this merchant Corfu's offer and that they might be reinstated as crew once again. Until we can be sure of them each will be watched over by one whose fealty is not in doubt. Those who offered no resistance and have expressed remorse will be given this opportunity. Myself, I think my mate too compassionate, but we need every hand we can get." She gestured toward the mainmast, where sailors were braving the frigid wind as they fought to set sail.

Others wrestled to bring in the ice anchors while Ta-hoding supervised the hasty splicing of the severed steering cables. Ethan ran to watch. September joined them a moment later, breathing hard.

"You didn't surprise them," Ethan said accusingly.

."Sometimes your target ain't as cooperative as you'd like. That's the real world for you, feller-me-lad." Behind the survival suit's visor his eyes shone like tiny echoes of Tran-ky-ky's moons. "We were lucky to do as well as we did. The bastards had beamers.

"One of 'em was off in a bathroom and got away before we could run him to ground. He's the one who saw us coming and raised the alarm. The rest of 'em divided into two groups. We took the first bunch easy enough but the others stood their ground well. I'm still not sure we got them all. But we did get these. Here." He tossed something small and silvery to Ethan. A beamer. Ethan clutched the illegal weapon gratefully.

"Older model." September grinned. "Bamaputra doesn't trust his Tran allies all *that* much, it seems. Not that it ain't an efficient killer." He displayed his own captured handgun. "Both of 'em about half-charged. Use it only as a last resort."

Ethan nodded briskly and clipped the gun to his belt. He was no soldier, but he'd done plenty of fighting this past year and the beamer was simple enough for a child to use. Or a primitive alien unfamiliar with advanced technology. You pointed it at a target and pulled the trigger as often as necessary until the charge ran out. He could be at least as accurate as any of Corfu's Tran.

The icerigger lurched, nearly throwing his feet out from under him. Ta-hoding turned away from the stern and moved to take the wheel.

"What do you think, Captain?" September asked him.

Ta-hoding hardly had time to reply. He was testing the wheel, supervising the storing of the ice anchors, and trying to set sail in an effective pattern. Shouts continued to come from over the stern, were relayed to him by another sailor straddling the aft rail.

"The steering will hold for a while, friend Skua, but not in a strong wind or at high speed. We'll push it for all its worth and when it snaps again we'll have to stop and re-splice it, but not a moment before."

"You'll get no argument on that from me." Then his eyes widened and he let out a warning bellow.

His beamer seemed to go off in Ethan's face, leaving spots dancing before his retinas. When he turned it was to see a Yingyapin soldier falling away from the rail, his face fried, skin and fur burning where the beamer had struck. As Ethan picked himself off the deck September stomped over to the rail and peered over the side, making satisfied noises.

"You enjoy killing, don't you, Skua?" He brushed at his survival suit.

The giant turned on him. "No, young feller-me-lad, you've got it all wrong. I don't enjoy killing at all. What I do delight in is confounding my enemies. That's always been part of my makeup and always will be."

The icerigger groaned and Ethan stumbled again. Several of the mainsails had been let out and now a pair of foresails filled with wind. Ta-hoding handled the wheel as delicately as a lady's ankle bracelet, making full use of the ship's adjustable spars as he edged it away from the dock. The first glow of morning was kissing the top of the main-mast with molten gold.

They were on their way.

It seemed to Ethan that every plank, every nail and bolt creaked and groaned as the captain guided his vessel out onto the ice. Ta-hoding was trying to steer the ship with wind and spars in order to spare the crudely spliced steer-ing cables as much strain as possible. September beckoned to Ethan to join him at the railing.

A small armed mob was gathering on the dock. There were no beamers in evidence. The arrows and spears they hurled at the retreating ship fell well short as Ta-hoding brought the icerigger's bow around, aiming for the harbor entrance.

A few of Massul's troops chivaned out onto the ice, more for show than anything else. They posed no real threat to the *Slanderscree*. They would make a rush, toss a spear or small axe, then fold their dan against their sides and wheel sharply to right or left to keep out of range of those on the icerigger. One bowman ventured too close and caught a couple of crossbow bolts for his trouble. That put an end to any incipient thoughts of pursuit on the part of their former guards.

They were beginning to move toward the open sea and still there was no sign of reaction from up on the mountainside. Ethan wondered how Massul would react to a thorough explanation of what Bamaputra and his people were up to. Would he believe that his patron humans intended not to help him so much as to cause the deaths of thousands of his own kind so they could then steal his world? That he would be an emperor in name only, lording it over a few sad remnants of a once proud and independent race?

And what of Corfu? What good would it be to possess a trade monopoly when most of your potential customers were dead?

Not that it mattered. Even if they could convince both Tran of the truth, Bamaputra would simply dump them in favor of more cooperative substitutes. There are always those among any race to whom promises are more important than truth. In any event he doubted he'd be given the chance to try.

Ta-hoding was spinning the wheel, heedless now of the potential strain on the spliced cables and shouting at his sailors to back sail. Ethan frowned. Back sail was the last order he expected the captain to be giving. He rushed toward the bow, September leaping from the quarterdeck to join him and landing so hard Ethan thought his huge friend would crash through to the living quarters beneath. The tough wood held.

Then they were standing side by side looking over the bow as the *Slanderscree*, which had just been starting to accelerate, slowed to a halt.

Shining in the rising sun and blocking the entire mouth of the harbor was a metal barrier composed of giant X-shapes made from construction beams. These were attached to a long thick metal tube like so many crosses strung on a post. Each X rested on a pair of metal skates not unlike those which supported the icerigger. The entire massive gate was hinged to a point of land just west of the city. Steady light shining behind windows of real glass hinted at an independent power supply. Even at a distance Ethan could see masses of armed Tran gathering on the rocky peninsula to protect the gate station.

The barrier completely closed off the harbor from the open sea beyond. Even if they could somehow cut the power to the tiny engines that moved the gate that didn't mean they could move it. Not if the hinge had been locked in place. The tops of the X's were four meters above the ice, the connecting metal tube or bar half that. No flimsy construct this, it looked solid and immovable. They were trapped.

A glance back toward Yingyapin revealed groups of Tran moving back and forth like clusters of ants. Probably someone was talking to installation security on a communicator right now. It might even be that Antal's security personnel had moved this harbor barrier into position by remote control. If that was the case, it explained the lack of reaction from above. There was no hurry. The escapees weren't going anywhere. Plenty of time to break out the skimmer with its laser cannon and escort the would-be refugees back to their cells. And Ethan knew they wouldn't be given a second chance to pull the recycle-the-monitor-view trick.

Meanwhile the *Slanderscree* rested on ice topped with three centimeters of water as those on board frantically tried to decide what to do next.

"Can we hold the ship?" Suaxus-dal-Jagger wondered aloud.

"Not against heavy energy weapons," Ethan told him.

"Suppose," Budjir said, "we threatened to burn it? That would not matter to the skypeople here, but this Corfu covets the *Slanderscree* desperately. He would at least argue with them that since we cannot flee they can wait and starve us out."

"Now that's a thought," September murmured. "Bamaputra's not the type to waste anything. And keep in mind he wants Hwang and her buddies alive in case any curious types from the outpost come calling to see what's happened to them. I think you're right, Budjir. I think they'll hold off any shooting. They can see we're stuck here, so why not just wait us out? Better for him if we give up quiet-like. Except we ain't giving up just yet. We're leaving."

Ethan eyed him sideways. "You just finished saying that we're stuck here."

"The *Slanderscree*'s stuck. We're not."

"Don't get me wrong, Skua. I don't want to go back up there anymore than you do." He jabbed a thumb in the direction of the mountain and its underground complex. "But at the same time I don't think we can make it back to Brass Monkey on foot."

"I'm not much on sliding myself, lad. That's why we're going to take one of the lifeboats."

"Are you seriously considering attempting a return to

your outpost in one of those tiny craft?" Hunnar asked him in disbelief.

"Not to Brass Monkey, no. But if we can make it to the southern shipping lanes near Poyolavomaar, we can hail a trader and buy ourselves passage the rest of the way. If we can make it that far, the young Landgrave will give us a decent ship and the crew to sail her back to the outpost."

"I am coming as well," Ta-hoding told them.

"Someone who can give orders has to stay with the ship," Ethan argued.

"Monslawic can handle command. Already he has proven that. Without me you will not have a chance."

"I'd argue you on that," September told him, "but fight it I won't. Be good to have you at the helm, Captain. I think we should take that Seesfar gal, too. She knows the territory between here and Poyo better than any of us."

"I would rather leave her behind," Hunnar growled.

"I ain't especially fond of her myself, but when you're trying to save your neck and the necks of your friends, personal likes and dislikes kind of recede into the background. You don't have to marry her, just sail with her. Now what about a representative from our scientific contingent?"

"Ought to be Milliken." Ethan looked down on the deck. Williams was deep in animated conversation with Cheela Hwang and Snyek, the glaciologist. "He knows what it's like out on the ice. The others don't."

Hwang and her colleagues agreed that the teacher was the best qualified of their number to make the journey. This Ethan expected. They were nothing if not sensible. What he did not expect was the ferocity with which Hwang kissed the teacher farewell. That was neither expected nor sensible. Amazing what a little casual conversation could accomplish between intelligent people, he mused.

"Six then," said Hunnar as they watched the crew unlatch one of the icerigger's two lifeboats. "Three Tran, three human."

"Go, husband," Elfa murmured softly. "Ride the wind back to me. I will be here waiting for you when you return." Sailors swung the small craft over the side, manipulating ropes and pulleys.

"Till the next evening." Hunnar put out his right paw, palm upward, and they locked fingers, then parted. September was already over the side, catching and stowing sacks of supplies. Williams followed, then Grurwelk Seesfar, Hunnar, Ethan, and lastly Ta-hoding, puffing hard and trying not to show it.

With only six of them aboard they had ample room to move about. It was a much smaller version of the *Slandnerscree*, equipped with four runners instead of five, a steering handle instead of a wheel, and a single folding mast. The raised central cabin provided the only shelter from the ceaseless wind. As they settled in and found places, sailors began to push the little iceboat toward the metal barrier. The central cabin barely passed between two of the welded-beam X-shapes and beneath the connecting bar.

Then they were on the other side, past the barrier. Ta-hoding, Hunnar, and September fought to raise the mast and lock it into position just forward of the cabin. The single sail was set and secured to the tip of the boom. As wind filled the woven pika-pina the metal gate, the mountains, and Yingyapin harbor began to recede behind them. The icerigger's bulk was clearly visible, imprisoned on the other side of the barrier. No one cheered their escape, no lookouts waved enthusiastically from their posts atop the masts. If they were lucky, they would slip away without being noticed by those on shore, whose attention should be concentrated on the much larger ice ship.

As they began to emerge from the shelter of the harbor

the sail bulged with west wind and they picked up speed. Freezing water splashed up and back from beneath the bow runner, splattering everyone aboard. Icicles began to form on the boom, the rails, and the roof of the cabin. Water was something no ship on Tran-ky-ky was designed to contend with.

Utilizing a spare sail from the lifeboat's storage locker, they were able to rig a crude screen between bow and mast. It slowed them slightly but kept the water off. Williams had been staring intently astern ever since they'd left.

"No skimmers. That means Bamaputra and his people don't know we've left. They might not miss us for quite a while."

"Don't count on it," said September, scraping ice crystals from the rim of his visor. "The first thing Antal will do is order a head count. They might not miss the lifeboat but they'll sure as hell miss us. I'm sure your lady friend will stall them as long as possible."

"Yes, Cheela ought to—" Williams halted in mid-sentence and eyed him sharply. "Lady friend? What makes you say that, Skua?"

"Why, nothing, nothing at all, Milliken. Except she pretty near had you right there on the deck by way of saying good-bye."

Fortunately for the easily embarrassed teacher, his skin was much too dark to show a blush.

XII

Tran-ky-ky's frozen ocean surrounded them, the rim of the southern continent was rapidly falling astern, and still there was no sign of the expected pursuit. Ethan was beginning to believe they'd pulled it off.

September stood on Ta-hoding's right, shielding his visor with one hand while peering into the rising sun. "Let's turn east for a bit, Captain."

"East? But Poyolavomaar lies north by northwest." The wind ruffled his dense fur. Like Hunnar and Grurwelk he appeared oblivious to the cold.

"That's the way they'll expect us to go. Better we waste a few days by sailing east before turning north. Once we're sure we're in the clear we can make a gradual swing back toward Poyo. Keep in mind that those sky boats' range is limited by the amount of fuel they can carry. The more they waste searching for us where we ain't, the less likely they are to find us. We sure as hell ain't going to outrun them. Not in this stuff." He gestured over the side.

It seemed to Ethan that the layer of water atop the ice sheet had deepened by half a centimeter just while they'd been imprisoned. That was impossible, of course. Such an increase would require months of heating. But it was hard to escape the feeling that at any moment their little craft might become a boat instead of an ice ship.

By midday the familiar cliffs which marked the limits of the continental plateau had replaced the unusual gentler slopes which embraced the harbor they'd left behind. The sun was bright and piercing, the air still warm to the three Tran, though not warm enough for the trio of humans to consider doffing their survival suits. At least they were able to flip back their hoods and visors. It was worth a little cold to be able to breathe Tran-ky-ky's pure, unpolluted air directly.

With your hood back you could also hear better, so everyone heard the low, buzzing whine at about the same time. It was loud enough to rise above the whistle the wind made as it passed through the little craft's rigging. September hurried to the stern where he raged at ice and a mocking fate.

"How did they find us? How?" He clutched the stolen beamer in one huge fist even though he knew it wouldn't be of much use against a heavily armed skimmer. Ethan gripped the other pistol.

"I'm not sure this time they'll give us the chance to ask questions." He gestured with the weapon. "Maybe they'll move in close to check on us and we can pick them off."

"Maybe." September's tone clearly indicated what he thought of their chances. "Depends who's on board; humans, Tran, or a mix."

Grurwelk had moved to stand alongside them. Now she pointed. "There it is."

Several minutes passed before the air-repulsion vehicle had come close enough for the less farsighted humans to pick out the silvery silhouette. It flew swiftly over the flat surface, keeping three meters above the ice.

"Good tracking equipment." September was muttering unhappily. "I was counting on them not having any portable stuff. Obviously I was wrong. Or maybe they just guessed lucky."

"Maybe it's our turn." Ethan slipped his beamer out of sight. "They probably know we took these but they don't know for sure that we have them here. It's possible they think they're back on board the *Slanderscree*."

September hesitated, then shoved his own weapon into a pocket in the pants of his survival suit. "Possible. Not likely, but possible. We'll find out soon enough." His eyes watered as he stared into the wind. "What about the heavy artillery?"

"I fear the weapon you refer to is indeed mounted on this sky boat." Hunnar's query was more hopeful than sanguine as he nodded toward the now concealed pistols. "Can you reach them with those smaller light weapons?"

"Not if they chose to stay out of range," September told him. "Better be ready to abandon ship if they start shooting. A heavy energy weapon'll make splinters of this boat. The air in the wood will explode and the rest'll burn."

"Abandon ship?" Ta-hoding clung to the steering mechanism and uneasily peered over the side at the layer of cold water their stone runners were cutting through. "What if we fall through the ice to the center of the world?"

"Don't worry about that," Ethan told him grimly. "You'd freeze before you could drown." The notion of swimming was as alien to the Tran as the idea of traveling through the vacuum of space. Not that anyone could stay alive for long in the frigid liquid. It was only six centimeters deep here. Be hard to drown in that. The captain's fears set him to wondering just how thick the ice sheet was this close to the continent. He knew it was thinner than elsewhere.

"Slowing up." September blinked tears from his eyes. "Damn. They must suspect we've got the pistols."

"Can you make out how many there are?"

"Two Tran for certain," said Hunnar evenly. "At least two of your kind. One steering and another seated behind the big light weapon."

"Taking no chances," September rumbled. "So what are they waiting for? Why don't they finish us?"

"Maybe they're having trouble with the gun," Ethan said hopefully. "Plenty of battles have been decided by weapons that didn't work properly at the critical moment."

"Taking a head count, more likely."

The delay did not last long, nor was there anything wrong with the laser cannon. An intense burst of amplified energy momentarily flared brighter than the sun as the weapon fired. It struck not the lifeboat but the ice in front and around.

Runners slid over nothing and the craft slewed sideways, the mast collapsing on top of them, as the ice gave way under the intense heat. They lurched wildly to port. Hunnar inhaled sharply and clutched at the steering column. Grurwelk cursed as she rolled over Ethan while Tahoding intoned a hurried prayer.

They did not sink. The ice sheet had been shattered all around them but it didn't melt completely. The lifeboat was partially supported by a large floe that remained beneath the starboard runner. As they listed to port water began to trickle in through the closely set decking. It pooled up around Ethan's feet as he struggled erect. The survival suit kept it from his skin.

"What the hell are they doing?" Even as he finished asking the question another bolt from the cannon blasted the ice off to their right. September had ducked below the railing. Now he raised his head to peer back at their assailants.

"Game time," he muttered tightly. Another flare melted more ice in front of them. "They're going to pin us in open water and wait till we sink."

"What happens if we don't?"

"I'm sure they'll find a way to accelerate the process. Blow away the stern or something."

Ethan pulled out his beamer. "We've got to take a shot at them. We can't just sit here!"

September put a restraining hand on his shoulder. "Maybe that's what they're trying to do, find out if we've got the pistols or if they're back on the good old *Slanderscree*. Save the charge. They're still out of range. If we don't fire, maybe they'll figure we don't have them and move a little nearer." He licked his lips. "They're pretty close now. Come on, boys, we're just as helpless as can be down here. Come on in and have a nice close look."

By this time they were drifting in the middle of a patch of open water the size of a small lake. Wavelets rocked the lifeboat, which refused to sink. Williams found a couple of pots in the central cabin and soon he and Ta-hoding were bailing like mad. No doubt those on the skimmer found this essentially futile activity very amusing.

Then all of them were thrown backward as the water heaved beneath them.

It must have been a fish. Ethan didn't know what else to call it because he didn't get a very good look at it. Williams had a better view and thought it surely the biggest *Holothuroidea* in existence. It had a mottled, leathery skin from which tentaclelike purple and red eruptions projected and it slurped down the hovering skimmer as easily as a trout would take a fly. It hung frozen against the sky, a streak of color shattering the pure blue, the aft section of the skimmer dangling from horny lips. As it slid back beneath the surface the two Tran seated in the rear of the craft jumped clear.

The wave created by its descent split more of the ice and rocked the floating lifeboat wildly. Only once before had Ethan and his companions encountered one of the monstrous lifeforms that lived beneath the ice in the dark depths of Tran-ky-ky's still liquid oceans. Undoubtedly the apparition which had inadvertently if momentarily saved them also had a warm-weather state, just as did the Tran and every other inhabitant of this frozen world. Perhaps in that state it had eyes. Ethan had seen none. In the cold lightless depths other senses came to the fore. Probably the swimming leviathan had sensed the skimmer's motion.

What would it make of the drifting lifeboat?

He forced himself to stay calm. In shape and movement their craft was little different from the ice floes drifting all around it. He climbed to his knees and peered over the side, his legs immersed in icy water. There was no sign of the skimmer. One minute it had been hanging in the clear air, tormenting them. Now it was gone, along with its advanced weaponry, communications equipment, and crew.

Well, not all its crew. As Ethan stared, one of the two Tran who had jumped clear at the last instant vanished beneath the roiling surface. The other clung to a small ice floe and somehow managed to pull himself out of the water. He lay there, breathing hard and soaking wet and terrified, staring at the ice corpse surrounding him. Ethan wondered how long he'd last. The Tran could tolerate extreme cold, but dampness was something their systems were not accustomed to.

Ta-hoding clung to the steering oar. "It will come for us next. We are finished, doomed."

"We're still afloat," September snapped, "and keep your voice down. That thing may have ears as big as its mouth."

So they waited, bobbing in the slush and water, expecting at any moment to be engulfed from below. They were not. Not in five minutes, not in ten. Half an hour later they were still drifting aimlessly.

September rose and whispered. "Anybody else see any eyes?" A soft chorus of nos greeted his query. "Then it doesn't see, or if it does, not well. Probably relies on high-pitched sound, or the pressure produced by other creatures moving through the water, or just movement. Maybe the vibrations the skimmer's engine generated brought it up. Maybe it doesn't even know we're here."

"It might be kilometers away by now," Williams suggested hopefully.

"Yeah, and it might be able to get back here real quick-like. So let's keep it quiet and slow."

"A legend," Hunnar muttered. "A creature from hell itself." He peered cautiously over the side, unable to see more than a meter into the dark water. "Something from the depths of memory. I hope it stays there. If that is the sort of creature we will have to deal with when our world warms and the ice melts, then I hope the seas stay frozen forever."

"What are we to do now?" Ta-hoding wondered. "Why do we not sink to the middle of the world?"

"We float." Hunnar had trouble with the little-used word. "The way a small pouch of *chiaf* floats in a cup of soup." He was studying their surroundings intently. "Somehow we must get back out onto the ice."

"What about that one?" Williams pointed to the exhausted sole survivor of the skimmer, lying on his ice floe.

"What about him?" Hunnar sneered. "Let him freeze; let him starve. He is already dead." He turned away, heading toward the bow. Grurwelk lingered in the stern, staring.

"We could paddle," Ethan suggested, "except we don't have anything to paddle with."

"And we don't want to make any vibrations in the water," September reminded him. He started hunting through the storage lockers until he found what he wanted. As they looked on he secured one end of the pika-pina cable to a serpentine hook in the bow. At first Ethan thought he was fooling with the ice anchor, but the anchor remained in its holder nearby.

"What do you have in mind, Skua?"

September grinned at him. "Been more than a year since I've been able to go for a swim. Expect I still remember how."

Ethan eyed him in disbelief. "You get in that water you'll freeze. A survival suit's not a spacesuit. It's designed to operate in air. Besides, you don't know what's swimming around down there."

"Reckon we're fixing to find out. One thing's for sure: We can't just sit here. In a little while this wood's going to get waterlogged. Then we'll all be swimming." He wrapped the loose end of the rope around his waist, then pointed to the left of the bow.

"There's a lot of big chunks over that way. If I can get some traction I can make it to the ice sheet, then try to pull the boat over. With all of us pulling on the cable we might be able to haul this thing out of the water. Remember, there's no hull. It's just a raft with runners and a mast. Not nearly as heavy as a regular boat." Slipping one leg over the side, he put a foot into the water.

"Your suit system's going to be overwhelmed," Williams was telling him. "The water will press it flat against your body. You'll lose the insulating layer of air. There'll be nothing between you and the material for it to heat. And if you get any water down your neck . . ."

He didn't need to finish the sentence. If the ice water got inside the suit, it would ruin the material's ability to distinguish inside from out. The confused thermosensors would interpret the water temperature as body temperature and adjust accordingly. Heating would effectively cease, and in the water beneath the lifeboat an unprotected human body would perish of hypothermia in a few minutes.

"Don't worry, young feller-me-lad. I've always been

pretty good about keeping my head above water." He
dropped the other leg over the side and slipped into the sea,
still holding onto the rail. Now he was submerged up
to his chest.

"How is it?" Ethan asked anxiously.

September smiled back up at him but you could see it
was forced. "Afraid it's starting to get a mite cool. We'll
see." The rest of the pika-pina cable was coiled over his
right shoulder. It was light and strong but there was still
enough of it to weigh him down.

Taking a deep breath, he let go of the rail and dropped
the rest of the way into the water, pivoted and began breast
stroking toward the solid ice a dozen meters in front of
the lifeboat.

Silently those on board urged him on, dividing their
attention between his swimming form and the dark water
surrounding him. Would the sudden presence of light attract curious dwellers from below? September continued to
make progress, swimming silently and strongly without a
single wasted motion. He reached the edge of the ice sheet
without anything arising from the depths.

Whereupon the next problem manifested itself. September was no seal, able to accelerate in the water sufficiently to leap out onto the ice. The edge of the sheet
offered precious little in the way of a handhold.

He tried several times but kept slipping back into the
water. Paradoxically Hunnar, who could not swim, could
have climbed out easily by digging his long powerful claws
into the ice. September didn't even have long fingernails,
which in any case were enclosed by the suit's gloves.

As they looked on worriedly he reached down into the
water and picked up a drifting chunk of ice. Using this he
began hammering away at a crack in the surface of the ice
sheet, holding himself partway out of the water by leaning

his left arm and shoulder on the sheet while simultaneously treading water.

Somehow he managed to chop a couple of shallow holes in the ice. Then using both hands he pulled himself out until he was lying flat. It was a measure of his exhaustion that he lay like that for a long time without turning to acknowledge the congratulations of his companions. Water formed a crust of ice on the exterior of his suit, which gradually brought his body temperature back up to normal.

Though it appeared plenty thick where the energy weapon hadn't touched it, September still crawled on his belly another three meters away from the water's edge, until he was certain the surface underfoot would support his standing form. Keeping the end of the cable wrapped around his waist, he dug his feet into another crack in the ice and leaned backward.

With infinite slowness the drifting lifeboat began to move. Using his body like a pulley, September continued to drag the waterlogged craft and its anxious passengers toward him. Almost an hour passed before the bow nudged up against the shore.

"I'll go first," Williams said. "I'm the lightest."

"Right. If you fall through, grab the rope and pull yourself toward Skua," Ethan advised him.

Williams nodded, then gingerly stepped over the bow and put first one foot down, then the other. The ice held.

"Solid," the teacher said with satisfaction. He walked over and joined September, adding his lesser but nonetheless welcome strength to the cable. Ethan was next, then Hunnar, Ta-hoding, and lastly Grurwelk, still gazing back at the lone survivor of the skimmer who continued to drift aimlessly on his ice floe.

Deprived of their weighty presence the lifeboat floated higher in the water. Under September's direction they all strained on the rope, using their weight as well as their strength, until Ethan was certain his arms were pulling loose from their sockets. Once they got the bow up on the ice sheet it became easier. They didn't let up, however, until they'd dragged the little craft a respectable distance from the open lake.

Ignoring the several centimeters of water that still sloshed beneath their feet they broke off the icicles that had formed along the sides and bottom of the boat. Hunnar and Ta-hoding struggled to reset the fallen mast while Williams straightened the sail.

Ethan frowned and walked over to where Grurwelk Seesfar was staring at the water. When he looked in the same direction he saw that there was no sign of the last Tran survivor from the ill-fated skimmer.

"Finally went under, huh?"

She nodded tersely, turned away. To his astonishment he saw tears in her eyes. It was extremely rare for a Tran to cry.

"I don't understand," he said, gaping at her. "He was one of those who tried to kill us."

"I know. One of those who allied himself with scum like this Corfu and his snotty little would-be emperor. He was also my husband. I ask a favor of you. Tell not the others. It means nothing now. It would not do me good."

Ethan swallowed hard. "I understand. I won't say a thing."

She managed the faintest of smiles. "I thank you for this small thing. It would seem that appearances and decency do not always go together."

Ethan stared after her as he strode back to join the others in preparing the lifeboat for travel. He noted that she did not again look at the place of open water.

* * *

The mast held, the sails held. They were off for Poyola-vomaar. Inside the small cabin, the three humans clustered around a stone Tran cookstove. Since the cabin had stayed above water, the stove had remained dry, along with its highly combustible contents. Now a small but intense fire crackled within, the smoke rising through a narrow pipe fashioned from a single bone from which the marrow had been removed. The blaze heated the stone walls of the stove which in turn radiated a luxurious warmth throughout the cabin. The heat would have driven the Tran to distrac-tion, but for the three humans it was an echo of home.

September had stripped off his survival suit and laid it out to dry and recuperate. His naked form occupied one whole end of the cabin. A couple of thick furs lay draped over his legs and like his companions he held his palms out to the fire until the skin threatened to crisp. He was no longer shivering.

"Terrific things," he said, nodding in the direction of his survival suit which hung from a hook like a discarded skin, "but they're not omnipotent. There at the end I thought I'd lost it all because I couldn't climb up on that damn ice. I could feel my legs starting to go numb, or is that a contra-diction in terms?"

"If you hadn't gone for that swim," Williams told him, "we'd still be floating back there, waiting to sink."

"Or be swallowed," Ethan added. "You think they'll send out the other skimmer to look for us?"

"I doubt it." September pulled back his hands and shoved them beneath the furs, a blissful expression on his face. "There's going to be a lot of shouting and yelling when that skimmer doesn't return. It'll be natural for Antal and his people to assume it might take a day or two to run us to ground. By the time they figure out their gunners aren't coming back we'll be too far out for them to find us. They can't have long-range tracking equipment."

"Why not?"

"No need for it, first of all. Even if they did they couldn't use the stuff. Emissions would be picked up by the survey satellite or in Brass Monkey itself. All they can do is assume their people got us and then crashed or something on the way back." He grinned at the thought. "Bamaputra's not going to sleep real well for a while, wondering what really happened." He stretched out on the combination bed and bench. "Now if you fellas don't mind, I'm a mite fatigued."

They were all exhausted, Ethan knew. No reason to worry with Ta-hoding guiding the boat. He lay down next to the exquisite fire and closed his eyes.

The last thing he saw out the rear cabin window just before he fell asleep was Grurwelk Seesfar, standing close by Ta-hoding and staring back the way they'd come.

Ethan could not penetrate the veil she drew over her emotions during the voyage to Poyolavomaar, but he was glad she'd come along. Whatever she was feeling inside she kept to herself and devoted all her energy to retracing the course they'd traveled on the journey south. When Ta-hoding's navigational abilities failed and Hunnar's instinctive sense of direction became confused she was ready and willing to choose a path based on her previous memories of travel in this region. Gradually the others came to treat her as a full-fledged member of their expedition and to rely on her knowledge. Ta-hoding accepted her boldness as a challenge and matched it with daring of his own.

An example of the captain's courage came five days out as they were overtaken by a *wyrsta*. While not as violent as a rifs, it presented a more subtle threat since it was composed of swirling ice particles. These created a complete whiteout. Anyone sitting in the stern was unable to see beyond the central cabin.

A less confident skipper would immediately have turned the bow into the wind, set the ice anchors, and waited for the storm to pass. Not Ta-hoding. With Seesfar assuring him no obstacles lay between their present position and their goal he kept the sail up and maintained speed. Half a day's travel found them through the storm, whereupon he was persuaded to surrender the wheel to Hunnar. Ice particles had collected in the captain's frozen fur and beard until he resembled a feloursine version of Father Christmas.

Williams looked back at the storm. "I imagine that's what a sandstorm must be like, only with ice substituting for sand."

"I could stand a nice, hot sandstorm right now." September leaned against the cabin while he perused the southern horizon. "Anything to get warm."

"Still no sign of pursuit." Hunnar reached out to tighten a loose stay. "Can your sky people devices track a fleeing vessel even through a wyrsta?"

"Depends on what instruments are being used," Ethan told him. "I think the ice might scatter high-res radar and I don't know what it might do with infrared. I'm starting to think that we just might pull this off."

"*If* we can find the spot where we brought the *Slanderscree* across the equatorial ice ridge, and *if* we can pull, push, or otherwise cajole this windboat back the same way," September reminded him.

Ethan's expression fell. "I'd forgotten about that."

"Do not worry," said Williams, trying to bolster his spirits. "We'll find the place again and we'll get across if we have to carry the boat on her backs. In any event the exertion will help to keep us warm."

"I'd prefer an induction heater," Ethan muttered, crossing his arms over his chest.

* * *

They managed the crossing—though Ethan was convinced his back would break and his legs give out—just as they made it all the way back to the wide, welcoming harbor of Poyolavomaar. Despite their exhaustion the Landgrave insisted on seeing them immediately, whereupon all adjourned to a private meeting chamber in order to avoid the stares and speculative gossip of the court. As T'hosjer T'hos listened quietly to their tale, interrupting only occasionally with a terse, pointed question, Ethan realized that fond as he was of Hunnar Redbeard, the Landgrave of Poyolavomaar was the Tran best suited to represent his world in the councils of the Commonwealth.

He was being premature, he told himself. There might yet not be anything left to represent.

When they'd finished, T'hosjer had a tray of hot drinks brought in. He watched in silence as his guests drained their goblets, the grateful humans not even bothering to inquire as to the nature of the contents. He spoke again as a servitor refilled the containers.

"I do not understand your kind, friend Ethan. What these people attempt beggars reason."

"Don't let it bother you." September leaned back in his chair, held his hot goblet against his forehead and put his feet up on an exquisitely carved table. "We humans have been puttering around with intelligence for about ten millennia now and we don't understand ourselves either."

"But why do such a thing? Why condemn tens of thousands of innocent cubs and elders to death? We would be pleased to share our world with any of your kind who would like to live among us."

September wagged a sardonic finger at the young Landgrave. "Ah, but in that case you'd have to be paid. Commonwealth law requires it."

"Whenever sentient beings are regarded as nothing more

than statistics affecting a profit and loss column, morality is the first casualty of the final reckoning," Williams solemnly declared.

"Clearly these people have to be stopped and an end put to their evil enterprise." T'hosjer spoke quietly, thoughtfully. "But how can this be done if they possess the magical light weapons you have spoken of?"

"We're hoping they had only one of the most powerful kind of light weapon, and we saw that vanish in the belly of something you wouldn't describe in detail at a polite supper." September handed his own hand beamer to the fascinated Landgrave. "If all they have left are more of these then we have a chance. Not to defeat them, but to keep them occupied until serious help can arrive from Brass Monkey."

Ethan nodded. "Milliken will return and confront the Resident Commissioner, explain what's going on, and see if we can't have a peaceforcer ship sent from the nearest base to shut these people and their operation down permanently." He glanced at the teacher. "He's better at explanations, and Skua and I are better at fighting."

"The fastest ship in Poyolavomaar will whisk your scholar back to your outpost to give the alarm," T'hosjer assured them as he rose. "Nor will you brave friends be returning alone. I will mobilize the fleet. But it will take time."

"It will cheer those we left behind just to know you are coming," Hunnar assured him.

"Begging your pardon," said Williams, "and I don't mean to denigrate your generous offer, sir, but I don't think that's a very good idea." Everyone stared at him.

"If we return alone, we might be able to sneak back into the harbor and aboard the *Slanderscree* without alerting anyone. If we arrive with the whole Poyolavomaar navy in tow, Bamaputra will know we got at least this far. He'll be forced to attack if only to find out what's going on. I suggest we allow them to believe we perished along with their missing skimmer. That way they won't be tempted to throw everything they've got at us in an attempt to take the ship. Let them continue believing they've achieved no worse than a stalemate. It will save a lot of lives."

September looked excited. "It'll do more than that, by damn. If they see us limp back to the *Slanderscree*, the first thing they'll think is that we didn't make it anywhere. Otherwise why return? We're not going to be giving any interviews and they won't have had the chance—unless they've managed to take the ship, which I doubt—to count heads except through monoculars from a distance. Six leave, five come back. I think we can fool 'em." He turned back to T'hosjer.

"How long for your best ship to make it to Brass Monkey and back?"

The Landgrave discussed figures with Williams, who transposed to metrics. The results left Ethan nodding with satisfaction.

"Not as bad as I thought it would be. Meanwhile, sir, if it pleases you to alert your forces, then do so. We don't know how Bamaputra will react to our return and you ought to be ready to defend yourselves if nothing else."

"Then all is settled." They rose to leave.

September stepped in front of the teacher. He towered over most men; Williams he dwarfed completely.

"You're going to be all alone for a bit, my friend. Just you and the Tran."

The smaller man smiled up at him. "I do not feel uncomfortable among the Tran. We've lived with them for nearly two years now. As for human companionship, I've spent much of my life living within myself. I'll be okay."

"Well, don't waste time, and don't stop to ogle the scenery."

"I intend to stop for nothing."

The three of them had been together for so long it felt unnatural to be standing on the end of a dock waving farewell to Williams. That was what Ethan and September found themselves doing the following morning as the sleek, narrow-hulled ice ship crewed by the best sailors in Poyolavomaar pulled out of the harbor heading north. Not that either man held any illusions regarding something as archaic as Three Musketeership. They'd been thrown together on this world by accident and kept together by circumstance instead of by choice. But the teacher had been a boon companion; soft-spoken, sensible, and silent unless he had something worthwhile to add to a conversation. They would miss his good counsel.

Skua September was anxious to head back to Yingyapin. His eagerness was matched by Hunnar's, who though he would not admit it aloud was obviously frantic to be with his Elfa once more. Ethan assured the knight that even if their adversaries had somehow managed to regain control of the *Slanderscree*, they weren't likely to engage in a massacre of the escapees.

By mutual consent no one discussed what they would do if for some reason Williams didn't make it back to the outpost. Tran-ky-ky posed plenty of problems for long-distance travelers without opposition from the likes of renegade humans. Stavanzers, wandering barbarians, drooms, storms of varying suddenness and awesome power—any one of these could obliterate a ship and its crew. T'hosjer tried to get them to relax. Williams was traveling on the best ice ship this part of the planet had to offer, assisted and watched over by the finest crew an ice-going city-state could put together. He would make it back to Brass Monkey healthy and ahead of time.

"I sure hope so," September commented, "or there's

going to be a lot of corpses lying in Yingyapin harbor, and they won't be of ice."

Ethan eyed him in surprise. "I thought you liked fighting, Skua."

"When it serves a purpose. A little war between our people and the citizens of Yingyapin won't do anyone any good. The Tran would be the ones to shed the real blood, and for what? You know, we're supposed to be the advanced race on this world. It would be to our credit to settle this trouble without spilling any more local blood than absolutely necessary."

XIII

Judging by the looks he drew from passing humans as he trudged toward the administrative complex, Williams knew he must have looked rather like a Tran himself. Weeks out on the ice ocean could do that to a man. His survival suit was battered and discolored, the face visible behind the ice-scoured visor haggard and unshaven.

His companions from Poyolavomaar drew equally curious stares from the local Tran, garbed as they were in their strange attire. For their part, the Poyo sailors valiantly if unsuccessfully strove to gawk at the peculiar alien constructs as inconspicuously as possible. They were fascinated by the distant shuttle port and the smooth, seamless buildings.

The first thing he'd noted upon their arrival was the presence of a shuttle on the ice landing strip. It was in the process of being lowered to the underground hangar dock. He badly wanted to spill his story to its pilot, who could then relay the details to the interstellar vessel lying in orbit overhead, but decided to follow protocol and talk with the Commissioner first. They would be in touch with the proper authorities soon enough.

If anyone had a right to know what was going on, it was the members of the outpost scientific establishment. But what was right and what was necessary didn't match up at the moment. He had to meet with the Commissioner so she could disburse the crucial information via the deep-space beam. Friends could wait for news of their comrades until the forces of law had been goaded into motion.

Contrary to Ethan's belief Williams didn't think they would need a peaceforcer to drive Bamaputra and his team off the planet. The mere fact that their presence and intentions were now known to the rest of the Commonwealth should be enough to send the would-be deluge makers packing. He could see Bamaputra and Antal scrambling to destroy incriminating records as they called frantically for a ship to evacuate the installation. It was an image he relished. Even so, he was willing to forgo the pleasure of seeing their faces again. It was good to be back in what passed here for civilization, good to be able to relax knowing that whatever else happened from this point on, Tranky-ky and its people were safe.

The single security guard seated outside the elevators hardly knew what to make of Williams as the teacher stumbled into the building and threw back the hood of his survival suit. Though the temperature inside was maintained at human optimum he found it almost unbearably hot. Maybe he'd acquired more than just the Tran look. He walked over to the small desk with its garland of advanced electronics, put both fists on the synthetic wood, and leaned forward.

"I insist on seeing the Commissioner immediately. It's a matter of life and death."

The guard eyed him as though he were some peculiar life form which had wandered in off the ice—which wasn't far off the mark, Williams reflected.

"I'll see if Ms. Stanhope is available."

"You do that." Williams stepped away from the desk, a bit taken aback by his uncharacteristic forcefulness. The result of spending more than a year in the company of one Skua September, he told himself. When this was over and done with, he would have to learn how to act civilized all over again.

The guard spoke into a pickup, listened quietly for a moment, then put the earpiece aside. "Marquel says for you to go right up."

"Marquel? Who's Marquel?"

"The Commissioner's secretary. She's over in Hospitality right now. He's calling her and says for you to go ahead and come up."

"Thanks." He turned and headed for the lift, feeling the guard's eyes on his back.

Guess I am something of a sight, he told himself as the cab ascended. By the time it reached the apex of the pyramidal structure he found himself wishing Skua and Ethan were there to back him up; Skua with his imposing physical presence and Ethan with his glib talk. He didn't feel comfortable with people like Stanhope, bureaucrats and exercisers of power. He was much more at home with Cheela and Blanchard and the other scientists. They'd treated him as an equal despite the fact that the degrees he held were considerably less impressive than theirs. Good folks. They were depending on him and here he was wasting time as he had so often in the past on useless second thoughts. Just talk, he told himself. The story would take care of itself. He was a teacher, wasn't he? It was time for a personal tutorial. Time to educate a Commissioner. She wasn't going to like what he had to say.

Tough. Standing a little taller, he pushed through into the reception area.

It was empty except for a man not much bigger than himself. Instead of waiting at his desk Marquel had apparently been pacing the floor waiting for Williams to arrive.

Now he rushed eagerly forward, the questions coming thick and fast.

"Ms. Stanhope will be here shortly. What happened out there? Where are your companions? What's going on?"

Anxious as he was to see the Commissioner, Williams saw no harm in giving her secretary a quick rundown on his experiences, concluding by explaining that Ethan and Skua had returned with Hunnar and Ta-hoding to help the *Slanderscree*'s defenders hold off any further attacks by the renegade humans and their Tran allies.

"You understand how imperative it is that this information be transmitted immediately to the nearest military base so that armed assistance will be forthcoming."

"Of course, of course." The secretary was thinking hard. "A terrible situation. No one here had the slightest idea anything of this nature was going on. You know, when you all sailed off in that native ice ship there were a lot of us here who never thought you'd be seen again, and those who thought you would return didn't expect you to find anything."

Williams nodded at the door that led into the Commissioner's office. "Would you mind if we waited in there? I remember there being some soft chairs and I wouldn't mind sitting down while we wait."

"No, of course not. Please forgive me." He opened the double doors and led Williams inside. "It's just that I was so enthralled by your story." The doors shut behind them.

"After I tell the Commissioner everything I just told you I'll need to meet with the heads of the various science departments to inform them of what's going on. Then I think I'll sleep for about two days."

Marquel was nodding sympathetically. "You look like you could do with a long rest." He pushed open a smaller door leading to a side room. "Make yourself comfortable. I'll be right back."

Williams settled down in one of the chairs that faced the Commissioner's desk. Thick insulated windows looked out over the outpost. Beyond lay the harbor of Brass Monkey with its Tran community and ice ships tied up at the three docks.

Marquel was not long absent. When he stepped back into the office Williams saw that the secretary had changed his clothes. His eyes widened. He didn't need to ask about the reason for the change. The new attire was self-explanatory.

He spun and bolted for the doors. They were locked. He started pounding on them and yelling.

"That won't do you any good, you know," said Marquel.

Williams turned and slid away from the doors, keeping his back against the wall and his eyes on the room's other occupant. "How did you lock them?"

"Remote inside the desk." the figure smiled thinly. "I won't show you where."

He knew it was Marquel behind the black and crimson hood. He recognized the voice even though most of the face was now concealed. The rest of the tight-fitting black clothing covered the man from toe to neck. It was mildly theatrical, but Williams didn't laugh at its wearer. There was nothing funny about what it implied. Besides, the slick black material had a practical use. It was highly water-repellent. It would also shed blood.

"You know," he said conversationally while Williams tried to find another way out of the office, "when you and your friends got rid of Jobius Trell it was a wonderful opportunity for my employers to put someone like myself in a position to oversee their interests here. Until now, though, I haven't had to do anything except perform as a secretary. I was hoping life would go on that way, but"—he shrugged—"sometimes things don't always work out the way we plan them. However, our training teaches us to be patient. I hadn't expected to have to practice my true vocation for the duration of my stay on this world."

Williams had never seen a Qwarm before, a member of the assassins' guild, but like most people he'd heard of them. They appeared so often in mass entertainment that myth became mixed with reality. As was often the case with professional criminals, their exploits were highly romanticized, something the Qwarm encouraged. The less seriously people took them, the easier it was for them to practice their art. Their services were very expensive, there weren't many of them, they were scattered throughout the vastness of the Commonwealth, and in two hundred years the government and the Church had been unable to stamp them out. It was difficult to arouse public opinion against malefactors who materialized but rarely and then vanished.

One had materialized now, across the room from Williams.

"I came aboard, you might say, with the new Commissioner. She's been very pleased with my work. So have my real employers. I could have killed you and your companions before you left, but if you didn't find Yingyapin, there was no reason to complicate matters and if you did, I expected Antal and his people to take care of you. Your return is a minor complication easily resolved. It was very thoughtful of you to come straight here, without telling anyone else your story."

"The security guard downstairs saw me come in."

"That's all it's his business to do."

"The Tran who brought me here will demand to see me again."

"You think the Commissioner is going to call for a peaceforcer on the advice of a few excitable natives?" He grinned humorlessly again. "Why do you think Antal didn't send his remaining skimmer and every ice ship he could muster out after you when the first skimmer didn't come back? It was because he knew I was here to look after things."

"Killing me won't save Bamaputra's operation."

"Of course it will. If your friends come back, I'll kill them, too. Right now I'm a little out of practice, but killing isn't something you forget how to do. It stays with you, like riding a bike." He cracked his knuckles, the sound loud in the room. "Your presence here will give me some practice. If you were that September fellow, I might be a little nervous about not having worked in so long, but you won't be any trouble, teacher."

This was without a doubt, Williams thought wildly, the craziest conversation he'd ever participated in in his life. At the same time he was coldly aware it might also be his last.

Still, as long as he was talking, he wasn't dying. Maybe someone would break in on them. Stanhope he didn't expect. That had obviously been a ploy.

"What about the rest of the scientists here? They're going to get worried when Cheela Hwang and her colleagues don't return."

"That's Antal's problem, not mine. He's a resourceful supervisor. He'll think of something." Marquel was starting to edge around the far side of the desk, his movements casual, assured. "Fatal accidents are not unknown on this world. The science staff here will accept a reasonable explanation, have a bit of a cry, then go back to their work."

"If you work for Bamaputra, then you must have some idea of what this is all about. Even so, I don't suppose it would do me any good to appeal to your sense of morality, assuming you have one."

"Oh, but the Qwarm are very moral, my inquisitive friend. Like everything else in life, however, morality is flexible."

"Not where I come from. So you don't care that tens of thousands of Tran are going to die if Bamaputra's plan becomes reality?"

Marquel shrugged. "I am in the business of death. Numbers don't frighten me. Just between you and me, I don't like the idea, no. But being a killer myself, I'm hardly in a position to question the motives of others for the killing they may do. In the case of the Tran who will fail to survive the rapid change in climate, they will never connect their deaths with a specific killer. There will be no personal contact involved, no face-to-face acceptance of responsibility. It will appear an act of nature and that's a shame. One should know who is responsible for one's passing. There's no intimacy to the act. As a professional I find that sad.

"With you and me things will be much different. You will know how you are going to die and by whose hands. You'll go to your grave without questions tickling your soul. Don't you think it's best that way? Much better than fading away like a song in some indifferent hospital bed, or being stricken by an attack on the way home from a job. Face-to-face assassination is a positive statement. Each of us goes to his death burdened by enough other unanswered and unanswerable questions."

"How are you going to do it?" Williams kept sliding along the far wall. If nothing else, he'd make himself a moving target.

"There are many ways. I'd like to be as inventive as possible, but your showing up unexpectedly precludes that. Besides, this is a very straightforward situation. Really no need to make it any more complex than necessary. The best thing for me, of course, would be to make it look like an accident in case I have difficulty smuggling your body out of Administration and over to the incinerator."

His hand dipped into a narrow pocket that was sewn

into one leg of the tight suit. When it reappeared Williams saw the tiny, collapsing stiletto protruding from enfolding fingers. Like Marquel's attire, the blade and handle were obsidian black.

"That doesn't look much like an accident."

Marquel nodded approvingly. "I'm glad to see you're taking this in the proper spirit. So many can't. They fall down and weep and wail and plead even though they know it's all a waste of time. It'll be a good change to kill someone who knows how to handle the inevitable like an adult." He held the stiletto up to the light, admiring it.

"You're right. This wouldn't look very accidental. But it's traditional. Much as I would like to use it, it'll be easier for both of us if you'll just swallow this." He held out a pill. For a change it was bright blue instead of black or red.

"Why should I make things easier for you?"

"Because this kills in less than a minute, quietly and bloodlessly. It'll be just like going to sleep. No pain. Efficient. If you don't take it, then I'll have to cut you. That will be slower, messier, and much more uncomfortable for you. The end result will be the same. This office is soundproofed but I'd still have to take the precaution of cutting your vocal cords first. Some people can get very loud."

He was moving purposefully toward the teacher now, gliding rather than walking across the floor. "Resistance on your part is useless. I'm considerably stronger than I look, much stronger than you, and a great deal quicker. Killing is my job. You know, I've never killed a teacher before. I'm not sure any Qwarm has had occasion to kill a teacher. There isn't much call for it."

"You're sure nothing I can say would make you reconsider? Not so much for my life as for all the others that are at stake here."

"Noble. I like that. Don't see too much of that these days either. No, I'm afraid there isn't. An assignment is an assignment. No matter how I might feel personally I have guild rules to abide by."

"Oddly enough, I do understand your situation." He sighed. "Well, I almost died out there on the ice half a dozen times this past year." He extended a hand. "Give me the pill. I'm not one for pain. You're sure it won't hurt?"

"Not at all." Marquel passed the blue capsule across. "Actually I rather envy you. That's tronafin, a very powerful narcotic. You're going to enjoy the biggest high of your life, even if it won't last very long. Not only won't you feel any pain, you're going to be overwhelmed with pleasure. You see, we're very businesslike, not cruel at all—unless somebody's paying for that, of course. We try to make every effort to . . ."

A startled expression came over Marquel's face. The black stiletto rose and struck. Williams ducked and rolled as the blade sliced down into a bookcase and the wall beyond. As he struggled back onto his feet the Qwarm turned and staggered toward him.

Tran artifacts and tools had been used in the decoration of the Commissioner's office. Very attractive, very ethnographic. One of them was a Tran dart thrower, a tiny, inconspicuous device fashioned from bone and horn. It utilized a small spring made of something akin to baleen to launch a fifteen centimeter–long dart. All the while he'd been chatting conversationally with Marquel, Williams had been shielding it with his body and arming it.

The angle was bad but he knew he wouldn't have time to remove the device from its hook and aim it. When he'd tilted back his head and raised the pill as if to swallow it Marquel's attention had been focused on the teacher's right hand. Just before swallowing, Williams had turned to his right to expose the dart-thrower and had used his other hand to flip the little trigger.

Marquel had been standing within arm's length. The

razor-sharp sliver of bone that the dart was cut from had gone right through his black suit to bury itself between navel and groin. It wasn't a killing blow but the shock was more than enough to stagger the assassin. Despite the unexpected pain he'd reacted quickly, stabbing with the knife. The pain had slowed his reactions sufficiently for Williams to dodge.

"Teacher." The Qwarm came toward him as blood began to drip from the wound and stain the floor. Williams kept retreating, trying to keep as much furniture between himself and the injured assassin as possible.

Yes, he was just a teacher—a teacher who'd spent almost two years surviving among sometimes hostile natives on the barren, deadly surface of an inhospitable world called Tran-ky-ky. Two years of battling lethal elements and carnivorous fauna. Two years on an occasional warship called the *Slanderscree*. Two years battling barbarians and duplicitous humans and their friends. Yes, he was a teacher. One who'd been hardened and toughened by the classroom called reality. His experiences had made him stronger, faster, and like the Tran, cunning.

Despite the long spike protruding from his intestines, Marquel continued to stalk him, the stiletto still clenched firmly in his right hand. Because of the location of the dart the Qwarm's control of his leg muscles was less than perfect. Sheer willpower kept him advancing.

This continued for several minutes until Marquel realized Williams had maneuvered him completely around the room so that the teacher was back by the artifact-covered wall.

The Tran sword he removed from its mounting was chipped from stavanzer bone. He held it in both hands and waited. No more chasing around the desk. "Come on, then." He tried to balance the weapon as he'd seen Hunnar

Redbeard and others do. Hunnar wielded it with one paw, but it was too heavy for Williams to attempt that.

Marquel's expression was contorted as he grimaced in pain. "Makes it interesting. Much better." His words were getting thick, Williams noted. "Better."

He lunged.

Avoiding the blow, Williams stepped to one side and cut down with the sword. Though slowed by the pain in his gut Marquel was still able to move fast enough to reach out with his left hand and grab the teacher's wrists, pinning both hands to the sword. The concussion raced up Williams's forearms. It was as though he'd been struck by an iron bar. The strength in the small man's fingers was incredible.

His right hand rose and light slipped along the flat of the stiletto. This time Williams was sure his assailant was smiling. His eyes glittered through the ocular openings in the hood.

"Very good, teacher, very good. Much more than I had any right to expect."

Williams tried to wrench his hands free, but the Qwarm's grip was like steel. At the same time the teacher brought his right knee up and round and slammed it into the assassin's lower abdomen, just below the place where the dart still protruded.

A tremor ran through the wounded killer. Somehow he still managed to strike weakly with the knife. It sliced through Williams's survival suit, the incredibly sharp blade lodging in his right shoulder. The strike was a little high. Marquel intended to drag the point down Williams's chest until he could use his weight to shove it into his quarry's heart, but the loss of blood and the continuing pain finally overwhelmed him.

Still holding the teacher's wrists in a death grip, the Qwarm crumpled to his knees, then fell over on his back dragging his quarry down on top of him. His right hand flopped loosely to the floor. The stiletto remained imbedded in Williams's shoulder. The assassin blinked; not at the teacher lying on top of him but at the lights in the ceiling.

"I'll be damned."

Using his foot, Williams was finally able to pry his hands free of the sword and the assassin's grasp. He rose and stumbled backward. Gritting his teeth he wrapped his fingers around the handle of the stiletto and yanked convulsively. The pain as the blade emerged from his flesh was tremendous. He staggered but didn't fall.

A steadily widening pool of blood was forming beneath the dead man. Marquel continued to stare at the ceiling, the look on his face one of astonishment and surprise rather than pain.

Williams staggered over to the Commissioner's desk. Inside a drawer he found a pop-up board lined with contact switches. Which one activated the sealed doors, which alerted building security?

He was still hunting when the doors unexpectedly parted, to admit not an ally of Marquel's but the elegantly clad Resident Commissioner. She stared at him a moment before her gaze was drawn to the body in the middle of the floor. Her expression tightened and she took a step backward.

"What the hell's going on here? Who—wait, I remember you. You're one of the three who—"

"Williams. Milliken Williams." He grimaced and clutched at his throbbing shoulder. Had Marquel taken him more seriously, he had not the slightest doubt the stiletto would have been poisoned. "Could I ask you to please call a doctor?" He gestured at the complex control panel. "I don't know which of these stands for what."

She walked over to him. Her fingers flew over a couple

of the controls. Williams was dimly aware of an alarm sounding somewhere in the bowels of the building. He sat down in her chair, suddenly unable to stand any longer.

"A Qwarm. I've read about them but I never expected to actually see one. I'm not that important," she said.

"How do you think I feel?"

"Stay there." She activated another panel. "Infirmary? Where's that doctor I buzzed for? Let's get some people up here *now*. I've got a man with a knife wound in my chair." She nodded toward the sprawled body of Marquel. "He was always weak on transcription, but I didn't have the heart to dismiss him. Never struck me as the violent type. It just goes to show. Is he dead?"

"I sincerely hope so."

"What's this all about, anyway?"

"There's a large illegal human installation operating on the edge of the southern continent. They took us prisoner; we escaped. Ethan, Skua, and the others went back to help those who couldn't get away. I came back to tell you . . . to tell you . . ." Suddenly speech was becoming difficult.

She leaned toward the intercom. "Where's that medic, dammit."

A crackling, then a voice responding. "This is Infirmary. What medic, Ms. Stanhope?"

"The medic I just—wait a minute, who is this?"

"Marianne Sanchez, Commissioner. Did you call for a medic?"

"You're damn right I did. Who took the call? Who was on a moment ago?"

"Not one of the physicians. Josef, I think. Josef Nilachek. He's with Administration. One of your people."

"One of . . ." She looked down at Williams.

The teacher had a phobia about swearing, but he ignored it now. "Shit. Marquel wasn't alone."

* * *

The shuttle had been unloaded and berthed for maintenance. Nilachek hung back in the shadows until the last member of the service crew emerged from the ship and moved off to chat with his colleagues. He knew what he had to do.

Marquel should have sounded the all-clear and called down for a body bag for his quarry. The fact that the Commissioner had called instead suggested any number of possibilities, none of them good. It was impossible to believe the Qwarm had failed, but then lately it seemed as though nothing was going right. Somehow he was going to have to contact either the company or Bamaputra.

But first he had to ensure that this schoolteacher's revelations remained on Tran-ky-ky. That meant disabling both the deep-space beam and shuttle-to-ship communications. The beam wasn't going anywhere so he decided to take care of the shuttle first. It shouldn't be difficult, and when the small packet of concentrated explosive went off inside the little craft it would attract enough attention to allow him to deal with the beam unopposed.

He had to move fast. First disable communications, then get to this meddlesome teacher and disable him before he could recite the details of his story. Without specific coordinates, the people isolated here at Brass Monkey would never find the installation.

No one saw him slip aboard. A quick glance showed that the shuttle was empty. He hurried down the aisle between the rows of seats. The door to the cargo bay was unlocked. He eased into the cavernous space, ready to deal with any stevedore who might have lingered aboard. There were none to be seen. The unloading process was largely carried out by machines supervised from elsewhere.

He was just placing the explosive when a voice said, "What are you doing there?"

His hand went for the beamer holstered under his shoulder, relaxed when he saw the speaker. A woman, one of the passengers judging by her attire.

"I might ask you the same question." He made sure the packet was concealed by his body. "Me, I'm staff. A little repair work." He nodded toward the doorway that led back to the passenger compartment. "You shouldn't be in here."

"Idiots lost a piece of my luggage. Thought I'd come look for it myself. How the hell do you lose baggage in space?"

"I don't know, but you'll have to leave. It's against regulations." Nilachek was beginning to get nervous. One of the maintenance people might show up at any minute. He started toward her. "If you'll just come with me, I'm sure we can find your missing luggage. Maybe someone's found it already." He took her arm and turned her toward the door.

She shook him off irritably. "These twits couldn't find their backsides with both hands. Why do you think I came to look for myself?" She turned back to the compartment, frowned. "What's that over there?"

"What's what?" He began to edge his hand toward the concealed beamer he carried.

"That plasticine packet over there, between those two conduits?"

"Just patching a small leak. Would you like me to explain how it works? I'd be happy to show you."

"Yeah, you bet I would. Especially why a patch on a leak needs a timer on it."

He started to pull the beamer. With unexpected speed the woman slammed the edge of her left palm against his elbow, simultaneously swept her right leg around in a wide arc to slam her heavy foreleg against his ankles. His feet went right out from under him and he landed hard on the metal decking, still trying to extract the beamer. She jumped on top of him and the wind went out of him completely. Stars danced in front of his eyes as he fought for breath. All wrong, this was all wrong. He could hear her screaming for help at the top of her lungs and tried desperately to slide out from under her, but she weighed more than he did. A good deal more.

Williams sat patiently as the doctor sprayed a coagulant and epidermal fixative on his shoulder, then slapped a square of fast-adhering artificial skin over the wound. Nearby, Millicent Stanhope was talking to her security people as the body of her former secretary was loaded onto a stretcher for removal. As Marquel left the office for the last time, she turned to the visitor occupying her chair.

"How did you do it?" She gestured toward the open doors. "Handle him, I mean. They're professionals. What are you?"

"A teacher, like I told you. Never been anything but a teacher. But a good teacher never stops being a good student. You learn a lot out there." He nodded toward the frozen landscape visible through the high windows.

"Your collection, or maybe I should say Jobius Trell's old collection, saved me. Marquel knew all about contemporary weapons but he didn't know anything about Tranky-ky. I knew he wouldn't let me get to anything obvious, like a sword or war axe. But that dart thrower is small and it looks more like a tool than a weapon. If he *hadn't* been a professional killer, I don't think I could have brought it off. A nonprofessional wouldn't have been sufficiently relaxed or confident."

Stanhope nodded slowly. Her desk buzzed for attention. The temporary new receptionist sounded slightly shaken.

"Someone here to see you, ma'am. She's very insistent. She—hey, you can't do that."

The doors had just closed in the wake of the coroner's

crew. Now they slid apart again to admit two young men. They wore side arms and their eyes immediately searched every centimeter of the office. One of them was half escorting, half dragging a smaller man. This individual's right arm had been bandaged and his face was puffy with bruises.

A large, extremely well-dressed woman sauntered in and stopped between her bodyguards. She indicated the battered Nilachek with a contemptuous flick of her wrist.

"I understand this belongs to you." She was staring straight at the Commissioner.

Milliken Williams sat up straight in the high-back chair and gaped at the new arrival as the doors closed behind her. At the same time she noticed him. Her eyes shifted from the Commissioner's face and a sardonic grin spread over her own features.

"Hello, Milliken. Long time not seen. What are you teaching this year?"

XIV

The emperor of all Tran-ky-ky gazed over the ramparts of his castle and was not pleased. He'd taken the advice of his human allies and waited for those on board the great ice ship to come crawling to him for food and shelter. Far too many weeks had passed without so much as a moan from the ship.

Eventually he had made the decision to wait no longer but to attack. For the past several days his imperial forces had repeatedly assaulted the defiant ones trapped in his harbor. His soldiers had tried and failed to set it afire with catapults. They had assailed it with arrows only to watch while the defenders took shelter behind the ship's solid wooden walls. They had even tried the small, magical light weapons of the skypeople only to discover that at least two of those on board had similar devices of their own, in whose employment they were far more skilled than his own troops.

As if that were not galling enough, the unspeakable Tran crewing the icerigger possessed strange horizontal bows which fired short, heavy bolts with enough force to penetrate the thickest hide armor.

Now he could only watch in frustration as still another assault was beaten off and his rapidly demoralized troops

270

retreated back across the ice. He turned furiously on the two skypeople who had promised him so much and thus far had delivered so little. Corfu ren-Arhaveg stood silently nearby.

Despite the fact that the taller of the two skypeople was the one who did most of the talking whenever they met, Massul knew who was really in command. He directed his fury at the smaller, darker-skinned human whose face was clearly visible behind the visor of his survival suit.

"Where is the great victory you promised me? Whence comes my dominion over the world? I cannot even control the harbor of my capital city."

"What are you worried about?" said Bamaputra via his translator. "They're trapped here. Of those who escaped all appear to have been forced to return. If any did not, we have arranged for them to be taken care of as soon as they return to the other skypeople place. It's more likely they drowned." The dumping of the lifeboat in open water had been reported by those on board the skimmer before its communicator had mysteriously gone silent. Bamaputra regretted the apparent loss of the skimmer as well as the large energy weapon it carried, but such losses had to be expected when dealing with combative primitives like the Tran. The important thing was that most, if not all of the would-be escapees had been forced to return to Yingyapin harbor.

When equipping the installation it had been decided that there was hardly any need for more than one large energy weapon. That decision was beginning to look short-sighted, though not insurmountable.

The endless ranting and raving of their emperor was becoming wearying.

"If I am to command my own subjects, let alone those yet to come, I must at least be able to demonstrate hegemony over my own state." He gestured violently toward where the *Slanderscree* squatted just inside the harbor barrier. "Why have we not been able to defeat those who mock me?"

"Because they are well-organized, well-led, determined, because they have a couple of stolen hand beamers of their own now, and because their people are better fighters than yours."

Massul turned away angrily to stare out over the parapet. "You said that you would train my soldiers, that you would make them into an unbeatable fighting force."

"Such things take time, and more than just better weapons." Antal nodded toward the icerigger. "Whoever's guiding the defense of that ship knows what they're doing. I suspect the giant has something to do with that. I didn't like his looks from the moment we set on eyes on him. Should've had him shot right off. The scientists are no problem. Then there's that other one, doesn't look like much of anything. The one who said he was a salesman. Funny sort. Tricky. I don't like him either. What was his name?"

"Fortune," Bamaputra murmured. "Ethan Fortune, I believe."

"Yeah, him. I can't figure him at all. Just when you think you had him pegged he'd say something unexpected. Should've shot him, too."

"Why can you not fly over and shoot down at them from your sky boats?"

"First because we've only got one skimmer left," Antal told him. "Second because their hand beamers have the same range as all our others. I'm not risking the skimmer unless I'm sure it's worth the risk."

"This is an affront to my royal person," said the outraged Massul. "What more reason do you require?"

Antal turned to the administrator and switched to Terranglo. "Ninety percent of what this stooge says is gibberish and the other ten percent is vanity."

"What concerns me," Bamaputra said, "is that one or more of those who went out on the smaller boat may have made it back to Brass Monkey. I wish we had some way of knowing for certain."

"Doesn't matter. Anyone gets through, Marquel and Nilachek will take care of things."

"I do not share your confidence in last-minute remedies."

"So what do you want to do?"

"I was wondering if we could increase output at the installation to the point where the warming of the atmosphere and the melting of the sea ice would increase ten or twelve fold. Even if the alarm has been raised, we could still hold out here for a while. If we could melt enough of the ice sheet, the process would become self-sustaining, with the sun heating the open water sufficiently to continue melting the ice."

Antal licked his lips. "I wouldn't want to try it. You run those reactors at that kind of rate and you're liable to have a containment field collapse. We didn't plan for that kind of output."

Bamaputra gestured toward the *Slanderscree*. "We didn't plan for that, either. We must proceed as if the worst has occurred, until we hear otherwise."

"You'll never get the technical people to agree to it."

"They have no choice. There is nowhere for them to go and they are involved as deeply as you or I. Even if someone from that lifeboat reached Brass Monkey, and even if they somehow avoided the attentions of our people there, it will take the authorities time to react. They will first seek confirmation of a civilian's story, then meetings will have to be held, group decisions made. Votes will have to be taken. Authorizations will have to be approved.

"While they dawdle we can strengthen our defenses here, dig ourselves in better, and acquire proper defensive armament."

The foreman didn't quite laugh at him. "This isn't a military installation, Shiva, and our personnel here aren't soldiers. A peaceforcer could blow us right out of that mountain without our even seeing it."

"I am aware of that. But they will talk first, try to avoid bloodshed. By the time they finally arrive and we finally agree to surrender we may have progressed to the point where it will be simpler for the authorities to adapt to the altered climate than to try and reverse it. We must try, anyway." He turned to Massul and explained what they were going to do.

The emperor did not react as expected. "No, you are wrong about one thing. We do have a choice. You may not, but we Tran do. I will do battle with my kin, but I cannot fight sky boats and light swords. You ask too much."

"Do you want to be emperor or not?" Bamaputra asked irritably.

"Better a live Landgrave than a dead emperor. I will fight Tran, but I will not fight skypeople with energy weapons. We will surrender."

"I beg your pardon?" Bamaputra said politely. "Surrender?"

"Do you take me for a fool? If those skypeople"—and he nodded toward the icerigger—"are more powerful than you, why should I not ally myself with them? Do you not think they will accept me? I think they will. Yingyapin is small today, but great cities often arise from villages. We can still serve as a haven for the disenchanted and disenfranchised." He waved a paw. "I disown you. Do what you will inside your mountain, but henceforth you may do it without my aid."

Antal confronted him. "Listen, you furry cretin, you

don't have the skills or the knowledge or the ability to command anything without our help! Have you forgotten, 'your majesty,' who put you on your crummy throne here?"

"You are not the only skypeople who are willing to help the Tran. I see that now. Perhaps you are not even the best. I no longer believe your stories." Again he indicated the icerigger. "Those who fight alongside the other skypeople do not act like the exploited and deceived. I begin to wonder on what they tried to tell me of your intentions. Yes, I begin to wonder. I have decided. We will surrender to them. I am still emperor here."

"That's right, you are." Antal stepped back and gestured sharply. Corfu nodded, whispered to two of the soldiers who had been serving as honor guard. The three of them grabbed Massul fel-Stuovic and carried him to the edge of the parapet.

"Put me down! Put me down this instant!" The wind caught his dan and they billowed tautly around him. "I am emperor here. I am emperor of all Tran-ky-ky, Landgrave of Yingyapin! I command you to . . ."

A moment later Antal stepped to the edge of the stone rampart and looked over the side. A couple of curious passers-by had gathered around the stain on the ice below. After a while they tilted back their heads to look upward. Then they turned and chivaned off in opposite directions.

The foreman stepped back from the parapet. "So much for one problem."

"Would that all our problems were so easily solved." Bamaputra turned to the merchant. "Corfu ren-Arhaveg, I hereby appoint you Landgrave of Yingyapin and Emperor of all Tran-ky-ky. Don't let it go to your head."

"At your service, sirs." Corfu executed that strange sideways Tran bow. "There may be some resistance among members of Massul's court."

"We'll take care of that," Bamaputra assured him. "You

understand what we're going to do here? We're going to try and speed up the warming trend."

"I understand, sir. I think it for the better. Why wait until one is old and stooped to enjoy success?"

"Why wait indeed?" Bamaputra muttered.

Antal put a hand on Corfu's shoulder. "Keep trying to take the ship. Don't risk too many of your troops. We want to keep them busy out there so they don't have a chance to sneak out. Eventually they'll get hungry and give up. Meanwhile we've got to get back to our work. We'll leave you a communicator, one of our 'wind-talkers,' so you can get in touch with us if anything unexpected turns up."

Corfu straightened. "Friend Antal, worry not. You can rely on me."

"Yeah, I know. That's why we've made you emperor. Should've done it months ago instead of sticking with that poor crazy bastard." He turned to leave.

"A moment." Bamaputra spoke softly.

Antal frowned, turned back to face his boss. "Something wrong?"

"Very wrong. Listen."

They did so, until Corfu was moved to ask, "The wind?"

"No. No, not the wind." Bamaputra's lips were taut, his expression frozen. "Not the thrice-damned wind."

"How much longer can we hold out?" Cheela Hwang was leaning over the railing, staring at the distant windswept city. Ethan stood nearby.

"A week," he told her. "Hunnar thinks maybe two or three."

"Then what?"

"Then we try to strike some kind of deal with our 'friends.'" He nodded in the direction of the harborfront.

"You can't deal with people like that."

"You can't starve to death, either. Besides which we're running low on crossbow bolts and beamer charges."

She sighed, turned to study him closely. "Then Milliken didn't get through."

"We don't know that. Not yet. Milliken's very resourceful. Deceptively so. There's still a chance."

"Yes, he's quietly competent."

Now it was Ethan's turn to stare at her thoughtfully. "You sort of like our friend Milliken, don't you?"

She looked past him, toward the mechanical boom that barred the *Slanderscree*'s exit. "Sort of."

He turned away so she wouldn't see him smile. As he did so he frowned. "You hear something, Cheela?"

She stared over the bow. "Hear something? Only the wind."

"No, something besides the wind. Higher pitched."

Others heard it as well. Those soldiers and sailors not manning defensive positions made a concerted rush for the bow. Ethan and Hwang followed, along with the ice-rigger's entire human complement.

"Skimmer!" he finally yelled when he was certain. "It has to be a skimmer!"

"Your excitement's premature, feller-me-lad." September had come up behind them. Panting hard, he strained to peer past the gate. "A skimmer it is for sure, but whose?" He held the huge Tran battle axe that had been a gift from the Landgrave of Wannome. With its edge resting on the deck, his left ankle crossed over his right as he leaned on the axe's handle for support, he looked for all the world like some silver-suited ghost resting casually on an ancient umbrella in some posh trendy neighborhood on Earth or New Paris. The barbarian boulevarder, Ethan mused.

"Could the evil skypeople have called another sky boat

from somewhere to come and help them recapture us?" Hunnar wondered worriedly.

"It's possible." Already Ethan was losing some of the initial enthusiasm the approaching skimmer had engendered. "If that's the case, there isn't much we can do about it. They might be supplied by skimmer at regular intervals. The critical thing is, how is it armed? I don't see them having another cannon. No need for two heavy weapons here. Maybe they had another skimmer out doing survey work and they called it back when the one tracking us didn't return. What do you think, Skua?"

"I don't know what to think, feller-me-lad. If our friend Antal had access to more heavy artillery, I think we'd have been treated to a demonstration long before now. So I can't explain what this one's doing showing up all of a sudden-like." He glanced back toward the city. "If this was going to be an attack, they'd be hitting us from both sides."

"By the same token it can't be from Brass Monkey," Cheela Hwang told them. "There are no skimmers at Brass Monkey. Only ice cycles. The presence of skimmers would violate . . ."

"We know, we know," Ethan said impatiently. "It's against regulations to utilize advanced transportation systems in backward regions of backward worlds. Too much of a shock to the natives. I'm getting sick of that regulation."

The humming grew steadily louder. "I don't think it's the one we first ran into out on the ice, the one whose crew we shot up that came back later with the cannon in tow," September declared hesitantly. "Sounds much bigger, like a cargo shifter." His wavy white hair fluttered in the wind like a glowing nimbus around his great head as he stared into the distance. Then he pointed with an arm the size of a foremast spar.

"There she is!"

"Can you see who's aboard?"

September could not, but the Tran could. "Many of your kind," Hunnar informed them. "It is truly a bigger sky boat than the one that tried to sink our lifeboat."

"Cannons, guns," September growled anxiously. "What can you see?"

"I see no such large weapons, no lightning-thrower." Hunnar leaned over the railing. "I see—by the beard of my grandfather!"

"What, what is it?" Ethan pressed him.

"It is the scholar!"

"The scholar?"

"Williams, he sees Williams," September said gleefully. "*Our* scholar."

"It is so. The respected one has returned with help."

"But that's impossible." Hwang had to stand on tiptoes to see past them. They could make out individual shapes moving on the deck of the huge air-repulsion craft, but not faces. "There are no skimmers based at Brass Monkey."

"I don't give a toot if the little bookworm pulled it out of his shoe!" September was dancing and twirling like a madman, scattering Tran and humans alike. "The teacher's come back and school's in session!"

"I don't understand." Ethan managed to be a bit more restrained in his reaction to Williams's return. "Where did he get the skimmer?"

"We will know soon enough," Hunnar said, "because the skyboat comes straight for us."

September was right about its size. It was a large industrial transport vehicle, fully a third as big as the *Slander-scree* itself. The survival-suited figures that lined its railing hefted weapons that sparkled in the sun. No cannon, but plenty of rifles, each with greater range and power than the most modern hand beamer and certainly more deadly than anything in Bamaputra's limited armory.

As they looked on, it floated effortlessly over the harbor gate to settle alongside the icerigger. Williams would have briefed its driver on where to hover. Then the diminutive schoolteacher was cautiously walking across the boarding ramp that the *Slanderscree*'s sailors extended over to the sky boat.

He'd survived the difficult two-way journey in good condition, only to find himself nearly smothered by the effusive greetings and congratulations of those he'd left behind. Cheela Hwang almost suffocated him all by herself.

"We ain't going to get any answers out of him right away." September grinned as he appraised the extended clinch. "Come on, let's go over and see where he found these folks."

Ethan followed his friend. "Maybe after a while each outpost automatically rates a small military contingent. Maybe they arrived in our absence just in time for Milliken to request their services and assistance. They could have come down as part of one of the recent monthly shipments."

"Maybe." September hopped off the boarding ramp onto the skimmer's deck. Ethan followed.

Men and women of varying ages watched them quietly. Many chatted among themselves and ignored the new arrivals. All looked competent and professional. This wasn't a group of volunteers Williams had recruited at Brass Monkey. These people were comfortable with weapons.

He continued to cling to his theory that for some reason a small military presence had been assigned to the outpost, until someone else emerged from belowdecks. At first he couldn't make out the face because light flaring off a window temporarily blinded him, but he recognized the voice instantly. A moment later she saw him.

"Hello, Ethan. It's good to see you again. I wasn't sure I'd ever be saying those words."

September grunted. "Now don't this just take the cake."

It was more eloquent than anything Ethan had to say. He was speechless.

She pouted prettily. "Can't you say something? Here I drop everything to come back to this frigid place just in time to save your frozen neck, and I don't even get a hello kiss?"

A powerful hand shoved Ethan toward her. He glared back at September, who only grinned broadly. "You heard the lady, young feller-me-lad. Kiss 'er."

Ethan gingerly touched his lips to those of the woman who'd emerged from the interior of the skimmer. She pulled back, frowning.

"If that's the best you can do I'm taking my people and going straight back to Brass Monkey. You can sit out here and play dice with ice cubes until your fingers turn blue."

"Sorry, Colette. I'm still in shock a little." He put both arms around as much of her as he could and bussed her good and hard. She responded passionately while the troopers on the skimmer looked on with interest.

September had sidled over to a tall, lean fellow about his own age who had the look of a Man in Charge. "Ethan there, he and Ms. du Kane go back a ways."

"No kidding." The soldier studied the on-going clinch casually. "I wondered why we were coming to a place like this. Ms. du Kane said she had unfinished business here. Always it's unfinished business, but none of us suspected this was what she had in mind." He glanced up at September. "You know her, too, then?"

"You heard about the time she and her paterfamilias were kidnapped?"

"Oh. You must be Skua September. Everyone's heard about it. They'd make a tridee sequence out of it if some production company thought they could get away with it, but the missus won't let 'em and she's got too strong a legal program on her side. So it's all true?"

"Yep. Every bit of it."

"None of us are surprised she came through." He nodded toward the embracing couple. "I've been with the du Kane family twenty years. She's tough as duralloy, but not a bad boss." He extended a gloved hand. "I'm Iriole, Roger Iriole. I'm in charge of the household troops, though most people would say bodyguards."

September's huge hand enveloped the slightly smaller one. "Thought it might be something like that. You folks couldn't have shown up at a better time. How'd you get those past customs?" He gestured at the energy rifles.

Iriole shrugged. "Ms. du Kane usually gets what she wants. Apparently she knows what this world is like and she wanted to make sure she came prepared." He turned and stared toward the city. "Mind telling me what's going on? What you're all doing here and why you're so glad to see a bunch of guns? Your schoolteacher friend gave us a quick rundown on the way out but I confess I didn't get much out of it."

"Not real complicated. Just your usual case of genocide for profit." He proceeded to explain in as few words as possible.

Meanwhile Ethan and Colette had walked to the side of the skimmer that faced the *Slanderscree*.

"The old ship doesn't look much different than I remember her."

"Not much has changed. You haven't been away *that* long."

"Feels like years. That's Hunnar Redbeard, isn't it? And Elfa Kudrag . . ."

"Kurdagh-Vlata," he corrected her. "They're married now."

"How is this union you stayed here to help get started coming along?"

"Well enough. Several important city-states are formally allied and others are debating joining."

"Sounds promising." A darker undertone abruptly slipped into her voice. "Milliken's told me all about what's going on here. We'll put a stop to that right now."

"It's not your problem. Why not let the authorities take care of it?"

"Milliken's worried about the time that would take and the damage these unmentionables could do in the interim. I don't just live for commerce, Ethan. I have larger values just like everyone else. We're going to put these people under citizen's arrest and haul the ringleaders back to the outpost. *Then* the government can take over." She indicated the crowded railing opposite.

"The Tran did well by my father and me. We owe them."

"How is your father?"

"Hellespont du Kane died four months ago. If you'll remember, Dad hadn't been well for years. His mind wasn't the only part of him that was failing, and dragging him across Tran-ky-ky didn't do him any good. He was too far gone for any kind of transplant, but I don't think he would've made himself a candidate anyway. He was tired. His passing wasn't unexpected. I'd been running the day-to-day operations of the conglomerate for years anyway. I told you that."

"I remember. You were pulling strings from behind the scenes."

"It's all out in the open now. Has been for four months. I liked it better the other way. Much easier when the old man was there to serve as a figurehead. He was a lot more tactful than I am. You probably remember that, too."

He tried not to smile. "I remember you always saying exactly what you thought."

"Precisely. That's no way to run a major commercial concern. I need somebody else to talk for me, someone who's experienced with business people and able to smooth ruffled feelings."

He swallowed. "You haven't, ah, bonded with somebody by now?"

"'Bonded'? You make it sound like I'm looking for glue." She glanced down at herself. "If I lost a hundred pounds, I'd need every one of these soldiers to keep the men off me. As it is there are plenty who try, but I know it's just the money they're interested in. The money and the power. They're terrific aphrodisiacs, Ethan, but they don't get you honesty." Those piercing green eyes locked on his and wouldn't let go.

"I could never be sure of any of them. Not the way I'm sure of you. Because of what we went through together more than a year ago. You told me then you couldn't marry me, Ethan. You wanted time, you said. Time to consider, time to think. That's why I've come back. You've had plenty of time to think."

"Actually there hasn't been time for long stretches of contemplation this past year, what with all the fighting and unifying and exploring."

"Don't tell me I've wasted this trip, Ethan. I mean, I'm glad I was able to show up in time to help out and rescue the lot of you and save the planet and all that, but that's not why I'm here. I'm formal head of the family du Kane now. I don't have to ask anyone's permission for anything. I know what I want."

"You always knew what you wanted, Colette." He smiled affectionately. "Ten minutes after you were born I'm sure you were telling the doctors how to handle you."

Her eyes glittered. "I had to. It probably took two of

them to carry me. Ethan, I need someone to share my life. You're the only man I ever met who accepted me for what I am. Whether it was the situation or what doesn't matter. You liked me for myself. I need a companion and a helpmate. I need . . . I need you. I've never needed anything else in my life.

"So I put all my business on hold and crossed a few hundred parsecs to ask you the same question you said no to a year ago. I thought that maybe after another year on this world you might be ready for some permanent luxury and relaxation. I won't make too many demands on you." She dropped her eyes and for the first time he had to strain to make out what she was saying. "I still love you, even if you don't love me. But if you'll give me a chance, I promise you I'll do everything I can to make it work between us. If it's a submissive woman you want or even a fully equal one, then there's no chance. I wasn't brought up that way. Blame it on my family, my father if you want to." She lifted her face and stared into his again.

"But if you say yes, I guarantee you'll never have to sell so much as a pocket communicator again and you'll lead the kind of life most people only dream about."

"Colette, I . . ."

"Whatever you're going to say, give it another minute. It's cost me plenty, both financially and emotionally, to do this. I'm not going to beg. If you say no this time, I promise you'll never see me again. But if you say yes, boy, if you say yes, you'd better mean it. I can't stand anything that's tenuous or halfway. It's all or nothing, Ethan. No partial commitments."

He turned away from her to stare past the *Slanderscree*, letting his gaze rove beyond the harbor gate to the vast ice ocean. Was there anything more he could do here? Anything else he could accomplish for the Tran? If he accepted, he would lose his freedom, but Maxim Malaika had taken care of that by sticking him with a permanent position at Brass Monkey. So if he was so worried about his freedom, why had he taken that post? Because it offered the prospect of being able to retire in ten years instead of twenty or thirty? Hell, Colette was offering him the chance to buy and sell people like Malaika.

Wouldn't he be in a better position to aid the Tran and their development as the titular head of one of the Commonwealth's most powerful commercial families?

All right, so what if Colette was no raving beauty? So what if there was enough for two of her? She might be ample but she wasn't unattractive. And how much did physical beauty have to do with living with another person for the rest of your life anyway? He was no tridee star himself. Life was what you and your mate made of it and you couldn't, shouldn't, prejudge it according to other people's perceptions of what was good and what was bad, what was attractive and what was ugly.

When he turned back to her he found those remarkable eyes waiting for him. They were pleading even as she couldn't plead aloud. He glanced across to September, found the giant smiling paternally and nodding slowly.

"What the hell. Of course I'll marry you."

She threw herself into his arms. The impact nearly sent both of them over the side of the skimmer. "Very sensible," she told him. Then she gave him a quick, firm kiss and hugged him to her so hard he thought his ribs would crack.

A few of her soldiers smiled and decorously looked elsewhere. The Tran on the icerigger labored under no such cultural restraints. They let loose with a farrago of appreciative growls and roars.

Finally she released him, still intact, and turned toward Yingyapin. "That's settled, then."

"There's just one qualifier."

She looked back sharply. "What's that?"

"I don't want it to be a Tran ceremony."

She looked puzzled, not understanding, while Skua September burst out laughing.

"Done. Now let's take care of this slime that thinks it can make an inhabited world its private development. Want anyone else to come with us?"

"Cheela Hwang should come along to represent the science staff. And Hunnar and Elfa. Also a young Tran named Seesfar, who I think deserves to see that we're not all motivated by self-interest." He unsnapped the beamer from his belt. "I'll leave this with Ta-hoding. With the firepower you've brought along, I won't need it."

"All right." She looked past him. "Roger!"

Iriole came over and saluted.

"You know what's going on here?"

The soldier jerked his head in September's direction. "I have been briefed."

"What do you think about it?"

"If I may be allowed to say so, ma'am, it stinks."

"You're allowed to say so and you're quite right. We're going to make a few citizens' arrests. We're going to shut this operation down. I saw that they finally put in a deep space communications system at Brass Monkey. When we get back there I'm going to get on the horn. I know the counselor for this whole volume of space. We'll have a peaceforcer brought in to haul the rest of these maggots off-planet in comfortable cells." She shoved a clenched fist into the air.

"Tran-ky-ky for the Tran!" Then she added in a softer tone, "That felt pretty good. In business you can't always be sure you're doing the right thing. No such uncertainty here. It's a nice feeling."

Hunnar, Elfa, Seesfar, and Cheela Hwang were brought aboard, the Tran marveling at the prospect of flying not across the ice but through the air.

"Roger and his people will take care of things up here," Colette informed them. "Why don't you go below until the arguing's over?"

"I'd rather stay outside," Ethan told her.

"No way. I'm not having my prospective husband's head shot off just after he's accepted my proposal."

"It'll be all right. They've only got a few hand beamers over there. When they see how badly we've got them outgunned, I don't think there'll be much fighting. You might have more trouble with their Tran allies. They're stubborn."

"I remember that much. No offense," she told Hunnar and Elfa through her suit translator.

"There is no offense in truth," he replied. "We *are* stubborn." He smiled, displaying sharp canines.

XV

Bamaputra did not look toward the harbor as he turned up another of the steep switchbacks that led up the mountainside away from Yingyapin. He did not have to. Antal's monocular had already revealed the unexpected presence of long weapons on board the unmarked skimmer. The new arrivals were obviously in league with his enemies on board the ice ship. His foreman had assured him there was no way they could win a pitched battle against well-disciplined people carrying rifles. All they could do for now was retreat to the installation and seal themselves inside the mountain.

Corfu accompanied them, wailing and raging at an interfering fate and wondering why they didn't stay and fight.

"Better it is to die for what one believes in than to run and hide in a hole in the ground!" He was having trouble keeping up with the humans, whose feet were far better designed than his for climbing.

"A foolish and primitive notion."

"They've got us outgunned," Antal told him. He gestured with his own hand beamer. "I'll explain it one more time. Our light weapons are not as powerful as theirs."

"Then what are we to do?"

"First we make sure they can't touch us." The foreman nodded toward the entrance to the installation which lay one last switchback ahead. "We lock ourselves out of their reach. Then we bargain. They could probably blast their way in, but that would mean casualties on both sides. I think they'd rather talk."

"Talk." Bamaputra wasn't breathing hard at all. "What is there to talk about? These are not government representatives. I do not know who they are but they are not that. Not that it matters. It is enough that they are friends of those whose destiny we once controlled. Their destiny was our destiny, and now that control has slipped through our fingers."

"We can still try to strike a deal with them," Antal insisted. "We can hold out till the regular supply ship arrives."

"Don't be a fool." They had reached the cleared area which fronted the entrance to the installation. As they watched, the huge door rolled up into the solid rock, admitting them to the complex beyond. "We are finished here. The project is finished. They will communicate with the authorities. We will not be given time to reach our own relief ship. Now if there was a way to disable their skimmer..."

"Not a chance. They've got rifles down there. They can sit around and pick off anyone, human or Tran, who tries to get close."

"As I feared." They were inside the complex now. Curious engineers and technicians looked up from their work as their supervisors walked past. Corfu was already getting hot, but he followed anyway. He had nowhere else to go.

"There's got to be something we can do," Antal muttered. "If they take us back, it means mindwipe at least."

"Better to die. The body lives on but the soul perishes."

Antal eyed him askance. "What do you mean, 'soul'? Mindwiping just removes whatever the psytechs identify as criminal tendencies. When it's over you're still the same person you were when you went in."

Bamaputra was shaking his head. "Are you so credulous as to believe the government's propaganda? They leave you enough to function with, but you are *not* the same person. Something vital has been taken away."

"Sure. The criminal part. Just the criminal part."

"But we are not criminals, you and I. We are visionaries. I do not think I could stand to lose the visionary part of myself."

The foreman frowned, but Bamaputra appeared to be completely in control of himself. "Yeah, well, I'll take care of securing the station, making an announcement about what's happened and what we can expect. There's only the pedestrian entrance and the cargo dock to seal. No matter how much portable firepower they can bring to bear I still think we can keep 'em out long enough to do some bargaining. Meanwhile you can start shutting stuff down."

"Shutting down, yes, of course," Bamaputra murmured softly. "There are records to destroy, chips to erase, people to protect." He turned on Antal so sharply that the foreman jumped in spite of himself. "Whatever you do, do not negotiate with this September person. Try to talk to the scientists. If we are fortunate, there may be a government official among them. Such types will go to almost any length to avoid bloodshed. I will see to the pumps and reactors while you brief the staff."

"Got it." They separated, leaving behind a confused and panting Corfu ren-Arhaveg.

Only much later did Antal reflect on his supervisor's words. Seeing to the pumps and reactors did not necessarily mean shutting such systems down.

* * *

There was some desultory resistance put up by the rag-tag imperial armed forces of Yingyapin. It didn't last long. Spears and swords weren't much of a match for beamers and energy rifles. Despite the pleas of Hunnar and Elfa, Colette directed her troops to shoot only to wound. After all, as Hwang explained to her, the citizens of Yingyapin were as much victims of the visiting humans' deceit as anyone aboard the *Slanderscree*. Once the truth could be explained to them they should become useful members of the expanding Tran union.

When the last soldier had dropped his weapons and fled, those on board the skimmer considered what to do next. Iriole was studying the entrance to the buried installation through a monocular.

"Door looks pretty solid. I'm not sure we can blast our way past."

"We shouldn't have to," said September. "They know it's in their best interests to surrender peacefully. They can't go anywhere. The threat of busting in should be sufficient to induce the lower echelons, at least, to come out with their hands in the air. Can the skimmer make the climb?"

Skimmers were designed to travel no more than thirty meters above a solid surface. They were not designed for ascending steep inclines. They were not aircraft. Still, if they moved slowly, Iriole thought they might be able to make it to the level area fronting the entrance. He looked to his employer for instructions.

"Let's give it a try."

Ethan put his arm around her. Somehow it seemed the right thing to do. Didn't feel bad, either.

"Everybody take a seat and strap down," Iriole told them. "We're going to tilt some and I don't want anybody falling out."

When the awkward climb had been accomplished and they landed outside the massive doorway, Grurwelk Seesfar wanted to go back down and make the exhilarating ascent all over again.

"Mr. Antal, sir?"

The foreman turned to the young technician who'd barged in on him. "What is it? I'm busy?"

"I think you'd better come with me, sir."

"Can't. I'm trying to do a dozen things at once right now. Didn't you hear me over the com system? Don't you know what's going on?"

"Yes, sir. But I still think you'd better come with me. It's Mr. Bamaputra, sir."

He removed his right hand from the sensor screen and turned to her. "What about Mr. Bamaputra?" he asked quietly.

"You'd better come quick, sir." That's when he noticed that she was so frightened she was shaking.

A crowd had gathered outside the central control room. It contained the master panels for programming reactor output. Armored glass enclosed it on all four sides, standard protection for the sensitive heart of the installation. Except for Bamaputra the room was deserted. It was also locked from the inside.

A single speaker was set in the glass next to the transparent door. "Shiva, what are you doing in there?"

The supervisor turned to smile back at him. "Preserving a vision, perhaps. Surely you recall our discussion wherein we talked about greatly accelerating the melting of the ice?"

The technician who had fetched Antal pointed into the room. As the foreman scanned the readouts she'd indicated the small hairs on the back of his neck began to tense. The figures he read belonged only in manuals, not on green screens. They continued climbing even as he stared.

"Shiva, you're going to overload the whole system! You've probably gone beyond several limits already. You need to let us in so we can emergency override and shut the system down."

"If we do that now, we will not be able to start up again," Bamaputra explained quietly. "I have ample food and water in here with me. I really can't allow override and shutdown at this point. It would interfere with the vision.

"I believe you underestimate the system's integrity. It will hold at these levels and we will accomplish fifty years' work in a few months. I am counting on you to bargain with these people to buy me that much time."

"You're going to blow the whole place!"

"I am not. Talk to the engineers."

Frantically the foreman sought out one of the installation's chief techs, asked her for an unbiased appraisal.

"He's right," the woman said. "Nothing will explode. It will melt. Not just the reactor cores: everything. If containment fails, there'll be a short, quick release of heat. It will dissipate rapidly."

"How much heat?"

She didn't bat an eye. "Millions of degrees."

"What do you think the chances are of maintaining containment?"

The woman turned to the older man standing behind her. His jaw and neck displayed the marks of an addict. "I'd say about one in ten."

Antal whirled back to the speaker. "Did you hear that? Your chances of bringing this off are one in ten."

"A better chance than a Commonwealth court would give us."

"The opposite side of that," the foreman shouted, beyond frustration now, "means there's a ninety percent chance you're going to turn the inside of this mountain into slag."

"Then you'd better hurry and leave, wouldn't you say?" Bamaputra's tone was icy.

"He is crazy." Antal stepped away from the speaker and the transparent wall. "He's gone crazy." He turned to the engineers. "What do you think we ought to do?"

The older man was sweating profusely. "I think we ought to get the hell out of here."

The foreman hesitated a moment longer, then jabbed the red alarm button nearby.

Bamaputura watched calmly from the director's chair as the panicky exodus commenced. He was not surprised. You couldn't blame them. None of them, not even Antal, was a real visionary. Throughout history those who had made the great discoveries, accomplished the memorable scientific feats, never had better chances than one in ten. Most of them began their experiments with worse odds.

This was the only way. The calculations had to be adjusted to take into account the greatly reduced time factor. He turned to the multiple readouts. The ice sheet would begin melting rapidly now. Very rapidly. At the same time, the quantity of water vapor and carbon dioxide being pumped into the atmosphere would rise twenty fold. The system would hold. A magnetic fusion containment field wasn't like a stone or metal wall.

Let them all leave. He could hold out alone, if need be. Despite the intereference he would accomplish everything he'd set out to do. If you had vision, you sometimes had to take a chance. Turning dreams into reality always entailed a certain amount of risk.

Better to depend on machines. The instrumentation surrounding him functioned silently and without complaint, doing its job in a predictable and dependable manner. He'd never liked people much. Come to that, he'd never been very fond of himself.

Better to risk one's life in search of the perfect abstract than to surrender to temporal temptation. He might die, but his vision would live on in the form of a transformed Tran-ky-ky. The money had never meant anything to him. Revelation lay only in achievement.

The skimmer hovered just off the ground as a squad of Colette's bodyguards climbed over the side. Those remaining aboard kept their weapons trained on the entrance to the installation.

Ethan began examining the walls on either side of the door. "There should be a speaker here somewhere. Surely they put in something that would enable them to talk with any Tran who might come up here."

Before they could locate the hypothetical speaker the camouflaged door began to open.

"Back to the skimmer," snapped Iriole. The squad retreated. Fingers tensed on triggers.

There was no fighting. The technicians and engineers, support and maintenance personnel who came stumbling out of the tunnel in their survival suits weren't armed. They kept their hands in view at their sides or held above their heads. As those on the skimmer looked on, the evacuees began staggering down the trail leading to the harbor below.

There was no sign of Shiva Bamaputra, but Hwang picked Antal out of the crowd immediately. There was no threat in his pose this time. All of the cockiness had gone out of him.

"We've got to get away from here!" he said wildly.

"Why? What's the hurry?" September folded his arms and adopted the stance of a man with all the time in the world. "We've things to do."

"Do whatever you want but don't do it here. Bamaputra's gone mad." He gestured back toward the dark tunnel. "He's running the whole system on intentional overload, way beyond its design peak. Locked himself in control central. You won't pry him out of there, not even with rifles. It's five-centimeter plexalloy paneling, molecular welded."

"Now why would he want to go and do that?"

"He's trying to accelerate the terraforming process. We talked about it lots of times, but not on this scale. He's got an outside chance of bringing it off. Way outside."

"What happens if the system fails?" Williams asked him.

"Melt down." It was the young female technician who spoke. "You get large-scale melt down. The containment fields in the reactors collapse."

"You mean the installation melts?" Ethan asked her.

She stared over at him. "I mean the mountain melts. Maybe more, I don't know. And I'm not planning on hanging around to work out the calculations. You better not either."

"Right. Resume positions," Iriole told them. They retreated back aboard the waiting skimmer.

"Wait a minute!" Antal rushed the craft, stopped short as the muzzle of a rifle swung in his direction. "What about us?"

"You've all got survival suits," September told him as the skimmer slowly drifted over the edge of the steep slope and commenced its downward flight. He pointed to the switchbacked path. Some of the installation personnel were already halfway down. "Better not run too fast or you're liable to fall and tear 'em."

Antal stared at the descending vehicle. Then he turned and joined his former employees in a mad scramble to get down the mountain.

Those on board the skimmer followed the frantic flight of their former adversaries as they drifted safely toward the harbor.

"What do you think?" September asked their teacher.

"I don't know. We don't have any idea what their setup here is capable of or where its limits lie. Obviously Bamaputra believes he's keeping within them."

"He seems to be the only one," Ethan commented.

"That doesn't mean he isn't right."

"I don't like the idea of going off and leaving him holed up in there," September muttered. "Won't do us much good to escort this lot back to Brass Monkey if we don't shut down what they've left behind."

"Let's get back to the ship and decide there," Ethan suggested. "Roger, what do you think our chances are of blasting into this control room and taking him?"

"Not good, if that other one was telling the truth. Plexalloy's tough."

"The foreman had one good point," Williams reminded them. "What *are* we going to do with them now that they've put aside their weapons?"

"Let 'em stumble around Yingyapin for a while," September said. "Let the Tran there see what their all-powerful friends are really like. By the time they make it to the harbor I don't think we'll have to worry about keeping watch over 'em. Maybe we can lash a couple of ice ships together and tow the whole bunch of miscreants back to Brass Monkey. They'll be too cold to give us any trouble. The trip back may not force confessions out of all of 'em, but it sure as hell will make 'em humble."

They were moving out across the ice, heading for the *Slanderscree*, when Ethan pointed toward the mountain that contained the terraforming station.

"Something's happening up there. Some kind of activity."

September squinted, cursed under his breath. "Can't see. Eyes are getting old, like the rest of me. Hunnar! Can you see anything up there?"

The knight joined them. "Truly I can, friend Skua. Clouds are coming out of the mountain. I think mayhap your mad kinsman is making a rifs."

Not a rifs in the traditional sense, but a massive storm front was forming with incredible speed above the highest peak. Lightning began to flash inside the boiling mass of cumulonimbus and thunder boomed across the harbor. The cloud bank continued to thicken until it dominated the visible sky. And then something else happened, something so extraordinary it stimulated excited discussion among the scientists and awe among the Tran.

For the first time in forty thousand years, rain fell on Tran-ky-ky.

"Liquid ice." Warm drops pelted the skimmer. "Water." Elfa stared in astonishment at the tiny pool that accumulated in her cupped paws. "Who thought ever to see such a thing?"

A shout from the mainmast lookout drew their attention. The heavy metal gate which had barred the icerigger's flight was slowly swinging open, sliding out of the way on its multiple runners. On board the *Slanderscree*, Ta-hoding gaped at the retreating barrier, then began bellowing orders. Sails were unfurled, spars adjusted, stays pulled taut.

"What of the humans who came out of the mountain?" Ethan asked Hunnar.

"They are . . ." The knight paused a moment to be certain of what he was seeing. "They are running through the city. The townspeople are staring at them. Now a few begin to throw stones."

A new sound, deeper and more ominous than the thunder. Shouts and yells from both those on the icerigger and in the city acknowledged its power. The rumbling arose deep within the solid rock of the continental shelf, a gigantic hiss. It was as though something monstrous was awakening inside the earth.

"Look at that. Even I can see that." September nodded toward the docks. In haste and confusion the personnel from the installation were pouring out onto the ice. They promptly began slipping and sliding all over the place. Their repeated failures only made them redouble their frantic efforts.

"Any arms?" asked Colette du Kane.

Iriole was peering through a military monocular. "None visible, ma'am."

"Hell. Pick them up and put them aboard the big ship, I guess. The prosecution's going to want as many witnesses as possible." She turned demurely to Ethan. "If that meets with your approval, my love?"

He didn't doubt for an instant that the question was rhetorical, but he appreciated it nonetheless.

"You have my consent," he replied grandly.

"Thank you." She actually batted her eyelashes at him. They exchanged a grin.

Then and there he decided this wasn't going to be a bad marriage after all.

The skimmer had to make several trips to transfer all of the refugees from the ice to the *Slanderscree*, which fortunately had ample room since it had been traveling with a minimal crew ever since departing Poyolavomaar. Body searches revealed that the technicians and engineers had fled the station unarmed. Most were too exhausted to have offered any resistance even had they wished to.

The foreman was in the second group. Antal didn't look in control of anything including himself as he scrambled frantically onto the skimmer's deck.

"Move, move, we've got to get out of here!"

"Not yet," Ethan told him.

"Why, what's the hold up?" The foreman was staring worriedly at the storm raging over the mountain.

Ethan gestured onto the ice. Led by Hunnar and Elfa, a group of sailors from the icerigger were chivaning at maximum speed toward Yingyapin.

"We still have to warn the people you were going to use." He eyed Antal accusingly. "You could have done that on your way out."

"No time, we don't have any time. Don't you understand?"

"Perfectly," said Ethan softly. "We've talked to your engineering people. If the installation melts, it won't affect us."

"Not the installation, not that." The foreman was on the edge of hysteria. "You can't imagine how much heat a complete and sudden melt down up there will release. There are three industrial fusion plants operating on overload inside that mountain, for god's sake!"

"We know."

"No you don't know. If the containment fields fail, more than the installation will melt. Rock will melt." He paused for impact. "Ice will melt a lot faster."

"Oh, hell," Colette muttered. Together she and Ethan turned away from the city. The *Slanderscree* was heading out of the harbor, loaded down with its contingent of Tran and scientists and refugee humans. It was accelerating slowly under Ta-hoding's skillful guidance, but was it accelerating fast enough?

"They'll make it," he murmured. "We'll wait here for Hunnar and Elfa and the rest." He favored Antal with a look of disgust. "What are you worried about? You're safe. A skimmer's as stable traveling over water as over a solid surface. Meanwhile I'm sure we can find a portable recorder or two. Why don't you tell your story? For the records?"

The foreman hesitated, licked his lips.

"Or maybe," Colette said sweetly, "you'd prefer to walk?"

"Or swim, as the case may be." September was looking at him hard. "Come on, man, the only way you've a chance of surviving your former employer's wrath is in protective custody. Tell it all now without coercion and you might even escape mindwipe."

Antal looked at him, then nodded to Ethan. Iriole provided recording materials, a guard, and privacy below-decks.

"People will do anything for money." Colette du Kane's jaw was set as she leaned over the railing. "I know. My father was like that. But he was lucky. He grew out of it before he died." She gestured toward the city as another violent rumble came from inside the mountain. "Hunnar and his people better get back here fast. They can skate like hell, but I doubt there's one among them who can swim."

Organizing a mass evacuation in a matter of minutes isn't easy under the best of circumstances. Fortunately the panicky flight of Antal and his crew helped Hunnar and Elfa to convince the citizens of Yingyapin that for the moment at least safety lay in abandoning their homes and striking out across the ice. Once persuaded, the townspeople moved swiftly. Yingyapin was so poor there was little in the way of goods to remove anyway.

Once a few of the more prominent families stepped out onto the ice the rest followed in a rush. Males and females supported their cubs between them. They formed a long, broad column chivaning toward the mouth of the harbor.

Last to leave was a repentant third mate, Kilpit Vyo-Aqar. "If there is any danger, it should fall upon me," he told Elfa. "I have no excuse for what Mousokka and I did except to say we were driven by the twin demons of homesickness and loneliness."

"You don't mutiny because you are homesick," she shot back as they raced across the ice sheet to catch up with the *Slanderscree*. "If so much as one citizen is left behind, I will hold your life forfeit. Later we may find a means to forget your treachery."

"Yes, princess." The joy and relief in the mate's face was overwhelming.

Rumbling continued to sound from inside the mountain as the icerigger and skimmer led the entire population of Yingyapin out to sea.

"We'll have to find an island or secondary inlet somewhere along the coast to settle them temporarily," Hunnar declared. "They can sleep and talk and wait for aid from Poyolavomaar."

"We can ferry supplies," Colette told him via her translator. "Portable shelters, food, medicine, that sort of thing. Later we can—"

She was interrupted not by an explosion but by a titanic blast of superheated steam from the side of the mountain facing the ocean. The pressure hurled rocks and debris a kilometer into the sky. Boulders as big as the skimmer were scattered like pebbles. Ta-hoding tried to find another place to hang more sail.

The initial eruption was followed by a second which punched a hole in the cliff that delineated the edge of the continental shelf. The powerful storm started to dissipate as rapidly as it had formed. Rain ceased.

"See," Hunnar murmured as he reboarded the skimmer, "the earth bleeds."

It looked as if half the mountain was glowing pale crimson from the heat within. The periodic rumbling had been replaced by a steady whisper from deep within the rock.

They were far out on the ice now, the *Slanderscree* steadily accelerating under full sail but with Ta-hoding moderating their speed so the population of Yingyapin could keep pace. City and harbor had fallen out of sight astern, though they could still see the line of cliffs that marked the rim of the continental plateau. As they stared, it began to collapse. Together he and Colette waited for the final explosion that never came.

The plateau imploded slowly, collapsing in on itself like a fallen cake as the tremendous freed heat of the three fusion plants spread out like a wave from the incinerated installation. As it melted, the rock absorbed the heat.

Grurwelk Seesfar continued to prove her name was not casually given. From the mainmast lookout bin she called down to the deck.

"The ice melts! Its corpse comes marching!"

"Waves," Ethan murmured. There was no word for "wave" in the entire Tran language.

A loud cracking sound precipitated a rush to the railings on both the skimmer and much larger icerigger. Small at first, the crack appeared beneath the *Slanderscree*'s right fore runner. It gave birth to several smaller cracks while it continued to widen. Dark water bubbled up from eons-old depths.

Screams and fear calls rose from the chivaning citizens of Yingyapin. No solid deck lay between them and the horror sweeping out of the continent. It was far more frightening than an earthquake.

The oceans of Tran-ky-ky were trying to make a comeback.

But the *Slanderscree* did not tumble down into the liquid center of the world, nor did the terrified evacuees. The melange of water and broken ice that initially appeared in their wake grew and then stopped. Even as he observed it through one of the skimmer's monoculars Ethan saw it beginning to refreeze. Gradually the spreading cracks receded behind them. The icerigger lurched once to port, leveled off, and stayed on top of the surface.

The energy from the overloaded installation had spent itself. Had Bamaputra truly believed he had one chance in ten of surviving the overload, or had he known all along the containment fields would fail under the strain? They would never know, just as they'd never known much of anything about that steely-minded, quietly megalomaniacal little man. His component parts were now mixed irrevocably with the minerals of the world he would have remade. He'd followed a private vision and now he was entombed with it.

Eventually they slowed to give the cubs a chance to rest. Sail was furled and the young and sick were allowed to come aboard the already crowded *Slanderscree*. There wasn't nearly enough room for all, but Ta-hoding had no intention of crawling back to Poyolavomaar.

Long unbreakable cables of woven pika-pina were dropped over the stern. The citizens of Yingyapin took hold and relaxed all but their arms as the great ice ship towed them effortlessly across the frozen sea, like a living tail at the end of a kite.

Save for a vast field of man-made lava now rapidly cooling behind them, there was nothing to show that the installation had ever existed.

An appropriate uninhabited island was located and the population of now vanished Yingyapin established as comfortably as possible. The *Slanderscree* resumed its homeward trek, leaving with the displaced a promise to send back help as soon as it arrived at Poyolavomaar.

T'hosjer T'hos, Landgrave of that fine city-state, listened with interest to their tale and immediately dispatched half a dozen large ice ships groaning with supplies to assist the homeless wanderers of Yingyapin. In an earlier time he might have sent pillaging soldiers instead. The Union was already proving its worth.

On the long journey between Poyolavomaar and Arsudun, Colette du Kane proved to Ethan that fusion stations were not the only thing in this part of Tran-ky-ky that could generate prodigious amounts of heat.

Millicent Stanhope, Resident Commissioner of Tran-ky-ky, stood bundled in her survival suit and watched as the hundred or so prisoners from the installation at Yingyapin were herded into an empty above-ground warehouse. They would be kept separated from the rest of the outpost's buildings in a heated structure, but with only minimal clothing. That would keep them from causing trouble for the outpost's constabulary, which consisted of exactly five people.

Already that morning she'd requested a peaceforcer via the deep-space beam to come and pick up this awkward contingent of law-breakers. It was going to be awhile before even a very fast ship could traverse the emptiness between its base and distant Tran-ky-ky. Meantime the prisoners were going to have to be fed and cared for and watched over. Their arrival blew her carefully laid plans for her six-month tour of duty all to pieces. She turned to confront Ethan and Skua September.

"I thought I told you two I didn't want to be bothered with anything out of the ordinary?"

"Well, I expect we could have let them go on destroying the planet," September replied. "That would've kept things quiet."

"Until after retirement. My retirement." She sighed deeply. "You did the only thing you could do, of course. I *hope* there are no more surprises."

"Just one," Ethan said hesitantly. She glared at him. "Maybe this isn't the right time or place, but I don't see why it would have to be done in your office."

"Why what would have to be done in my office, young man?"

Hunnar looked at Ethan, who nodded and moved aside. The knight took Elfa's paw and the two of them approached solemnly. They towered over the Commissioner but she didn't back away.

Elfa cleared her throat, an intimidating sound in itself, and recited the words Ethan and September had helped her prepare.

"As ranking representatives of the Union of Ice of Tran-ky-ky, we wish to hereby formally apply to you, the Resident Commissioner, on behalf of all our people for application to associate membership status in the government of peoples and systems known as the Commonwealth."

Colette clapped politely when she finished, though her survival suit gloves muffled the sound. Behind his visor September grinned broadly.

"Well," Stanhope said finally, "is there to be no end to the day's surprises? You are aware what requirements you must meet? In order to qualify as a recognized planetary government you must be able to prove suzeranty over a substantial portion of the population."

"With Wannome, Arsudun, Poyolavomaar, Moulokin, and many smaller city-states now united under the same articles of cooperation I believe we of Tran-ky-ky can now satisfy your regulations."

"They qualify easy," said September, "and by the time the sector government gets around to completing the paperwork this here Union will have doubled in size."

"Can I be certain everything they tell me is true? After all, I'm still new here. I wouldn't enjoy being fooled."

"Milliken Williams knows Tran-ky-ky as well as Ethan or I. Why not appoint him your personal adviser for native affairs? He'll be straight with you."

Stanhope considered. "The schoolteacher? He's not leaving with you?"

September and Ethan exchanged a grin. This time it was Ethan who replied. "Our friend and a member of the science staff here, a Cheela Hwang, have formed rather a strong attachment for one another. Don't be surprised if you're approached in the near future to perform a marriage. Resident Commissioners are qualified to do that, I believe."

"Yes. Dear me!" She shook her head tiredly. "Will I never be permitted to rest? I will certainly make use of Mr. Williams's unique body of knowledge. That's an excellent suggestion, young man." She turned her attention back to the patiently waiting Tran.

"As for your application, I will take it under advisement and pass it along to those specialists most familiar with your situation. If they approve, I'll see to it that recommendation for approval is given to the sector council." To Ethan's surprise, she turned to wink at him.

At which point he realized that there were no specialists on Tran-ky-ky's situation—except for three travelers named Fortune, September, and Williams. He winked back. She was asking them to approve their own request.

"We will need weapons," said Elfa excitedly, "and sky boats, and wind-talkers and all the other wonderful devices we have seen and . . ."

"Easy, easy," Stanhope admonished her. "First your request has to be drawn up and passed along. Then it has to be read and dissected, discussed and argued, voted upon— oh, lord, the paperwork, the forms!" She shook her head, already exhausted by the prospect of the work ahead. "And

I thought this was going to be a simple, relaxing few months."

"Consider though," Colette told her. "Upon retirement you'll be bringing a whole new world into the Commonwealth family, a new sentient race. That is an honor few diplomats even dream of supervising." ·

"That's true. Yes, that's true." Stanhope straighted perceptibly. "Instead of slipping silently into oblivion, I expect it will be my duty to go out in a blaze of glory. Well, one must make sacrifices, I suppose. I'll just have to force myself to see this through.

"Now if that's everything, I have much to do and I'd like to begin by getting out of this infernal wind."

"Infernal wind?" September spread his arms wide. "Why, this is nothing but a light breeze on Tran-ky-ky."

"You can have it. And so can my successor when my tour of duty is done." Her voice dropped and she began muttering to herself. "Have to have the formal ceremonies celebrating Tran-ky-ky's inclusion into the Commonwealth before that, of course. Yes, a lot of paperwork to do." She turned and headed for the nearest entrance to the administrative complex, a small but nonetheless impressive figure receding into the blowing ice. Ethan watched her knowing that the immediate future of Tran-ky-ky was in good and capable hands.

"Now we must see to our ship." Hunnar put a paw on his shoulder. "Can you not come down to bid us farewell?"

Ethan looked up at the knight, seeing for the last time the membranous dan fluttering in the wind, the sharp teeth, the large feline eyes, and the dense red-brown fur. The Tran were going to cause quite a stir when their first representative appeared in council. Of course their appearance would be mitigated somewhat by the special suits they would be forced to wear to keep comfortable. Survival suits designed to cool instead of heat. Comfort was a very relative term between intelligent species.

"I'm afraid we can't," September told him. "Ethan and I, well, we've been away from the fleshpots too long as it is."

Grurwelk Seesfar stared at him. She was returning with the Sofoldians to Wannome. She would eventually return to Poyolavomaar as their official inter-state representative. It would allow her to do a great deal of traveling, which she loved above all else.

"You practice cannibalism on your home world?"

September swallowed, coughed. Some terms just did not translate properly.

"Understand," he told them, "we haven't regretted a minute of our stay among you. Well, maybe a minute or two, but on the whole it's been enlightening, yes, enlightening. Bless my soul if it hasn't."

"Ta-hoding will sorrow," Elfa said, sounding none too in control of herself at the moment.

"Maybe we'll come back for a visit someday," Ethan told her. "When it's a hot summer where we are. Or maybe we'll run into you on another world."

"Another world." Elfa tilted her head back and stared out of wide yellow eyes at the perfect blue sky. "A strange thought." Then she reached out and embraced him so hard he could feel her claws ripping into the back of his survival suit. First Elfa and then Colette du Kane. What was there about him that made him irresistible to amazons of two races?

Then there were no more farewells to give, no more good-byes to say. The Tran whirled and chivaned down an icepath leading to the harbor and the tall-masted icerigger that would, at last, carry them back home.

"If you cry with your visor up like that, young feller-me-lad," September warned him, "you'll get ice on your cheeks."

Colette du Kane put a protective arm around her husband-to-be. "Let him cry. What are you, some kind of emotionless man?"

"Not emotionless," he replied easily, "just some kind."

Together the three of them turned and headed for the warmth of the nearest sealed corridor.

ABOUT THE AUTHOR

Born in New York City in 1946, Alan Dean Foster was raised in Los Angeles, California. After receiving a bachelor's degree in political science and a Master of Fine Arts in motion pictures from UCLA in 1968–69, he worked for two years as a public relations copywriter in a small Studio City, California, firm.

His writing career began in 1968 when August Derleth bought a long letter of Foster's and published it as a short story in his biannual *Arkham Collector Magazine*. Sales of short fiction to other magazines followed. His first try at a novel, *The Tar-Aiym Krang*, was published by Ballantine Books in 1972.

Foster has toured extensively through Asia and the isles of the Pacific. Besides traveling, he enjoys classical and rock music, old films, basketball, body surfing, and karate. He has taught screenwriting, literature, and film history at UCLA and Los Angeles City College.

Currently, he resides in Arizona with his wife, JoAnn (who is reputed to have the only extant recipe for Barbarian Cream Pie).